The Stairway Guide's Daughter

The Stairway Guide's Daughter

John Burgess

RIVER

BOOKS

First published and distributed in 2017 by
River Books
396 Maharaj Road, Tatien, Bangkok 10200
Tel. 66 2 622-1900, 224-6686
Fax. 66 2 225-3861
E-mail: order@riverbooksbk.com
www.riverbooksbk.com

Editor: Narisa Chakrabongse
Production supervision: Paisarn Piemmettawat
Design: Ruetairat Nanta
Copy editor: Tom Lent
Cover design: Narisa Chakrabongse and Ruetairat Nanta

ISBN 978 616 7339 87 0

Printed and bound in Thailand by Bangkok Printing Co., Ltd.

In memory of Alice Stevens Burgess
1919-2015

Who kindled in me a life-long fascination
with the ancient Angkor civilisation
by taking me to Cambodia when I was a boy.

Characters

Jorani – the Stairway Guide's daughter

Pik – the Stairway Guide

Chantou – Jorani's stepmother

Bonarit and Pen – Jorani's brothers

Kamol – Jorani's suitor

Abbot Vamashiva – high priest of Preah Vihear, the Temple in the Clouds

Bouray – the Abbot's son

Priest Sar – the Abbot's deputy

Abbess Parvati – head of the nunnery

Ritisak – the Abbot's nephew

The Commander – head of the militia

Darit – the princely contender

Lady Sray – holy woman who visits the temple

Prelude

Close to a thousand years ago, Hindu priests divined that a clifftop in what is now the far north of Cambodia was a unique portal to heaven. Masons arrived to build the great temple that is today called Preah Vihear. Made of sandstone quarried on the site, it was the work of the same civilisation – the Khmer Empire – that left the world the fabled temples of Angkor.

In modern times, Preah Vihear has sadly become known as the prize in a border conflict between Cambodia and Thailand. But in antiquity, it was one of Southeast Asia's prime hubs of spiritual devotion. Generations of priests and acolytes performed rites to venerate the Hindu god Shiva – they called him 'the Lord of the Summit' – in hopes of securing his aid to continue the cycle of human existence.

Yet inscriptions found at this Temple in the Clouds suggest that it was also very much caught up in the real-world political currents of the times. It served as a repository for documents that established the lineage and legitimacy of kings. There are hints of military threats to Preah Vihear and the construction of fortifications there.

John Burgess's previous novel, A Woman of Angkor, takes place during the twelfth-century reign of the great Khmer king Suryavarman II. The Stairway Guide's Daughter is set in this same period. Its title refers to a stairway by which pilgrims ascended from lowlands to the temple's heavenly heights. Sections of the steps remain on the mountainside in ruined form. In researching the novel, Burgess climbed them to gain an appreciation of the strength and devotion of those ancient visitors.

It seems likely that, in view of extreme steepness and the dangers of strange spirits, pilgrims made the ascent in the company of guides. The story that follows centres on a family of such guides. One member of the family will come to appreciate better than all the others how the great temple at the top straddles the spiritual and the secular. She is Jorani, the Stairway Guide's daughter.

Part 1

Ascent

On the clifftop is a boy who has never built a fire, but needs to now. He has seen the job done by servants and the forest priests who once cared for him, and each time it involved a live coal, so he has brought one, carried in a small pot that he has taken (not stolen, he tells himself) from a cooking hut. He has also come with a straw bag containing thirty-three strips of palm leaf that are engraved top to bottom with religious verse. The strips are now in front of him, stacked atop a waist-high obelisk that is used for ritual destruction by fire.

He hesitates an instant, then tilts the pot. The coal inside is meant to set fire to the strips, but it skitters past them and falls to his feet. He frowns. He has imagined the efficient creation of a strong, righteous blaze, with deities sympathetic to his task guiding his hands.

But the coal has not broken. It glows, seeming alive and ready to help, and he finds encouragement in that. He scoops it up with the lip of the straw bag and places it carefully atop the stack of strips. He leans close and blows. The coal brightens in response and sinks into the strips, burning a red-ringed hole. Wisps of smoke cross the boy's face. He smiles; the help he had hoped for is being provided. He blows again, and a flame pops to life. He begins a chant.

'Lord of the Summit, with this act your servant strikes a blow against the false doctrine that has taken root in your sacred abode. With this act, your servant destroys the deceitful words recorded on these strips in defiance of your will. Protector of the Universe, your servant seeks nothing for himself. He seeks only that your law will receive its due respect in the human community that you in your infinite compassion and wisdom oversee.'

Prayer is something the boy does know, and these words come easily. He fans the pile with the straw bag. Before long flames are consuming all of the strips. He shuts his eyes against flying cinders.

The air had been still when he arrived, but now a breeze carries the smoke away, over the edge of the clifftop on which the boy stands. He finds himself suddenly enveloped in clear, cool air. His eyes reopen. Gazing into the sky, he imagines the false doctrine dwindling into nothingness there, dispersed beyond recovery even by gods.

1

The Errand Up the Mountain

People say that the great schism at the Temple in the Clouds was a struggle between two groups of priests and the deities who took their sides. That is true, but I can tell you that it also drew in common folk too many to count, myself among them. We can all remember precisely when it first made a mark on our lives. In my case, it was the day Father ran out of merit certificates, the kind that allows the bearer to accept some help in climbing the two thousand steps.

Where can I get one? This was the question on the lips of many of the pilgrims who arrived tired and dusty at the base of the mountain. Perhaps they were old or ill and couldn't make the ascent without a steadying hand or a place in a palanquin. Or they were gentry who felt that the long journey they'd made already from one faraway province or another had earned them the right to assistance in this final exertion.

Any pilgrimage to the Temple in the Clouds is of course carefully planned with a goal of acquiring maximum merit towards rebirth on a higher spiritual plane. Each step, each prayer, each bead of sweat along the way accrues for the traveller a discrete quantity of the sacral substance. A particularly large amount is to be had from the journey's demanding final stretch, the two thousand steps to the summit. Yet some of that portion can be lost if the climb is made not entirely by one's own strength and determination. So, pilgrims who accepted help could obtain a merit certificate, for two pebbles of silver, by which the gods would graciously make up the deficit.

Now, a pilgrim could get a certificate from an acolyte at the summit, but when welcoming new arrivals at the mountain's base, Father (and we children too) sometimes made it sound as if you couldn't be sure you'd find that acolyte once you reached the top. We can provide what you need right here, we'd say, and it's just as good, written out on a square of palm leaf by the Abbot himself (though I knew from my own eyes that those supposedly hard-to-find acolytes were often the authors). If you kneel and pray before the climb, palms together, the little square held between your forefingers, chances are good that a deity will gaze down favourably upon you, murmuring, 'Let us welcome this supplicant who has parted with silver to support the holy community of men and women who honour us.' We children sometimes affected a deep and wavering voice for those words, in a way we imagined a god would speak. All in all, it was powerful logic, so most people said yes. We handed over a certificate; they handed over two silver pebbles. One found its way to the temple's treasury room, the other we kept. Please forgive me if this seems like we were taking advantage. But we did believe the logic ourselves, and it was through this support that, generation after generation, our family could serve the temple, as guides on the great stairway.

You will understand, then, why Father always kept a stack of certificates at our house at the foot of the two thousand steps. But I should say almost always. A larger-than-expected party of aged pilgrims had availed themselves of every last one, and Father realized this only after rising the next morning. There was no time for him to head up top for more; he and my two brothers were due in the village across the rice lands from our house to greet the next group of pilgrims. So the job of replenishing the supply fell to me.

'Go up and bring down forty,' Father told me. 'Come right back, please. No stopping to play.'

I was twelve years old, still slim like a boy, but soon to leave the body and concerns of a child behind. I remember a twinge of disappointment that Father thought I wouldn't understand how important an errand this was and would stop to, as he put it, play. So I mouthed a prayer and set out at a run. He would see how wrong he was. One, two, three, four – I took the first of the stone steps springing like a doe. I turned to steal a glance over my shoulder. Father was smiling at me from the door of our house. That made me smile back, though I think this watered down the effect of mature determination that I was trying to achieve.

Every pilgrim knows that the great stairway has two thousand steps. And before the first climb, every pilgrim believes that the stairway is as broad as a royal avenue, each step made of crystal polished and pristine, marred by not a single bird dropping or dead beetle. Each step carries the pilgrim aloft at a gentle angle towards a golden gleam that signals that the glory and virtue of Heaven lie ahead, within human reach. Perhaps a few sky gods flutter overhead. I know this is how the pilgrims think because so many times I saw how perplexed they became at their first encounter with the real thing. In places, the stairway is in fact wide like an avenue, but in others it narrows to almost nothing to pass between boulders. Some of its steps are uneven, even broken, and certainly none are made of crystal, but rather the sandstone that the holy mountain offers up all over its slopes in pieces great and small. Birds and animals feel free to leave their deposits wherever, even around the little shrines to local gods that the pilgrim encounters here and there on the ascent. The stairway sometimes flattens out to run almost level, then a few steps farther it matches the mountainside's angle to become so steep that you feel you're climbing a tree. You use your hands and wish your feet could grasp like a monkey's. (In these places, my family has strung ropes to give people something to hang on to.) I never saw any sky gods, and no bright lights ahead. Indeed, in rainy season, mists can steal in, making it hard to see more than a few paces ahead.

But perhaps what most surprises pilgrims is that, though they've heard the figure two thousand, they are simply not prepared for how long the ascent goes on. Each time they think they're nearing the top, and sheepishly ask us guides if it's so, they're told, no, not yet. Always, it seems, there's another height to struggle up. Not a few fit young noblemen, having begun the ascent confident they'd have the wind, would quietly ask for a merit certificate halfway up and accept the strong, reassuring hand of Father or one of my brothers.

I'd known the steps since I was a baby. I was a strong and healthy girl, but still I couldn't maintain a run the whole way up. So after I passed out of Father's sight (foliage embraces the stairway in many places, another surprise to the newcomers), I slowed down to the methodical steady pace that he'd taught me. Brittle dry-season leaves lay scattered across some of the steps, crunching under my toes as I passed. I almost stepped on a land crab that was late in scurrying out of my way. Other than that, I have no real recollection of the climb that morning. My memory only resumes when I scrambled up the stairway's last steep section and arrived at the top of the mountain's crowning cliff.

This is a special place. The physical trial is past. An extended stretch of level walkway begins; the temple is finally near. We would always announce this to the pilgrims and oh, how their spirits would soar! That day, I paused when I reached this point of the climb. Not to play – certainly not. To catch my breath, that was all. Then a hint of smoke tickled my nose.

Now, at this place there is also a narrow dirt path that leads off to the left through bushes, ending after a few steps at a large rock that lies buried in the soil at the edge of the cliff. At the centre of this rock is a thick stone obelisk, standing about waist-high, the top of which was a place for burning. The burning of what? This was supposed to be a secret but we all knew: holy texts that had crumbled with age. They were set alight here by priests in rites of destruction.

When I smelled the smoke that day, I thought that priests must be at the rock, burning texts. Time for me to get going. Yet before I did, something made me glance down the path.

Normally you couldn't see to its end, but this was dry season and the bushes' leaves had fallen away. I saw the son of the Abbot, standing at the obelisk. He was a boy of about my age, dressed in the white garment of a Brahmin. I had seen him before, though usually at a distance, as my family is of course not of priestly stock. Now he was alone, tending to a fire, and I could sense right away that something furtive was going on. He was alone, fanning the flames with a straw bag, as if he wanted whatever was burning to burn quickly. I couldn't see what it was. Then he looked up and our eyes met. That was a shock. Yet I didn't immediately look away. Then, another surprise: he gave me no look of admonishment. Rather, he nodded just discernibly to acknowledge me, in a not unfriendly way, and then looked back to his fire. How calm and yet determined he seemed.

I was at a loss for what to do. My palms went quickly together to show respect. Then I hurried on, along the level stretch of avenue. With each step, I tried to put the glimpse of the son from my mind, but it would not leave. There were many things about the Brahmin existence that I did not understand, and this, I told myself, was just another. I had committed no offense; I had merely happened along. But still I felt disturbed. It seemed that the son and I now had a secret.

Soon I drew near the temple's Entry Court. Its red tiles and soaring eaves, held aloft by stout stone pillars, shelter our temple's main guardian god. I murmured a prayer asking that someone as humble as I be allowed to pass beyond his abode. I crouched, picked up my pace to cross the temple's processional avenue, and in this way reached the other side of the court. There I turned onto a rocky trail that led up a hillside to a clutch of simple wooden lodges. I felt better now; this was a friendly place. Acolytes lived in these dwellings and they all knew me.

At the first lodge, I called a greeting up its steps. A young man appeared at the door above me and agreed to gather up forty certificates. But I had to wait so that he could go to another lodge to get the full number. I drank a cup of water that another acolyte offered. Then the forty were handed over in a straw bag, and I was making my way back towards the stairway. But near the Entry Court I stopped, uneasy again. I did not want to pass the Abbot's son a second time. I began thinking I should give him a bit longer to finish whatever he was doing and leave.

Just then I heard hurried footsteps behind me. I turned and saw two temple watchmen, human helpmates of the guardian god, rushing at me. Their rough hands seized my upper arms. I was stunned; not a word was said by either of them. I was simply marched back up the trail, almost dragged like a piece of prey. I don't think I screamed. More likely I cried, both from the pain their hands and nails were causing and the humiliation of whatever was this thing that was happening. I was no stranger at this level of the temple; members of my family had a right to be here. We knew how to behave and show respect. Yet now I was being treated like some kind of thief or blasphemer. Why hadn't they just asked me to come with them? I would have, without a fuss.

We approached the acolytes' quarters and I wondered if I was somehow suspected of stealing the merit certificates. This I could disprove – the young men inside would back me up. But I was pulled right past the lodges, then onto a rough path that headed up the hill.

This was another place that children were told to avoid, and avoid we did, to the point that I had never set foot on this trail. Up it, we were told, lies the house of the august Vamashiva, Abbot of the Temple of the Clouds. I had seen him too, from a distance. He was a large, fully whiskered being whom we all knew was in constant commune with the cosmos. His knotted hair, his golden jewellery, his white garment marked him as a man above all others, as did the attendants who were always trailing behind him. He walked with a stick that to me always seemed better fit for striking errant children than aiding his step. His eyes were always fixed ahead. This was something for which I was always grateful, because I couldn't imagine anything more terrifying than their being directed at me.

The guards did not ease their grip, dragging me past priestly residences, storehouses, and small pools in the rock that captured water for drink and bathing. Each time I thought we must be where we were going, we went up farther still – I was quite like one of those pilgrims, only terrified. But then there it was, a grand teak house situated just steps from the edge of the cliff. I was feeling the worst kind of dread. We were indeed going to this house.

Wooden steps led up to a veranda, and right now the great man was standing square at the top of those steps! In the brief instant in which I dared look his way, I saw fulsome anger on his face, and yes, my worst fear – his eyes focused right on me.

At the bottom of the steps, I was pushed to a crouch. Yet even in that position, the guards kept their hands on me.

'Well, tell me what you saw!' The words fairly boomed from the Abbot's mouth, conveying the anger I'd seen on his face. 'Tell me! I have been informed that you arrived at the top of the stairway at the same time this boy was there. Don't deny it. You were seen there.'

'This boy' was the Abbot's son. I only now realised that he stood next to his father, held in the same kind of grip that I was. The scene at the overlook came back to me. I had in fact witnessed something secret.

'Well, go on – speak! What did you see?'

For an instant, I locked eyes with the boy. And for a second time, I didn't see what I expected, fear or resignation that he was about to be exposed. There was in his face the same calm but this time a look of empathy for the ordeal to which I was being subjected.

'I saw...I saw...'

Before I could continue, one of the guards slapped the back of my head, knocking my face painfully into the dust. What a shock, what a humiliation it was; I raised my nose just barely and spat out a pebble.

When I looked up, the boy was struggling to escape his father's hand – I sensed he was trying to come down to me. But a servant strode up from inside the house and, after an instant's hesitation, clutched the boy hard by the other arm, immobilizing him.

The Abbot's eyes came back to me.

'Answer, then!'

'I saw your son, Holiness.'

'Of course you saw him! Now where did you see him?'

'At the stone overlook, Holiness.'

'And what was he doing?'

'He was standing near the edge, Holiness.'

'But what was he *doing*?'

'Doing, Holiness? He was standing there, Holiness.'

'To what purpose?'

Why did I say what I said next? I believe that a spirit entered me and created courage or recklessness to do something the purpose of which I had no inkling at that time.

'I cannot be sure, Holiness. Perhaps to feel the breeze, or to throw stones off. Boys do that sometimes.'

'He was not burning something?'

'Burning?'

'Yes, burning.'

'I saw no burning, Holiness. Only a boy standing.'

'Don't lie to me!'

What terror I felt! But I managed to murmur, 'I have not, Holiness.'

That was all. On a signal from the Abbot, the hands released me. Had I not already been on the ground, I would have fallen down. The great man strode back into his house, dragging his son in that same grip, like a prisoner. But the boy looked over his shoulder and gave me with his eyes a faint, silent thanks.

I sprang to my feet and began racing down the trail. I sobbed as I ran. I wondered if the spirit that had directed me might be a demon. Had it quickly departed me, its work done, or had it taken residence in me for a long period with the intent of doing more evil through me? Or was it in fact a god, having used me towards some purpose that had Heaven's blessing? I could not know. That day, all I could do was run.

2

Little Champion Climber

I was born under a crescent moon in the fifth year of the reign of
Our Lord King Suryavarman, the second to bear that sacred name.
The midwife from the village beyond us had been sent for but arrived
too late. I was already out of the womb and in this world, not two
hours after my mother's water broke.

A beautiful child asleep in the arms of a beautiful mother – that is
how Father always described his first view of me. I heard the story of my
birth many times but as I grew old enough to comprehend such things,
I came to know that the word beauty was not really to be applied to
me. I had seen my face reflected in pond water and in polished metal
and it did not include the square jaw and almond eyes that define the
feminine ideal. I won't say that I am displeasing to look at, but still, my
body could be narrower at the hips and shoulders, my hair possessed
of a bit more lustre. No, as my childhood passed, Father began praising
me less for beauty and more for aspects of character. From the very
beginning of life, he said, you were eager to get things done, and
quickly! You struggled out in just two hours! How proud I felt hearing
him talk of sharpness of mind and firmness of determination. Such
traits were more easily assessed, because they required no reflected
glimpse. I could sense them within myself, all day long. Certainly I was
faster to speak up than other girls, sometimes to the point of drawing
admonishing looks from adults. I learned my numbers without
trouble. If I saw a problem – a column of ants stealing into our home's
vegetable basket, perhaps – I would take it upon myself to act, rather

than waiting for someone older. And though I lacked the physical strength on which so much of our family's hereditary station relied, from a young age I showed the kind of responsibility that was equally important.

How many generations has our service spanned? I can tell you precisely. Eleven. Father could not read or write, so he had no written record, but he could recite all the names and all the dates by which our family had toiled faithfully for more than two centuries, back to the reign of Our Lord King Yashovarman, founder, patron, and first worshipper of the Temple in the Clouds.

Our service began with a dream. Not in the King's slumber, of course, but in that of a young male servant attached to the staff that oversaw the special garments and jewellery worn by the sovereign at times of ritual. In the year that the construction of the temple was completed, this servant was part of the royal party that travelled here from the capital for the consecration. The party passed the night at the village at the mountain's base, then climbed the holy stairway, which was then as new as the temple itself. On the final night aloft, a god appeared in the dreams of this servant to announce that now that he had tasted of the challenges of the climb, he must devote his life to assisting the many pilgrims who would attempt it too. On waking, he begged leave from his superior to carry out the god's instruction. We believe that our forebear's request made it all the way to the King himself, who graciously gave leave. The young man descended the mountain with the royal party but bade farewell at the village. Soon he married a young woman from that village, whom he'd met during the overnight stop before the climb. The couple built a house that stood – that still stands – a few paces from the sandstone gate at which begins the holy stairway. It was in this house that I was born, as the midwife hurried towards it.

By the time I was three or four, I was helping in the family's work. Each morning, we rose before sunrise and prepared for a new group of pilgrims. We swept the ground at the sandstone gate, we drew water from the stream that passed a short distance away, we shook out the mats in the rest pavilion that stood a few steps from the house. When the first pilgrims arrived, we offered water and snacks.

We offered those merit certificates as well, of course, and to people who said yes, a pledge of help on the way up. If they were aged or clearly infirm, we provided transport by palanquin. We always called it by that fancy name, but the thing that we normally used was more of a hammock, slung from the ends of a sturdy length of bamboo. One of my brothers took the front, the other the back. Several times a year, when a very high-ranking pilgrim arrived without transport of his own, we brought out a real palanquin that we stored draped in a cotton shroud in a shed behind the house. This was the proper way for such a personage to ascend. The conveyance was an elegant gold-painted wooden thing with a sunshade, mat, and, as its handles, four carved Naga serpents.

Bearing it required the strength of Father, both my brothers and a young man from the village, hired for the occasion for wages. They crouched two to a side, giving off not even the hint of a groan as they raised it to their shoulders. The resulting ride was more dignified but a lot less comfortable than in the hammock conveyance. And potentially quite frightening, though we never mentioned this in advance. At the truly steep sections, the four bearers turned the conveyance at a right angle to the stairway and inched it upwards, two men below bearing its weight on their shoulders, two men above pulling at it, holding onto the palanquin with one arm, a stairway rope with the other. It required a dance of considerable precision to keep things rising steadily and evenly, never listing. The carried personage would often grow very still, hands gripping the sides, certain that the palanquin was going to tip over and tumble full down the stairway, taking the personage with it. Father always advised the person to keep eyes to the right, to the stones of the rising stairway, not to the side with the drop. And I can tell you that there has never been such a fall, not in all the years of service that my family has performed. The gods of the mountain would not allow it, and I believe that the stout arms and formidable discipline of the men who bear the conveyance played a role too.

I could not carry the palanquin, of course, but I had my own role in helping the ascent. This was a break with tradition.

Through the many generations of service, the females of our family saw off each group of pilgrims, wishing them well, then remained behind at the house to get ready for the next (and to guard the silver the previous one had left). The story is that one day when I was quite small I began to cry very noisily on seeing Father prepare to climb the stairway. The pilgrims he was leading were at that very moment kneeling and murmuring their first prayers (with merit certificates tucked between fingers), and I so impinged on the dignity of the occasion that Father scooped me up and placed me on his shoulders. I went quiet instantly and rode all the way to the top! The next morning, of course, I wanted to go again and I cried twice as hard, so go again I did. I became a regular sight on the stairway. For some of the temple's acolytes it became a joke that, riding on Father's shoulders, I needed a merit certificate of my own. And because on that perch I could be said to always beat Father to the top, they gave me the nickname 'Little Champion Climber.' For many years it stuck, though my real name is Jorani.

When I became too big to ride this way, I was not willing to surrender the privilege of going up. But I knew I had to provide Father with a justification. So I assigned myself to be special helper to the women and children in each group. I led them. I announced the names and stories of the spirits honoured in wooden shrines that sit atop stone blocks that flank the stairway, marking zones of holiness of the climb. I carried water or a pilgrim's bag, sometimes a baby. I shooed away insects. It all had effect – the females of the groups moved more easily when I was there. I once overheard a woman say that she had taken me as an example. 'If this girl can prance up the steps so easily, chattering all the way, why can't I too?' (I don't think I really talked as much as that, though.) And I believe that for everyone, whether men or women or children, there was reassurance in seeing a young girl in what was after all such a potentially foreboding place, where who could say but a god might take offense at something and let fly with a thunderbolt. I and my childish exuberance were a signal that all was going well.

I was blessed to have brothers who did not resent something that I can appreciate now, that I got attention and tips that might otherwise have been directed to them. Bonarit, the elder, was in effect Father's apprentice and would one day succeed him. Father was quite proud of him, and for good reason. How serious he was about the family's vocation, how determined to carry out the duties without a flaw. Father liked to tell pilgrims that Bonarit had the strength of a boy three or four years older and the spring of a boy three or four years younger. Sometimes, when Father had important things to tend to below, Bonarit was allowed to lead parties himself. I remember the first time that happened. Father simply came up to him as an ascent was being readied and told him to take charge. Other boys might have been taken by fright at this first test, given without warning, but Bonarit responded as if it were as natural as being asked to dust off the palanquin. I went up that day too. As the party cleared the first fifty steps, Bonarit called me forward, looking grave, and I thought that something was wrong. But then he smiled and said, 'Now, Little Champion Climber, don't expect to ride on my shoulders. You're on your own.' My other brother, Pen – he was two years older than I – had been brought in on the joke. 'Nor on mine,' he said, appearing suddenly at my side. I laughed, they laughed, and then we all turned back to the business at hand, getting this group safely to the top.

I kept this up all through my childhood years, and as I approached womanhood, I formed the idea that this was not something I would grow out of. It would be my vocation. It was a strange notion, of course. A young woman of good character looks forward to marrying and having children, of course, and I too wanted those things. When I went to the village, I looked with envy and curiosity at young mothers walking about with infants balanced on their hips. I wondered, what would my own children be, how many, and by what man? But I also took note that these same mothers worked. Some weeded paddy fields, some tended beehives, some sold fruit in the market. So why couldn't my work be the leading of pilgrims up the mountain?

I will not claim that my motivation was all for service to Heaven and pilgrims. This work of leading filled me with purpose in its own right. I liked how perspiration formed on my brow as we neared the top, how my breath quickened. I liked how people who had paid me no attention at the bottom listened to my every word as we negotiated the stairway's more trying sections. I liked the view from the top, the breeze there that cooled you off. I liked everything about being a guide, really, and could not imagine giving it up.

Nonetheless, I did not tell Father or my brothers or any of the pilgrims about this ambition. As long as I kept it to myself, it seemed attainable. If it were known, it might evoke smiles and laughter, and I wondered if that would make the idea seem absurd to me as well. But I did tell Mother, at the shrine by the big gum tree behind our house where we honoured her spirit.

Forgive me – I have not mentioned that Mother is no longer in the human world. It is painful to speak of it because I am the reason she is not here. I emerged from the womb quickly, but, with no midwife on hand to grasp and direct me, I caused a tear in my mother's flesh. The tear became infected, and ten days later her spirit departed. But at the earliest age at which I could appreciate visitors from the world beyond the human world, I sensed her spirit keeping near, at my side. I am quite certain that she did not blame me for her death. Rather, she felt remiss in having left me so soon in this life, unable to do the many jobs that a flesh-and-blood mother does for a child, and she was now eager to do what she could from the spirit world. I could feel her love, and I returned it, yet, as a child, I will tell you, I often also sought to use her for selfish gains. There are limits to what a spirit can accomplish in this world, but I was always trying to test them, thinking of new things she might do for me. When I brought the family's offerings of rice and fruit to her, I knelt and whispered the words of homage that one says at such times, and often I followed with a private plea. 'May this girl, your daughter, who regrets deeply that her birth caused such tragedy, may she nonetheless request a favourable consideration of her wish, however undeserving she might be.'

One day the wish might be for sweets, the next that there would be no pilgrims, so that Father could sit with me in the rest pavilion and tell me stories. Of course, Mother knew what I wanted already, having watched for years over our family, and I think me in particular, from her place in the spirit realm. Sometimes she gave me what I requested, other times she did not. And still others she gave me things that I had no idea I would need. One day I stepped on a scorpion and yet suffered no sting. On another I fell into a fever that the village healer could not contain and in my dreams she come to me and took my hand, smiling serenely. From that moment I began to recover.

So much she had done for me, yet on one particular day I requested – perhaps it was really that I demanded – yet more. I wanted her to help me settle my life as a guide. And, do you know, as I knelt in prayer I sensed no admonishing response. Rather, she was conveying sympathy for my wish and making a mother's promise to once more do what she could.

That day I remained on my knees at the shrine longer than usual. I shed a tear. That was unusual, but I found myself wishing I could make this request to a mother of this world, not the other, and feel her draw me near. I tried to recall her face from my fevered dream, but I could not. I could only recall the love that her smile had conveyed onto her undeserving daughter.

3

The Old Water Jar

As I raced down from the Abbot's house that day, I cried hard, like the child I felt I no longer was. There were many reasons behind my terror. I had been brought before Heaven's supreme representative like a criminal. My face had been pressed to the dirt. The rough men had squeezed my arms cruelly hard – I rubbed them as I hurried down unfamiliar trails, fearful I would take a wrong turn and blunder into some forbidden sacred place. Each time I passed a priest or acolyte, I tried to slow and cover my tears, but I knew that each one could see that something terrible had happened.

By the time I reached the Entry Court, another thought was taking hold. My good relations with the people up here, on which rested my ambition to be a guide, had been upended. Word would spread through the temple community and down the mountain too. No pilgrim would want to be guided by a girl whom the Abbot had treated in such a way. And Father would hear, though I had already decided that he would hear directly from me.

How unfair it was. The girl the guards had dragged in wasn't a criminal. I had never stolen anything; I had never insulted a god. And yet, as I continued my flight down the stairway that day, there welled up in me a thought that at first had been masked by the terror. In the brief time I had been before the Abbot, I had *become* a criminal. I had lied. I had given a false account of what I had seen.

I have already said that some spirit caused me to speak as I did, and so in part I don't bear responsibility. But I can say that it was also due

20

to something very much of the human world. I was discharging a debt. I will tell you how it happened.

There were in fact quite a number of children at the temple. Some were like the Abbot's son, born of Brahmin blood. They lived with parents and servants in wooden houses near the temple's upper reaches, located like the Abbot's along the long cliff line. These children wore the white garments of the holy sect. The boys had top knots and spent so much of their time in special pavilions with tutors that to us other children they seemed like prisoners. That was their life – they were undergoing instruction by which they would fulfil their destined roles. They learned to read, they learned to write. They learned to perform magic rituals. They learned holy words that, chanted, carried all the way to Heaven. They learned to chart the movements of the sun, moon, and planets and determine their influence on events on earth.

There was a much larger group of children without Brahmin blood. Some were sons and daughters of masons (there was always a stonework project underway at the temple). Others were from villages down on the plain or in the highlands to the north, part of families that for a few weeks or months at a time had been consigned to help maintain the temple grounds or provide labour in stonework projects. Still others, like me, were children of common folk who lived here permanently to serve the temple.

Normally I saw the Brahmin children only at a distance, tiny figures coming and going near the upper precincts of the temple. Very occasionally we actually mingled. Sometimes it happened when a senior priest was coming or going from the temple. At those times, priestly boys came down to the Entry Court and formed two lines outside it to pay obeisance. One morning, such a rite was taking place just as Father and I reached the top with a group of pilgrims. We of course stopped and knelt when we saw what was happening. A departing priest passed between the two lines of Brahmin boys, conferring blessings right and left, then boarded a palanquin to begin his journey northward. When he was gone, we continued on with our group and got them started on their visits. Then I sat down on a rock to rest while Father went off to tend to some business.

I had been carrying water that day in a green earthen jar, a cheap old one that was rough to the touch. There was just a tiny bit left, but it had become warm and I felt no interest in drinking it. So what did I do? I got rid of it. But I didn't simply pour it onto the ground. I splashed it to my left, without looking. And who happened to be passing behind me just then but one of the Brahmin boys who'd bid farewell to the priest.

The water caught him full across the chest. I gasped, one hand going to my mouth, the other putting down the bowl. Apologies began to spill out of my mouth, but he would have none of it. His eyes bulged, he tried to speak but couldn't – that was how angry he was. Then he found his wits and seized me by the arm. He pulled me along a stony trail that ran up the hill through tall grass, the same one that went to the Abbot's house. I was digging in my heels, but he was too strong for me. I saw now that another Brahmin boy, a younger one, was following, bringing my jar. I stopped resisting, thinking I was only making them angrier. My captor was now laughing softly to himself, as if picturing terrible things he was going to do to me, and I began to feel truly afraid. I knew what can happen to a woman who comes under the control of bad men. These boys were not old enough for that, but they were treating me as they would have treated another boy, really, and in that, boys can be extremely cruel.

Near the top we turned off onto a side trail. Ahead was a wooden house. That gave me hope, because surely the boys would not behave this way with a Brahmin adult watching. But they seemed not to care. We passed the house, and I understood – it was unoccupied. We were coming closer to the edge of one of the mountain's cliffs, I could tell, one that faced out to the west. I was feeling wind on my cheek, and that made me even more afraid. Then we stopped by a wall of tall grass. I was handed over like a prisoner to the younger boy. He pinched my arm as hard as he could, to impress the first boy, who now took the jar in hand. He made an evil little smile and, keeping his eyes on me, made a show of holding it up high, right over a rock. It had been a gift from a pilgrim family some years earlier; they had told me that its greenish tint was common among jars made in the province where they lived.

'No, please don't,' I said.

That, of course, was what he wanted to hear and so he dropped the jar. It shattered atop the rock.

Perhaps my punishment was now complete. But the elder boy looked me square in the eye. 'Now we'll throw you off the cliff!'

This time they both seized me, from either side. My feet barely brushed the ground as they propelled me along a path that passed through the tall grass.

Then suddenly, there it was – the great green expanse of the lowland plain. Far below. We came to a halt just short of the cliff's edge. Grinning, the older boy pressed his face close to mine. He wanted to see terror in my eyes.

Now, I am not afraid of heights. I have experienced them all my life. But I had always done so in perfect safety, knowing that friendly spirits and my own sure-footedness would prevent a fall. There was no such protection now; I was powerless like a fish in the jaws of an otter. The boys stood me right at the cliff line. The elder boy brusquely pressed my head down, as if to say, take a last look, that's where you're going. Far below, trees stood bare of their leaves. I imagined a rapid fall, ending with a horrible thud, branches impaling me through my belly.

I let out a scream. They seemed to like that and to want to hear it again. So they backed me up a step or two, then propelled me again to the edge. I screamed again. But how quickly the elder grew bored with this. 'Lay her down,' he said to the other, 'on her back.' Suddenly I wondered if these boys were older than I'd thought, but I was too frightened to resist. They forced me onto a rocky surface and shoved me outward. My head suddenly had no support – it was hanging over the edge! Now I was truly panicking, both hands grasping at these boys, desperate to keep myself from going over. The elder pushed me again so that even my shoulders were out in the air, then pulled me back, then pushed me out again. 'Go on, go on, let's hear it from you.' I did scream, just as he commanded.

Then I felt hands yanking at my feet. I was slid roughly away from the edge.

Somehow I managed to look up. Behind my two captors was a third boy. One of my brothers? No, another Brahmin – the white of his garment told me that – coming to take part. But I was wrong.

He asked: 'What did she do? Why are you tormenting her this way?'

'I don't need to tell you,' spat back the older boy. 'But she splashed her filthy water all over me. Disgusting!'

He looked at me. 'That's true? You did that?'

I was confused. I felt it was an adult speaking, not a boy. Yet he was barely older than I, with a visage that was both sweet and determined.

'I did, sir.' I could barely get the words out. 'But it was an accident. I beg to apologise.'

'Well, please do it then.'

I managed to look to the elder boy and say, 'Sir, I deeply apologise.'

'There you are. She's sorry. You can let her go now.'

'Leave us alone! This isn't any business of yours. We're going to whack her with sticks.' I felt relieved to hear that the cliff was no longer the plan.

The third boy looked my way, then back to the others. 'Don't hit her. You can hit me instead.'

'No! We want *her*.'

'Hit me. I can take it.'

'I don't think you can.'

'I can.'

That was that. A challenge had been made. The second boy was told to go back and find a stick. My protector helped me to my feet and walked me the few steps along the path and into the open by the wall of grass. How grateful I was; I clung to his arm, trembling.

The second boy reappeared and passed to the tall boy a long, crooked stick that made me afraid, even if it wasn't intended for me.

'Go on,' said my protector. 'I said I can take it.'

The tall boy was losing his nerve. But he had his honour to defend and so he backed up, raised the stick over his shoulder, then brought it down hard at an angle, striking right above the hip. My boy went down, letting out a yelp that seemed to me louder than the blow deserved.

The tall boy stood gloating for an instant, then dropped the stick and ran off with his assistant.

My boy lay unmoving. I didn't know what to do. Should I slink away? Go up to him? I settled for a bit of both. I edged away but I also called out, 'Thank you so much, sir! Are you all right, sir?'

He sat up suddenly. He smiled; he had been lying still to frighten the other boys. And just as quickly he got to his feet, dusting off his garment.

I said again: 'You're all right, sir?'

'Yes, pretty much.' He wasn't much good at swinging that thing, really.'

It was only then that I recognised who this was. It was the Abbot's son. I had seen him before, part of the entourage that trailed behind his imperious father. Strangely, a somewhat unwilling member of that group, I always felt. He should have been walking right up with his father, but he seemed always to drag his pace, to be near the end.

Now I became afraid all over again. I had caused the Abbot's son to be struck with a stick. So what did I do? I turned to run off. But he stopped me with a question.

'Please, may I know your name?'

'I am Jorani, the Stairway Guide's daughter.'

He seemed to take interest in that very ordinary information. 'Jorani, may I know what brings you up the mountain?'

'Why, sir, because I am his daughter, but I am also a guide.'

'But I thought that guides are men.'

'Sir, I am a guide and I will always be a guide.'

How I dared say something so forceful, and to him, I don't know. It was, really, the first time I had intimated my dream to anyone.

He had no answer, and I took that as permission to turn – and run.

Later, when I'd reached home again and calmed down, I told Father that I'd stumbled and dropped the jar. He was not angry. It was old and cracked, he said. We'll get a new one.

How much time passed between that day and the day I was brought before the Abbot? I think it was less than a year. But a feeling of debt remained. Sometimes before sleep at night I would picture in my mind's eye the boy who had prevented me from being thrown off the cliff, for now I had concluded that that was what was intended. I would reflect on how kind and brave the son had been, on what his life atop the mountain must be, how different from mine. I wished I somehow hadn't run off and had had more time with him, and I wondered whether he felt the same about me. I have used the word debt to describe my feelings, but I thought at such times that it was more than that. I dared even to think that in that brief period, we had formed some kind of bond.

And then we had been brought together for a second time, however brief and painful it was. So without hesitation, I lied to the Abbot and said I had only seen a boy standing at an overlook, perhaps to throw stones and watch them fall. It was scant repayment for what this boy had done for me.

4

As Tall and Glorious as Heaven Intended

Pilgrims can be talkative folk, even in the middle of a strenuous climb, and of course a favourite subject is the place from which they've just come. Often it's another stone temple. So I learned as a girl that the empire has a great many of these. In fact, it seemed that the far-away capital Angkor was as much a city of temples as of people. Walk this way or walk that, the climbers would say, and you'll run right into another one! How beautiful, how imbued with Heaven they are! Over and over, I heard of temples standing on great squares of flat ground marked by moats and the straightest of walls, with gates that face east so that each morning they welcome the rays of the rising sun.

I could not help but think that what I was hearing as we climbed was quite different from what our own temple is. This was often confirmed to me when we approached the Entry Court and the visitors got their first look. How their faces lit up with wonder, or sometimes bewilderment.

This temple, they could now see, is doubly close to Heaven. It is a mountain resting atop a mountain. In the mists of history, Heaven constructed this great peak so that men could build on it and create our community. Divorced from the flatlands and the concerns of life there, the peak allows a unique focus on Heaven and spiritual accomplishment. In what other place can men and women pray so close to stars and Our Lords the Sun and Moon? In what other place can they not only see but *feel* Heaven's clouds, the mists passing right through them? Rather than watching from below and wondering what hides inside the luminescent mantle of clouds, here they can inhale that very essence.

Heaven gave one other signal of the holiness of this place. It built the mountain not of soil but of holy stone. Our masons have no need to use slaves and elephants to haul it from far away, certainly not up the slopes. Stone, all that could ever be needed, is right here beneath our feet on the peak, waiting to be chiselled free. In some cases, our masons left it in the ground where Heaven placed it, and carved it to become steps or foundations or other parts of the temple. At other temples, I have been told, the builders use brick for some parts, because stone is too difficult to obtain. But our temple? It's almost entirely stone, save for its roofs, which are great rippling slopes of red tiles.

Now, you will recall how I said that pilgrims who reach the foot of the mountain expect that the great stairway will be straight and even, and that they are puzzled to see that it narrows and widens and never keeps to an even incline. Well, as they climb the mountain, they begin to think that the temple must be like that too. So they are surprised all over again to reach it and find that it is in fact much as they imagined the stairway to be. The reason this can be so is that the mountain at its upper reaches abandons the random crags and contours up which the stairway climbs and becomes a smooth and gently rising ramp. I once heard a priest say that the quest for enlightenment is this way, with a long journey of moral turbulence giving way in its final stages to calm and order and steady progression. On this ramp is our temple built, and it is like nothing else in the empire. Temples of the flatlands are square or rectangular. But our temple's prime quality is that it is *long*. It is a great thoroughfare heading straight and gently upwards on a course to Heaven. With each step, the pilgrim moves closer to the absolute. Along the way are five courts. These consist of wondrous pavilions, terraces, shrines, gables, statues, bathing pools, and holy linga shafts, each holier than the one below it. The holiest place, the First Court, stands at the very edge of the cliff.

I describe to you all of this, but for many years I knew only the

Fifth Court, the one we called the Entry Court. It was the only one to which people of our rank could go. The eastern stairway led directly there, and from it you could look up the temple's great processional avenue and see, far ahead, the foot of a set of steps that gave access to the gabled Fourth Court, which sat on a massive base of stone.

Pilgrims were startled by the temple's length but also by its orientation. The ones they knew from the lowlands point east and west, but our temple looks north and south. I saw more than one pilgrim check his sense of direction by glancing upwards to see the sun's position in the sky. Sometimes Father was asked how such an orientation was possible. He would say that to us of the temple community, it was only natural that the Lord of the Summit, a manifestation of He of the Third Eye, should look north and south from his sanctuary. Does not his mountain provide a perfect vista in both directions? For what reason would our Lord choose to cast his gaze in a direction at odds with the patterns that He in his wisdom had chosen to create here? Some of the pilgrims were learned men. I could see that they found Father's answer interesting, but that before deciding what to believe they would put the question to priests at the temple.

Now, so awed were pilgrims at what they saw from the Entry Court that sometimes they forgot themselves and made to continue their ascent right away. It was now up to us guides to remind them politely that there were other things to attend to first. Foremost, they should say the initial prayers of their visit. Oh yes, of course, they would reply. Then they would kneel with palms together on the paving stones outside the Entry Court or pass up its steps and through its door so as to directly address the guardian god who presided in gilded glory inside.

With these prayers completed, there was one more thing to do – make a donation to a special fund. Years before I was born, the Abbot had decreed a new form for the temple's supreme tower, which stood in the First Court. However tall and glorious it was, he believed, it was not as tall and glorious a home for the Lord of the Summit as Heaven intended. Masons were now working to render it as it should be. They had long since dismantled the old tower, and were nearing completion of one that stood more than twice as tall. You could not see it from the Entry Court, but it was visible from down on the plain if you walked a bit away from the mountain's base. The former tower had barely shown from down there – you might even have mistaken its tip for the top of a distant tree. But this new one – what a marvellous sight! It jutted straight up from the mountain's summit, adding height to what Heaven had created there in ages past.

The masons' work on the tower proceeded using funds graciously sent from the capital by His Majesty the King. But the Abbot had deemed that each pilgrim deserved a personal chance to help advance this great project and thereby win added merit for the next life. So for many years now, acolytes had been stationed at a mat outside the Entry Court, with a treasury box and ledger sheet in front of them. Father and sometimes we children explained why these young holy men were there and how far the project had progressed. (And we would neglect to say that these very acolytes could also provide merit certificates.) Most every pilgrim gave something for the tower, occasionally something of substantial value. More than once, I saw golden jewellery placed in that box. Names and items given were duly recorded so that neither Abbot nor Heaven would forget the generosity.

Now we would offer final hints and suggestions on how to proceed with a successful visit. Up near the Fourth Court, we'd tell them, to the left of the avenue, you'll find a large pool for your ablutions. We spoke as if we'd been there ourselves. An acolyte there will explain to you the proper ritual of this cleansing. You'll find lotus blossoms and fruit and other offerings for sale outside each court.

Before departing the Entry Court, pilgrims would variously settle tips on us or look elsewhere and pretend they didn't know that such things were customary. Some strode up the avenue full of purpose and energy. They were eager to reach whichever court was their destination for devotions. Others moved timidly, pausing every few steps for silent prayer right there in the avenue, as if fearful of what lay ahead. Sometimes I would play a whispered game with my brothers Bonarit and Pen to guess which kind of walk each pilgrim would assume, based on what we'd noticed of that person on the trip up the stairway. I was rarely wrong.

The upper courts, of course, were not quiet and empty, waiting for the prayers of the pilgrims. They were filled with priests and acolytes carrying out the various functions of the temple. The most senior priests, often the Abbot himself, tended the First Court's linga shaft, in which resides the Lord of the Summit. By bathing the shaft in water that became sweet and holy at the touch of the stone, the priests both reassured the god of the esteem in which he was held and beseeched him to allow life on this earth to continue.

Other priests up top had tasks involving the temple's very large volume of holy texts. Do you know how villages have storehouses for rice, filled to the brim? Some of the temple's buildings are like that, almost as full, but with texts. Stacked on musty shelves, or on top of each other, sometimes in an absolute jumble, there could be so many that it was hardly possible to move about inside. The texts had been written out in ancient times on palm leaf, and though the temple priests take care to handle them gently, no text could last forever up here. That is because for so much of the year everything is damp. In wet season, rain clouds pass right through the temple's windows and doors, leaving behind a hint of the water that the gods give them to carry. Stones perspire, the shine on silver bowls grows dull, beads of moisture form even on the jewellery that adorns the chests and arms of priests. Just as a garment worn by a village woman will eventually rot and crumble in these conditions, so do the texts – Heaven did not choose to make them immortal. So, new copies were made, and the old ones retired. But not, of course, just thrown out. As I told you, priests and acolytes brought them in procession to the overlook and set them alight atop the stone pedestal.

Most of the temple's texts explored the mysteries of the cosmos, drawing on the epics from mother India that recount the holy armies that took to the field in eons past to address the conflict between good and evil. But there was also another kind of text, kept in a separate depository. These recorded the names and authority and glories of our human monarchs, going all the way back to the founding of our empire, back even before the time of Our Lord King Yashovarman, first worshipper at the Temple in the Clouds, fourth King to rule over our race as benevolent father.

I talk as if I knew all of these things at this time. I did not. I could not ascend beyond the Entry Court and see these things, and the temple's workings were not something that anyone saw fit to explain to a common girl from a family of guides. This knowledge would only come several years later, when events took me to places I had never seen before.

But, to return to the pilgrims whom we had just dispatched up the avenue, I am sure that some of the priests were annoyed with their constant comings and goings and ignorance of the temple's customs. But that was not our concern. For now our work was done. Father would clap his hands, the signal that we should all hurry down the temple's northern stairway. I haven't mentioned this one before. It's the second means of access to the temple; it and our eastern stairway come together at the Entry Court, but from different directions. Compared with the number of steps that ours has, the northern one has almost none at all. In a flash we would reach its bottom, where there's a large flat area that contains the temple's main market. Pilgrim guesthouses large and small are found here, as are stalls selling things to eat and drink, or amulets or cures for disease. We always went straight for a stall that had coconut milk. There we sat and laughed and of course paid only a fraction of what pilgrim customers paid. Everything that had happened that morning would be tossed about: the size of the tips, the look of relief on the face of the litter's occupant when we reached the top, the cuteness but constant naughty behaviour of a party's twin little boys. Father would gently scold us for speaking this way of our betters, but we all knew he shared our feelings on things like that.

Perhaps we were not really always in such a carefree mood. But this is how I remember those days and a life that now seems so remote.

5

The Abbot's Benevolence

When I reached our house on the day I was brought before the Abbot, Father saw my distress right away. He led me to sit in the rest pavilion. Thank goodness no one else was around. I got the story out, in some detail. Father listened, a hand on my shoulder. I knew that what had happened gave him great concern too, but he concealed it from me, instead whispering sympathetic words that his girl should not be too upset, that it wasn't her fault, that she had simply stumbled onto something that was not her concern, that he would say prayers seeking dispersal of any ill will created. I was trembling all over again when I got to the end, and not just because of the terror of it all. It was because I had told him the same lie of omission that I had told the Abbot. I had said the son was merely standing at the precipice. The fire and smoke were so troubling in my memory that I did not want to involve Father in them. Whatever they meant, telling him would make it worse. And I suppose I was discovering that a lie, once told, must be told again.

When I was done, Father took a breath and told me what I knew he would tell me. I would no longer be going to the top. 'It was never really natural in the first place, you coming along with us,' he said. 'It's time to take your place down here like the other women. I've been thinking about this for a long time. I was going to have a talk with you.'

'No! Please!'

But I stifled whatever else I was going to say. I had told him a lie, and now he had told me one. If anything, I had been gaining in his confidence as a member of the escort team. He had only today sent me up the stairway on my own for the certificates.

Father could see what I was thinking.

'Jorani,' he said, 'it's also better that the Abbot and his people don't see you for a while.'

I looked away.

'My girl, we simply can't risk it. The Abbot is Heaven's representative on earth, but he is also our family's benefactor.'

'I know that, Father. I just...'

'Perhaps you don't know it in the way you think you do. Some past Abbots have ignored our family. This one has helped us. Before he began to do that, we were horribly poor. We were thinking even of turning our backs on our duties to the pilgrims and taking up farming. It seemed the only way to survive.'

I had never heard such a thing. The family chronicle had always been one of unbroken service and devotion.

'It's a shameful thing, Jorani, something a parent would not want to share with a child.'

'But when? When was it?'

'It was well before you were born, when I was younger even than you are now. All right, all right, I will tell you. Everything.'

I edged closer.

'You know that our service here began with our ancestor who begged leave from his King to serve as stairway guide. The duty is vital, but for a man to devote his life to it, he must have food to eat. Our ancestor married a woman from the village down the trail that you and I have visited so many times. It was such an honour for her to become wife to a man of such critical duties that the village took it upon itself to support the couple in their service. Each week, members of a different family provided supplies of rice, fish, vegetables, and cooking oil – the basic sustenance to maintain a household. This arrangement proceeded for many generations, allowing our family to focus on the holy task. But it broke down during the time of my father – your grandfather – when he was a young man.

'It happened because the headman of the village took a liking to the young woman whom your grandfather was courting – my mother, you see, though I was not yet born. The headman was already married; he wanted her as a minor wife. He had known her for many years as she grew up in the village. One day when she returned alone from the fields, he fell in alongside her and began telling her how pretty she was, how delightful her voice, how comfortable she would be as part of his household. But my mother replied that she had to be going home. She bade him goodbye politely, then turned down a path she didn't normally use. Leaving him behind was rather a brave thing to do, because she knew that just that morning he had approached her parents with promises of silver and other kinds of help a headman can provide. Her parents had a dispute with a neighbouring family over rights to a plot on which banana trees were planted – they could expect some assistance when those rights were decided. But she loved your grandfather already, and I suppose that she knew that as eldest son of the stairway guide of the time, he would one day inherit the post and she would become mistress of the stairway.

'The headman refused to give in. For months, he kept trying to win her acceptance. She declined, again and again. The politeness she had at first shown was giving way to refusal in sharp and definite terms, but he chose not to hear. One day he waylaid her just outside the village, taking her hand, saying he would not let go until she agreed. Your grandfather happened along just then and before long there was a fight. It ended with the headman on the ground, his nose bleeding, and my father standing over him. Immediately your grandfather realised what trouble this could bring, so right there he offered a very elaborate apology and a hand to help the headman up. Both were rejected. The man got to his feet on his own, giving an angry glare, and set off back to the village.

'But the headman did not approach her again and she and your grandfather began to think that the danger was past, that the headman had grasped that he had behaved badly. Three months later your grandparents were wed as planned.

'Now normally a bridegroom goes to live with his new wife's family, but because of the special duty of the stairway, your grandmother came to live in our house. One week later, it became clear that the headman had not forgotten. On the appointed day for the delivery of supplies from the village, nothing arrived. Our family assumed there was some mistake and that the things would come the next day, but that day too passed with nothing. So, your grandfather's father walked to the village to inquire. He knew which household was scheduled to deliver, so he went directly to its door. He was met by a very apologetic young mother who explained that she could not provide. The reason was that the headman had called a meeting two days earlier and announced to the people of the village that they would no longer be feeding this family that produced nothing. It was burdensome and unfair, the headman said. How had it gone on for so long? Where was the written authority for it? He had consulted with a seer and learned that our welfare was the responsibility of the temple community up top. Some people spoke up to protest, of course, but got nowhere and soon there were murmurs going around that the true reason was my mother's rejection of the headman. But such is the power of a headman that he was able to enforce his will. No food was delivered that week, or the next. None officially delivered, I should say. Some people brought things on their own, at night, but never in amounts sufficient to make a real difference. The fact is that there were some households in the village that welcomed the lifting of the obligation to supply us. It meant that much more to sell in the market or to wholesalers or simply to eat themselves. After a month or two, it became clear that our family was cut off permanently.

'Now, this food was not our only source of support. Some pilgrims who were happy with the service we provided during the climb would tip us at the top – you've received those tips yourself, Jorani. But you know they would hardly be enough to support a family. My father's grandfather tried to take up the question of support with the priests atop the mountain, but it seemed that none of them really wanted to help. Each one sent him to another, who sent him to another, who told him that he should trust in Heaven or solve the problem on his own. It was said that even the Abbot of the time thought this way. I think that the headman was correct in saying there was no written order from His Majesty or the temple for such support. It had simply arisen as a tradition.

'So there began a long decline in the fortunes of the family. We had never been wealthy, of course, but the house that the original guide had built so solidly had been maintained well. When floorboards warped, when thatching leaked, skilled craftsmen were called in to replace them, sometimes hired from several villages away. We all had several sets of garments and no pilgrim was led by a guide wearing anything but a new and freshly laundered one. We never had more than one lamp in the house, but it always had a good supply of oil. And we ate well. The people in the village did not just supply us. They gave us their best. We never received leftovers or damaged goods.

'That situation was long gone by the time I was born. I grew up in conditions much harder than what you have known, Jorani. Our rice was poorly milled, our fish were bought in the market past their prime, or caught as best we could in the stream. When the house needed repairs, your grandfather did them himself. He was now stairway guide and had many skills, but working with wood was not one of them, and gradually the house came to have a ramshackle look. We wore our garments until they were in tatters. But we kept up the guiding and I don't think that my mother ever regretted her marriage. Still, our situation weighed heavily on my father. It was his great shame that the headman's words about life being more comfortable for her under his roof had come true. This feeling did not show as anger, rather as morose resignation. She tried to cheer him up. Each time that he would suggest that she use some of what little we had to buy a new garment for herself, she would laugh it off and say that garments were not what made her happy. A happy husband was the only thing that could.

'Things continued like this until I was about fifteen. One afternoon, a fearful storm swept through the region. It was so strong that it did terrible damage to the priests' houses up top and other wooden buildings, notwithstanding magic incantations that the Brahmins had chanted as the storm closed in.

'Our house suffered grave damage too. The winds carried away the entire roof, beams as well as thatch. Chickens that we kept in a pen below the house were blown away – we never saw them again. In the forest, whole trees came crashing down. It was all quite frightening, as you can imagine. When the storm finally ended, we built a makeshift shelter with banana leaves. Our mats, our rice, our clothing – everything in the house was were ruined or soaked through. We spent days afterwards clearing fallen trees and trying to dry out our possessions. As we worked, my father's eye went constantly to where the roof had been.

'I asked him: "How will you replace it, Father?"

'"I don't know, I don't know..." That was all he could say. He hung his head. I had seen him demoralised before, but never like this. It was frightening.

'The flow of pilgrims had stopped during the storm. But several days later, some new ones arrived, expecting the usual escort. For the first time, my father did not lead them. He sent me. I felt proud to be entrusted with the job on my own, but I was anxious over how it had happened.

'When I descended that afternoon, I found him sitting in the rest pavilion, staring blankly. I tried to tell him about the climb, but he waved me off. 'I don't want to hear. It may be the last trip, so why should I be concerned?'

'I asked my mother what had happened, but my question merely caused her to weep.

'In later days, my father did elaborate. There was no way to fix the house, he said, unless we gave up our stairway guiding for several years and went off to some far district to work fields as hired hands and build up some savings. But if we did that, there was the chance that some other family with means would step in to claim the house and our vocation.

'Now, it was just at this time that Heaven intervened for us. An acolyte brought us a summons to escort a priest down the stairway the following morning. My father hardly paid any attention, so it was I who went. I arrived at the top before the appointed time. I was surprised and a bit frightened when I saw approaching not "a priest" but the Abbot himself. Our Abbot of the current day, Jorani, at that time a much younger man. He had only recently taken up the post and was escorted by half a dozen other men of holy orders.

'I worried that our family would be perceived as giving offense by sending only me and not my father for this duty. I knelt as the Abbot's party approached. One of the lesser priests looked askance at me. But the Abbot seemed not to notice me at all. But then, why should a great priest pay attention to a boy? Now, when he had first arrived at the temple to take up his post as Abbot, he had come from the north by the route that leads to the northern stairway. He had not yet ever set foot on the eastern stairway, nor seen our house.

'We began the descent. I got up my courage and did my best to facilitate, showing him silently how to grip the ropes and plant his feet safely on the steps. I did this keeping my distance and implying that these were skills that he could only know already. We made reasonable time—he was quite slim and fit in those days. As we neared the bottom, he caught sight of our roofless house.

'He spoke for the first time: "Now why did no one tell me there was this kind of damage down here?" One of his aides – he was perspiring, due to nervousness as the exertion of the descent, I think – replied that word had not reached the top.

'My father spotted our party as we completed the descent. He came quickly out of the house, having realised that whatever his state of mind, when the Abbot came calling, he must give the proper honours. He went to the dirt before the Brahmin, but, as with me, the man seemed not to notice. His eyes were taking in the damage to the house and the rest pavilion, and the fallen trees that had not been cleared away. His eyes kept coming back to the house. It was, of course, the first structure related to the temple that arriving pilgrims saw.

'"When will the house be repaired, Stairway Guide?"

'"Holiness, I beg your forgiveness, but I cannot say precisely. We lack the money." My father said nothing about quitting the vocation to work in the fields.

'The Abbot looked around and, seeing my brothers, said: "Assign those two to work on the house exclusively. It must be fixed."

'My father swallowed and, still on the ground, he said: "They are strong boys, Holiness, but they lack the skills needed for the job. And, please, as I said, sir, I lack the money."

'The Abbot showed some annoyance at that. He proceeded to ask a string of questions that quickly extracted the facts of our family's destitution. He now noticed, I think, how my own garment was tattered at its hem, how my sister had not even a wooden comb in her hair. All this displeased him. Just as the house was the first thing that pilgrims saw, we were the first people. My father remained on the ground as the Abbot pondered this situation. He was a man of fearful power, of course, but his authority terminated right here at the base of the mountain. It was beyond his sway to instruct the village to resume its support of us. He would have to find another way.

'Then something like a miracle occurred. He turned to one of the assistant priests. "What was it that that pilgrim was asking you the other day? I overheard it. You know, the estate lord from south of the capital. He had a question about merit."

'The assistant replied: "Holiness, he had received help from the Stairway Guide during the ascent. This man here. He wanted to know how much less merit he would accrue compared with his brother, who completed the climb without help."

"'Yes, that's what it was. Stairway Guide, do you ever hear this question?"

"'Sometimes I do, Holiness."

"'And how do you answer it?"

"'I try to answer truthfully, Holiness. I say that the merit deficit would depend upon how much help he had accepted. A great deal of help would mean that almost no merit would accrue. It is Heaven's law, but they don't like to hear that answer, Holiness."

"'Yes, I'm sure they don't. But suppose that pilgrims who accepted help were able to do something that made up the lost merit. Theirs would be the same as for people who had no help. What would be their response?"

"'I think, Holiness, that many of them would want to do that."

"'I imagine they would. And I think that Heaven would feel that it's only fair that a person whose physical state no longer allows an unaided ascent should not be penalised in terms of merit. There are many texts that would support that contention. Now, this equalizing of merit could be provided as a gift, a sign of divine compassion, but pilgrims would be ashamed to offer nothing in return, would they not?"

"'They would, Holiness."

"'They would feel obliged to give something. Now, Stairway Guide, you know these people. You know how much silver they typically arrive with. What would be a suitable amount to give in return?"

'My father considered that for a moment. "Two silver pebbles, Holiness. At a minimum. Those who could give more would give more."

'The Abbot seemed to like that answer. "That seems right. Now, you would keep one of those pebbles, Stairway Guide, and the other would go up the mountain to the temple treasury."

'It took a moment, but my father became almost delirious with joy! His mind was good at sums and he could see that what the Abbot was describing would more than guarantee an adequate living for all of us. He put his forehead back to the dirt and breathed out thanks and more thanks. Just then, one of the assistants spoke up to say that perhaps a split of three pieces to the temple and two to the family would be more appropriate. But the Abbot cut him off, saying that a simple, easy-to-understand division of half and half would be the better way.

'Turning back to my father, he said: "And there will a full and honest accounting of the silver collected, will there not, Stairway Guide?"

'"Honest in all ways, Holiness! There has never been reason to question the integrity of this family. Not once. That will not change!"

'"It's settled, then. You will make sure that the first silver that you collect goes to repair this house, and in a proper way. Go out and hire artisans. The house must fully uphold the dignity of the temple community. As must you. No more tattered garments, for instance."

'He gestured in my direction. It was a great mortification, Jorani – imagine! Everyone was looking at me in this disapproving way, but my father quickly spoke up.

'"Holiness, all will be conducted as you instruct!"

'The Abbot then told one of the priests to go back up the mountain and explain these new arrangements. Right there on the spot, he ruled that to give pilgrims peace of mind concerning parting with their two silver pebbles and to help keep the accounting straight on the temple's ledgers, certificates would be written out. The priest who was being sent back would bring the first batch back down, hand them over to my father, and then catch up with the travelling party. "Don't be slow," he told the priest. "We will need you in the capital. There's a lot more work on the question of finances to be done."

'And with that, the Abbot departed, not even looking back. As soon as he was out of sight, my father told me to change out of my garment and burn it. I didn't mind – he told me in the old sure sense that had vanished from him.

'It turned out that the Abbot had planned this trip to the Capital for weeks, since long before the storm struck. The purpose was to seek funds to build the higher tower in the supreme sanctuary. Now there was added urgency for his trip, to get help to repair the many damaged structures. Later there were people who said that he intended that this benevolent gesture to our family would lead Heaven to help with his much larger requests in the capital. And indeed those requests were granted. But my father insisted that everything the Abbot did for our family came not from such mercenary calculations. Though the Abbot might on the outside seem to – how did people say it? – be somewhat lacking of a benevolent heart, acts of this type proved that such a heart did in fact lie within him.

'My father's health and spirits revived. He lived another ten years and never missed an ascent until the final six months of his life.

'All through that time, right up to now, as you know, Jorani, the income from the certificates has maintained our family in a dignified manner. Some years ago, the priest who manages the temple's finances began to think that their treasury should have rights to collect both silver pebbles. They changed the arrangements so that it became also possible to obtain a certificate at the top, after the climb. But as you know, most pilgrims choose to obtain their certificates here, from us. As a matter of fact, you're rather good at helping them make that decision!'

He was done. He put his arm around me; I smiled.

'On your feet, then! Let's get on with the day.'

'Yes, but Father...'

'There's more?'

'No. Just this.' I held out to him the bag that contained the forty certificates.

'Of course. I should have guessed. You got them and brought them down, even with everything you've been through.'

For the rest of the day, I took some comfort in Father's story. The Abbot no longer seemed quite as frightening a personage. Still, I could not forget the fierceness with which he had stared at me and gripped his son's arm. I could not escape the feeling that whatever was this thing occurring in the temple community, the silent compact between me and the Abbot's son would assure that I had some further role in it.

6

Courtship

I knew the change would be hard, but it was only the next morning that I found out how hard. Mustering for the climb was the latest party of pilgrims: a toothless old woman who had asked for the hammock conveyance; the woman's son and his wife; four children of varying ages, an infant; and two people I took to be servants. Father called the group to order, led them in a brief prayer, then off they went – without me! Father looked to me in sympathy, then, realizing that this only made things worse, he turned his head. I walked away from the house and stood with my forehead to the trunk of a tree to hide my tears. How long I cried I don't remember.

When Father had said that I had to remain down here 'like the other women,' what he meant was, like the past generations of our family's women. There was only one woman now and it was from her eyes that I was hiding my tears. Her name was Chantou and she was Father's wife. I think that at this time she was in her nineteenth or twentieth year.

There is something you need to know about Father's character, and that is that he never showed any ill will towards me for my role in depriving him of his first wife, my mother. We are taught that such things may be caused not by human action but by that of a spirit, yet so many people, being unable to avenge themselves against the spirit, direct their anger at the person whom they believe was the spirit's tool. Yet Father never showed any of that kind of ire in my direction. Instead, on my mother's death he wrapped me in a cloth and carried me to the nearby village. I spent my first years there, suckled by a young mother alongside her own child. Father came often to visit me, saying he would not allow his girl to grow up a stranger to her sole remaining parent. And when I was old enough to eat rice and fish, he came again to retrieve me. I grew up in the company of Father and my two brothers. My mother's spirit was also present, but despite her efforts, we remained essentially a household of males. The food we ate was not always skilfully cooked, our house could have been better swept. Some people have said that for years I seemed a bit more boy than girl.

But let me return to Chantou. It was perhaps eight years after my mother's death when Chantou came to live with us. It is unnatural for a man to be with no woman and so she came, from that same nearby village, sent with the good wishes of her parents. There were other young women available (Father was the holder of the Stairway Guide post, after all), but for one reason or another, he did not care for any of them and settled on Chantou. She was quite a few years younger than he. I will be frank – I think that her prospects for marriage to a boy closer to her age were not good. Heaven had chosen to make her powers of thought somewhat unsteady. She found numbers difficult, she failed to notice things that were plain as day to the rest of us. She could become confused over a pilgrim's simple request for a cup of water. She could set aside a gutted fish and forget it, allowing it to spoil. But all in all, she made Father happy, I think. She worked hard, she was loyal, she was pretty. She had a good heart. And she added some mirth to the house. One thing I remember well is her ability to mimic the song of birds. She liked to do this in the evening as we all sat eating rice in the house. 'How did a bird get in here?' Father would ask, looking around in mock exasperation. 'Jorani, go and put the poor thing out the door.' I would get up, take a reed broom in hand, and wave it back and forth as if driving a bird to the door. Chantou would stop the call and look about innocently, and we would all laugh.

I came to love Chantou, but I never viewed her as my mother. She was like an older sister, or sometimes even a younger one.

So now my days were passed with her. The males of the family would disappear up the stairway and she and I would get down to the business of maintaining a household and pilgrim station. If there was no rainwater in the jars, I drew what the stream had to offer. I washed my brothers' garments. I walked to the village to buy charcoal and rice and other supplies. Chantou went about her own work in her contented way, sometimes humming a village song to herself. She liked having me as company, I could tell – her sense of contentment increased, which was one good thing that came of this change, I suppose, though on many days I felt resentful that her elevation of mood came at the cost of the decline of my own. As I came and went with the chores, I found myself thinking, over and over, that in not so long the Abbot would forget whatever it was that had happened. There would be no harm in my being seen up top again. And the bond with the Abbot's son? I must have just imagined it.

But as time went on, I found it hard to remain patient. Often after a party of pilgrims had left, I bided some time, then invented an excuse to go outside. I stepped back from the bottom steps to a spot that gave an unobstructed view for a long way up. My brothers came to expect me to appear there just before they reached a place at which they would pass out of sight. They always turned and waved. Father waved too, though after a while he stopped because he didn't approve of this sign that I had not accepted my new life.

Perhaps two years passed this way. It was in this time that I became a woman. For this I was happy to have Chantou. However much my spirit mother could do, she couldn't show me how to deal with things such as the monthly flow. Chantou took the job in hand. She showed me how to wrap myself and assured me that the aches and bad temper would last only a few days at a time. And she began to instruct me on how to behave like a woman. It wasn't anything intentional, I think, just an instinct on her part. However weak her powers of concentration might have been, her instinct was always strong. She insisted that I break my boyish gait, stand straight, and do the proper shuffle of a proper girl. She showed me how to show a hint of calf beneath my garment, how to put up my hair with wooden pins. She corrected my language. And she told me of the dear kind of love that can exist between a man and woman and how it can lead them to do certain things together. I didn't need that part of her instruction. What child has not awoken in the middle of the night and seen parents clutched close beneath a sleeping cloth that is moving in unusual ways? I knew that whatever the differences in age and mind, there was this deep kind of love between Father and Chantou, one that did not threaten the link that he and I had.

Chantou brought up the subject, I'm sure, because she had noticed the attention I got from the new boy who came from the village to be the fourth set of shoulders when the palanquin was borne. I say boy but really he was a young man, with strength to heft that heavy and unwieldy thing. His name was Kamol. He came for wages, but Chantou used to tease me that he would gladly lift the palanquin for free, even pay for the right, just for the few minutes that he got with me at the start and end of a job. I did not reject his attention. It was a welcome diversion. Certainly Kamol was fine looking, with firm shoulders and a well-shaped chest and torso. He smiled often. He had a particular motion that I recall – he would snap tight the waist knot of his sampot garment with a certain kind of flair just before he bent down to lift the palanquin.

'Pretty Jorani, will you be here when I return?' He whispered that to me one morning as a pilgrim party stood waiting for an ascent.

I whispered back: 'Of course. Where would I go?'

'Away somewhere, if you didn't want to see me.'

'If I didn't want to see you, I could just turn my eyes away.'

'Please don't!'

'Oh, hush! My father will hear.'

I did look for him when he returned. I brought him water and we walked a few steps into the forest to sit together on a large rock. We bantered until the sun was low and it was time for him to go home to the village. I was interested, I think, in Kamol and the things that go on beneath a sleeping cloth. But I kept waiting for the other thing, love, to appear and on that day, as on others, it remained just out of reach, like a grasshopper that springs right when your hand comes close to catch it. I will confess what happened on that day, as on others, when Kamol had gone home. I sought out a place alone by the stream or in the rest pavilion, and there I allowed myself to wonder what had become of the Abbot's son, and whether he might be playing some role from the top of the mountain in love's refusal to appear down here at the base. How many times I recalled that look of gratitude that he gave me as his father pulled him through the door of the big house. I would wonder what would happen if somehow we were to be in each other's presence again. I would wonder that, and then feel foolishness come crowding in, and with tears in my eyes I would hurry to rejoin the family.

Those two years passed. I began to think that, though love remained unsighted, perhaps Kamol and I would be married. It would simply happen. Who else was I likely to meet? All the other young men in the village were spoken for; the men who passed through as pilgrims were of other places and higher stations. A few of them flirted when I served them those coconut shells of water, but I knew it was for amusement only. When Kamol caught sight of that, he said nothing. It was not for him to speak up against a gentry boy, of course, but I think that he felt no need to. He had come to feel secure that he and I would be together. What was his work with the palanquin if not a form of bride service? I could tell that Father welcomed the idea of a match. Many times I sensed him watching with approval from the corner of his eye as Kamol and I joked about this or that. Certainly Father had practical matters in mind too. It wouldn't hurt to bring a third son into the family, to end the bother of having to arrange each time for Kamol to come from the village to do special duty with the palanquin.

'So when will we announce our plans to marry, Jorani?' Kamol asked this late one afternoon as we strolled in the forest.

'Oh! We don't have to think of that now. What is the need to hurry?'

'When two people love each other, there is always a need to hurry.'

'But it can be sweeter if you wait, don't you think? The heart grows all the more afire.'

'Jorani, my heart is burning like a giant pile of rice husks already!'

'Kamol, what nonsense you talk!'

'You wound me, Jorani.' At such moments he resembled a scolded puppy.

'Please, please! Now come on, I need to get back to the house, and you need to get home to your parents. Your mother will be wondering.'

I said these things, but still I might have married Kamol soon after. Everyone around me was behaving as if no other outcome were possible. But we can never see the future. The day after Kamol and I took that walk, there came one of Heaven's unexpected interventions.

7

The Summons from the Mountaintop

Father arrived at the base of the stairway wearing a long face. 'Jorani,' he said, 'the Abbot has summoned you.'

I was sweeping the open area in front of the house. The broom stopped of its own accord; I stood there, too stunned to make any response.

'I don't know what it's about,' Father said. He was as concerned as I, but trying to hide it. 'I know only that His Holiness has called you to his presence. I was told just before I came down.'

For so long I had looked forward to climbing the stairway again, and now it would happen in a way that would be terrifying.

Father put a hand to my shoulder. 'Really, Jorani, whatever it is, I'm sure we'll make it right. I'll go with you, of course.'

That was some comfort, but still I hardly slept that night. In the morning I went to the shrine by the house and prayed to my mother for courage to face whatever it was that was coming.

With no pilgrims to tend to that morning, Father and I climbed alone. I dragged, I dawdled. Father had to urge me forward. We passed the Entry Court and took to the upward path that I had been hustled along two years earlier. We reached the Abbot's house, whose size and soaring eaves seemed every bit as frightening as before. There was no putting it off any longer. Father went ahead of me, spoke with a temple guard, who spoke with a servant who disappeared inside. Shortly afterward, the servant came out and spoke to the guard, who spoke to Father, who came walking quickly back to me. I cannot describe the relief on his face! 'The word conveyed from inside the house is that there was no summons. "Why would the holy master summon a girl like your daughter?" That's what was said to me.'

But it was clear that someone important wanted me, so Father took me to look for the acolyte who had conveyed the original summons. And we got to the bottom of it. Not the Abbot. The *Abbess*.

There are so many priests and acolytes at the temple that sometimes people forget there are saintly females as well, living in a colony a short walk to the west of the temple's lower precincts. It is a closed community, supplied with rice and fish and other necessities by outlying villages that were assigned to its support generations ago by princely authority. How many women resided in this place? Perhaps fifty, and from all over the empire. They passed their lives behind a bamboo wall that ran this way and that up and down ravines and hillsides to mark off holy ground and keep out the prying eyes of men. Its gate was normally shut tight to all outsiders, male or female, but once some years earlier I had entered the colony briefly, guiding a prominent pilgrim woman to see a niece who had taken vows there. Inside was strange ground, occupied mostly by enormous boulders! Wherever there was a bit of space between them, bamboo huts had been erected. In each lived one nun, alone with her prayers. In the only real open space stood the main prayer pavilion; behind it, against yet another of the giant rocks, was a house of some size that I was given to understand was home to the colony's leader. I didn't see her that day, but I knew, as everyone knew, that she was a stern woman who bore the holy name Parvati.

Now Father led me along the trail that led to this community. No sooner did we reach its gate than it swung open to reveal the Abbess.

'There you are, Stairway Guide. I was wondering when you'd come. Thank you for bringing your girl. You may leave now.'

Some people you hardly notice. Others are in such possession of themselves that they demand attention. Such was the Abbess. From inside the door she inspected me in a way that took for granted my total submission and obedience. In the few instants before I looked to the ground, I saw that she was tall, with hair streaked in white. I gained the impression that she was past her fiftieth year, and yet in her foreboding face there remained the traces of youthful grace and beauty.

I stood silently, gripping Father's hand harder, unwilling to let him go.

'Holy Mother,' Father said. 'I would like to know, for what purpose is my daughter summoned?' I was happy he had found a way to delay his departure.

'They didn't tell you? I require a servant and have been told that your daughter would be suitable.'

'You wish her to *live* here with you, Holy Mother?'

'Of course. How else could she be my servant?'

That was it. An order from this woman bore almost the same authority as an order from the Abbot. We were to be separated. I don't know which of us was the more heart-broken. I hugged him hard, eyes closed, and suddenly tears were flowing down both our faces.

'Father, you'll come look for me sometimes, won't you?'

'Often! You're going to see me again very soon, in fact. We haven't brought even a change of clothes for you.'

'That's enough, Stairway Guide. It's time for you to leave.'

The Abbess was quite experienced at having tearful young girls handed over to her custody and I found out later that she was following her standard prescription: keep the parting as short as possible, get the inductee started immediately on the rigors of the new life.

But first Father knelt and put palms together. 'She is yours, Holy Mother. She is a gem. May she serve you well.'

Then I was pulled inside by the Abbess's firm hand. The door swung shut with a bang that made me jump.

Part 2

Devotion

The acolyte remains crouched at the Abbot's feet, praying there will be no more questions. But then comes another.

'You mean to say, boy, that the stone has nothing to say about the lack of a nephew?'

'It does not, Holiness!' The young man shudders, realizing that in his distress he has almost shouted. 'There is no mention of such a deficiency.'

'You took rubbings of all four sides?'

'I did, Holiness. The complete text. And I have brought the full set for you this morning. Please, Holiness, understand that I did all I was told to do. I beg forgiveness, but I can only state the facts as I discovered them.'

The acolyte keeps his face to the mat, wondering if there will be a stroke to his back from his master's walking stick. But the Abbot's response is only a laboured breath and a word: 'Leave.'

'Yes, Holiness!'

'But those things you brought will remain here. And you will of course say nothing to anyone about them, or about being sent to the lowlands at all.'

The acolyte crawls gratefully towards the door. The Abbot follows him with his eyes, frowning, then picks up the topmost of the sheets of blackened Chinese paper. He takes some time reading it and then the others.

He turns to the priest who acts as his deputy. 'The boy is right. There's nothing here. So...' A cough makes him stop. 'So, take these things to the depository and keep them safe.'

'I will, Holiness,' replies the priest, understanding that 'safe' means 'hidden.'

'And you will continue looking for other scriptural support.'

The Abbot puts his palms to the mat. He emits a grunting noise, prelude to an attempt to get to his feet. No servant is present, so the deputy steps forward quickly and, murmuring a request for permission to touch the holy body, places hands to armpits from behind and lifts.

The Abbot begins a slow walk in the direction of the door. 'Holiness,' the deputy whispers from behind, 'the poison will be cleansed from you! We have found the means to accomplish that. We can be sure: A god does not renege on a pact.'

'It is better not to comment on the behaviour of a god,' replies the Abbot, not looking back.

8

The Myriad Duties of a Maid

My first act in this new life was to climb the steps of the Abbess's house and bring down soiled garments and a jar of washing ash that lay by the door. These I carried, following the holy woman, down into a ravine where a stream flowed. 'Wash the garments *here*,' she instructed, pointing a finger at an eddy. 'Place them to dry on the bushes *there*. Then come back and find me. There will be another job.'

'Yes, Mistress.' My tears were still showing. I wiped one away.

'Gracious, girl! Don't stand there and cry. You'll get nothing from me for it.'

Do you know, when I had first heard Father address this woman as Holy Mother, I felt a flash of hope. I wondered if I was about to get the mother of this world of whom Heaven had deprived me. Right there, I told myself that I would do my best to be an attentive, responsive, and obedient daughter to this woman; she would reward this effort with love and guidance and protection, and words of support. Yet then so quickly had come those words: 'You'll get nothing from me for it.' No mother would say such a deeply wounding thing.

I was soon locked into a cycle of constant labor, and I suppose this helped keep me from dwelling on that disappointment. I rose before dawn to the strike of a bell that woke the entire nunnery community. I assisted the Abbess with her bath, pouring water over her with a coconut shell. Then she went to lead the nuns in first prayers in the main pavilion; I went to her stove to fan coals back to life, being careful to move the stove if the air carried smoke in the nuns' direction. When prayers were done, my mistress returned and I laid out her breakfast of rice and fish on a tray at a rattan table on the house's veranda. How many times she scolded me that I was cooking like a farm girl! Afterwards I cleaned up. Her scraps were my breakfast. The rest of the morning was taken up with sweeping and straightening and tending to whatever tasks were sent my way by the Abbess, who was now usually at her writing and study board. There was no midday meal to serve, due to fasting, and the Abbess deemed that I should take no food either, lest the nuns see me eating and feel the sinful stir of envy. Past noon, I squeezed in more washing of garments at the stream. At mid-afternoon I began making her dinner. I served it, and later, out of her sight, ate what pickings remained, and washed the eating plates in the stream.

Much of my life, then, revolved around that stream. It flowed into the colony through a passageway beneath the wall, meandered about, then passed out under a wall by which our privy stood. It was wet season when I began my service, so the stream was giving off a pleasing splashing song as it crossed our community. Water was plentiful. But when dry season set in, the challenges became enormous, though I got no sympathy from my mistress. 'If we're running low on water,' she would say, 'then go get some more.' As the stream dwindled, I built little dams of rocks and mud to trap water. When the bed had gone completely dry, I hunted around the colony grounds for rocks that had cracks that continued to give forth drips of water. The nuns, of course, were on a similar hunt for their own needs, and at times there was some unseemly competition among us, but I at least had the advantage of priority in that my labors were for the fullness of their mistress's jars. Whatever I did manage to collect, I husbanded carefully. I used not a drop more than required when cooking rice. By use of multiple clay pots, I figured out how to catch and reuse water when washing garments, though this I never told my mistress. Overall, I did not make her garments as clean in dry season as in wet, but she never scolded me for that. I can only conclude that age had weakened her eyesight to the point that she could not see these things.

Another challenge of dry season was its air, which Heaven had deemed would be so much cooler than at the base of the mountain! Nights I slept with a cloth clutched to my chest yet I never felt fully warm. My dreams were long and unnerving. Yet in the waking hours, the chill helped me get by with less water. Normally my mistress was not given to conserving when bathing, but in this season, when I poured water over her, she always urged me to hurry up. As for me, sometimes I skipped a bath entirely rather than have to explain an empty jar. How I disliked doing this, but again, the cool air was my helpmate, reducing my need to bathe.

So, water was my constant concern, except for one particular kind. It was contained in a gilded jar that held a place of honor atop a stand of lacquered teak in the Abbess's house. That first day, I saw this jar and sensed that a maid should not handle it, yet its sides and top were marred by dust and fingerprints, and I could not restrain myself. I took up a cloth and made to dust it.

'Don't touch!'

Startled, I pulled back. 'Of course, Abbess.'

'If "of course," why were you about to touch it?'

'Only to clean it, Abbess.'

'That is not part of your duties. Only I will handle that jar. It holds water that has been sanctified at the linga of the Lord of the Summit.'

I quickly learned how important this water was. It was central to her daily devotions, in fact. Before saying even the smallest prayer, she moved the jar to her shrine, so that its content's powers would infuse her every word. But this jar was not only for her. One day, she broke a nun's fever by sprinkling drops of holy water on the girl's face and breasts. On another, drops were scattered across a small vegetable garden that the nuns cultivated within the walls, so as to assure the fertility of seeds planted there. The Abbess was sufficiently generous that she used all of it up in a few weeks, at which point an acolyte arrived at our gate to take the jar back to the linga to be refilled. The jar came back clean, but before long dust and grime had collected on it again. As far as I know, my mistress never cleaned it. Again, I think fading eyesight was the reason. But her eyes were good enough to find many other things for me to do.

I recount all this not to suggest that I was near worked to death. I did get time to sit by myself and eat, and sometimes when I lay down on my mat at night I would deliberately put off sleep, so that I could listen to the song of crickets in the dark. It did take discipline to forgo the midday meal, but I was rarely truly hungry. In fact, for the two meals that I was allowed, I generally ate better than I had in my old life. The quality of the fish and greens that I served my mistress reflected a station in life quite higher than my family's. And I learned early on just how much she would eat and so prepared enough to assure that the leftovers were sufficient.

And there were periods when the work ebbed. It was when my mistress turned over authority to the senior nun and left our compound for a day or more. She never offered any explanation as to where she went, though I could see that she walked towards the north. There was always something purposeful in her gait at those times. I formed the belief that she had a shrine in the forest where she went for a special retreat away from the noise and sometimes petty bickering of the nuns. It was of course for me to keep up my work in her absence and have everything in order when she returned. But still, with her demanding presence removed, these interludes lightened my load and I very much looked forward to them. So too did the nuns. More than once, they brought out contraband in the form of dice games and even little jars of rice wine.

As the weeks progressed, I would sometimes take comfort by imagining things that must be happening at the house down the stairway and would be happening when I returned. The bustle and sense of purpose as a new pilgrim group arrives in the morning, the peace that sets in at night as everyone settles down under mosquito nets, the scent of the lamp's extinguished wick in the air. I don't know why, but I found particular solace in recalling sounds—a floorboard creak that endured no matter how many times Father tried to fix it, the rustling call of leaves overhead as a breeze passes through. And of course at quiet moments I would sometimes allow my thoughts to stray to a certain son and whether he might visit the nunnery, though of course that was quite impossible. Feelings of foolishness still followed when I imagined such things.

Gradually I came to accept my life here, for however long it would continue. But what I could not get over was that Father was never allowed to visit. On that first day, the Abbess had not objected to his promise to come. Yet when he returned with my clothes he was not permitted to see me. He was told just to leave them at the gate. He tried many times after that, I know. I could hear him. Fruit and other things he brought for me were either given to the nuns or channeled to me long after he'd gone back down the stairway. And Kamol? He tried to see me too. Once his somewhat raised and irate voice carried into the colony from outside the gate, causing several of the nuns to glance up from the texts they were studying. To him my presence inside seemed like nothing more than a kidnapping, I think. But his efforts were as futile as Father's. I will confess that I was not entirely upset by that. I would not be marrying him as long as I served the Abbess. Hearing Kamol's voice brought to me mainly a thought that a young man will do reckless things when he is separated from his sweetheart.

Now, there is one duty that I have not described to you, and it was something that I actually liked. It was assisting the Abbess when she was at work with texts. She would sit on a mat, before a low writing board. Whenever she did this, it was my job to obtain a lotus blossom to put on either end of the board. I did not ask, but I think the blossoms were meant to clear her mind of worldly concerns. I brought many other things too. To her right, I placed a pile of thin black sheets of stone—slate, she called it. To her left, on an old plate, I put stubs of charcoal. These she used to make marks on the slate. For hours at a time she would sit there, writing, writing, writing. I could not go far, no matter what other work was waiting. I could never be sure that she might turn and tell me to take up a knife and shape the end of a charcoal stub. 'Make it sharp like an arrowhead, girl. The letters will be clearer that way.'

Her charcoal texts were intended just to order her thoughts. Later I came to think of them as discussion with herself (and perhaps with helpful spirits) concerning what should be in permanent texts. These were written on dried palm leaf. For these my duties were much more demanding – it took me many months to learn them properly. She instructed me in how to use a knife to cut the leaves into strips of a very specific size. She taught me how to mix ink from various powders that were stored in tiny vials. Just the right amount of water, just the right portions of powders resulted in a blue-black liquid of the deepest richness. Often I finished my sessions with her with the tips of my thumbs and fingers stained. I had to wait until all was dry before I could gather up the strips on which she had written and store them away in one of the teak boxes that lay against the back wall of her house.

I didn't realise it at the time, but I was learning the skills of a scribe's assistant.

And then one morning she surprised me with an announcement that I would accompany her to a meeting of the temple's Brahmin Council.

'But why, mistress?'

'What kind of question is that? Because I will need you there.'

'And where is this meeting?'

'In the Third Court.'

This was too many shocks at once. I would make my first trip outside the nunnery. I would ascend not one but two courts above the Entry Court. I might be in the Abbot's presence again. And, I will confess it: the face of the Abbot's son flashed in my mind's eye. I might see him again too.

Whatever my face revealed of these emotions, she paid no attention. 'You will bring a change of your newest and cleanest garment. Mine as well. And charcoal and slate.'

So on the appointed day, I gathered up the things in a straw bag. I followed her out of the nunnery, feeling a sense of liberation. We said brief prayers at the Entry Court. And then we began to walk, just as the pilgrims always had, up the great avenue that I had never travelled. And I was like those pilgrims who were fearful of what lay ahead. I dragged; the Abbess told me to hurry up. On we went, passing the stone posts that lined the holy thoroughfare. We came to the ritual bathing pool, which I had told so many pilgrims about but never seen. Its four sides were carved as stone steps that gave access down to the water's glistening surface. The Abbess signalled that we would stop.

'Clear your mind of all but virtuous thoughts.'

I removed my garment and did my best to follow her instruction, though I think that the thoughts that remained were not particularly virtuous. They were merely yearnings that I would commit no error of propriety in this place.

We descended the steps. I slipped into water that was strangely warm, as if gods had breathed on it. The Abbess murmured a blessing. 'May we be pure and fit to enter the holy court and may we carry out our duties to Heaven.' She submerged her head, and I did the same.

I dressed her in the fresh garments I had brought, then saw to my own. We resumed our ascent. We came to the Fourth Court. What a sight it was close up – a long stone building with flaring eaves like the wings of a bird. It rested atop a tall stone platform that stretched east and west. We said another prayer, then began climbing steps to its centre door.

'You! Go around to the side!'

From above, a temple guard shouted those words down on us and they were meant for me alone. I stopped, frightened, but my mistress tugged at my arm. 'We will keep going as we were,' she told me. 'It is my right to bring whomever I choose through the center door.'

We stepped by the guard; I avoided his eye but could still feel his admonishing glare.

This court was mostly open to the air. We passed through it, me whispering prayers in the direction of shrines erected on either side of the passageway. We stepped out into the light again, with another section of ascending avenue before us.

The Third Court was even grander than the Fourth. 'We will be with the council shortly,' my mistress said as we climbed its steps. 'Stick close by me and remain silent.'

In the entry hall, an acolyte motioned that we should pass into a chamber to the left. It was long and brightly lit by windows. Red drapes adorned walls; gold bowls and cups gleamed. Two priests were seated on mats. They paid us no attention. Neither of them was the Abbot, so I breathed more calmly. I noticed now that each priest had an assistant behind him, seated on a smaller mat, and that the mats were part of a circle of mats and writing boards that filled most of this room. So, would my mistress take her place on one of those in the circle? She would not, I now learned. Instead, she turned to the acolyte and told him to lay out two mats outside the circle, in the corner to the left of the door through which we had entered. A large mat for her, a small one for me. And a writing board.

I took out the charcoal and slate that I had brought and laid them out neatly on the board.

Soon more priests and assistants entered the room. It took a while, but all the mats were filled, save for two at the chamber's head, which I now noticed were larger than all the others. Then came a bell's chime and an acolyte's chanted call. We all put heads to the floor. With my face down, I glanced furtively in the Abbess's direction for cues. When she sat up, I waited a moment before I did the same, lest I seem to be placing myself at her rank.

And then—I saw the son, seated at the head of the meeting. It had been more than two years since the mysterious fire, and in the instant that I looked at him now, I saw that he had made the same transition as I. He was now a young man, his Brahmin whiskers having come in, his hair in the top knot of an adult rather than hanging loose as a boy's. He sat calmly, comfortably. He showed no particular emotion just then, other than polite engagement with the gathering. I looked longer than I should have. Then his gaze drifted my way and what a change came over him! You might have thought he'd discovered he was sitting on a scorpion. His eyes widened, his mouth trembled. Perhaps I remember his reaction as stronger than it was, because I felt some pride in being its cause. But then he recovered and gave me a silent nod of acknowledgment, or welcome, or empathy, I couldn't quite tell. In me, notions of feminine modesty taught by Chantou took over. I gave a prim smile and looked to the floor.

I noticed only now that sitting next to the son was the Abbot. Thankfully, he had taken no notice of me. His face bore a scowl. If it is possible to sit in an intimidating way, His Holiness was doing it, the very arrangement of his limbs seeming a statement of threat to everyone in the room. Yet I was also left feeling that he had aged, by much more than the two years that had passed. Though his eyes exuded commanding energy, his cheeks were sunken, flesh sagged on his chest and his arms seemed like sticks. I got the sense that just the few steps from the door to the spot where he sat had been something of a trial, conveniently obscured by the communal lowering of heads.

A priest called us to order. We (or rather, everyone else) chanted a blessing, touched our foreheads to the floor again, and the meeting began.

Except, it was in a language I could not understand. Brahmins are schooled in Sanskrit, the holy tongue of India, and when they discuss religion, they often do it in this language. So the Abbot began what turned out to be a lengthy discourse on...something. His voice went up, it went down, it seemed to be insisting that everyone in the room agree with it. Whatever he was saying, he had a voice that matched the force and energy of those eyes. He took in hand a dark sheet. At first I thought it was palm, but then I saw it was some other material that

I didn't recognise. Normally texts have dark letters on a light surface. But this one was the opposite, white letters on a dark surface.

My mistress was busy with her charcoal stub, writing words quickly in something less than her usual careful hand. Many priests did the same. Two very ancient ones, however, seemed to be committing the words to memory, their eyes closed. Yet, based on frowns that I saw around the room, I formed the impression that about half of the priests could not agree with whatever it was their master was saying. How this could happen I could not say. I had always thought that the Abbot's every word was taken to heart and obeyed.

He finished. I sensed that my mistress wished to pose a question, but knew she could not in this company. The Abbot's eyes had come her way not once during his presentation, and it occurred to me that the fact that no mats had been laid out for us meant that she had not been invited to this gathering. She had sent herself.

A priest who was sitting just in front of us put a question to the master. The answer seemed to be yes, or at least not no. But a second question from this priest was received with eyes closed in impatience and an answer that seemed to dismiss it. For a bit there was a sort of hubbub, with some priests speaking up to try to question the Abbot, and others leaning close to consult one another.

Then, with nothing resolved, silence settled over the room. It was the Abbot's son who broke it. His was the sonorous voice of a man, so for a moment I had trouble matching it with what I'd heard when we'd exchanged those few words at the cliff two years earlier. He spoke with what seemed clearness of intent, though for not nearly as long as his father, and I sensed that his words caused the same division of opinion among the priests in the room.

The Abbot spoke once more, in a somewhat combative way, as if abandoning attempts to reason and simply demanding that they accept his message and ask no more questions. Then, on a signal from the Abbot, a bell sounded to close the meeting. We all put faces back to the floor. We held them there for what seemed an unusually long time.

From the swish of feet on floor stones I gathered that servants were helping the Abbot rise and make his exit. When we brought our heads up, the son was still there, and his eyes came to mine. I should have looked down, but I did not. We exchanged something, I don't know what, across the length of the room.

'Go wait outside, girl,' said my mistress.

I did. But before long, I found myself edging to the door to take one more look. The priests and scribe assistants had all departed. Remaining were just the Abbess and the Abbot's son, exchanging whispered words. I should have wondered what they were saying; rather, I focused instead on wishing that I were in her place.

9

The Insights of a Fortune Teller

As I knelt to put out breakfast the next morning, the Abbess announced that she would go to the lowlands and I would accompany her.

'To the village on the plain, mistress?'

'Goodness, no. Much farther. We will go to the capital, Angkor. Really now, you look quite uneasy, Jorani. Have you never been beyond your home village and the mountaintop?' There was an unfamiliar tone of sympathy in her voice.

I admitted that I knew only those places. 'Well,' she replied, smiling, 'it will open your eyes. Be grateful. Some of the nuns in our community here would love to be in your place. But they commit to a life of prayer and I'm not going to let them be exposed to the temptations of six weeks in the lowlands.'

'*Six weeks*, mistress?'

'Why, yes. Perhaps more. However long it requires. We will leave in three days. You'll have a lot to do to get ready.'

'Yes, ma'am. But may I know, why are we going?' I felt emboldened to ask this, I think, because I had accompanied her to the council meeting and done her proud – no stumbles across thresholds, no errors of protocol.

'Because every other year the Holy Mothers of the nunneries of our order come together there in convocation for two weeks. On the way back, perhaps there will be a stop at a temple or two.'

'I see, mistress. Now, would you like Father to arrange for an oxcart? He knows everyone in the village down below.'

'No, no. We won't be going that way. We'll leave to the north.'

My heart fell on hearing that. There would be no descent down the stairway, no reunion with Father and my brothers and Chantou. But I have to confess I was also thinking that each week I was away would be a week in which I would have no chance to again be in the presence of the Abbot's son. What nonsense had swirled through my mind the night before as I lay on my mat. There had taken hold in me again a notion that our brief encounters, those few seconds when it was just he and I, had created some sort of bond. A bond between an Abbot's son and a common village girl – how absurd it was, yet the rule that our eyes should not meet had been broken, so easily, with no offense felt on either side. I could not accept that there would not be more such times and perhaps even the trading of words.

But the next morning's light, then news of a journey, brought me back to earth. Right away there was so much to do that my thoughts and energies were all taken up. First to prepare breakfast, then to clear up, then to begin packing garments and jewellery and hair brushes and other essentials for the Abbess's travel.

On the day of departure, the Abbess recited a prayer to transfer authority over our community to the senior nun. Then, with two hired men helping with the bags, we walked to a clearing just north of the temple. A covered oxcart waited – I had arranged it through a man in the market. I helped the Abbess climb up and settle onto a mat in the back. I remained where I was; I was preparing to use my feet.

'Girl, it's too far to walk to Angkor. Get up here with me.'

'Yes, mistress!' Again, kindness to which I was not accustomed.

The first stage of our journey was a long descent. Our cart followed a track that wound left and right between hilltops. I studied rocky slopes, wondering what spirits lived there. Mostly the place was wild, but here and there we passed small cultivated fields scratched from soil along streambeds. Two men using hoes looked up as we passed, staring right into the cart. I silently shifted closer to the Abbess. It was not that I was afraid of strangers. I had grown up serving them – all pilgrims were, after all, people I had never seen. But the interactions had always been on ground that I considered mine – our house, the pavilion in front of it, even, in some sense, the stairway itself. Here it was *I* who was the stranger. I was passing through places that belonged to other people and other spirits.

'Don't worry, girl,' the Abbess said, seeming to read my thoughts. 'Those men were merely curious about us. An unknown cart passing by their plots is a big event. They may be talking about it for days.'

By mid-afternoon, I was feeling more secure. The rocks and crags of the temple zone had given way to the familiar greens and browns of lush vegetation. We had reached the northern base of the hills that held our temple up to Heaven. Ahead were perhaps fifty houses arrayed along a stream.

'Is this the capital, ma'am?'

'Goodness, no!' She laughed. 'This is just a village, not even a big one. We have a long way to go. We'll see *much* bigger than this.'

There was no hiding my ignorance, so I tried to change the subject. 'You have travelled often, then, ma'am?'

'Yes, when I was young, I went many places. I haven't been in a nunnery all my life.'

I hoped she would say more, but she did not, instead looking back to the sights of the road.

We turned to the west. The track took us along the stream's bank. At late afternoon, as a monsoon shower prepared itself overhead, we came to a crossing. The water seemed rather deep, so our driver went to find help. The first raindrops were falling when he returned with two local men, who coaxed our oxen forward into the water with whispered country endearments. Through cracks in the cart's floor, I watched water rise towards me. Wading alongside, one of the men assured me it wouldn't flood me out, and though it did come awfully close, we remained dry. On the other side, our driver gave them a bit of silver, and they wished us a good journey.

In a short distance, with rain beating hard on the cover of our cart, we came to a temple rest house, our first stop. I hurried the Abbess up its steps and helped her bathe and change her garment for evening rice. Early the next morning we resumed the travels. For two days we headed westward, mountain ridges always on our left. Then we came to a place where Heaven had split the mountains. Our cart rolled through the gap; lowlands showed themselves far ahead. Our pair of oxen got a break from their labours – they had only to walk and the cart followed of its own weight. We reached the plain. From here, the mountain range's majestic southern face showed itself, and I looked down its length, hoping to sight our holy summit, but I could not see it. Still, this place below with its flat expanses and paddies and clay termite nests felt comfortingly familiar to me.

It took six more days of travel to reach the capital. But we did not reach it all at once. Rather, I became gradually aware that villages were becoming closer together, that there was hardly any rice land in between. We crossed a bridge made of stone, then another. The road became wider and busier – farm carts, soldiers, work elephants, and pilgrims all vied for space. In places it was alive with people who seemed just out to stroll and chat among themselves. Enticing, unrecognizable scents, chimes wafting from shrines cloaked in foliage, vendor women calling out their wares – all these told me we had left the countryside behind.

I stepped down from the cart and walked alongside, the better to experience it all.

At late afternoon, we were following a track that ran some distance along the base of a tall, straight embankment. This brought us to the nunnery that was to host the convocation. It was a large, clean, well-swept place, with a meeting pavilion and stone shrine, surrounded by huts in which individual nuns lived. Trees planted in precise rows crossed the grounds, providing shade and a contemplative air. In all, this place seemed elegant compared with ours atop the mountain. An aged nun greeted us and showed the way to the hut that would be ours – they seemed even to have spare huts here. I unloaded our bags and helped the Abbess get settled and bathe. Later she released me for the evening. After a while I grew bold to wander out the nunnery's gate.

On the ride in, I had felt that the embankment was hiding something. Now I climbed it and at the top had my breath taken away. I was looking out over a vast body of water, its surface rippling with the myriad reflections of a late-day sun. The far bank was so distant that I could scarcely make out a thing on it, other than the green of trees that lined the bank, some of them leaning low as if to lap up the water. Small waves lapped at the shore before me; fish darted about just below the surface.

I looked to the left and I saw something marvellous far away, a temple that seemed to rise from the very surface of the water. A pair of golden towers jutted towards the sky. Just now the rays of the setting sun were bathing those towers, lighting them up. I recalled what I had heard so often from pilgrims, that Angkor was a city of temples as much as a city of people.

I went down on my haunches to rest and better experience it all. Darkness slowly fell. Out at the temple, lamps began to show themselves, warding off the approaching night.

'Ma'am, I had no idea we would see the great Freshwater Sea,' I said as I prepared my mistress's sleeping mat that night. Some of the pilgrims had also spoken of this body of water, which expands every wet season to fertilise the empire's most fertile rice lands.

'Goodness, girl, that's not the Freshwater Sea. It's a holy reservoir, dug by the strength of men's arms three reigns ago.'

I reddened. There was so much to learn.

Other heads of nunneries arrived that evening and the next day, until there were more than a hundred. The convocation began. For two weeks, the women sat dawn to dusk in the nunnery's main pavilion. They prayed, they listened to sermons. Much of the talk was in the holy language, so I could only guess as to the subject, though I am confident that even had I spoken that holy tongue I could not have grasped the ideas. For the most part, things were serious, but at other times gales of laughter carried out from the pavilion, as if they were a group of village mothers passing the time at a well.

Sometimes my mistress had me sit with her as scribe assistant. But other times, there was little for me to do. The nunnery's own servants provided meals for the holy women. So I took to wandering some more. Often I was drawn back to the shore of the holy reservoir, and I tried to imagine how it was possible that this sea was dug by the hands of ordinary men. Surely giants had done it. Perhaps the Abbess was mistaken.

Other times I passed time at a market that lay a short walk from the nunnery. I knew markets from home, of course, but this one was so much larger and so much better supplied. I couldn't come close to listing everything the vendors had on sale there: ducks, crabs, water spinach, lotus bulbs, rambutans, rice. Fishnets, pots, lamps, sleeping mats. There were also fortune tellers, physicians, a man who specialised in relieving toothaches, scribes. The Abbess had given me a bit of silver, warning me to guard it closely. 'Markets in the capital always have tricksters on the prowl for country folk and their money.' Sometimes I bought cut fruit and wandered eating it, attempting the carefree airs that I saw in other girls here. Young men called after me sometimes, but I always kept walking. I knew that my money was not all they were after.

But I did part with some of my money to have my fortune told. At the market's entrance there sat every day an ancient man whose legs were withered and useless. 'Come here, young lady, come here and let us see what the future holds.' If he was unoccupied, he called to me like that each time I arrived from the nunnery. Each time, I walked past, but then I began to think that perhaps I could learn something from him. And so on the morning of the convocation's last day, I strode deliberately to the market and sat down before him. I felt rather self-conscious being there alone because normally he told the fortunes of couples.

He said nothing, just took my right hand with both of his, rubbed the palm, squeezed it, then brought his eyes very close and spent quite some time examining.

Then he turned a doleful pair of eyes up to mine. 'You must sit very still while I make my reading. Can you do that?'

'Yes, sir, I can.' I thought I had been sitting still already.

'Sometimes young girls squirm and I can't get an accurate view.'

'Please sir, I am not like those girls. I can sit still for however long you need.'

'Very good. No need to say anything more.' He continued his examination.

Suddenly he dropped my hand. I thought he had seen something bad, but he merely remarked: 'You have come a long way, I see. And not just to have your fortune told.'

'You are correct, sir.'

'Yes, yes, that's quite clear. You serve faithfully. Your mistress is a woman of high holy orders.'

'Why, yes, she is, sir.'

He took my hand again, kneading the flesh between thumb and palm. 'She is appreciative of your service, yet...at times she does not recognise the full breadth of it.'

I did not answer.

'You help her with so many things. She could not lead her life without you. You help even in the texts that she writes.'

'Why, yes!'

'There will come a time when she sees the full value of your work.'

He closed his eyes to bring on more revelation. 'Now, I can see too that you have come from a place where for part of the year it is cool at night.'

'Indeed, it can be like that.'

'It is far to the north. I see hills and mountains. You live in a holy community and I sense that you are pious, yet you have not taken the vows of any order.'

So much this man was discerning from just a palm. Whatever self-consciousness I had felt, it had left me now.

'You miss your family. Because your service is in a place that they cannot visit. There are walls around it, so that you cannot even gaze upon your family at a distance.'

'It is like that, yes.'

'You miss your family, but that is going to end, perhaps soon, perhaps somewhat later than that. It is not clear. You will receive a visit from family members.'

'I await that most anxiously, sir.'

'And you will hear too from someone who is not family but who is quite dear to your heart.'

I gave no reply, because I was trying to think whether he was seeing Kamol or the Abbot's son.

I took a breath and asked, 'Please, sir, which do you mean? There are two such.'

'So it is with many young girls.' He closed his eyes. 'Ah yes, I see more clearly now. There are two, and I can make out that one of them is, well, quite different from the other.'

'Yes, it is like that.'

'You tell yourself that one of them is the most suitable for you, and yet you find yourself thinking more often of the other. You wonder which one will come to you, but I can see that both will.'

My eyes were glistening now. The fortune teller looked up again. 'You face a choice that faces many young girls. Quite a few of them have sat right where you are sitting. Some allow family to make the decision. But I can see that you are the other kind, who with the assistance of Heaven will make her own choice.'

'But, sir, you must tell me which boy it will be!'

'I cannot. That has not been revealed. But, let me try again.' He took my hand and spent some time examining it again.

'I can tell you only that whichever one it is to be, the union will entail your being together below, not above. Does that have meaning to you?

'It does, sir.'

His divination revealed the only realistic outcome, but not of course the one I wanted to hear. Nonetheless, I paid him well, for a servant girl, at least.

When I returned to the nunnery, I saw that I had passed more time with him than I had thought. I was late for my next duty. My mistress was already standing in line with her sister Abbesses and their attendants. I hurried to her, whispering an apology.

Looking back, I'm sorry that I received the divination when I did, because it put me in a dark frame of mind that was not fully open to what followed.

We all walked in silence up the embankment and down to the shore of the holy sea. At a dock there, a collection of sampans was waiting. I helped my mistress settle down into one, then sat behind her. Our man with a paddle set us quietly gliding towards the temple out in the middle of the waters. The Abbess said nothing, gazing on the sea's late-day shimmer in hopes of spiritual inspiration, I think, inviting me by example to do the same. I pretended to, though in fact I was still parsing the words of the fortune teller. I don't know why I bothered – there was no misinterpreting what he'd said.

Gradually – we must have travelled for close to an hour – we drew close to the temple. It was in fact one with the water, awash in it, in fact. We climbed out of the boat at a dock over which waves lapped gently. An acolyte directed us through ankle-deep water to a pavilion where we sat and pulled our feet up. I dabbed my mistress's dry, though I knew they would soon get wet again. I sat, having no idea what we would do at this place and how I should behave; my lateness in returning to the nunnery meant I'd had no explanation from the Abbess.

Before long we were led through more water to a stone gate, at which an acolyte handed each of us a lotus garland. Silent, we stepped through the gate. I came to a stop. Ahead was the most remarkable god I would ever see, lit by a ring of lamps. Larger than ever a man could be, he reclined on the water, his torso covered in white blossoms. With one of his four hands, he supported his head in repose, no, contemplation of the absolute. With his other hands he held aloft sacred objects whose significance I could only guess. What I recall most vividly is that his eyes were animated, seeing things, twinkling in the lamplight. He gazed upon me with a benevolent power that was at once exciting and disconcerting. I did not deserve such attention from a god. I turned my eyes away. It was only then that I became aware of his greatest miracle. From the navel of this god there leapt a jet of holy water. It arced high into the air and came down into a bronze receptacle.

'This way, Jorani.' My mistress was whispering to me.

A flooded walkway circled the god. The other Abbesses and assistants were processing slowly around it and we followed. I sneaked further looks towards the god. I could see that he wore a jewel-encrusted headdress and neckpiece, and that even his garment sparkled. We passed back to his front and I again lowered my eyes. After a pause for the women ahead of us, we hung our garlands before the deity, then went to our knees. For what did I pray, as I knelt half-immersed in this great god's holy water, absorbing his divine energy? I prayed that the fortune teller's divination would be wrong.

It did not take long to convey this request, and in any case I did not want to demand too much of the god's time. But I did not get up because my mistress remained in prayer, for so long that a woman waiting behind us began to grumble softly.

Finally the Abbess stood up and we moved to the bronze receptacle into which was falling the jet of holy water. I stooped to avoid the water's flying arc; she stunned me by placing herself directly in it. For an instant the god's waters kissed her face.

Trembling, she took a moment to recover, then motioned for me to do the same. I balked, she nudged me forward. Before I knew it, the god's water was washing my cheeks and my eyes, cool and restorative, yet invested with an indiscernible power and purity. I cannot say for sure, but I believe that I was transported for an instant to the realm of this god, where I became for just that instant a devotee in his court, and then I was back again to being what I was, a servant girl standing in the presence of a reclining god and unsure how to behave.

Later, as our boat carried us back to the nunnery, my mistress spoke.

'Our Lord Vishnu, Jorani. We have been in the presence of Our Lord Vishnu. He slumbers beneath the cosmic ocean and dreams our world into existence. You saw for yourself.'

'He was sleeping, mistress?"

'Yes, that is what I said.'

'But mistress, I...I felt that he was awake and bestowing his benevolence on his worshippers.' I did not dare say that he might have been showing *me* attention.

'He is a god, Jorani, and can be asleep and awake at the same time.'

'I see, mistress. And the jet of water, mistress...'

'From the navel of Our Lord Vishnu springs a fountain that gives birth to the god Brahma in each cycle of existence. And you and I have bathed in that fountain's water.'

'We have, mistress.' About that I still felt uneasy.

'We have bathed in this water and received its protection. I dare say that in the months ahead, Jorani, we will need that protection.'

She turned from me and said nothing more as we neared the nunnery's dock.

10

The Holy Monolith

Early the next morning, I carried our things to the cart. Then I stood to the side, awaiting my mistress and the driver. I was surprised to see them arrive together, he carrying something we'd not arrived with, a teak box. It was quite heavy. He grunted while hefting it into the cart's covered compartment, then pushed it deep inside to fit into a corner. My mistress looked on in smiling satisfaction.

'Time to go,' she announced.

I expected we would return to the road by which we had come, but instead we took one that led us deeper into the capital. I thought I was now accustomed to all the city had to offer, but everywhere we went, it seemed, were sights that startled me all over again. One moment we passed a corral filled with stomping elephants, the next a field where soldiers marched in formation, thrusting the points of their spears into the air. Next, a place of entertainment – how was it possible that a man was walking along rope pulled taut between the trunks of two trees? Then a settlement filled with people doing nothing more than passing the time on the steps of their houses. And temples, of course. But now I wondered whether the pilgrims were completely right in saying the capital was more a city of temples than people.

The driver seemed to have specific directions, and after an hour, we came to a long stone wall, too high to see over. It seemed to mark off holy ground. We rolled along it for some distance and came to a stop at a large stone gate. Inside, men in Brahmin garb were walking about.

The Abbess got down. 'You will wait for me here.'

The driver stayed with the cart; I wandered, though not far, having no idea when she would return. After an hour she emerged, trailed by an acolyte who carried a bag from which the tops of palm texts showed. As with the teak box, I was left with the feeling that this bag was heavier than it looked. I noticed too that a man – I took him to be a temple guard – had followed my mistress out the gate, as if to keep watch. But he stopped in the shade of a tree and did not approach.

The acolyte placed the bag in the cart. I helped the Abbess climb in, and off we went again. I was facing out the back, but I was aware that behind me my mistress was opening the teak box in the corner and placing things inside. Of course I wanted to look, but I felt she would scold me if I did.

The driver now returned to the road on which we had entered the city. I welcomed that—I was eager to begin the journey home. We left the city and travelled perhaps an hour through villages and rice lands. We came to a road leading off to the left, and the driver got down to ask directions at a farmhouse. We took the left road. So we were not to go home, at least not by the same way.

The villages became far between, sometimes too far to see from one to the other. But we did not feel alone. This was a major trunk route and we frequently passed people coming in the other direction, in carts and on foot. One time it was a column of dusty soldiers, their officers on horseback putting palms together to greet us. Nights we passed at rest houses. The Abbess and I slept inside; the driver slept in the cart. He had not done that during the journey to the capital, but on that leg we had not had the teak box, which now always remained in the cart. Again, the Abbess's manner encouraged me not to ask why.

On the fourth day, beyond a stand of trees, we saw a golden tower, glinting in the late afternoon sun as had the island temple's. It was not as big, but it served as a signal of civilization and holy precincts all the same.

'Bhadraniketana,' said the Abbess. 'That's what the priests call this temple. It means Great Holy Place of Worship in the language of the gods. To the local people, it's Prasat Sdok Kok Thom, Temple of the Big Reed Lake.'

We approached from the east, passing a holy reservoir, but how small it looked compared with the one in the capital. Swans glided across its surface, and I did see some of the reeds of the name the local people used, filling one of its watery corners. Ahead was a stone wall, with a gate at the centre. We did not go in, of course, but followed a track round to the right, which delivered us to the temple's settlement. There a servant showed us to a rest house. We waited a bit, and then the Abbot came to greet us, or rather, to greet my mistress. I was relieved to see that he was not a frightening figure like the Abbot I knew, but a peaceful man in the final stages of life.

After baths, we went to eat rice at his house. She climbed its steps; I was directed underneath to the place where the servants ate. The driver stayed with the cart.

The next morning, the Abbess told me: 'Today you will come with me inside the walls of the temple.'

'Inside the holy walls, mistress?'

'Now, really, do you need to repeat back to me what I said, young woman?'

'I am sorry, Abbess. But were we not blessed sufficiently at the temple of Our Lord Vishnu?' I was recalling her words on the boat coming back from that place, and wondered how it was we needed still further protection.

'That's not it,' she laughed. 'There will be no blessing here. You will come inside because I will need your help with something.'

Later the Abbot led us through the temple's east gate. My mistress carried a bag over her shoulder; I carried only my usual apprehensions about violating some rule of behaviour in a holy place. Naga serpents looked down upon us from the gate's tower; I gave obeisance to each in turn, trying to maintain a pious frame of mind. We passed into an outer courtyard. There was not much of anyone here, just an acolyte with a broom, sweeping the paving stones of the processional avenue which my feet now touched.

Ahead was a second gate. It took us into an inner courtyard, bounded by columns and galleries on all four sides. Directly ahead stood the temple's principal sanctuary, the golden lotus tower with yet more carved Nagas. At the top of a set of steps, a door gave access to its holy of holies chamber. The Abbot directed us not there, but to the right, where we stepped between two of the courtyard columns. This brought us into a narrow corridor. At the Abbot's direction, we passed a few steps along it to come to a small chamber at the courtyard's northeast corner.

It was gloomy in here, but as my eyes adjusted I made out that we were in the presence of a holy monolith. It was smooth and four-sided, resting on a pedestal and standing almost as tall as I. It took me a moment more to see that it was covered with writing.

'Words given of Heaven,' the Abbot declared. 'They were committed to stone by my great-grand-uncle ninety-six years ago.'

'The bloodline has remained pure, then,' the Abbess said approvingly.

'It is Heaven's will. And my great-grand-uncle was himself the nephew of the previous Abbot.'

My mistress mouthed a prayer, then brought her face near and began to read, her lips forming words as she scanned each line in turn. After a moment, she turned to the Abbot.

'Holiness, I would like to read all of Heaven's words. It will take time. You of course have many things to tend to, and I hope I will not keep you from them.'

With thanks and apologies, he excused himself.

The Abbess turned back to the stone and resumed reading. I remained where I was, uncertain what my role here was to be. I felt skittish in the presence of so many words from Heaven. After a while, my mistress went down on her knees, but not to pray. Rather, she was reading lines that were extremely low on the stone. She almost prostrated herself to read the very bottom one. After that, she got back to her feet and passed around to the back of the stone, where the whole process began again.

Perhaps an hour later, she let out a single word: 'So!'

Now she stepped back and took from her bag a number of large square sheets. I thought they were palm leaves, but when I looked closely I saw that they were some kind of very smooth material. It seemed, in fact, to be the same material that our own Abbot had displayed in that meeting with the priests.

She handed a sheet to me. 'Hold this against the stone – just here.' She pointed to a spot.

'Ma'am, I am to touch the holy words?'

'You may, without concern. I have asked permission of the resident god.'

I did what she told me, but she wasn't satisfied.

'Hold it firmly. Use both hands. Don't let it slip!'

The Abbess took a charcoal stub from her bag. But instead of writing something with its point, she turned it on its side and rubbed it hard back and forth across the paper I was holding. I couldn't understand. But then I saw – forming on this sheet were ghosts of the words beneath it! I felt suddenly very uneasy again. We seemed to be stealing the words. Or perhaps the god of the temple was presenting them to us as a gift. The Abbess seemed to have no such concerns. She kept going, her face displaying a very industrious look, until she had covered the entire sheet with charcoal blackness.

'Now, put that aside. Hold this next sheet lower down on the stone.' We repeated the process; more ghost words appeared. White words on a now dark surface. Again I remembered the Abbot's document.

'Are you sure this is allowed, Abbess?' I was whispering, worried that our host would return and see.

'Of course. It's done all the time.'

'Are you certain?' How bold I was, but this was the strength of the concern that I felt.

'Quite certain, young lady. Now enough of your questions, please.'

After we had done all four sides of the stone, she announced that the job was complete. She placed the sheets carefully into a straw folder. We walked back out through the gates. She took leave of the Abbot, politely declining his offer to put us up for another night, and then we were in the oxcart travelling the road.

We headed farther west. The Abbess had the trace of a smile on her lips.

Presently I asked, 'Ma'am, may I know what those sheets are?'

'They're called paper, Jorani. They come from China. There people use paper to write on, like we write on palm leaf.'

'Yes, but those ghost copies that we made. May I know what...'

'Too many questions,' she replied. That half-smile returned, and I could see that she was more relaxed than she'd been at any point on this journey.

At sunset we reached another temple, but there the Abbess had no special business that I could discern. We were merely travellers putting up for the night.

As we departed the next morning, she announced that we would now finally head home. We would connect to the road that had taken us along the mountain range those weeks earlier and arrive back at the temple's north entrance.

11

The Smile of Heaven

Several days later we passed the same rest house at which we had slept the first night of our journey. We forded the same stream that flowed near it. The water was lower now, so there was no delay – we did not need the local men's help. I smiled broadly as our cart clattered up the far bank and so did the Abbess. We were both tired of life on the road.

All afternoon, our oxen pulled us faithfully up the curving track that led to the temple. The day's light was fading when up ahead the market area came into view. Vendor women were packing up for the day; a hint of the scent of charcoal fires reached us. My heart warmed. Everything seemed just as we'd left it.

Then four men appeared, walking very deliberately in our direction.

The Abbess watched, suddenly concerned. 'The one at the front is a priest called Sar, Jorani. The Abbot's aide, an unpleasant character. The others are so-called temple guards. Now, quickly! Place this under the mat.' She passed me a leaf folder. I guessed right away that it contained the charcoal rubbings and the texts she had obtained from behind those walls in Angkor. 'Don't let them see it, do you understand? Sit on it.'

I did as I was told, though the folder, however thin it was, created what seemed an unnatural bulge beneath me.

One of the guards signalled our driver to stop. The priest stepped around to the back.

'Abbess, on behalf of our master the Abbot, I welcome you back from your journey.'

Courteous words, yet I sensed no sincerity in them. Nor, for that matter, piety in the man. He of course wore the white garment and gold jewellery of a Brahmin, but on him they seemed emblems of a kind of authority that required three rough men for enforcement.

'Thank you, sir,' my mistress replied, though in a cold tone. 'I am happy to be back.'

'My master invites you to take rice tomorrow evening with him and other members of the Brahmin Council.'

Again, courteous words. But he was standing so as to block our stepping down from the cart. He seemed even to be enjoying making us prisoners for a moment. I looked away, worried that he would find reason to address me directly.

'That's a great honour,' said the Abbess. 'Please convey my thanks. I will of course attend.'

'Very good. He is eager to hear about the convocation in the capital and... about any other places you may have visited.'

'Of course. As I said, please tell him that I will attend.' The Abbess signalled the cart's driver to start again, but he could not. The guards had placed themselves in front of the oxen.

'Now, pardon me,' continued the priest, pretending he'd not noticed, 'but I'm afraid that in your absence, the Abbot has initiated new policies concerning holy texts that are brought onto the temple grounds. All of them must first be vetted for theological correctness by him and other members of the council. Have you perhaps brought some back with you?'

'No new ones—only the basic devotional texts that I took with me when we departed. Everything new that I encountered I recorded in memory, not on leaf.' 'That's the best way!' He flashed a toothy grin. 'There is no need to clear space in your house for more packs of palm strips. But I'm afraid that our master insists that we confirm with our own eyes that no texts enter the grounds unofficially.'

'I have told you that I have none.'

'Still...' The priest shrugged, to say, argue all you want, I have time to wait you out. 'It's the same for everyone, Abbess, I assure you. No matter how high the rank.'

'Well, then, have a look.' She got down from the cart. 'Give our bags over, Jorani.'

I did not like that this priest now knew my name, but what could I do. Taking care not to move from my spot atop the texts, I handed him my mistress's three bags and my single one. What did he do but place them on the road – right in the dust! – and thrust his hands in to rummage. I winced at this violation.

Of course he found nothing beyond the devotional strips she had mentioned. After handing the bags back, his eyes began inspecting the inside of the cart.

'Now, what about that box?'

'It contains no texts.'

'All the same, I must have a look.'

'Then look.'

This time she did not tell me to help. I expected him to call one of the guards to pull out the box; he surprised me by hitching up his garment and crawling into the cart like a common labourer. As he did, he sent a scowl my way to convey his distaste at being so close.

He lifted the box's lid. 'Goodness! What's the purpose of all this?'

'The primary shrine in our nunnery is in need of repair, Priest Sar. So are the huts of the nuns. My fellow Abbesses have kindly donated to allow us to fix them.'

He considered that. 'But it's very dangerous to transport things like this without protection.'

'Perhaps it would be for you. But we have travelled for many days without any problem at all. Heaven has seen to our safe arrival.'

He looked again into the box, as if to confirm he'd actually seen what he'd seen. 'I must turn this box over to our master.'

'He is your master, not mine, and you will leave it where it is.'

'I must take it.'

'You will not. You said yourself that on the Abbot's order you were only checking for forbidden texts. You can act only on authority that you've been given.' With that, she turned her back on him.

He had no answer to this kind of logic, so he looked into the box again. A moment passed; he was considering how to salvage some dignity.

He did that with a final demand. 'What about the mat? I'll need to look under it.' He meant the one I was sitting on.

'This is insulting!' the Abbess declared, turning around to face him. 'There's nothing there!'

'How can you be sure? There may be all kinds of forbidden things underneath. Servant girls do things that their mistresses know nothing about.' He gave half a grin; there was a lewd suggestion in it.

'Not this one!' The Abbess was losing her composure. 'Are you saying I haven't trained her properly?'

But the priest was not to be deterred. I shifted, as instructed. He lifted the mat and found nothing.

My mistress was dumbstruck; I was afraid the priest would take note, but he did not. 'Very well, then,' he said, trying now for an accommodating tone. 'We've finished all we needed to do. We welcome you home again.'

The cart rolled on. As soon as I dared, I whispered: 'Mistress, I leaned out and threw the folder behind a shrub by the road while he was checking the box. I shall go back for it.'

What a sigh came from her. And then she hugged me.

'Abbess!'

She said nothing, keeping me in her arms. We rode on.

'Abbess?'

'What?'

'Will Heaven be angry that I mistreated the holy texts? First I sat on them. Now they'll have dust and grit on them. The same as the bags with our clothing.'

'No, girl. Heaven will smile on you. You protected them. You have done a great service.'

When the cart stopped, I got down and carried our bags toward the nunnery. Following was the driver, perspiring as he hefted the weight of the box. He put it down at the gate. From there, a nun and I moved it to the house of the Abbess and up its steps, all the time under her close supervision. We set the load down in the corner that was farthest from the door. Then she went outside to the pavilion to be received by the women of the community. They were kneeling in two lines, palms together. By the power of a quick prayer, authority was transferred from the senior nun back to my mistress.

I saw and heard the rite only in passing, from the house – I was busy putting her things back in their appointed places. Every so often I cast a wary glance at the house's new furnishing, the teak box, and wondered what the true purpose of its contents was. The shrine and huts were not in particular need of repair. It was part of the vows that each nun would keep dwelling in good condition and keep them they did. But how clever the Abbess was in giving that explanation. It could never be checked, because the shrine and huts were hidden behind walls through which the priest could not pass.

And of course I worried about the folder lying out by the roadside. Surely someone passing would see it. So as soon as it was dark, I hurried back to the spot. There it was, undisturbed, right where I'd thrown it. I breathed a prayer of thanks and brought it back.

Inside her house, the Abbess was waiting. She took the folder from me. All she said was: 'In a day or two you will deliver it somewhere for me.'

With that job still to be done, I slept poorly that night. But I was also beginning to feel aggrieved. A maid owes her mistress whatever is demanded, yet for tasks like this, a mistress owes her maid an explanation, and I had received none.

12

The Bloodlines of Priests

The next morning, the Abbess sat down after breakfast with her writing instruments. I brought her a cup of water.

She drank it down, then said, 'You did well, Jorani.'

'Thank you, mistress. But...'

'What is it?'

I had determined when I woke up that morning that I would be bold.

'May I know, mistress, may I know, why such a thing was required of me?'

She let out a sigh. 'All right. It's time that I tell you something of what this is about. Well! Where to begin? Perhaps with your family.'

'My family?'

'Yes. Your father is Pik the Stairway Guide. When he dies, and die he will, like all of us, who will take over from him? Who will be the new stairway guide?'

'Why, my elder brother, Bonarit.'

'Yes. That is how it is in most of society. The elder son takes over from the father, and everyone knows many years in advance that he will. But did you know that among the priests of this world there is a different custom?'

'I did not, mistress.'

'Yes, by order of Heaven, the rightful heir is not the son but the nephew.'

'The nephew...' I did not understand.

'The nephew, but only a nephew who is son of the current priest's sister. A brother's son cannot be heir.'

'I still don't...'

'It is like this: An infant takes form in a woman's womb for nine months. The child's very flesh and blood come from the mother's flesh and blood. It is not too much to say that the infant is a copy of the mother, an extension of her. By comparison, the father's role is small. I know you are young and fresh and have not had the experience, but he is contributing just his seed. The role of the mother is so much larger that Heaven has deemed that with priests the bloodline flows only through the mother.

'Now, suppose that a priest holds a position in a temple that is only for a man of a certain bloodline. The priest is of that bloodline, but his son cannot be, because the son was born of the priest's wife, who is from outside the line. The heir can only be the child of a woman who shares the same blood as the priest. That woman is his sister. Through her, purity of blood is maintained.

'This truth was revealed in ancient times in India. When the great Brahmin Kaundinya came to our land from that place in the mists of history and entered into marriage with the Princess Soma, daughter of the Naga King, to found the Khmer race, he brought with him this custom. It has been followed ever since among priests. It is the way of the Brahmins.'

'I am trying to understand, mistress.'

'You will, don't worry. Now, this system is Heaven's will, yet Heaven does not always provide the means to fulfil it. Suppose the priest has no sister? Or perhaps he has sisters, but they have given birth to no children at all or only to girls. In such cases, it may be acceptable for the brother of the priest to succeed him. The brother's blood is the same as his, after all, as they share the same mother. But this merely postpones the question of a proper succession to the next generation. When this brother dies, the same problem arises. There is still no sister who has given birth to a son who can take the post. So you see, the perfect succession is impossible. In such cases, Heaven will allow the priest's son to be the heir.

'But I will tell you there is another obstacle to a perfect succession, and it is this one that more often gets in the way. It is the tendency of fathers to favour their sons. Regardless of their station in life, fathers want their sons to succeed them. Is it that way with your father?'

'It is, mistress. Father has mentioned it many times.'

'Yes. Fathers know and love their sons. They have watched them grow up. They have had them close at hand for entire lifetimes and trained them in whatever is the family trade or calling. A father wishes to establish security of occupation for his son and he wishes to establish his own security of rice and shelter in the old age of himself and his wife. What better way than placing the son in the father's position? For common folk, Heaven allows this. The farmer's son succeeds the farmer. The blacksmith's son succeeds the blacksmith. For Brahmins this is not the way, yet priests are men too and some of them look to the common folk and wonder why they cannot do the same.'

The Abbess asked for another cup of water. I hurried to get it.

'Now, what I will tell you now you must never speak of, never repeat.'

'Yes, mistress.'

'You sound nervous, Jorani.'

'I am, mistress.'

'You're whispering.'

In fact, I wanted to put an end to this conversation now. The whole subject made me nervous, as if I was treading somewhere I did not belong. But how can a servant break off with a mistress?

'Now right here, right here in the Temple in the Clouds, we see these conflicts. The Abbot has a son. He is very intelligent, very well educated. You saw that on display at that meeting so many weeks ago, did you not? He is pleasing to look at too.'

I did my best to assume an expression of neutral acknowledgement.

'The Abbot intends that his son will succeed him. He has felt this way for many years, and now his determination has been strengthened by a decline in his health. Did you notice the Abbot's appearance at the meeting, Jorani?'

'Yes, mistress. I've always thought him to be a strong, vital man and yet he seemed to have not the energy to even lift his arm.'

'It is that way, Jorani, though on some days he is better than on others. Brahmin physicians have come from the capital to treat him, because the treatment that he gets from our own physicians at the temple seems to have no effect. I believe he is anxious to settle this issue quickly because he sees his own mortality.'

I asked: 'Then, there is a nephew, mistress?'

'Yes, there is a nephew, born of the Abbot's sister. But the Abbot continues with his plan nonetheless. Now, anyone who wishes not to submit to Heaven's will looks for explanations that it is not Heaven's will at all, that Heaven in fact wants what this person wants. The Abbot has grabbed onto such an argument. It originated in the capital, Angkor. There is a Brahmin monastery there whose own Abbot has authored a treatise suggesting that Heaven's will on succession patterns has long been misinterpreted. He points to many places in the scripture where sons succeeded fathers. Did not King Dasharatha of Ayodhaya grant his throne to his son Our Lord Rama, incarnation of Vishnu? The Kings of the epics were really priests, this Abbot says, as evidenced by their many powers and virtues. He cites examples like these and makes many other learned arguments in his treatise. It won't surprise you to learn that he himself has a son.

'The Council of Brahmins in the capital's royal palace has remained silent on this issue. Its focus is the construction of a great state temple for His Majesty. But in the meantime, copies of the treatise of that Abbot in the capital have begun to show up at temples across the empire. Several years ago, a copy arrived here, brought by a runner, we think at our own Abbot's request. He has since studied it with great interest. He is now writing a commentary of concurrence and elaboration. He is trying to lead other Brahmins in the community here to lend their weight to the notion that a terrible mistake has marred priestly succession for centuries, and that we have a sacred duty to correct it now.

'This is what the meeting we attended those weeks ago was about. You saw the document that he was showing. It was not his commentary but a reproduction of part of a great inscription at the temple that is known as Sdok Kok Thom.'

'The temple at which we stopped.'

'Yes, that one. Earlier this year, our Abbot sent two trusted senior acolytes to that temple. They were allowed inside, just like us, to inspect the great stone on which the inscription is carved. They made a rubbing of a passage from that text and brought it back – that is what the Abbot was displaying at the meeting. The words recount that the august Vamashiva, chaplain to the very King who established the Temple in the Clouds, Our Lord King Yashovarman, was the grandson of the chaplain who had served our empire's founder, the blessed Jayavarman. *Grandson,* you see. Not grandnephew. By Heaven's doctrine, that would have meant dilution of the blood. The Abbot asked the gathering, how could this word in the text mean that the august Vamashiva was unfit for the post? That Heaven cursed his appointment to it? Well, look around you, the Abbot said. Could Heaven have opposed his vocation if it allowed so holy a place as this to be constructed in Vamashiva's term as chaplain to His Majesty the King?'

She paused there to let me consider. After a bit, I said: 'I felt, mistress, that some of the priests at the meeting disagreed with the Abbot.'

'You are right. But they don't do it directly. No one dares to. One priest—you recall him, he was seated just in front of us—raised the question of whether during those two generations there were sister-mothers fit to give birth to proper heirs. The Abbot replied that yes, there were such women. They were mentioned in the inscription, he said. So it could only be that Brahmin elders of the time had ruled that father-to-son succession was the correct way. Then this priest asked if the group could kindly see the reproduction of those particular words, the ones that showed the existence of the sister-mothers, but the Abbot said there had been a mistake on the acolytes' part. They had accidentally left behind copies of passages that mentioned the sister-mothers, and did not discover their error until they returned to our temple. So there was talk among the priests about whether other acolytes should be sent back to the other temple. The Abbot said that was not necessary, that the proof of divine approval of father-to-son transmission was the very existence of the Temple in the Clouds.'

'And please, mistress. What did the son say?'

She took a moment before answering. 'He said what he would be expected to say. He said that priests should respect their master's interpretation.' She looked away, and I was left with the feeling that she had tailored her words in some special way.

'But do you see, then, Jorani? The Abbot said it was unnecessary to send acolytes a second time. So I went, we went, in their place.'

'And...may I know what my mistress found?'

'I will tell you!' She showed a flash of triumph that did not sit well with me. 'There is no mention in the temple's inscription that there were sister-mothers at that time. No mention at all. It can only be that there were no such women, and for that reason the succession was allowed to pass through the male line. And you recall that we stopped at that Brahmin centre in the capital before we left? There I obtained a commentary that a priest who is our ally has secretly written. That was what was in the folder that you safeguarded. It entirely discredits the notion that an heir can be anyone other than a nephew.'

'Who is the Abbot's nephew, mistress? Is he here on the mountain?'

'He is. He is a young man named Ritisak. He lives with his mother in a house just to the north of the temple. He attends instruction there. He is of good health and is acquiring all of the wisdom and liturgical expertise necessary to be an Abbot. It is Heaven's will that he will lead the temple when his uncle passes.'

She was finished. A silence lengthened, and I was left with the impression that concerning this Ritisak, she had chosen her words, rather than just letting them flow from the heart.

She made to dismiss me, but I said: 'Mistress, pardon me, but you said nothing about the box that we brought back.'

'Yes, that. It contains things that will make it possible to pursue our campaign—jewellery. Each Holy Mother at the meeting in Angkor contributed something gold or silver from her own body, some of them more than one. We will barter these things as necessary to meet Heaven's objective. It was safer if I didn't tell you, Jorani. The things will be safe enough here behind our walls. But on the road – that was different. Despite what I said about Heaven seeing to our safe arrival, it's always better to limit knowledge that a cart is carrying something that would interest bandits. You understand, I'm sure.'

I didn't really. I felt wounded that she did not trust me to keep quiet on so important a subject.

'What kind of things will you buy with the jewellery?' I could not imagine how this campaign would depend on having the means to buy things.

'Whatever is required. Now, we've spent enough time talking here. It's time for you to get back to your work.'

Later, as I scrubbed the day's laundry, I again pictured the Abbot's son that morning at the overlook, burning something so diligently, and then looking up and catching my eye. I began to wonder if what he was burning was in some way related to the question of succession. Perhaps it was a magic text to empower the rite that would elevate this cousin Ritisak to the post. But in that case, the Abbot would likely have known and approved of what his son was doing. So why did he question me about what had happened? I could not make sense of anything. But the more I thought about it, the more distasteful it became to me that I was serving a group that was working to deny the son the honour of leading Heaven's work at the temple, this son who had shown such selfless courage and compassion for me that day at the cliff's edge.

13

The Voice in the Dark

Two days later, the abbess instructed me to take the ghost rubbings to the convent's gate just before dusk. I did. Waiting there was an acolyte whom I did not recognise. Perhaps he had come up the mountain from some other temple. Without a word, I handed the rubbings over, then ran back to my regular duties. It felt good to be rid of this dangerous material.

Life proceeded as before for quite a few weeks. I washed, I cooked, I bore water. My mistress went off on her visits away. I welcomed the dull routine of it all.

Then one night I dreamed that a male voice was calling to me from across a stream. I peered in its direction, trying to discern whose voice it was, but it was coming from behind a stand of trees. I made to descend the stream's bank and wade across, but the soil beneath my feet was as hot as stone heated by the midday sun. I tried to call out to this person; my mouth opened, but no sound emerged. All of this required effort, and this effort led my eyes to open.

Next to me in the dark was a human form, seated calmly. The call to me continued, but now it was whispered.

'You're awake, then, Jorani! How happy I am.'

'It's you, Kamol?'

'It is, lovely young woman.'

I sat up, startled, clutching my sleeping cover to me. 'Go away quickly! You're offending a thousand spirits by being here.'

I was of course thinking too of my own honour. So many times it is said that an unmarried girl is like a piece of raw cotton. If dropped in the mud, it never becomes clean again, no matter how many times it is washed.

Kamol said: 'I am happy to offend a thousand more, if this is my reward.'

'Go! And I'm not a reward.' He would do better to think of his punishment, in this world or the next, for an offence like this, and one committed for a girl who was not worth the risk.

'I've been denied my sweetheart for a whole year now. How can I just go when finally I'm together with her?' He wasn't afraid at all, it seemed. His voice had assumed the same playful tone that I remembered from the times we had sat on the big rock near the house below. He was trying to draw me to answer in kind. 'And now she's looking pretty as a lotus bud.'

My fortune as told in the Angkor marketplace was coming back to me. One of the men special to me but separated had found his way to my side. 'The union will entail your being together below, not above.' I remembered the augury word-for-word. And yet even with the truth of it before me here in the hut, I found myself resisting.

'How can you say she's like a lotus?' I asked. 'You can't even see her.' I might have said words like that in former days, but not in the reproachful tone I was using now.

'I can say it because my mind recalls every detail of her lovely face. I can see her even if there's no light.'

'Crazy!' That silenced him.

He made no move to leave, and, as we sat there in silence, I began to look past his offense. 'Kamol,' I whispered, 'I am touched that you took this risk to come here for me. But this visit must end now. You are defiling sacred ground. There can be no male presence on soil that is consecrated to female prayer.' I had heard the Abbess use words like those when she lectured her flock. It did not matter to me that what the fortune teller had said suggested that his presence was not so repugnant as that. This man was here to confirm a seer's prophecy of marriage.

When he answered, the playfulness was gone. 'If I am to go, Jorani, I must first know, do we still have an understanding? Will you become my wife when you return to the house down the mountain?'

'Kamol, I...I feel towards you precisely as I felt before I was called to service up here.'

This was true in a strict sense, but the moment the words left my mouth, I knew they would only prolong his misconceptions. They would be repeated down below to Father (though without an explanation as to where they were said) and to everyone in the house, and from there across the paddies to the village. Jorani has renewed her pledge to Kamol. On the day that I returned below, I would be a fish in a bamboo trap, the same trap as before.

But Kamol had come just to hear those few words, not, as many other men would have, to try to draw close in the dark and take things between us to a new stage. I began to feel more and more ashamed.

'I will leave, then.' He said it simply, but I could hear joy in his voice.

He rose and began stealing his way to the hut's steps, my eyes following him.

'Jorani?'

I froze. It was the Abbess, calling across the space between her house and my hut.

'Yes, mistress?' I did my best to sound like her voice had woken me up.

'You're all right?'

'Yes, of course, mistress.' How frightened I was. 'Do you need something?'

'I don't need anything. But I thought I heard voices just now.'

'I must have been talking in my sleep, mistress. I'm sorry I bothered you.'

Kamol was standing motionless at the door.

'Talking in your sleep isn't like you, Jorani. There must have been

something bad in the food we ate, something that riles the stomach.
I'm feeling something myself.'

'Yes, mistress, that's what it must be. I feel that way in the belly too.
I'll be more careful with the preparation.'

'Yes, do that, but now sit up for a bit. That will help it clear.'

'I will, mistress.'

That was all she said. I lay back and waited for a telltale snore from
her house. But there was nothing.

Kamol knew that he could not leave just now. So, quiet as a cat, he
moved ever so slowly back to my mat. When he had lowered himself, I
whispered: 'Sit there until we hear sounds of her sleep.'

'I will.'

'The moment we hear it, you'll leave, do you understand?'

'I do.'

I lay there in silence. My sympathy of a short time earlier was
evaporating. I kept thinking of that saying about cotton, and so I
rolled onto my side to face him.

'Kamol.'

'Yes, Jorani.'

'Before you came tonight, did you stop to think that if you were
caught here, someone else might get in trouble as well?'

'I did.'

'Then why did you come?'

He was silent a moment. 'Because I knew that with you, it wouldn't
be so. If I were caught, no one would gossip about you in the way you're
suggesting. No one would make trouble for you. Everyone would know
that the fault was entirely with me.'

'Foolish! They would talk, and they would talk some more!' I tried
to keep my voice down. 'And in the end you wouldn't want a girl whom
no one could respect, whom everyone regarded as lewd in character.
What would it be like walking through the market with her?'

Now Kamol rolled slowly onto his side so that that he was lying
alongside me on the floor. There was hardly a hand's length separating

our faces. 'That would be a fabulous experience, Jorani. Because, whatever you say, the men would look at this girl and envy me. The women would look at her and envy her. They would wish they could be of such beauty and virtue. They would not talk about her in any untoward way. And, if there was some fool who did, male or female, that fool would have to answer to me and would quickly wish that such things had never been said. But, you know, in the end it would make no difference to me. What other people think is of no concern. I know what resides in my heart for you, and no one can shake that, certainly not with idle blather.'

This year apart had made such a difference. Kamol was almost a poet, it seemed! He had dropped the playful tone he usually employed when making a declaration of love.

I lay back in the darkness a while before I answered. 'I am flattered to be the subject of feelings so strong, Kamol. But however strong this love of yours might be, you should think too of your own safety. It is not only spirits you are offending by coming here, but temporal authorities. Do you know what the punishment might be if you were caught here? Soldiers would come and take you away. Are you prepared to be put in a prison cage, or whipped, or even worse?'

'It would be a small price to pay for the pleasure of sitting in your presence in a darkened hut, even if you take the opportunity to do nothing but berate me.'

'If I do, it's because I fear for your safety.'

What a pure, devoted soul Kamol was. How he deserved to hear me whisper that I had been longing for this visit and had known he'd come, that the risk of his presence here was worth it to me too, that he must find a way to come to me again.

Instead what he got was me breaking off and rolling onto my back. Looking up into the dark, I could sense his presence so close by. I felt even that I could read his mind. He was telling himself that no girl worth having would have responded in any way other than as I had responded. No girl worth having would have done anything but

THE STAIRWAY GUIDE'S DAUGHTER

express concern that he'd be caught. Yet even then he would feel he had obtained what he had come for, a reassurance that my feelings hadn't changed.

Wind rustled the thatch on the roof's hut. I prayed that it would subside so that I would hear when the Abbess resumed her sleep.

Soon, there it was, a hint of a snore from across the way.

'Kamol! Leave now and leave without the slightest sound.'

He followed my instructions. He was so quiet, in fact, that after a few moments I rolled back onto my side to look his direction, convinced he must still be there. But the spot was empty. He was gone, making his way on cat's paws, I was sure, to the hole beneath the wall that let the stream through.

The next morning, things were as before. I prepared my mistress's breakfast. She made no mention of my talking in my sleep. Perhaps in the depths of her own she had forgotten having asked me.

14

A Priestly Ruckus

Ten days later my mistress and I attended another meeting at the Third Court. The room was laid out with mats and writing boxes just as before, with none for us. The same collection of priests took the same places on mats, and we on ones ordered up from the acolytes. I was of course watching to see if the Abbot's son would come. He did. For just an instant before sitting down, he sought out my eye. That was all. But it was more than sufficient reward, confirmation that to him I was something more than a servant girl.

The Abbot arrived. The convocation began with the usual prayers chanted in the holy language, proceeding to discussion in the same mysterious tongue. I would have liked to move my eye to the son, but I knew I must not, so I turned my gaze out a window and studied a mynah bird hopping about as it foraged in a plot of grass. I thought of the birdsong that Chantou used to mimic over evening rice.

But then I was pulled from my reverie by the voice of a priest. He was almost shouting! I looked, and there he was, holding high some black sheets of paper, turning them left and right so everyone could see, making some very forceful point. I knew right away that they were the ghost rubbings of the inscription stone, brought back by my mistress and me. Propriety deserted me – I looked straight to the Abbot's face and first saw alarm, then an attempt to hide it. He adopted an air of impatience, drumming his fingers on his writing desk and jotting notes, or trying to. It was remarkable – the priest ignored him, continuing all the while with his very rash exposition.

Now the Abbot's play-mood shifted to disappointment with the priest's behaviour. He looked away – let the priest say what he will say; I will wait him out. But then he thought twice of that approach too. He called towards the rear door, in the common language. 'Come in here and get me those things.' In a flash, two temple guards appeared. They must have been waiting just outside for such an order. One of them was the man who had gripped me from the left that long-ago day, but he had no interest in me now. He and his partner strode straight past me into the room, without any apologies or preliminaries. Stepping rudely between priests seated on the floor, they closed in on the one who had the papers and even now was continuing his declamation. But instead of surrendering the papers, he held them to his chest as a mother holds a child. 'Go on, I dare you! Put hands on a man of holy orders!' He too was speaking the common tongue now. The guards looked to the Abbot, who nodded gravely. But then two other priests sprang to their feet – I was surprised at how nimble they were – and placed themselves in front of the one with the papers. Next came some pushing and shoving, and shouting of words that I had never thought priests capable of.

Then another, bigger shock. The papers were passed in a flurry to the Abbess who passed them to me with an order: 'Run, Jorani, run! Take them to the nunnery!'

I always obeyed her and now I did so again. I was on my feet in an instant and flying out of the room. Behind me I could hear grunts and slaps as priests did their best to delay the guards. By the time those two men emerged from the room, I was down the Third Court's steps and had a lead of perhaps a hundred paces. I ran madly down the hill, keeping off the holy avenue. Stone in the ground bit at my feet but I ignored the pain. I mouthed prayers to deities I passed, apologizing for not stopping, and all the time breathing harder and harder, far beyond what I normally do with exertion. From behind me I heard shouts demanding that I stop, couched in more bad language, but the guards lacked the prowess that I had acquired in years of climbing the sacred stairway. And yet as I ran, I felt also that I was being sped by a spirit, the one that had caused me to say what I did that day I was brought before the Abbot. It now seemed to me a sympathetic one, not a demon.

I burst through the gate of the convent and kept going the short distance to the Abbess's house. I skittered right up the steps. Panting, I came to a stop at the place where she did her work with texts. I had no idea what to do next. From the direction of the gate came male shouts. I considered going out through the wall's stream gap and running farther. But the Abbess had told me to bring the papers to the nunnery. I would stay here. The shouting was continuing, but not coming closer. My pursuers had stopped at the gate; for men to enter the convent would be a severe act. I relaxed a bit and in my mind I hurried the Abbess to me.

Soon she was running up to the house, breathing as hard as I. I had never seen her in such a state. But what relief I felt to be no longer alone.

'You did well, Jorani.' She could barely get the words out.

'Thank you, mistress!'

'I had no idea I was getting a girl with such determination.' She took from my hand the pieces of paper. 'You have saved four sheets that will allow us to defeat a grave challenge to Heaven's will.'

What a compliment that was. But I barely heard it, because suddenly my mind went to what the Abbot's son must think of me now, having seen with his own eyes that I was among those working to deny him his father's position.

As our breathing slowed, she explained what had happened. The sheets I had saved were in fact the ones I'd thought they were. In previous days, various people on the temple grounds had made close copies of them on palm leaf and these had found their way to priests who opposed the Abbot's plan and some of those who were undecided. The copies, of course, did not have the magic powers, so it was not necessary that we keep those sheets out of the Abbot's hands. But not so for those that my mistress now held.

Later in the day, we heard that Priest Sar, the man who had searched our cart, was visiting the quarters of each priest in the company of those same burly guards, demanding to know whether a copy was there. Some priests surrendered theirs; others refused, leading to searches that turned holy dwellings upside down. In the end, six priests were ordered confined to quarters. These happenings were recounted in whispers by furtive visitors at the stream hole – it was not now safe to do so at the gate.

We couldn't see any of these events ourselves, because by now we too were confined. Priest Sar and his detail appeared at the nunnery's gate, demanding to speak with my mistress. She strode to the gate, me following. We remained just inside the threshold, out of the grasp of his ruffians.

'Abbess,' he began, in an officious tone. 'I come to convey our master's demand that you surrender the rubbings. It is imperative that...'

She cut him off. 'Priest, there is no need for you to deliver the full message. My answer is that the rubbings will remain here.'

'But our master cannot accept...'

'He will have to. I will not give up texts that uphold the doctrine that no reasonable person can contest.'

Now he dropped the civility. 'Abbess, you will regret this. You will regret it and the vile little minx beside you will regret it too, I promise.' What terror I felt! Quick as I could, I jumped behind the open door, trying to escape his eyes. But they caught mine for an instant, and he let off a small laugh.

'Priest Sar, you stoop to threatening a girl, an honourable one? Your threats mean nothing. What we do is holy duty.'

'You call it that. But anyone who comes out this gate will be seized and taken before our master. And nothing will be allowed in. No food, no supplies, and certainly no sanctified water. Do you understand?'

'We will make do without.'

He withdrew, but not before loudly telling one of his guards to settle in outside the gate and grab anyone coming or going. The Abbess frowned, then turned her attention to practical concerns. She ordered an inventory of all food and drink on the grounds. The nuns had permission to keep certain kinds of snacks in their huts, so when these things and our regular stocks were laid out on mats in the main pavilion, it looked as if we all could eat, in a very basic way, for about two weeks. My mistress gave orders concerning the size of portions that would be prepared for the evening meal. Everyone would sacrifice equally, she said.

Water for cooking and cleaning would not be a problem. The stream was flowing through the nunnery grounds with wet-season abundance. The question of holy water was the most troubling of the issues of supply, and I think my mistress was happy that the nuns had not been within earshot when the priest said it would be among the things withheld.

She led me inside her house and, whispering a prayer, took down the gilded jar. 'About half full,' she announced. 'We will no longer use it for fertilizing the garden. Just for prayer and healing.'

'I understand, mistress.'

She looked to me. 'Jorani, you must not fear this man.'

'I try not to, mistress.' I was still shaken.

'Heaven praises you for what you have done. The insults he delivers show only how far from the course he and the Abbot have strayed.'

'Yes, mistress.'

'And you will be safe here. No man will dare come through that gate.'

She turned to her texts. I was surprised at how calm she was. As for me, I began to pace about the house, only now realizing what I had done. I had defied the Abbot, Heaven's representative on earth, and openly joined in a campaign against him and his son.

15

The Lady's Intervention

Two days into our confinement, we heard a male voice calling from outside. 'Send the servant girl Jorani to the gate!'

I was with my mistress at her writing board. She nodded that I should go, and that she would too. 'Just stay inside the threshold. Don't put even a toe outside it and you'll be all right.'

My concern was for other things, though, because I knew who this must be. I was surprised that he hadn't come sooner.

The gate swung open, and on the other side was Father, in the presence of a temple guard, whose voice we had heard. It was my first time with Father since I had begun my service. What I did next was shameful. I looked to his face for some sign that he was acting under duress, that the message I knew he would deliver was not really his own. Imagine – I hoped that force, even torture, had been applied to my own parent. But there was no bruise on his cheek, no twitch of secret communication in his eyes. What I saw was anger, the same as had showed on the Abbot's face. But Father's was anger with me alone. You will recall how our family's fortunes had risen when the Abbot assumed the post. I knew that when word reached him of what his daughter had done, he could have only one response.

Trembling, I went to my knees, putting hands together to seek forgiveness. I opened my mouth to begin a little speech I had thought out in advance. But not a word came out. I dared glance up and saw a look that I saw only once during childhood, on the night when I almost burned down our house. Father had a rule that children did not touch the oil lamp. But one night, after he and my brothers went out to collect crickets, I began playing with ours. I overturned it, and set the floor on fire. The house was saved only because a friendly spirit turned Father's head as he stood across a paddy field and he saw the flames.

No matter how old you are, your parents have the power to make you feel whatever age they choose. Now I felt myself shrink down to become that careless little girl with the lamp.

'I come on behalf of our master,' Father declared. He was bellowing, really, and I can't tell you how frightened and demoralised I felt. He had never used this tone with me, even on that night of the fire. 'He demands that the demon-inspired scraps of paper be turned over to proper authority. And I demand it too.'

I still could not speak. I put my face to the ground.

'Return the paper, daughter, and our master will give merciful consideration to forgiving the transgressions of all people associated with the papers' creation and misuse.'

There was a pause. Then the Abbess spoke up from above me. 'Whatever you have been told, Stairway Guide, the papers are blessed of Heaven. They will remain in my possession until such time as they are not threatened by ungodly forces. I ask that you understand that this girl Jorani, your daughter, was acting only upon my order. She is in my service and as such could not disobey. Heaven desires these papers to be protected and has made me their custodian. You may tell the master that any discussions about them must be with me, not with a servant girl.'

How I wanted to spring up and put arms around Father and cling to him until he forgave me. But I did not. I was serving the Abbess, but I was also serving a spirit, and I felt its presence quite strongly just then. It kept me down at Father's feet, silent. It was more powerful than I, and submit to its will was all I could do, even at the risk of destroying the standing and livelihood of my own family.

The Abbess closed the gate and sat awhile with me. I was incapable of work just now, and I think she recognised this.

Our imprisonment continued. We grew hungry on the partial rations allowed us. But despite Priest Sar's words, we were not completely cut off. At the same hole below the wall where we had learned of the Abbot's action against the priests, we soon received small bags of smuggled food, which my mistress insisted on putting aside for that time when our own supplies ran out. I was surprised at how many people came at great risk to themselves to leave gifts. One day we would feel heartened by support like this, then next our hopes would sink. Late one morning, for instance, we heard male voices from the hillside above the nunnery. I looked over the wall and saw men with picks, trying to divert the stream that flowed into our colony. All day they worked, but by dusk the flow was still strong. Either the job was beyond them, or they were secretly sympathetic and refusing to do it right.

Perhaps a month passed like this. Then we learned from a food-smuggling acolyte that some influential god had been attentive to our prayers. A woman renowned in the capital for piety and generosity of spirit was due at the base of the stairway in four days' time. She would climb the mountain to say devotions, and after those were completed, there might be an opportunity to appeal to her for help.

We waited as patiently as we could. She arrived on the appointed day. She passed two days in prayer at the upper courts, then a third, staying the nights in a house near the Abbot's own. All this was whispered in daily messages through the hole in the wall. But there was no sign she had shown any interest in us. Once she had completed her prayers, she might simply proceed back down the stairway. Our hopes wilted. But isn't it true that Heaven always works in a way different from what humans expect? We try to gaze into the future, but if we saw correctly, we would not in fact be humans.

On the sixth day, a man called from outside our gate.

'The Lady Sray seeks permission to enter the holy grounds.' It was not the demand of a rude temple guard, but a polite request from a voice we did not recognise.

The Abbess hurried to the gate. 'Permission is granted with great gratitude.'

The gate swung open and a woman stepped through. I looked beyond her, out the gate, because, I will confess, I assumed that she was an attendant. There was no glitter of gold about her – no jewellery on her head, her wrists or ankles, nothing around her neck. But outside I saw only a soldier of midlife years, a stocky man with a knife at his waist. He was peering at me as intently as I was at him.

He addressed me. 'You must see to my Lady's safety, please. I cannot enter this place.' I was a servant, but again, these words were not delivered as an order, just a sincere request for help.

'Of course, sir. There can be no danger to her on this side of the gate. There are only women of faith inside here.'

I turned around. My mistress had gone to the ground, but the visitor was urging her to stand. 'If anything,' she was saying, speaking the common language, 'it is I who should bow. What devotion you have shown! You have led this holy community for more than fifteen years, I am told. Is that correct?'

'It is, Lady.' My mistress seemed surprised that she was not being addressed in the priestly language.

'That is an accomplishment that must please Heaven.'

'I am hopeful it does, Lady. But it is not for me to know.'

The Abbess rose and beckoned the visitor to come sit in the nunnery's pavilion. I went for water and refreshments, such as we had, and placed them before the Lady, who gave me the kindest smile of appreciation.

I backed away, but I could not help stealing glances in the direction of this Lady Sray. She wore no gold, yet I sensed now that she was richer than anyone I had ever encountered – rich in virtue, in knowledge, and in the most fundamental kind of natural beauty. I especially liked her look in profile. How old was she? I guessed that like the sergeant, she was more than midway through this life, but every mark of age seemed somehow to enhance her beauty. Perhaps she had children. Would they be of about my age? I guessed it was so. These were the kinds of thoughts that she caused in my mind. That such a woman would visit us here was confirmation to me that Heaven must be taking our side in the conflict.

Later on, I found out that when the Lady had arrived at the base of the stairway, Father had the ceremonial palanquin waiting. But her soldier guard took him aside and disclosed that the Lady wished to climb with her own strength. He was quite protective of her, this soldier. As they took the first steps, he was right behind her, though never so close as to impose. Father was in escort, and I'm sure he thought he'd be called upon for help when she reached the stairway's steepest sections. Yet somehow, the Lady never sought it. Each time, she gazed upwards, mapping out in her mind the best way to negotiate the challenges of the next section. It was as if her virtue carried her up the stairway effortlessly.

The Abbess and Lady remained together for close to an hour. From where I sat, awaiting instructions, I could not hear, but I could see that the visitor mostly listened, sipping at her cup of water with delicate hands. I kept my eye on that cup, and what a privilege it was to go forward and refill it. Each time, she gave me that same type of smile and I felt like the most accomplished servant girl in the world. I decided I would put the cup aside as a keepsake when she was gone.

The Lady left us, gliding out the gate in the same way she had arrived. It came to me that holy people normally have attendants all around and this somehow makes their every action seem holy, as if Heaven has provided a corps of worshippers to bear witness. But this Lady did not need such attendants. It was clear that her every motion was inspired by Heaven, whether there were witnesses or not. As she passed through the gate, I saw relief light up the face of the soldier as she returned to his protection.

My mistress told me nothing of what had transpired. But perhaps two hours later there came another sound at the gate. The Lady and her soldier were back – but with the Abbot! I wanted to hide. My mistress, however, had no such fear. She told me to get two mats. One I placed for her just inside the gate. The other I passed to the Lady, who, remaining outside, placed it on the ground there. Soon Abbot and Abbess were seated, facing each other across the threshold.

The Lady said: 'I hope you will talk to one another now. I will sit sometimes with you, Abbot, and sometimes with you, Abbess.'

Talk they did, for the rest of the afternoon, with the Lady moving back and forth as she had promised. I provided tea. With darkness falling, I placed a lamp on the threshold. As before, I could not hear most of the words exchanged, and when I did, I couldn't always understand, because many were of the holy language. Several times, they seemed to run out of words, and just sat on their mats, glowering one at the other. Each time this happened, the Lady shifted her place and began speaking, to both of them.

Then, with no warning that I could discern, Abbot and Abbess were standing up. He disappeared up the trail; she remained behind. The Lady gave a goodnight to my mistress, then turned to follow with her soldier. The Abbess watched until she had passed into the darkness too, then turned to me.

'Jorani, we are no longer prisoners! Everyone eats double portions tonight!'

Later she told me how the change had come about, but also that it only temporarily ended our troubles. Abbot and Abbess had agreed that their dispute would be put for judgement before a Brahmin in the capital who was known as sage and incorruptible. Both sides would draft preliminary appeals in the next two days; these the Lady would deliver to the capital herself. Two months later, the Lady would send a retainer to the mountain to collect the full written arguments of the two sides. She was confident that a ruling would be rendered within six months. Both sides would undertake to respect that ruling. And in the meantime, life at the temple would continue as before. There would be no confining to quarters, no curtailment of food and, most importantly, no forbidding of discussion of the succession issue.

'Mistress, the Abbot agreed to all *that*? You didn't return the rubbings?'

'I did not return them and he did agree, Jorani. We are free.'

She could see how puzzled I was. 'It's like this, Jorani. There was another factor, brought up by the Lady at those times when the Abbot and I reached a point where we had nothing more to say to each other. The Lady agreed to pay for the quarrying, carving, and installation of two large Naga serpents. Their seven heads, raised to Heaven, will bless pilgrims who have climbed the eastern stairway's final steep section.'

'I know exactly the place, mistress!'

'Of course you do, Jorani.'

'I've been hearing about the stone Nagas since I was a child. Each year they're supposed to appear, but each year passes without them.'

'It takes more than wishes, Jorani. There has never been the silver necessary to bring them about, and what does exist is devoted to the work to build the new tower. But the Lady has changed this with a generous donation. The Nagas will finally come into corporeal being. They will be husband and wife. The pilgrims will walk between their long bodies on the final approach to the temple, absorbing holy energy with each step.'

I felt a spirit stir inside me.

That night, in the light of a lamp, the Abbess took out a stack of holy texts. One of her priest collaborators came to the gate, carrying a load of his own. I expected him to gather up hers and take them away; instead he entrusted his to her.

My mistress saw my surprise and explained that she was to be the principal author of our side's argument. 'Heaven's group has decided that I will be the writer, lest it be said that the Abbot influenced its contents.'

'But why...why won't the writing be done by the true heir, the Abbot's nephew?'

'Because our treatise will by necessity contain high praise for him. It will discuss in detail his education, his mastering of magic and ritual at an earlier age than other boys, his tireless reading of the Vedas, his concern for the poor, and his willingness to sacrifice everything if it might bring the world's moral alignment one degree closer to Heaven's. Now, what would you think if you heard a person saying such things about himself?'

'I would think he was boasting.'

'Of course.' She patted my wrist in approval. 'That is why someone else must say these things, not the nephew. The treatise will reflect my voice. It can be no other way. And it will be the same with the Abbot.'

'The same, mistress?'

'Why, he will not write his side's treatise, not officially, at least. How could he praise his son in the way that the treatise must and yet retain the humility of a priest? Rather, he is now taking advice from lesser priests on what his side's treatise should say. He will decide, write it out, then instruct another man to copy it. It will be presented as the voice of that priest, not the Abbot.'

'It will not be as strong as what you write, mistress!'

'Of course it won't, young woman. It will be weak because it will go against Heaven's will. It will also be based on flawed advice. So much of what the Abbot is hearing from the priests up there comes not from the heart but from some lesser place in the soul that exists only to placate the powerful.'

'How different it is here,' I said. 'There's no one among us who doesn't believe absolutely. Surely, that's a sign Heaven is on our side.'

She smiled. 'Heaven blesses you, Jorani.'

The following day, my mistress began writing the preliminary statement. Because time was so short, and because what she was drafting was not a full exposition, she wrote in charcoal on slate tablets. Still, I stayed near her through the task. I sharpened her charcoal, I provided new slates when she had filled those she had. All day she kept at it, and into the night. She finished only at close to midnight.

'The Lady will leave the temple grounds at midmorning, Jorani.'

I had been dozing but now I awoke. 'I see.' I was disappointed, though I knew she could not stay.

'I will go to the Entry Court and give her our tablets as she leaves.' I smiled when she added: 'You will accompany me.'

But when we reached the court the next morning, I wondered how we would ever get them to her. I am not exaggerating when I say that almost the entire population of the temple had assembled to bid her goodbye. Soon she and her soldier began descending from the upper courts. As they passed down the processional avenue, people ran to position themselves at either side. They knelt on the paving stones as she passed. Some called out to her to bless them.

My mistress of course had special standing, and when she made to take her place where the avenue ends at the Entry Court, people parted way to let her (and me) through. The Lady approached. The Abbess stepped forward and offered the slate tablets with both hands. The Lady accepted them graciously, thanked her, and then, to my complete surprise, turned to me.

'Young woman, I like the devotion with which you serve your mistress. At my home in the capital, there is a servant girl just like you, attending my daughter. I am happy to have her, and am sure your mistress is happy to have you.'

She continued: 'I don't claim to know how Heaven intends to settle the dispute that has divided your community here, but I do know that serving a mistress in the way that you do requires great faith and devotion. And, I think, sometimes unusual methods. They told me about it, up on the mountain.'

That was all. Now she was moving through the throng, her soldier a single step behind.

I never saw the Lady Sray again, but her piety and beauty have remained in my heart ever since. And so has the pride, I will admit it, of the Lady noticing me and paying such a compliment. I believe that courage to do things that I was called on to do in later months arose in me from a spirit but also from the knowledge that the Lady expected it of me.

Part 3

Rebellion

Inside the box are quite a few gold and silver implements, but the commander, peering in, has expected more, given the rank of his visitor. One by one, he removes the things and lays them out before the box, doing sums in his head for what they would bring when traded to merchants at the market town up the road.

'With respect,' he says, 'these would cover wages for my men for perhaps two weeks at most. And really, it's hard for me to give you a commitment to send the men if I don't know what you need them for.'

'As I said, we need them to provide security.'

'Yes, but security against what?'

'Against a threat we face.'

The commander looks to the floor, wondering if negotiating with a holy woman is always so vexing. He's had no such experience. Normally it is other military men who come seeking to hire the militia that he oversees.

'I'm afraid then that I must tell you that we cannot go. Please accept my apologies.'

The woman pauses a moment, eyes closed. The commander believes she is seeking divine guidance; in fact she is deciding to say more than she had wanted to. 'Commander, you should treat what you see in this box as preliminary payment only. You and your men would stand to gain much more. I say this because your mission would entail the suppression of...heresy.'

'Ah.'

Until now, he has assumed that she wants protection from some kind of bandit threat. At best there would be the payment in the box, and as a bonus the few weapons and amulets that could be stripped from dead thieves' bodies. But heresy adds the prospect of the jewellery and polished stones by which wicked doctrines are practiced.

It tips the balance. 'We will be at your service in one week's time, as you request. We will serve you with strength and commitment.'

He puts his head to his mat, and she blesses him. As she does, her mind is elsewhere, exploring how she will find a way to assure that only a fraction of the heretics' goods goes to these men. The holy implements will be needed when right doctrine is restored.

16

Seven Groups of Seventy-Seven

How long did the peace last? Certainly through those first two months, when the full treatises were being drafted for dispatch to the priest in the capital. I remember it as a time of abundance, even inside the nunnery. Rice and fish and spices were again delivered to our gate. Our holy water was replenished. A priest arrived from the upper court carrying a gilded jar full of the lustral substance, and took away the one that was in our possession. It was nowhere near empty, in fact. There had been no illnesses during our imprisonment, which we had taken as another sign of Heaven's support, and the Abbess had otherwise husbanded the water closely.

The Abbess had a new bamboo pavilion constructed just outside the nunnery's gate, and there she received priests who were on her side, or, as she always said (and told me to say), Heaven's side. They came down the hill carrying stacks of palm-leaf commentaries. As far as I know, the Abbot's people did nothing to prevent these visits. The pledge to the Lady that there would be no forbidding of debate over succession doctrine pending the final decision in the capital was respected. I served tea to the visitors, then withdrew. My mistress sat with them for hours at a time, listening, speaking, contemplating, praying.

Then came the day when she told me to devote the rest of the hours to doing my various chores in advance, because in coming days there wouldn't be time. She would need me beside her at all waking hours as scribe's assistant. There were more waking hours than before, it turned out, because she had us working well into hours when we would normally be asleep.

Our focus at the start was what she called 'drafts.' All day and into the night, she wrote, she rubbed out, she wrote again. I sat at her side to provide slate and sharpened charcoal. Anything else that she required I sprang up to fetch. I was surprised to find that, even on this concern, Heaven's words did not come to her perfectly the first time, nor even the second or third. She could commit nothing to the slate without soon finding fault with it.

We worked like this for perhaps three weeks. Then she announced that she grasped the precise words that were needed. We would now make them permanent and beautiful.

As I'd learned to do some months earlier, I cut strips of palm leaves and presented them to her. She took up her long copper stylus, and, after a brief prayer, she cut grooves that I could barely see in one of the strips, which she held delicately before her. The grooves were words. She smiled a tiny smile of contentment each time she finished one. When a strip was filled, it was my job to spread ink over it with a brush. Then she wiped ever so gently with a cloth to remove the excess so that only the grooves that she had cut were filled. In this way, the words of Heaven magically appeared – I always leaned close to catch that sight. Of course I had no idea what words they were. But I can say that to my mistress, and to me in my own way, they seemed ideal, perfectly selected and perfectly drawn. I could not imagine that anyone could read them and not be convinced of their justness.

It was good that I was so busy, because it kept my mind off Father, sometimes, at least. At night when I finally lay down to sleep, I was exhausted yet I could not stop picturing his face that day at the gate. I told myself that surely the Lady's intervention, having calmed the passions of so many people, would calm his as well; wherever Father was at this time, his heart was cleansed of his anger against me. But a week after the Lady's departure, I learned otherwise. I had decided I must see him, so I went to the Entry Court late one morning, supposedly to continue on to the market at the base of the northern steps. Keeping the Abbess fed was still part of my duties, whatever else I had to do, and she liked special things, duck embryos among them, that weren't sent by the villages tasked with supporting the nunnery. As I'd hoped, I caught sight of Father approaching the court with a party of pilgrims. I am certain he saw me, yet as he drew closer his eyes refused to engage mine. Instantly I was again that little girl. I trembled. Again I had an impulse to throw myself into his arms. I would weep, I would plead for forgiveness, I would beg to be taken back down the mountain to resume my old life there. He would understand if only I had the time to explain. But something made me suppress this impulse. I just stood watching. Perhaps it was the same spirit at work, having need of me up here in events that were still to come.

Father ignored me the next time I came across him. So did Bonarit and Pen, who on this day were walking behind him. I had hoped for some kind of covert signal from my brothers, something to let me know that they had sympathy for me and were trying to persuade Father. But there was nothing like that, just eyes that refused to come my way. I never caught sight of Kamol. It seemed that when an extra pair of shoulders was needed for a palanquin, some other young man from the village below was hired. I was certain I was the cause of this substitution – Father worried he would lack authority with Kamol to keep him back if he saw me. Perhaps Kamol had confided to him his night-time visit.

We finished the treatise the night before the Lady's courier was due to arrive. By lamplight my mistress laid out the leaf strips as seven groups of seventy-seven, chanting a prayer of blessing as she worked. Such was her thoroughness that she had asked each of the visiting priests to predict the most auspicious number of strips, then made her own decision. She told me that night that the number she had chosen reflected the seven worlds in the universe, the seven seas in our world, and the seven gurus who impart wisdom in the Vedas.

I tied them up as seven bundles. We were done. I prepared my mistress's mosquito net.

'Place the texts inside the net, Jorani.' I did, though it seemed an odd thing to do. I helped her arrange herself between the bundles. 'Don't worry,' she told me as I worked. 'The spirits aren't offended by this. And I'll sleep much better, knowing everything's safe and right at hand.' And with that she closed her eyes and slept as if her soul had flown clean out of her.

The Lady's courier arrived at the temple on schedule the next morning, accompanied by four bearers. We handed over our treatise at the nunnery's gate. Somewhere in the upper courts, the Abbot did the same with his.

17

The Naga Masons

A week later, word reached the nunnery that twenty men had climbed the eastern stairway that morning, each with a bag of tools over his shoulder. We all knew they must be the masons whom the Lady had promised, sent from the capital. Nuns are nuns, but they are also females, and before long I found myself getting requests to go out and see what I could see. The Abbess expressed some curiosity too, so before long I was on my way. For some reason I thought I'd get a private look, but as I drew near the Entry Court I saw that practically everyone in the temple community had dropped what they were doing to hurry down to the base of the northern steps. Children, groundskeepers, guards, even junior priests – it was almost as well attended as the Lady Sray's departure. We all found the men. They were sitting on mats in a shady area of the market, taking rice soup served up in clay bowls free of charge. The vendors were generous in part because these were a good-looking bunch, with strong arms and closely cropped hair and a vital kind of energy on display even when they were at rest. Yet they'd have eaten free however they looked, because they were going to bring about a religious project that we had awaited for many years.

We Khmers, of course, are kin to the great Naga serpent. We are the proud issue of a union of primeval times, when a Brahmin came from India and married a Naga princess who had taken human form. We have remained one with the serpent god ever since. There are people, in fact, who say that our temple was built by a Naga King who sent labourers and material. My family knows from our long service that it was actually the work of human Kings, starting with Our Lord King Yashovarman. But certainly Nagas have kept it safe through the ages. Husband and wife Nagas look down from the top of the northern stairway. Their bodies run the full length of a thirty-pace section of the grand procession way; each holy serpent has seven heads sheltered by a hood that stands twice as tall as a man. Through this benevolent presence is safety assured at this important point of access to the temple.

But even a Naga has limits to its power. Everyone knew that these two could not properly care for the eastern stairway as well. So when I was a young girl, the priests prayed in hopes of calling another Naga couple to serve at the top of this entryway. The prayers were fruitful. A holy pair came, as spirits. I remember the rite of welcome. Father carried me up on his shoulders to witness it. With sacral water, incense, and more than an hour of chanting, the priests thanked the two serpent gods for agreeing to make their home here. Be certain, they told them, that you will soon be given stone form in this world. From that day, the serpents carried out their duties at that place, at the top of the eastern stairway, one on each side of it. They fended off unwelcome ghosts, they guarded over pilgrims. I could sense the presence of the two serpents every time I reached the top.

Now, creation of a stone Naga, particularly of the size that we all contemplated, is a very costly task. Each New Year, the Abbot would pledge that this year it would be done, that the necessary labour and silver would be found. Yet each year would pass with the job unbegun. It was at this same time, you will understand, that another group of masons was carrying out the replacement of the central tower of the main sanctuary. That work was never on schedule, however. So year after year, the Abbot announced that because of the tower's delay, the Nagas' construction would have to be put off again. But he let it be known that he and his priests had been in communication by prayer with the Nagas, and that the two gods had acquiesced to this postponement of their transformation into corporeal form.

For some years, all was well, but over time we began to get hints that the holy serpents were becoming cross with us. For me, at least, it began with a vague feeling of unease when I passed between the twin presence at the top of the stairway. Father felt it as well. Some months later, there began a series of troubling incidents. A woodsman working the slopes down below lost his grip on his axe and split open his calf. From beneath a rock, a cobra struck at the heel of a climbing pilgrim, barely missing it.

But the most direct communication of this displeasure came by means of my stepmother, Chantou.

I have told you how her mind was at times not strong like other people's. But one day, I learned that it could function as a portal from the absolute. It was during the period when Father had told me to remain below with her and do proper woman's work. Early one afternoon, I left Chantou in the house and went to draw water from the stream. Returning, I called to Chantou from outside but got no response. She must have gone out somewhere, I thought. Now, it happened that just then Father reached the bottom of the stairway, in the company of a priest who was beginning a journey to the capital. Father went into the house; I busied myself pouring the drawn water into a large bath jar. Suddenly, Father was calling for me in very urgent tones. I ran inside. I found him bent over Chantou, who was lying, arms splayed out, near her charcoal stove. She seemed lifeless; Father turned her over tenderly and tried to make her comfortable on a mat, all the time whispering to her. 'Hello, Chantou! Time to wake up, Chantou!' She did not respond. I was troubled by what seemed to be white foam on her lips. Then she stirred, and we both felt relieved. Her eyes opened, looked around aimlessly, and then closed again. Her breathing turned difficult and her entire body tensed. Something made Father and me draw back from her.

And then we heard a voice, rather high and rasping. It was not hers, though her lips were forming the words. *Why have my mate and I not received corporeal form? We came here with a promise that it would be provided right away! Yet these many years later, there is nothing. Why do we not receive proper homage? Why is there not gratitude for all the help we have given on this mountain?*

We froze. We knew right away that this was a Naga speaking, and there was no denying that such a promise had been made. Of course it was not due to us that the stonework remained unrealised. We hoped that the Naga did not feel that *this family* was ungrateful. But Father and I both knew we should not offer excuses. All we could do was put our heads to the floor and hold them there to show our deepest respect.

The voice trailed off. When it seemed safe to do so, I looked over to Father and whispered: 'I'll get the priest!' It was very important that he should hear the voice too.

I explained this remarkable event as best I could as I led him quickly inside. He knelt quietly. Father was leaning over Chantou again, trying to rouse her. She remained still. I was feeling anxious that the Naga spirit had completed its message and the priest would not believe us. But suddenly, the words began again, causing us all to start.

We will wait no longer! It is time to bring in the masons and begin the work. We will accept nothing less!

That was all. Within the hour, Chantou was sitting up, back to her normal self. You'll recall how I felt she was skilled at mimicking birdsong. But after that day I felt it had nothing to do with skill. It was the spirit of birds speaking through her, ones that had used up their time on this earth, and now sought the continued satisfaction of song through the lips of my stepmother. I imagine that she was not really aware that this was happening, just as she had no memory of the Naga's voice after she awoke.

Father and the priest spent some time speaking privately that day, and then the priest climbed back up the mountain to convey the Naga spirit's message. Father remained with Chantou all the rest of the day. But she was soon on her feet and working. The possession had ended.

A panel of Brahmins conducted a preliminary rite of inquiry to see if the Abbot should be informed. They determined that the possession was, as Father and I already knew, the work of a Naga, and so the Abbot was told late that night.

Early the next morning, a lone pilgrim arrived at our house. He declined any assistance from us, even a cup of water, and began climbing. Not long afterward, we heard panicked shouts from above. When Father and my brothers reached him, he was dead, the back of his head crumpled against a stone. He lay a good way off the stairway; no one could explain how his body had travelled that far unless propelled by a very strong spirit.

Word of this spread quickly. Of course, people assumed that the death was the work of the Nagas. Given the affront they had endured, it was said, a strong statement of this sort could only be seen as inevitable and justified. The serpents' patience was exhausted. It was said that the Abbot would now immediately relieve some of his masons of tower duties and assign them instead to carving the Nagas. Yet again nothing happened. Word filtered down from the upper courts that the master was unconvinced by the priestly panel's findings. He had been in communication himself with the Naga spirits, he told his subordinates, and they had denied possessing my stepmother or causing the pilgrim's death. When it was learned several days later that the deceased pilgrim had climbed bearing a heavy load of sin, the murder of a rice merchant in a dispute over payment, the Abbot cited this as confirmation. The man's death was justified. So how then could it serve as a warning? The carving could wait another year.

None of this sat well with people who served the temple. Father was respected among them; his account of the Naga's message was not questioned. Fearful that the holy serpents would take them to be complicit in the broken promise, people made to organise on their own to raise money and bring in masons from outside. But the Abbot found out and forbade it. He sent word that so important a change to the temple and its corps of divine guardians could proceed only by his own leadership and funds.

So you will appreciate why the Lady Sray's pledge of masons for the Nagas brought general jubilation. It was viewed as overriding the Abbot's refusal. The wait was finally over; the great obligation would be discharged. And now, on this day, here was proof that she had not forgotten us: twenty robust men, finishing up their free bowls of rice soup.

Later, their labourer assistants appeared, having made the climb separately. They sat down on their haunches beneath another copse and were served with equal enthusiasm by the market women. And whom did I see among them but Kamol. Spotting me, he put down his bowl and walked over, smiling oh-so-broadly.

Immediately he fell into the old ways. 'Sweet Jorani...' He was doing his whisper. 'You have come to greet me, the man whose heart belongs to you.'

And immediately I fell into those ways. 'And why would you assume that? I was just passing by. And there are lots of men to see here. Some are better looking than you.'

'But none holds this girl so dear. Sweet Jorani, you know this – your eyes have betrayed it. You hold this man in special affection too. He can tell.'

'Can't a girl go out in public without being approached and bothered? Go on back and finish your soup!' I gestured playfully at his bowl.

'Look at me now and tell me truthfully that you really want me to go away.'

I dropped the tone. 'Oh, Kamol, I am happy to see you. You do know that. I've never taken holy vows, but up here I lead the life of someone who has. All day long, in the presence only of girls and women!'

'That's not natural. Come back down and live again below.'

'I can't. But tell me, you're a stone labourer now?'

He gave me a wounded look for changing the subject. 'Yes. The masons recruited twenty of us down on the plain. The pay will be in rice and silver. We'll be here for the full length of the project, eight months at least, they say.'

I wasn't sure how I felt about that, so I said nothing. But I did not leave. After a while, we walked a few steps into a wood and sat together on a rock. Kamol took my hand, and I did not bat him away. How like the old times it was, despite all that had happened.

'How is Father?'

He paused a moment before answering. 'He wants you back below, just as I do.'

'To punish me?'

'No! He worries over you. He worries that you are falling under the influence of bad people.'

'I am in the hands of the Abbess. How can bad people be around me?' I paused to wonder how much Kamol knew about the melee over the inscription rubbings.

'So!' said Kamol, to fill the gap that had opened in the conversation. 'Since you cannot come to me, I have come to you. I am sorry I was delayed. Every day I waited for a call from your father to come bear the palanquin. Yet that call stopped coming. But aren't you glad that I've now found a way?'

The next morning, the masons and labourers built thatch huts near the site where they would do their work. The same crowd came to watch, me included (the nuns wanted reports every day). People brought rice and fish, water in jars, sleeping mats, and they forced these on the newcomers.

The chief mason had worked here as a young man, so he knew the mountain well, including of course the location of stone waiting to be quarried. At midday he took three assistant masons on a walk. Perhaps half of us watchers tagged along. Presently we all came to a hole where blocks had been cut away some years earlier. Shrubs were partially obscuring it; the mason gave orders to clear them. Assistants swung long knives; it was remarkable how quickly they finished. Now the mason squatted and inspected the hole. From his waist he pulled a small chisel, and he spent some time poking at the stone, testing it, holding samples up to his eyes. He broke away chips and rolled them between thumb and forefinger. Then he stood up fast. We were all given to believe that the stone in this place was not to his liking. He led assistants and the rest of us for a short walk to another hole in the hillside. There the same process was repeated, with the same result. It was only when we came to a third spot that he found what he wanted. Everyone smiled when the assistants brought out measuring cords and chalk and began marking off squares on the stone's surface. Other masons arrived; they wanted the actual cutting to begin right away, and so did we. Word was sent to the Entry Court requesting a priest to come bless the start of work. Soon a priest appeared and voiced some incantations.

With the rite completed, the masons got down on their haunches to work. There followed a true cacophony – twenty hammers meeting twenty chisels, cutting long grooves in the stone along the lines marked by chalk and taut cord. But it was such a beautiful sound. Such smiles it brought to all our faces!

I watched for perhaps half an hour. I was about to leave when I noticed a group of priests striding in our direction, holding the hems of their garments up to prevent them catching in brambles. Rank indignation – that was what I sensed in them. At the head was Priest Sar. 'Put down your tools immediately!' He did not say this, he roared it, waving his hands. 'Stop right now!'

The masons, of course, could hardly hear through the din of their work. Many kept right on going. The priest reached forward and seized a hammer being raised to strike.

The chief mason stepped forward, baffled.

'These men answer to me,' he said. 'If there are orders to give, I will give them. Now, please, Holiness, what is your business here?'

The masons were looking to their master, unsure whether to resume work. But none of them did, I think because they wanted to hear the rest of this exchange.

'My business? It's to stop this work. You have no permission for it.'

'We do. This quarry was blessed an hour ago by one of your own priests.'

'His name?'

The mason gave it.

'Well, I can inform you that this priest was acting without authority. Heaven has not been propitiated. Only the Abbot can authorise such a rite. Have you not even paid respects to him?'

The chief mason made a frown. 'I have not.'

'Then I suggest you do. Perhaps you proceed by the capital's customs of work, but we have different ways here.'

The chief mason turned to his men. 'Stand down, then. We'll continue as soon as our work has been properly blessed.'

'Before they put tools away,' said the priest, 'have them fill in the cracks that they've cut already. Everything must be as it was.'

The chief mason mulled over that one, then nodded to his men, as if to say, let this fool have his way.

I got a lot of attention that evening back at the nunnery. The women wanted a full account, not just of the confrontation, but of the men themselves. I could see that their attention was much sharper when I described the style of dress and how strongly the masons swung their hammers. The Abbess, however, was more interested in the confrontation.

Later, as I put up her mosquito net by lamplight, she asked me to describe the event all over again, in more detail. She wanted to know which of the priests I had recognised, and whether I had any explanation for why the chief mason had not first gone to the Abbot. I failed her, I'm afraid. I recognised none of the other priests and I had no idea about the chief mason.

She sat down on her mat. 'I'm worried, Jorani, that something else is the motivation here.'

'Abbess, what kind of thing?'

'You know that for many years the Abbot has put off the creation of the stone Nagas. He says that each time, the Naga spirits have made no objection. Now he has dismissed the finding of his own priests that through the possession of your stepmother, the Nagas demanded immediate work. A group of masons has come to the temple grounds, ready to begin the job. They are fully financed by the Lady. It won't cost the temple any silver at all, nor slow the completion of the tower. And yet there is again an obstacle from the Abbot. I can only wonder if he has some other reason that he has not shared with us.'

'I don't know, mistress.'

'Of course you don't! Be happy that you don't have to worry about such things. That's all, then. You may blow out the lamp.'

Late that night I awoke with a start. I sat up filled with the conviction that the spirit wife Naga had visited my heart, and that the creation of her stone form was only part of what she desired to be brought about. Suddenly I knew something of enormous import – it was she who had been in me that day when I was brought before the Abbot, and it was she who had given me the courage to do what I was doing now in the succession struggle.

One imagines feeling honoured by such a visit, but I lay fitfully the rest of the night, unable to sleep. It was true relief when dawn made its first mark on the room, a square of blue-grey light on a wall above me, admitted by a window that gave onto the east. I arose, lit a lamp and began my morning chores. I felt better not having to think about the Naga. But I decided to say nothing to the Abbess, lest she think I was trying to exaggerate my role.

18

The Tea that Grew Cold

The following morning, the chief mason put on his cleanest garment, and with assistants in tow strode up the processional avenue to meet the Abbot at an upper court. Two hours later, the men were spotted returning. I was there waiting, of course, both to be able to inform the Abbess and for my own curiosity.

People dared rush forward and crowd around the chief, asking what had happened , but he waved off every question. He kept right on walking to the Entry Court, then turned to the right onto the eastern stairway to go to the place where his men had built their huts. I think he wanted to tell them privately about the meeting, but he saw that we weren't going to go away. So he ignored us and called all his men to order before him.

'I have seen the Abbot,' he said. 'He has welcomed us all to this place.' He paused, and everyone was saying, *go on*, with their eyes.

'He asks that, before we carry out our assignment here to give form to two holy guardian Nagas, would we please first attend to certain other projects that require our skills.'

There were instant cries of protest from the men and from many of us.

'Quiet! Quiet, please! I have told the Abbot that while we serve at his discretion, we are here to carry out that project for which the Lady Sray has commissioned us. It is my understanding that this work was agreed to by both parties to a doctrinal dispute, in which we masons take no sides. And that therefore, while we would be honoured to carry out these other projects that the Abbot desires, we respectfully submit that they would have to be carried out after our primary job is done.'

People felt heartened; this man was doing service to the Nagas.

'Now, I have told him that we respect the customs of this great temple, and that we intend to wait here in our work huts until our quarries receive his blessing and we are free to proceed with our proper work.'

The man sounded so confident that I believed the blessing would occur immediately, that the Abbot himself might arrive in full procession at that very moment. But there was no sign of him that day, nor in subsequent ones. The masons and their assistants settled in to wait. Some slept long contented hours in their huts, happy to be paid for no work, while others busied themselves with tasks such as sharpening tools and improving their shelters. As this wait lengthened, I am sad to say, we paid less attention to the men. The novelty of their presence had worn off.

My mistress, however, absorbed these events with compounding anxiety and frustration. I wondered what secret knowledge she had.

The next day she went off on one of her mysterious errands. She soon returned and right away resumed her meetings with supporters in the pavilion outside our gate. But then one morning those contacts ended. Two priests who had promised to come did not appear. Tea that I put out for them grew cold as the Abbess waited, her face becoming graver by the hour.

Shortly before midday, she told me to come with her back to her house. 'Bring out my ceremonial garment,' she said, 'and put on your best garment as well. We will go see the Abbot.'

I did not like this idea, but I did as I was told. When we began the walk up the processional avenue, I could see a priest and three temple guards waiting just below the Fourth Court. Soon it was clear who the priest was—Priest Sar. As we approached, my mistress picked up her pace and made to pass the group, but one of the guards stepped directly in front of her.

'Good morning, Abbess,' called the priest. 'It's an honour to see you here. And your sweet little servant girl.' He gave a frown in my direction; I did my best to ignore it. 'May I know how I may help you?'

'Thank you, Holiness, but there is no need for help.' Again she tried to proceed, first to the right, then to the left, but the guard matched her every move, as if performing steps of a dance. He kept to a respectful distance, of course, but made it so there was no way forward.

'I'm so sorry!' said the priest, with a hollow laugh. 'Apparently word hasn't reached the nunnery.'

'Word of what?' The Abbess was trying to keep her temper.

'Our master has announced that as we await the decision from the capital concerning our arguments, the temple community will again obey him in every way. There will be no meetings or discussions concerning heretical doctrine. To that end, he has decided that nuns must not come above this point in the temple, and that priests must not visit the nunnery. This, of course, will also have the effect of enforcing rules of proper moral behaviour.' Again he looked distastefully at me.

I don't think my mistress noticed. Her eyes had drifted to one of the trails that pass through scrub on either side of the avenue, worn by the feet of people making informal climbs to the upper courts.

'Our master has also decided,' the priest said pointedly, 'that temple guards will watch all of the side trails. It's in everyone's best interests.'

'Holiness,' said my mistress slowly. 'Let us put aside pretence. The Lady's compromise guaranteed that members of our community would be free to debate this issue until there is a decision from the priest in the Capital. I am attempting to exercise that right by calling upon the Abbot, and you are placing a hooligan in my way.'

'Please! I'm sure the Abbess doesn't mean to insult this man, who serves faithfully to keep our temple safe. He is only doing what all members of our community here must do; carry out the orders of the Abbot.'

'Those orders are valid only if they reflect the will of Heaven.'

'Are you saying they don't? If they don't, why has Heaven not removed the Abbot from his position? Why does it allow him to continue governing our community?'

'Priest Sar, if you have truly read the scriptures, you will know that sometimes Heaven relies on its folk on earth to see to its will.'

It was always that way. My mistress was able to out-argue this priest, forcing him to fall back on his connection to temple authority. 'Abbess, speaking for our master, I respectfully suggest that with such statements you are verging on something untoward. I call on you to reflect and rethink. The Abbot is eager for all members of our community here to come together. As you know, he is a forgiving man.'

We could do nothing but turn back.

That evening, we were informed by an acolyte (they were still free to move about) that the two priests were not just barred from coming to see us. Each was confined to quarters, with a guard at the door. What's more, the acolyte said, the Abbot had deemed there would be no more delivery of sanctified water to the nunnery. When he left, I watched as my mistress checked our jar. It was empty, or very near it.

The next day, the Abbess wrote to the Lady Sray, informing her of the situation. A young man at the market was engaged to carry the message down the stairway and straight through to the Lady's hand in the Capital. He set off, yet at dusk of the same day he re-appeared at the nunnery's gates.

'I was turned back,' he said apologetically. 'There was a man at the bottom of the stairway. He demanded to know what I was carrying and where I was going. I'm afraid that I no longer have your letter, Abbess. He took it from me.'

'This is an outrage! Who was this man?'

He glanced at me, hesitating. 'It was the Stairway Guide, Abbess.'

How disheartened I was. I had allowed myself to think that perhaps Father was making his way to our side of the dispute. Kamol had described him as wanting me back, open to reconciliation. But now I pictured him again as he had been that day at the nunnery's gate, filled with righteous anger. Again I felt like the little girl I had been. I turned from the Abbess to hide a tear; I wondered if the Naga spirit would give me strength to endure this, but then I thought, no, she will expect me to find it within myself.

The next morning, the Abbess announced that we would go on another trip. She would not tell me where, only that we were going north. I prepared a bag for her; she surprised me with an instruction also to bring the box in which the jewellery was kept. It was heavy, but I managed to bundle it to our hired oxcart. We rode for two days, she with hands protectively on the box much of the time. Then she began directing the driver to turn first this way, then that, showing a familiarity with the cart tracks that surprised me. At mid-afternoon, we came to an estate settlement. She asked a passing woman to direct us to 'the commander.' I had no idea what that meant. But shortly afterwards, our cart was parked, its animals released to forage, and the Abbess was sitting in a pavilion with a man whose arms were thick and covered with war tattoos. He was examining the contents of the box.

19

The Young Brahmin

I had always wondered why my mistress was not in touch with the man who would be the successor, the son of the sister. She knew where he lived – with his mother, she had told me, atop a wooded hill north of the temple, just outside its precincts. You could see this hill from the Entry Court. The house was hidden, but many times I had pictured it. What I saw, really, was the Abbot's house transported to a new location, with the same rich teak and tiles and carved gods. The heir I observed in my mind's eye passing long periods in retreat at a pavilion some small distance off in the forest, alone with texts and the essence of Shiva. Now, I understood well enough why he could not write the treatise. Even were there not the problem of vanity that my mistress had cited, the practical demands of such a task would disrupt his life of prayer. Yet with my mistress devoting so much of her day to the cause of proper succession, it seemed unnatural that there would not be consultations with him (perhaps in that very forest pavilion) or with his mother, or with at least someone of that branch of the family. My mistress had told me such things would happen, yet day after day they did not.

But ten days after our return from the north, she announced that we would go to the heir. Tomorrow? I asked. No, she replied, right now.

'And you will carry this,' she said, passing to me a bag that was deceptively heavy. I knew right away what it contained: the jewellery, removed from its box.

We climbed a trail that led up the heir's wooded hill, she walking faster than normal, me more slowly because of the weight of the bag. After half an hour, the house came into view. That was the first surprise. It was not so different from the one I had grown up in. No tiles, no carved teak. A simple dwelling with thatch on the roof and steep steps to the door.

Atop those steps stood a woman much younger than the Abbess, her waist enclosed by the white garment of a Brahmin. Even from here, I could see that it was tattered from many wearings and washings. Now, we often think of Brahmins as blessed with Heaven's wealth, having earned temporal rewards through godly service in this life. We think that way because, I would say, so many of them do in fact have great wealth. Certainly the garments that our Abbot wore were new and of the finest weave. Certainly his house had taken the labour of many tens, if not hundreds, of skilled men to build. Yet I knew there was another class of Brahmins who choose a life of impoverished wandering. Alms placed in begging bowls support their travels. Each morning these mendicant priests (and there are a few nuns of this sort too) get to their feet, take up their walking staffs and resume their journeys, as if the truth they seek lies just across the next stream, just over the next hill. Sometimes small boys or girls accompany these seekers, carrying those begging bowls and whatever other simple implements are required to sustain life on the road. From time to time, we used to receive this kind of Brahmin at our house on the plain. I knew to keep my distance (they could be a choleric bunch, and the children's service was said to be not always by choice). Certainly I never offered them merit certificates. It would have been an insult, suggesting that they needed help with merit or had the silver to pay. These Brahmins, most of them, at least, desired nothing but the most physically rigorous ascent of the mountain. Often they insisted on climbing in solitude, and I saw more than one carry a bag of stones to make each step the more taxing.

So, as my mistress and I continued to approach this very modest abode, I was feeling some confusion. Was there yet another type of ascetic Brahmin that I didn't know about, who chose to seek Heaven in poverty but in just one place?

The woman spoke. 'He's not here. He's with the men.'

'Good. He should stay there.'

That was the next surprise: no greetings, no enquiries as to health or praise of Heaven. My mistress was much the elder, but with this woman she spoke in a tone of familiarity, and in the common language. I could only conclude that these two had known each other well for many years and, as with so many other things, my mistress had chosen to tell me nothing about it.

She took the bag from me and began climbing the steps. I made to follow her, but she signalled me no.

So, I was left to entertain myself. I walked away from the house, hearing behind me a few more words in the common language. I stopped and turned, to see if this house was truly as modest as I first thought. It was. Beneath it were two large jars of rainwater and a small enclosure of bamboo strips that in the evening would hold chickens that must now be out scavenging.

I wandered to the edge of a thicket, where I came to a log. I sat down.

It was pleasant here. A breeze cooled my brow and stirred leaves overhead, and there was something inviting too in knowing that I might idle the whole day away right here. My mistress had given no sign of how long she'd be. I felt a brief pulse of contentment, but then I remembered about Father intercepting my mistress's message. It was troubling, so I tried to put the thought aside, and imagine the situation at the old house, as it had been. What was Chantou doing right at this moment? Was she all on her own, Father and my brothers off with a group of pilgrims? I know that at the time I had resented my life alongside her, but now it seemed something to be longed for. Yet now I found myself considering that Father might have hired a female from the village to take my place in the preparations for pilgrims.

This woman might right now be bending over a clay rice pot that had been mine.

'Who are you?'

It was a male voice and it startled me, coming from directly behind. I sprang to my feet, feeling suddenly like a trespasser. I turned around and saw a young Brahmin. He'd emerged from a forest trail that I only now noticed. I was standing in his presence! Down I went, to a crouch.

'Do you speak? I asked who you are.'

'Jorani, maid of the Abbess, sir.' I was addressing the ground.

'And why are you here, Jorani?'

'I am accompanying my mistress, sir. She is inside the house consulting with...with.... I was told to wait outside, sir. I apologise that I have chosen a bad place.'

'She's here, you say? Talking with my mother?'

'Exactly, sir.'

He let out a breath of exasperation. 'Tell me, did she bring a copy of that text of hers, the one she's written? Is that why you came, to carry the load?'

'No, sir.' I knew not to say that I had carried something else. 'I came along only as a maid does with her mistress.'

'Well, it's good you came. It got you out from behind the walls of that nunnery so we can have a look at you.'

What was I to make of that? The only response I could think of was: 'I am not a nun.'

'I can see that. Though it can be more fun when they are. You know, it's all pent up.'

I blanched. Surely this was just a young man's boast! Surely none of the women of our community had behaved in the way he was suggesting.

I was trembling now. I realised now that this young Brahmin, this man who had said so many shocking things in such a short time, was the rightful heir to the Abbot, son of his sister. And it settled on me right then as well that he was the boy who those years earlier had threatened to *throw me off the cliff.*

He made a smirk, as if he enjoyed my discomfort. But it seemed he was done with me. He turned and made to head back down the trail from which he'd come. But suddenly, there was a call from a window of the house. 'Ritisak! Come inside.'

It was my mistress. He stopped, seemed for a moment to consider this command, because that was the tone of it, then turned and headed to the house. He avoided my eye as he passed.

What was I expected to do? For some reason, my legs concluded I should follow him, though not too close. As I walked, I heard behind me what seemed like voices in the forest, male voices. But when I looked back, I saw no one.

When I reached the base of the house's steps, the young Brahmin had already climbed. I placed myself to the side and waited. I hadn't intended it, but every word that was said inside carried down to me.

'How many men are there?' It was my mistress speaking.

'Close to forty, Abbess.' He spoke in the tone of a chastised boy. I couldn't believe this was the same young man who moments earlier had addressed me in such a crude way.

'And where are they?'

'In the clearing just down the hill, Abbess. The place you saw the last time you were here.'

'And why did you come up here?'

'Well...Abbess. It's so rough down there. I just wanted to lie down on my own mat for a while. I was going to go right back down after that.' Again, the voice of a scolded boy.

'They will stay there, do you understand? You will go rejoin them. It's not safe for you here.'

'He always does his best, sister.' Sister! It was the mother speaking.

'Yes, you've told me that many times. I wish it were true.'

'It is, sister.'

The Abbess let out a deep breath. 'Now, listen, both of you. It *must* be true this time. It is a critical moment for you and for all the rest of us.'

'Abbess, I pledge that I...'

I think he said more, but I didn't hear it. My attention turned to five or six temple guards who were sprinting towards the house.

20

A Fight at the Entry Court

The guards rushed right past me and clambered up the steps, making everything shake. Shouting and scuffling erupted inside. 'Hold him, hold him!' 'Take your hands off!' 'Get back from there!' There came a stamping of feet; something crashed to the floor. And then the men were hustling their prey, this young man Ritisak, out the door. He thrashed, trying to free himself, but there were too many of them, one on each arm, one clutching his waist, one daring even to grip him by the neck. They propelled him down the steps. My mistress followed right behind, screaming invective I'd never heard from her. I turned and saw Priest Sar standing perhaps thirty paces away with several more guards. With a small motion of his hand, he signalled to one of them to deal with my mistress. This man stepped in front of her, blocking her way, moving to the left and the right to obstruct her without touching her, as had happened at the temple avenue that day. There was more shouting and struggling; I could no longer see the heir. The Abbess chose this moment to throw herself against the guard. He stood firm as a tree trunk, and she tumbled to the ground.

I went racing to her, but she was already getting up. 'Did you see that? Did you see that?' How hard she was panting. 'They've taken him like he'—she paused to catch her breath – 'like he's some kind of criminal. Well, we're going to get him back!'

She hurried up the steps of the house and returned with the bag in hand. Then she strode tothe trail from which the heir had emerged.

'What are you doing?' It was the mother, standing in the door of her house, terrified.

'You will see!'

I followed her along the trail, which wound down a wooded slope. At the bottom we stepped into a clearing that contained several roughly cut bamboo pavilions. And lots of young men, variously lying about, eating, or going through drills one-on-one with spears and knives.

'Where's the commander?' she asked the nearest of them. 'Get me the commander.'

Barely a moment passed before a stocky man of perhaps thirty years presented himself. 'Commander, the heir has been abducted by the Abbot's men – right from his own house. They're taking him to the temple. You must get him back. Here are your initial wages.' Saying that, she thrust the bag at him.

So it was that just a few minutes later, forty fighting men were running up the trail, shields, knives, war clubs, and spears in hand. The commander, in the lead, began chanting a call for battle-god strength and protection. The men joined in, clattering swords on shields as they did – I had never heard such a din. The Abbess and I stood to the side. She did look troubled, but only, I felt, concerning the heir's safety. I saw nothing that suggested doubts of the correctness of this course of action.

When the men were gone, my mistress and I climbed the trail. At the house, the Brahmin mother was still standing at the doorway, distraught. The Abbess barely acknowledged her, but announced that we would remain here with her for now.

I asked: 'Who are these men, mistress?'

'Men whom I have called to protect the heir,' she replied. 'I've been worried for some time that the Abbot would resort to kidnapping.' She turned away, and I think she was rebuking herself for having called the heir to come into the house. Of course I was now recalling her visit to the estate to the north and her conversation with the tattooed man whom I now recognised as the commander she had just paid. I wondered if the holy women who had provided what was in the box during our visit in the Capital had any idea how their gifts would be used.

We waited, eyes glancing in the direction the heir had been dragged, hoping to see him. I'm not sure how much time passed. Then from far up the hill came more of those war chants and the clang of metal striking metal.

'Heaven will remember that the Abbot insisted on violence,' the Abbess observed gravely.

The sounds continued off and on for perhaps half an hour. Then silence for close to an hour. Then – there he was, the heir, walking under the protective escort of the commander and three of his fighters. The Abbess hurried to them, ebullient. The heir went to a crouch.

She asked: 'You're not hurt, then?'

'Not at all, Abbess.' He raised his arms and turned around, to show there was no wound on his body.

'Heaven protected you, as we knew it would. Come to the house and bathe. We'll keep these guards around you, or else this might happen again.'

The commander spoke up. 'Abbess, I think that is unlikely.'

'Why?'

'Because the Abbot's men are now confined to the upper courts of the temple.'

'What? I gave no such instruction. You were only to retrieve the heir.'

He shrugged apologetically. 'We caught up with the group who took him, but it was only when they had already reached the Entry Court. We tried to get them to turn him loose peacefully. But instead they circled around him. We saw some more guards coming down from the upper courts, so we did the only thing left to us. We attacked. There was fighting. Those extra guards arrived and we fought them too. We repelled them all and then, well, none of our men wanted to retreat, so we held steady on our ground. We hold the Entry Court. The Abbot's men have fled to the upper courts.'

'And you said they are confined to that area?'

'Yes, Abbess. No one can leave the upper courts. We control all the access ways. The avenue and the informal pathways.'

'The priest who came here with the guards – what happened to him?'

'He escaped to the upper courts with the others.'

'I see.' My mistress turned from us and walked slowly away. I knew not to come along; I would be shooed away as disturbing her concentration. The heir, standing calmly now, ignored me. But, you know, I got the feeling that had my mistress not been nearby, his eye would have come my way in a leer, even at such a time. I wondered if he remembered me as the girl he'd threatened to throw off the cliff. He'd given no sign.

The Abbess turned back to us. 'Commander, you will go back to your men and you will tell them to remain where they are. You will keep the Abbot's men contained in the upper courts, but you will do nothing further without my instruction, do you understand?'

'I do, Abbess.'

'Perhaps we will fight more, perhaps we will persuade the Abbot and his men to leave. In either case, it will be by my order.'

'Yes, ma'am.'

'And one more thing. Your men are now in possession of the Entry Court. It is holy ground; it is not of the heretics. None of the images, none of the bowls, none of the hangings and fittings there can be taken, do you understand? When your men are in control of the full temple, *then* they will be able to take things as payment, but only from houses that I identify. Is that clear?'

The commander frowned. 'Abbess, if I may say, letting them take at least something now would be better. They would know that their bravery is appreciated and that there will be more to take later on, if they can win. They would fight better.'

'No. Everything they control now must be protected. It's up to you to make sure that they fight well. You're their commander and Heaven is on our side.'

It was as if she were speaking to me, her servant. She would not brook a reply. The commander bowed and withdrew.

We returned to the nunnery. My sleep that night was troubled by more of those metal-on-metal sounds from the temple's direction.

At first light, my mistress told me to go have a look, with admonitions that I must take no risks and observe only from a distance. How unprepared I was for what I saw. The shocking sights began at the base of the processional avenue, by the Entry Court. Four shrouded bodies had been laid out on the paving stones—the commander had said nothing about deaths. I had seen corpses before, of course, but never in this number. To each side of the departed ones, there knelt comrades with torn clothing and bloodied faces, hands together in prayer. I glanced up the processional avenue. There was movement on either side of it. It seemed that the Abbot's men were building a barricade of bamboo and wood, as if to keep our men out of the upper courts. I noticed now the scent of smoke in the air, far stronger than what comes from morning cooking fires. At the top were black wisps, thrown this way and that by the wind. Something big was burning up there.

Now I became aware that there were armed men in many places around me, standing, sitting, each of them clutching a spear or dagger or war club. Some seemed to be nursing wounds. I did not see the heir, just these men. All of them wearing red bands on their right arms.

My mistress had told me to stay back, but I had come this far with no trouble, and so I felt drawn to see a bit more. I made my way to the base of one of the informal trails that ran up the hill. No one was there. Something possessed me to climb a short distance and see what I could see. Very quickly I came to two more of those men with red armbands.

'Go back, go back, you don't belong here,' declared one. He had a dagger tucked in his waist.

The other broke in. 'You're lucky we were here. Ten more steps and you'd be in the hands of the Abbot's guards.'

The smell of fire was stronger here. I saw the remains of a lodge, the winds pulling wisps of smoke from it. It was one where acolytes had lived.

Suddenly I felt sticky dampness beneath my foot. I looked down. The soil was blood-red. I gasped; the soldiers laughed. 'Go on, you heard me,' said the first one. 'Pretty soon there's going to be more muck like that. Theirs, of course.'

I hurried down the hill, with a mind to head straight back to the peace and safety of the nunnery. But I didn't, because by the Entry Court I came upon a sort of victory procession. The heir, his white Brahmin garment gleaming in the morning sunlight, was walking towards me, escorted by the commander and a few other men. It took a moment, but the fighters who had gathered around the court looked his way and recognised him. They fell to their knees, raising a general cheer as they did. I knelt too. The heir waved in acknowledgment. I expected him to stop and bask in the adulation, but he strode straight on. Then I understood – he was going to the shrouded bodies laid out on the avenue. At their side he went to his knees, palms together. Everyone fell immediately silent. With what intensity did he pray! He closed his eyes as if straining, he whispered unheard words, he rocked his head up and down. Then he went still, as if listening for Heaven's voice. It was all done with such respect and piety and grace of motion that I had trouble believing that this was the same man who had spoken to me so coarsely the previous day.

Glancing to my right, I saw that the Abbess had come too. She was keeping back, kneeling with a clutch of local people who'd come to watch. It seemed odd at first that she would kneel for him, but it came to me that she was both paying respect to the martyrs and signalling to anyone who noticed her presence that the heir was the supreme authority now.

He got back to his feet. Standing up straight, he motioned that people should step closer. I moved to be next to my mistress.

'Brave warriors, brave supporters from the villages,' he began, and what a voice it was deep, strong, and clearly enunciating each word. I could imagine that it would carry up to the Abbot's men. 'You have waited so long for this day. But now the forces that oppose Heaven's will have finally been put on the run. You can see them up the avenue, planning new iniquities. That is their way, they will never change, but this time they will not succeed. Their time in power has come to an end. Their gods are abandoning them now in the face of the greater ones who graciously apply their magic to guide our swords and clubs.

'For your service, your loyalty, your sacrifice, I give my most heartfelt thanks!' That set off more shouts and cheers.

'Yet I must tell you that I save my very deepest thanks for those of our comrades who now lie still beneath the shrouds. The departed souls, I know, are gazing down on all of us at this very moment, imbued with virtuous pride for having brought about the results that we now see. Before long, with their service completed, these souls will depart to find new lives, ones with even higher planes than the ones they have now completed with such glory. And let no one doubt that the families they leave behind will be supported. No widow will lack rice or a stove to cook it on. No child will go unclothed or lack a place to shelter from the monsoon showers.'

This drew more shouts of approval. Then silence returned and we all looked on, waiting for more. But he seemed at a loss for his next words. His glance went this way, then that, then our way. Something made me look at just that instant to the Abbess. She formed words with her lips: 'From this day forward...' And then the heir took a breath and said, in that same penetrating voice: 'From this day forward, we pray there will be no further violence on this holy ground. We pray that the man in the upper courts will realize that his time there is finished, and he must vacate the holy precincts. If he does, he will face no interference from us as he and his people descend the mount and make their way to whatever new homes they choose.'

'I call on all of you, then, to stand firm here, to keep your spears sharp and ready, but to initiate no violence in any form. You may feel that as fighting men, it is your duty to finish what we have begun. But let me say it again – I call on you to wait, though it may be a wait of many days, so that events here may be completed in the peaceful way that Heaven intends.'

The Abbess nodded quietly in approval of all this. Not one word had surprised her. I could only conclude that she had composed his words and had him commit them to memory.

21

A Single Act of Recklessness

Back at the nunnery, I sat down on the steps of the Abbess's house, convinced that there was still blood on my foot. I looked to my sole, feeling revulsion, but saw only dust. My mistress told me to go to the stream and wash.

'Those were terrible things you witnessed today, I know,' she said when I returned. 'But everything you saw was done in service to Heaven and correct doctrine. I want no wealth or power, Jorani. You know that. I want only that the Abbot will depart and leave the nephew as his heir.'

Mention of the nephew brought a look to my face. Before I could hide it, she leaned forward and asked: 'Now what did the heir say to you? Tell me! I saw from the window that he spoke to you as you were sitting outside.'

It took some courage to be truthful. But what I told her drew not a denial or a scolding but a sigh of resignation. 'Heaven tests us in this way, Jorani. That is the only explanation. The heir's bloodline is pure. He is Heaven's choice. Yet Heaven provokes us to see if we will lose faith and turn away. We will not. What we will do is improve his character and make it fit for the holy post he will assume. We will strive to be at his side when weighty issues come up for decision. We will make sure that he selects the just course.'

'My mistress has great faith.'

'And you must too, Jorani. So many times it has seemed set that the Abbot would succeed in giving his son the post, and then Heaven has stepped in to keep the correct outcome alive. It happened again today. You saw it yourself.'

'Yes, of course, mistress.'

'I can sense, Jorani, that you have questions. Perhaps you feel they are not questions that a maid can ask a mistress. So I will now tell you some things, so that you will understand. I will start with things that happened many years ago. You will come to see what they all mean. Will you be patient?'

'I will try, mistress.'

'Good. Now, those many years ago, a girl was born into a prominent Brahmin family who were lords of a settlement four days' travel north of here. Heaven and earth were in harmony in this place. The family had obtained the land as a grant from His Majesty the King and on it they erected a temple and linga of our god Shiva. All rites were conducted properly. Beyond the temple, fields were laid out, gardens were planted, reservoirs were dug. The family and their villages prospered.

'This girl was blessed with the happiest of lives as she grew up. Her parents were loving and attentive to her every need. She ate only the purest, best-milled rice. She was protected from all danger, whether from sinful people or wild animals. She studied the holy texts, she gave alms to the destitute. She spent long hours in prayer. She became known in the wider community of Brahmins, in fact, as someone specially touched by Heaven. I do not mean to suggest that she was without flaws. No one is. There was vanity in her; she pretended to be unaware of the talk in her favour, but she secretly listened for and treasured it. Though she was determined in her studies and spiritual quests, she could fall into despair when she encountered an obstacle and remain without hope for too long before she regained her resolve. And she had one other flaw that I will tell you about shortly.

'When it came time for her to marry, a groom was nominated, a young man from a Brahmin family in the next province. This girl was not supposed to know the suitor was coming, but there were talkative servants in the house and word did reach her. At the hour of the visit, she crept to the doorway of the room where the young man was being received. Ever so carefully, she peered round the doorframe, and, do you know, she instantly fell in love. How handsome and strong he was! Yet what a kind voice he had, what decorum he showed as he sat sipping tea with her parents. She felt in her heart the deepest kind of longing.

'The young man returned to his province, but before long, he returned. This time he was to be introduced to the young woman. Love of this kind, based only on sight, can expire when first words are exchanged, but nothing of the sort happened. He turned out to be just as attractive, just as kind as he had seemed that day when she spied upon him through the door. They spent many hours together in a pavilion outside the house, sitting close enough to touch. They were not alone, of course – there was always a maid or a parent or her brother nearby – but they were so engrossed in each other that they felt as if no one else were present.

'Now, this girl's brother was newly married, and already had a son. The young woman would see them sitting together on the porch of their house, the father instructing the son in right thought and action, and she would sense the devotion that father felt for son. This sight caused in her a hope that she would have her own sons and love and instruct them in a similar way.

'One day, she told her brother of the love that she felt for her suitor.

'"Before long, we'll be married," she declared.

'"You're sure?"

'"Of course," the girl replied.

'"But is it wise to rush a decision of this sort?"

'She looked at him strangely, wondering why he would ask such a thing. Everything was already arranged, after all. "We will be married," she repeated. "And we will have a dozen sons. We will love our sons every bit as much as you love yours."

'Now, she thought about having children but she also thought about the carnal relations that bring children into the world. These relations must of course await the completion of wedding rites, which were set for a date in the rainy season of the following year. But as time went by, this young woman began wondering if she could wait as long as that. It was taking only a certain kind of glance from her groom-to-be, or an accidental brush of his fingers across the back of her hand, to bring to life in her mind all manner of acts in which the two of them might engage. She would think of stealing into the chamber where he slept at night during his visits. Each time they parted, she would retire to her private shrine and say prayers seeking Heaven's help in casting off thoughts of these acts, but even as she said the prayers, she would be thinking again of those very things. This, you see, was the other flaw of character that I mentioned.

'One day, the groom-to-be arrived for a visit on the first day of a local festival. The whole family was going to go, and he would come along. Everyone put on fine garments, and off they went at dusk, her brother acting as chaperone for the two betrothed. The festival was noisy and crowded. Everyone was drinking honey wine. A cup was placed in her hand. She and her suitor strolled, following her brother. People bumped into her. Several times she contrived to do the same with her betrothed. Before long she found herself and her betrothed at the edge of the festival. Her brother was gone. She peered left and right—there was no sign of him. Her mind formed a sinful plan. She led her betrothed into the dark, where the lamps of the gathering did not reach. She grew bold to take his hand and lead him down a paddy dike to what she knew was at its end, a shelter where farmers sleep at harvest time. The groom-to-be protested that they should return to the festival, but she told herself that his heart was not in his words. She pretended not to hear, and took him on to the shelter. There she lay with him. The act was accomplished; it was by her will entirely. And do you know, when it was done, she fell asleep and did not wake until there was a lamp shining by her face, held by one of the family's maids sent to look for her.

'What infamy it was that followed. The betrothed was sent back to his settlement, straight from the festival ground. She was reproached severely by her parents, then taken back to her house and made to stay alone in her chamber. She descended into one of her pits of despair. She barely ate, she was barely able to move, in fact. All day she lay on her mat, reflecting, reflecting. Before too long, her mother and father put aside their anger and became worried. They came in to try to speak with her. She wept. They wept. Many times this happened. As time passed, it became clear that there would be no child. Now, in such a situation, an indiscretion of this kind can be kept quiet, and her parents began to make suggestions that perhaps that was the course to take. They were prepared to forgive, and they were sure that with proper prayer and offerings Heaven would do the same. One day, they entered the chamber and were astonished to find their daughter sitting up and eating. She was almost her old self. But a change had come over her. She announced to them that she would repair to a nunnery and seek a life of prayer and reflection. She had sinned against Heaven, she explained. She had known full well the temptations she faced, the wrongness of her actions, and yet she had followed her will anyway. Life in a nunnery was the only proper response. Her parents resisted, asking that she wait, saying there was no cause to be hasty in such a decision. But she insisted, insisted, insisted that she could do nothing else.

'So one day an oxcart carried her to a nunnery that lay a few hours' journey away. She was assigned a hut and given a set of garments and the basic implements of eating and sleep. She rose with her novice sisters at dawn the next morning for two hours of prayer. It was all very hard at first. Many times she dissolved into tears when alone in her hut. But over time she discovered that if luxury had departed from her life, so had anxiety. She discovered that this was the life intended for her. The well-milled rice, the silk sleeping covers, the help of servants at every turn – how distant they seemed, and how unimportant.

'Once a year, she was allowed visits by outsiders. Her parents and brother came, their faces long, but each time she greeted them cheerfully, letting them know by word and action that she had found peace with Heaven in this place. Sometimes her former servants came as well. One day there came the very maid who had discovered her and her betrothed in the farmer's shelter. This maid clearly had something she wanted to say. It took some coaxing, but when it came out, it was an apology. "But what," asked the nun, "is there to apologise for? The sin was by my own action alone. What followed has turned my life in the direction of virtue. You can see that here." The maid replied, "Yes, mistress, it's that way, I know, but sometimes I think, what if your brother had not suggested that I check the shelter? You would still be at the great house. I would still be serving you. We all miss you so very much."'

I let out a gasp.

'Jorani, you are a sharp-witted girl. You recognised right away what the maid's words meant. But for this young nun, it took some time. She bid good-bye to her former servant and retired to her hut feeling a vague sense of diminishment. Each brick of the foundation of her spiritual life had been set carefully in place; now one had been wrenched awry. She found herself doing something that her vows as a nun forbade – deliberately recalling the precise events of the evening of her sin. No, not the act itself. Over the years in the nunnery, she had devised the spiritual means of resisting thoughts of this type of thing. Rather, her mind reviewed the chain of events before and after. Her mother was going to be chaperone, but her brother had volunteered to take her place. She had heard him make the offer – she was quite certain of that. She and her betrothed had strolled together; she recalled the scents, the sounds, the taste of the honey wine. Who had obtained that wine? She was quite sure that it was her brother. He had led them to the edge of the festival and then he was no longer to be seen. But her mind kept coming back to what the maid had said. Her brother had suggested looking in the farmers' shelter.

'By morning, she had reached the same conclusion that you did, Jorani. She was convinced that her brother had set out that evening to enable her sin and then to assure that it was discovered. Why would he do that? Well, there was no question about that. To secure the future of his son!

'I have told you that the nun's family was prominent. Her mother's brother was Abbot of a great temple to the south of their settlement. It had been known for many years that on the death of this Abbot, he would be succeeded by the nun's brother. This was proper and in line with doctrine – he was the Abbot's nephew, you see. For years, the brother had been carrying out all the necessary studies and vigils for this post. Yet even as he did, even before he had set foot in that temple, he had become transfixed with the idea that his own son would one day succeed him. Imagine – the doctrine that would bring him to the post would be rejected by him for the succession that followed! The nun could only conclude that some demon had entered him on the day of his son's birth and set him against Heaven's teachings. The best way for him to defeat those teachings would be if there was no nephew – no son born of a sister. And yet, his sister was betrothed and had been telling him of the sons that she was going to bear after her wedding. If she bore just one, it would end any chance of the post passing to his own boy.

'Now, for days after her realisation, the nun was possessed by the rankest anger. She remained within her hut, claiming illness, and all day she lay on her mat. Dark fantasies crowded into her consciousness. She imagined renouncing her vows and going back to the family settlement. She would steal up on her brother while he slept and drive a knife into his belly, then revel in the blood. Yet then Heaven intervened. She awoke one day aware that it was her duty to resist this anger. She emerged from her hut and, though it was quite difficult, she resumed her normal activities and cycles of prayer. Gradually she restored her serenity. The desire to give this life up faded.

'Her brother continued to make those annual visits to her at the nunnery and she never confronted him with her realisation. She knew that ultimately the sin was her own doing, that he had merely encouraged it, and that, had she followed a moral path, his plan would have come to nothing. Such was her victory over anger that she felt nothing but serenity when he told her on one of his visits that the Abbot at the great temple to the south had died and he was now called to assume his post. He might not be able to come visit her for some time.

'Several years passed. There came another annual visit, from her father and mother. Now what should the nun see but that her mother was with child! Everyone had believed she was well beyond that age, but then a new life had been conceived within her. The nun rejoiced and after her parents left, she said special prayers at her hut's shrine for many days. Her prayers gave thanks for her mother's good fortune, but they also sought guidance concerning an idea that had formed in the nun's mind. She waited very patiently for the next annual visit and what should she see but her mother arriving with a baby in her arms. A girl! It was confirmed, then – Heaven willed the course of action that the nun would now take and which she had by now thought out very carefully.

'She knew that she would have only one chance to begin it, right then, as her parents visited. So she told her mother that she had had a dream, just the previous night, that the new baby was a girl and that this girl was in mortal danger. All had been explained in this dream. An evil spirit had taken up residence in the fields by the family settlement and it wanted to do this baby harm. It would bide its time, and begin with just small things, such as causing a looseness of the baby's bowels. Had there been anything like that? The mother thought and said yes, she could not deny it, there had. Well, then, said the nun. As much as you love this baby girl, you must take her to some faraway place and leave her to be raised there. You as the mother will have the power to keep this place secret from the spirit, but you must tell no one, not even your husband or son, because the spirit will be able to steal into their minds as they sleep and learn the place. The mother of course resisted this idea, but the nun kept talking and talking. By the time the visit was over, the mother was despondent, but convinced that survival for her new daughter depended upon her being brought up elsewhere. The mother did follow the directions, explaining to her family members the reason, but telling them nothing of where the child would go. She went away for two weeks and placed the baby with a childless couple two provinces away.

'The child was safe now; that was the nun's only objective. Many years passed. The nun rose in her order. She was given the holy name Parvati. Many nuns take on a study specialty, and hers was the Yajur Veda, source of so much of our faith's liturgy. She wrote lengthy commentaries on it and beyond her nunnery, I think, she acquired a reputation for scholarship. She took quiet pride in letters that arrived from distant nunneries and monasteries seeking her views on questions large and small concerning this Veda.

'One day, her Abbess called her and told her that the order was expanding and would establish a new presence at the great temple to the south. You have shown obedience and piety in unusual quantities, she said. I discern that Heaven is calling you to lead this new community. I know that your brother is Abbot there; perhaps there is a plan from Heaven that after these many years your religious life will place you close to your own blood. Now, the nun began to ask questions. How many women would live in this place, from where would the resources come, what was the state of the temple community, was the Abbot in good health—or would the handover to his son come soon? To that last question, the older woman replied that there was no son, that he had died a few months earlier in a riding accident, and that the Abbot's other children were all female. It was unclear, she said, who would ultimately succeed him.

'Now, you can imagine the shock and also the joy with which the nun received this news. Not joy at the boy's death, of course, for a death is always a tragic event, but joy that Heaven had seen fit to block the heretical succession. And perhaps it was also opening the way for a correct one. Within a day, Heaven had placed in the nun's mind another plan. She accepted the call to head the nunnery at the temple. But first she travelled to see her own mother. In short order, she found out where her sister – that baby girl, now sixteen years old – was living. She went there and retrieved her from the couple who had raised her. She returned this young woman, her sister, to the family seat, telling her mother that the demon that wished harm had departed. She wrote letters to various Brahmin families seeking a husband for her sister. She found one. That she succeeded in all this could only mean that Heaven was behind her. And do you know, within a year of the wedding the sister had given birth to a baby boy. Here was yet another sign of Heaven's design. This boy would one day fulfil his destiny to become Abbot of the Temple in the Clouds, for this, Jorani, as you of course have discerned, was the temple in question.

'By now the nun was heading her order's new community at the temple. It was time to bring the baby boy here so that he might begin his education and prepare for his rightful role. The nun sent word to her sister and her husband that they should hire a cart and come with their possessions. But she did not reveal something that might have led them to stay away. The Abbot had taken a new wife, a young one, and from her he had obtained another son! This boy was of approximately the same age as the rightful heir.

'It was only when the young family arrived that the Abbess revealed the existence of the Abbot's new son. The sister grew in turns angry and despondent, her emotions compounded by the decision to keep this information secret from her. And there was of course immediate conflict with the Abbot. He refused to bring the sister's family into the Brahmin community up at the mountaintop or give the boy proper schooling. He allowed him only occasional participation in ceremonies and mixing with other Brahmin boys. He and his parents were forced to live outside the precincts, and in a house not fit for an heir to a great temple.

'The father died of mosquito fever two years after the arrival. Yet somehow the Abbess rebuilt the mother's trust and prevailed upon her to remain with her son, making her believe that the day would come in which her son would be Abbot. The sister turned out to be a weak parent, doing little to teach her son the texts and correct moral behaviour, so the Abbess stepped into that role as well, instructing him herself or engaging tutors. He proved to be not the best of students. At those times when he was under her direct supervision, he could apply himself, even grasp the right track necessary to carry out his future assignment. But when she was elsewhere, he could often succumb to temptations. Several times the Abbess caught him in immoral behaviour – the telling of lies, the beating of servants, or the secret drinking of wine with the young women who served at the stalls in the market.

'So Jorani, now you understand. For years there has been an unhappy co-existence. Now it has descended into violence. But Heaven intends that it will end in the proper way and I will not waver from that objective. And neither, with Heaven's help, will you.'

My sweeping, my washing suffered for the rest of that day, because I could not stop thinking about this story. On my first day of service, I had seen distant beauty in the Abbess's face, and now I could picture her as that young woman of wealth and standing, removed from the temporal world by a single act of recklessness. What drive, what energy it must have required to pursue for so many years her goal, recovering each time from the many setbacks and periods of despair. She spoke of doctrine and Heaven's will, but I wondered if there was another thing, that she saw this young man Ritisak as the son she should herself have had. She had many daughters already, her nuns, but this was the first son, the only one she would have, and it was up to her to assure his place in the world and guide him to correct character and acts.

I wondered too how it was that my mistress could so quickly launch an enterprise that was drawing blood. How calm she had been when the commander informed her that men were going at each other with spears and swords. All she had done was take a short walk to think through this turn of events. She had decided so easily that violence would be used in achieving her objective. It was really she who was the commander, not the officer. He had accepted her authority in the blink of an eye. Perhaps he had seen the heir's own submissiveness to her, and sensed where Heaven's blessing lay. As I thought more about the story she had told me, of the young nun sitting in her hut for so many years without surrender to anger or bitterness, I began to think that she had more discipline and perhaps even more physical courage than the men now carrying arms on her behalf.

Such were my thoughts. But every so often that afternoon, they were pushed aside by the sudden recollection of that awful red dampness under my foot.

22

A Lamp in the Forest

There were no more sounds of fighting from the temple the next day, or the next. But up the avenue from the Entry Court, the confrontation continued, armed men facing armed men, albeit now silently. How quickly we came to accept this situation as normal. My mistress and the nuns resumed their daily cycles of prayer and offerings, though of course she was in frequent contact with the commander. I resumed my chores. The market at the foot of the northern stairs came back to life. Day after day, we expected that something decisive would happen. Yet day after day – nothing. Perhaps neither side was eager to repeat the abomination of spilling blood on holy ground. Perhaps the Lord of the Summit had decided that things should wait. I could not know.

One afternoon, the Abbess told me that after sunset I must go to the top of the eastern stairway. My help was needed there; she gave no explanation.

When I arrived, at the place where the two Nagas were to take their eternal places in stone, I found a priest and the commander.

'Your mistress says you know this stairway well,' said the soldier.

'I do, sir.'

'Now, is there any place along the stairway from which a trail leads off along the mountainside? An ordinary trail, I mean, not part of the holy stairway.'

We had always told pilgrims that you could go up the stairway, you could go down, but Heaven would allow nothing else. The entire mountainside was a holy zone; it was only on the stairway's stones that human feet could tread. But, truth be told, there was a series of paths through the forested part of the mountainside. Local men and women sometimes asked permission of the Nagas to enter to hunt birds or gather berries and firewood. Children did too, to help with tasks like those or simply to wander and pass the time. I had walked the trails many times as a child, so I knew them well. In places, they did cross the holy stairway itself. But they were not well worn; you had to know how to look for them.

The commander's question made me answer as I would have in the old days. 'Sir, Heaven does not intend that anyone should step off the stairway.'

I could sense him grinning at me in the dark. 'Heaven does not intend it, you say, but does it happen?'

'I suppose it does, sir.'

'At what point on the stairway?'

'At several, sir.'

I looked beyond him and saw that perhaps ten fighting men had joined us. They stood with the bases of their spears in the dirt; the points showed against the nearly black western sky.

'Is there a trail that leads to points below the peak at its southernmost point?'

There was. 'It is perhaps two hundred steps down from here, sir. But the spirit Nagas will not welcome outsiders.'

'Of course. But we will show them first that we respect them and mean no harm.'

The commander called his men to attention. 'Listen to this young woman. Pay no attention that she is not a man. What she tells you may assure that you get through this mission without injury.'

In the old days, pilgrim groups newly arrived at our house below received words of instruction from Father. Now it was me saying the words, and I found I remembered them perfectly. Yet I had to reverse the order, because Father of course always began with tips about climbing and followed with ones for descent.

Face the stairway as you descend, I told the soldiers. Your toes are nimble, your heels are dull. Feel first that you have found a full step; only then put your weight down. Here and there water seeps across the steps; on these take particular care. Keep your eyes to the stone in front of your nose; don't succumb to the temptation to look down and behind you. Keep some distance from the person ahead and behind; it can be very dangerous if you step on the fingers of the person below you. Hang on to the ropes. There is no shame in this – Heaven recognises that at many places the stairway's slant is too great to do otherwise.

When I finished, the commander turned to the priest. We all knelt for a series of prayers to the spirit Nagas to accept the entry of these brave men this night, these brave men who were daring to enforce the will of Heaven and restore right doctrine to the temple community. A half-moon shone overhead; I only now noticed it. It would help light the way.

With the prayer completed, the commander made to dismiss me. I had expected this, and so I turned and faced him.

'Heaven allows no one on the stairway without a guide.' This was not true, of course, but I said it anyway.

'We are not pilgrims, young woman. Heaven will see to an exception.'

'There is a reason for this rule, sir. It is dangerous enough in daylight. Without a guide, you will fall or be injured in some other way. You may have to turn back before your mission is complete.'

He looked over the edge, and saw the logic of this.

So that is how I again became a stairway guide, if just for this night. I knew of course that the soldiers might be headed towards something horrible, yet I couldn't pass up a chance to do again what I had done for so many years.

There were two ropes in place here, so I took in hand the one on the right and went over the edge. In the darkness, my toes felt the old pleasure of knowing each step, its width, the coolness of its surface.

On a descent, the stairway starts off very steep, for a distance of perhaps the height of three men, then almost flattens out for a few steps. I reached that place and stood waiting. In a moment or two, the commander caught up to me. But what a contrast with his confidence at the top! He was breathing hard and his cheeks were dampened with sweat (I could see its glint in the moonlight). He seemed more like a confused boy than a military commander. But he quickly recovered his composure (perhaps he sensed that I had noticed) and turned to supervise his men making their own first descents. Grunts and whispered curses signalled that many were having the same trouble. The commander stepped forward and admonished them to stop the bad words and show proper respect to the spirits that were graciously accepting their presence.

We descended farther, me in the lead again, stopping every so often to allow the men behind me to catch up. I saw them only as shapes in the darkness.

It was slow going, but before long we came to a place where a trail crossed the stairway.

'Here it is, sir.' I was whispering.

'Where?'

'Right there, sir,' I said, pointing into the gloom to the right.

'I don't see anything.'

'If you can't see it, sir, your toes will feel it.'

Now, I had walked this trail a number of times in the light of day, but even for me it was hard to do it solely by moonlight, and moonlight filtered by leaves.

'Watch where I put my feet, sir. Then put yours there too.'

We began. How long did we progress in this way? I would say for two hours. We were like a great caterpillar that has forgotten how to make its many legs work together. Not all the men could see just where to put their feet, and as we went on, some of those feet became bloodied. I whispered prayers to minor spirits over whose holes we were passing. But slowly, slowly, we made our way along the eastern slope of the mountain, the dark drop to our left, the rise to our right. Over and over, the commander asked how close we were to the place just below the southernmost cliff of the mountain. I was reminded of those hopeful pilgrims of the old days and I answered as I always had, that no, not yet, we need to keep going. Yet when we finally did reach this southernmost point, the commander was not satisfied and said we must continue some distance more. In this way, we reached the western slope of the mountain and began advancing along it.

And then, through foliage to our right, somewhere up the mountainside – a lamp. Winking on and off as unseen leaves shuddered in a breeze. The commander whispered an order to stop and prepare. There were quiet rustlings and clinks as arms were made ready.

'You will remain here, Jorani.'

For the first time, I became nervous. I stepped to the side as soldiers filed quickly past me, each man now moving with agility that had been so lacking at the first descent. Then there was a great shouting and rushing forward in the dark, up the hillside. I cringed, listening for the clank of sword on sword, but I heard none. Rather, the sounds of a headlong race through heavy foliage continued, punctuated by grunts of pain and confusion. I think the commander had misjudged how far up the mountainside the lamp was.

Then I heard distant voices. 'No one? No one at all?' 'Gone already.' 'Ours, ours!' Then some general joyful whooping.

And then, the sounds of a scramble *down* the mountainside. Had the soldiers not been celebrating, they might have heard too. I turned around. One after the other, three figures lit like ghosts by the moonlight crossed the trail behind me and continued their descent. Then came a fourth. But this one paused. He glanced my way. I gasped. I was alone and now this man was advancing on me.

'Jorani!'

'Father!'

'It is you indeed. Thank Heaven!' In the blink of an eye, he grasped my wrist and began pulling me back along the trail.

'Father, wait! Let me go!'

He paid no attention. We had almost reached the place where the other three men had crossed the trail.

With some pain, I pulled free. We stopped, both of us breathing hard.

'I won't go!'

'Jorani, it's not safe where you are. You'll return below with me.'

'I'm needed up top.'

'It's no business of yours, anything that's going on there. No business of anyone in the family.'

I should have been backing away, but his voice had somehow disabled my legs. He reached for my wrist again. I dodged his hand and took off.

He came after me, but at his age he was not catlike in the dark. After a few steps he missed his footing and stumbled, cursing softly. I kept going and, making out a crevice in rocks to the right, I lay quickly down in it. I closed my eyes hard, as if that would make me invisible. He passed my hiding place, but I could sense that he stopped just a few steps past. He knew I was close; he was listening for my breathing. I struggled to control it.

I don't know how long things continued this way. He passed me again. 'Jorani, please come out. You must!' Tears were filling my eyes, but I resisted.

Finally, these words: 'Jorani, you break my heart.'

I was left alone, lying in discomfort on my stomach, my sorrow mounting.

After a while, I got up, brushed off my garment, and picked my way up the mountainside to join the soldiers. Ahead the lamp was still burning; it had been set in the crook of a tree. It lit a small clearing. At the far side was a wall of bare stone – the bottom of the cliff. Ropes hung down it in disarray. The spearmen were on their haunches, weapons laid aside, taking count of bags of rice, bundles of greens, and other things they had pulled from baskets that now lay strewn about.

These were the cause of the whooping—proceeds of war that the men would now divide.

'No one to stab in the belly, but we do get this,' said one. The man beside him laughed.

I approached the commander, who stood watching.

'This is what we were looking for, sir?'

'Yes. The Abbot's people have been getting supplies from here.' He gestured at the ropes and the baskets. 'We'll leave a couple of men behind to make sure there's no more of that.'

Of course I said nothing about the encounter with Father, but it was all I was thinking about as our group made its way back to the stairway. I had broken Father's heart. I had broken the heart of the man who had raised me without help of a wife, who had never blamed me for taking her from him, who had carried me on his shoulders up the mountain a thousand times.

23

The Point of a Spear

Dawn was just commencing when we reached the stairway and turned toward the top. This is a beautiful time of day, when Our Lord the Sun peeks above ridges to the east and banishes darkness from the whole of our mountainside with the sweep of a dazzling hand. Leaves regain form and colour that they had shed for the night; rays seek out dewdrops on steps and tree trunks to turn each into a jewel. But none of this made any impression on me that morning.

At the cliff edge, home of the Nagas, we knelt as the priest chanted prayers to mark our safe return. Afterward, the commander thanked me for my guiding, but I barely acknowledged him. As soon as I decently could, I hurried on to the Entry Court. I wanted to be away from people. But I wasn't for long. Just in front of the court, the heir stood chastising three of his fighting men with very crude words – a few carried to me as I scuttled past. The revulsion of my own first encounter with him returned. Away from the counsel and control of the Abbess, this was the kind of man he became.

I reached the nunnery. My mistress was not in her house, so I went down to the stream to wash some garments left from the day before. I hoped the routine of work would calm me. But as I scrubbed, nothing came right. Over and over I recalled the soldiers' disappointment that there was no bloodletting to be had in the clearing, the venom in the heir's words. How could Heaven's will be advanced by men harbouring such brutal passions? I suppose I dwelt upon these things to avoid the more painful recollection, those words from Father. So short, so simple. You have broken my heart.

Perhaps if my mistress had been home, she would have ordered me to sit with her and share what troubled me and she would have made sense of it for me somehow. The weight would have lifted. But she was not there, and so it was that on this morning, right there at the stream, I conceived an idea to leave her and the nunnery and make my way down the stairway to home. I would kneel before Father and confess my misdeeds, remaining at his feet until he forgave me, enduring whatever beating he might inflict. I would take my place again alongside Chantou to see to the needs of pilgrims before the ascent. I would marry Kamol and have children, and give up these improper feelings for the Abbot's son. I would find a way to serve the wife Naga, but from down there. I would pray to her and somehow make her understand that continuing my service at the top was beyond my strength and abilities.

I scrubbed at the stream longer than I needed to that morning. With my mind made up, I now wanted to avoid my mistress. If saw her I would feel I should confess my intentions.

Around noon, I became aware of distantshouts and clanging, not from the direction of the upper courts, but from the hills north of the temple. At first I gave them no thought, but they did not die out and I began to grow uneasy. I spread the garments out to dry on some scraggly shrubs and went back to the huts. Some of the nuns had stepped down from their huts to listen. And my mistress was back. She stood by the gate, telling a nun to close it and make it extra secure. But then it swung wide open, pushed from the outside by a terrified woman whom I recognised from the market.

'Get out right away, all of you! A force of soldiers has come from the north to support the Abbot.'

'Heaven will protect us,' replied the Abbess.

'It did not protect my family. All slaughtered! Get out now! The soldiers are coming this way.'

This was heard by every woman in the community. We looked to our mistress. Her eyes told us to maintain discipline, to remain where we were. But then one young girl, a newcomer, broke ranks and raced for the gate. Then others, then all of them were scurrying out, right past their mistress, daring not meet her eyes. She shouted commands to stop and come to order, but not one of the nuns did. I felt the same urgings of panic pushing me toward the gate, but I did not go. I would like to say it was because a maid's place is by her mistress. But the real reason was that I lacked the courage to commit an act of disobedience in front of her.

She turned to me. 'Well, it's just you and I, Jorani.' There was a hint of a quaver in her voice; I had never heard anything like that.

'Perhaps we should leave too, mistress.'

She looked at me blankly and I repeated my suggestion.

'Yes, of course. But we must take some things with us.'

I knew she meant her writings, which we kept bound in packets in a teak cabinet. I raced up the steps. Inside, I threw stacks of strips into straw bags, murmuring a prayer that I be forgiven for such disrespectful handling. I rose to leave, but realised too that we'd have to take her jewellery. Each nun had little more than a clay lamp and hairpin (a maid had even less), but she, like the other holy mothers at the convocation in Angkor, had necklaces, bangles, earrings, metal hand mirrors, quite a few of them, all made of gold or silver. I turned and saw her at a box seeing to that, though not with any urgency. I willed her to move faster.

I was breaking her rules, but now I went quietly to the box we'd brought back from the lowlands. I lifted the lid. There was nothing inside. All the last contents, it seemed, had been handed over to the fighters.

I was growing fearful again. 'Please, Abbess, hurry!' The noise was stronger now and, glancing out the window, I could see no sign of the woman who'd warned us.

Soon we descended the house's steps, me carrying bags over my shoulder—I can't remember just how many. It was just then that a pack of armed men came racing through the gate, spears pointed at us.

I froze, and so did the Abbess. I cannot describe the terror I felt as these men came closer, then began to circle us. One put the point of his spear to the knot of my garment as if to unfasten it. I dropped the bags and brought my hands to my waist. This drew cruel laughter from the throats of the men. With a start, I realised that these were not newcomer soldiers from the north. They were the same men I'd accompanied down the mountainside.

I looked to the Abbess, expecting some sharp words to bring the men to heel. But she had been rendered motionless, her lips quivering slightly, her eyes as wide as a pair of eggs. I doubt that in her entire life she'd ever been threatened with bodily harm. Certainly not as the privileged Brahmin girl she'd been, nor as an Abbess behind the protection of her nunnery's walls. Those tiny bronze points drained from her all the courage that she thought – that I thought – she possessed.

It was up to me. 'This is a holy woman, protected by Heaven.' I tried to sound firm and fearless. All I got was more laughter. But then it broke off because attention went to the bags. One man put down his spear and squatted at the one filled with jewellery. He pulled out a pair of earrings, held them to his ears, and leered at his comrades. 'A lot better than what we got down the mountainside,' he said. A second man moved to thrust his own hands into the bag, but was pushed away by the first. The remaining men dropped their weapons and, all at once, went for what could be had. I made to move back and pull my mistress with me, but one of the men noticed and brought a spear point back up, this time right to my chest. The men had now pulled all the jewellery out. Others were emptying bags of holy texts, right onto the ground. What defilement it was! But they seemed certain that more shiny metal things were hidden there, and when they found none, they turned to me and my mistress.

'You've got more – show us where!'

One man seized me by the arm. I struggled, but he only tightened his grip. He began to propel me toward the Abbess's house.

'Please, sir! There's nothing more in there. We brought everything out.'

'Don't worry, sweet girl. I'm sure I'll find something worthwhile in you.' The grip on my arm tightened, and I sensed his intentions. The panic that had eluded me before came on in full force. I thrashed. I flailed. I kicked at his legs. He slapped me; I turned, craned my neck, and bit his arm. He yelped and raised his fist.

'Leave her alone!'

The shout came from the gate, and what force it carried. All the men went instantly quiet. The hand fell away from my arm; men who were holding jewellery knelt and began hastily placing it back in its bag. I looked to the gate and saw the commander. His eyes were on the holy texts, which lay scattered about on the ground, some of them trampled by the soldiers.

He barked an order to save the texts. Again, how fast the men moved to comply. I was reminded, in fact, of how the heir responded to my mistress's admonishments. The men began hastily repacking the texts into bags, brushing off the dust. In a few minutes, all the bags were filled again, after a fashion.

I rejoined the Abbess, feeling safer alongside her. The commander looked to us. 'I apologise for this behaviour. These men will be disciplined.' I noticed now that he and all the others were wearing green bands on their right arms.

His eyes went to the house. 'I will need to look inside.' As before, there was not a word of protest from the Abbess. He climbed the steps. We could hear him moving from room to room inside, shifting things around. Teak boxes were opened and closed. I felt good that there was nothing for him to find.

Outside again, the commander called his men to order, then turned to us. 'Come with me, please, Holy Mother.' The title – I hoped that hearing it would restore her to form. But she seemed not to notice and made no effort to move. So, taking her arm, I nudged her towards the gate. 'It's best that we do what he says, Abbess. Please.'

We walked up the trail that led to the Entry Court, the commander in the lead. The Abbess moved only through the force of my urgings. The newly cowed fighters carried the bags behind us, but when we passed some abandoned houses, two of them broke away to look inside. They returned quickly carrying garments and cooking pots. The commander looked back on the two, showing no sign of caring about this particular theft.

Outside the Entry Court, the fighters placed our bags in a row on the stone pavement, then were dismissed. The Abbess and I were directed to sit on a mat laid alongside.

The commander stooped at one of the bags and began examining its contents.

I felt I should say what I knew the Abbess would say. 'Please, sir, I hope the texts will be treated with the respect they deserve.'

'Of course,' he replied. 'They are Heaven's words.'

He seemed not angry with me for speaking, so I asked: 'Where are the nuns, sir?'

He answered without looking up. 'They went down the eastern stairway – that's what I've been told. And the masons too. They did not need to, though. The criminal gang that had taken control of the temple is banished now.'

Kamol would be safe then. I gave the commander a few minutes to continue his inspection, then asked, 'And we, sir, are my mistress and I free to follow them?'

He laughed, though in a not unfriendly way. 'No, you must stay here for now.'

'Why, sir?'

'For your safety, of course.'

'But you said the gang has been banished.'

'It has been here. But some members escaped down to the plain and may harm you if you go there.'

He followed with a serious look that said I'd asked enough, but I was not ready to be silent. 'Surely, sir, you understand that a maid like myself can only be puzzled. A short time ago you were accepting orders and wages from my mistress.'

For the first time, he looked at me. 'That has changed, of course. But you will have noticed that I have protected her, and you, and forbade my men to take any of her possessions.'

'Yes, but...'

He motioned for my silence. 'The temple is now in the hands of forces loyal to Prince Darit, and my own lord has declared for Prince Darit.'

I had never heard this name.

'Prince Darit is the rightful King,' the commander said, seeing my confusion. 'A vast army of men and war elephants is coming together in the north to bring him to his rightful place on the throne.'

'If you say so, sir. But how is that cause served here, sir?'

'The Abbot requested the help of Prince Darit's forces to drive off the criminal gang.'

None of this made sense to me, but I asked nothing more.

As dusk approached, we were given water. I made the Abbess drink. We were given permission to visit a pilgrim privy and I led her there. As darkness fell, a soldier brought more water, and I began to wonder if we would pass the night right in this place. I laid my mistress down on the mat, and joined her on it. My eyes grew heavy. I began dozing.

A hoarse cry roused me in an instant. My eyes flew open and I saw a man racing at the commander, wielding a hammer like a sword. The commander had time to spring to his feet; two of his soldiers raced in from the side and, throwing themselves headlong, knocked the attacker off his feet. He hit the pavement stones terribly hard. The soldiers jumped upon him to hold him down.

'Let her go, let her go!'

Kamol! Of course. Somehow I had not reckoned on another

impulsive act for a woman who would not be his wife.

The two soldiers tightened their grip on him, laughing at his squirming efforts to free himself. One was reaching for a knife. I blanched. My eye went to the commander. He seemed to have no plan to intervene.

Quickly I knelt before him, palms together. 'Please, sir, please! Can you forgive him?'

'Forgive him? He was about to bring that thing down on my head.' He pointed to the hammer, which had fallen a few steps away.

'Sir, it's just a hammer.'

'That doesn't matter. It's dangerous.'

Kamol coughed out some words: 'It *is* dangerous! And I *will* bring it down on your head!' One of the soldiers slapped him hard on the back of the head.

The commander shrugged and looked to me. 'You see?'

'Kamol, hush!'

Of course that surprised the commander. I quickly said, 'Sir...this man is a man who has proposed marriage to me.'

'Really? Well, you'd better find someone else to marry. He will not be in this life much longer.'

But I sensed some kind of softening in his tone, if not words. 'Sir, he does not deserve to live. That I acknowledge. He has come at you with a weapon. But it was done to confront what he believes is danger to me. Any man with courage would have done the same. Yourself included, I think. He does not realise that I am not in danger, that I am under your protection. I ask that you give him pardon as a special favour to this young woman...this young woman who got you and your men across the holy mountainside in darkness without a single one of them falling, without a single scorpion sting, with no greater injury than a bloodied foot or two.'

'The prayers of safety from the priest are more to credit for that.'

'The prayers prevented spirits from being a problem. I prevented you yourselves from being a problem.'

The commander considered this. Then he addressed Kamol. 'Will you apologise?'

'Kamol, apologise!' My voice was the louder.

There was no reply, so the commander turned back to me. 'Well, if he won't...'

I knelt down to Kamol and put my face just a few inches from his. I whispered. 'Kamol – you must do this. Don't be stubborn. Do it for me.'

He whispered back. 'Only if you promise.'

'Promise what?'

'You know very well what.'

'Well, then...all right. I promise.'

'Say it again.'

'I promise.'

What relief came over him, even as he lay pinned under those soldiers.

'You really are safe here? I heard what you said just now. This man is not taking advantage?'

'He is not. He is entirely honourable.'

'Still, I don't like it.'

'Of course you don't. But you must accept it. Well, go on, then.'

It took a moment, but then Kamol said, just faintly: 'I apologise.'

The commander shrugged and I again felt afraid, but then he gave an order: 'Get him on his feet. Take him to the eastern stairway and send him down.'

What a sight it was that followed. Kamol was lifted like a sack of rice and spirited away, giving no resistance. He gave me a final glance of gratitude and affection before I lost sight of him.

I turned to the commander. 'Thank you, sir, thank you! Heaven smiles on you.'

'Perhaps. But I think it smiles on you, young woman. It has sent a very brave young man your way. Those were quite some risks he took just now, all for you.'

'As I said, sir, he did only what you too would have done.'

'I'm not so sure I'd have had the courage,' he said, laughing. 'Those men who tackled him had very sharp knives. But you did make me think for a moment that I would. Very cleverly done.'

He looked to me for a reply, but he got none. I did not want this conversation to go further. In a moment, I stepped back to the Abbess. How quickly a familiar kind of guilt was returning. I had promised Kamol, but I had said nothing about what I was promising. In my heart, the promise was to do whatever it took to get myself back to Father.

24

The Path through the Tall Grass

A short time later, with dusk settling in, I saw four men descending from the upper courts, their way lit by the light of a torch that one of them carried. I was appalled to see that it was Priest Sar and his burly temple guards.

The priest came to a stop standing over us. 'Holy Mother. I'm so happy to see you weren't harmed by the criminals. And your little servant girl too!'

My mistress gave no response, so he continued talking. 'We will protect you, don't worry. Members of the criminal gang are still on the loose but you'll be safe from them. We will take you up the mountain to a secure place.'

I spoke up. 'My mistress prefers to remain here.'

'Abbess! You allow this girl to speak for you?' How he was enjoying taunting her. 'May I remind you that this place is still in the grip of conflict? I've assured these soldiers here that you would cooperate in full, that you're a friend. They wanted to bind your hands!'

The commander gave a small shrug to deny that any such thing had been contemplated.

The Abbess spoke, in a trembling whisper: 'We will go, then.'

With the torch again lighting the way, we walked up the trail that lay to the avenue's west side, the one that led to the Abbot's house. I carried the jewellery bag, one of the guards carried the texts. I glanced back every so often to assure myself that they had not been made off with. But one moment, the guard was there, the next he was gone. I could do nothing but keep walking.

We passed the Fourth Court, then the Third. Despite the disturbances, evening devotions were underway inside it; windows glowed and occasionally we caught the gentle tingling of bells. I began to worry we were being taken to the Abbot. But then Priest Sar turned us all onto a side trail that led away from the temple. We shortly came to a wooden house that stood by itself near a wall of tall grass.

'For you, Abbess, and your maid,' the priest announced. 'I will send some men to your house at the nunnery tomorrow and they will bring up all images, clothing, and other articles that they find. Nothing will be lost or defiled. You will be able to resume your life of prayer here. It's a better place, as you will see. Closer to the energy of the mountain.'

I asked: 'Please, sir, will the guards return my mistress's texts as well?'

'Certainly not. She would not want them. She knows those texts are poison, and she would not sleep in the house if they were present there with her.'

Again, my mistress was silent. Priest Sar stepped closer to her. 'Isn't that right, Abbess? Now that the band of criminals has been destroyed, you are free to renounce your allegiance to the false doctrine. Our master the Abbot knows that you never took that belief to heart. You were only pretending to be a heretic out of concern for your personal safety. You will now be able to take part in the ceremonial life of our community, alongside our master. He rejoices at your return to the true and proper doctrine. He looks forward to welcoming you and seeing you take part in water rites at the linga to thank Heaven for its gift of the true doctrine.' He paused to let that sink in. 'Now I must go, but I will be back in the next day or two with word as to when you will attend these rites.'

His departure was the signal for one of the guards to produce a lamp, which he lit from the torch and handed to me. I climbed the steps into the house to take stock. There were basic implements— mats, mosquito nets, a brazier. And a broom. I picked it up and quickly swept, trying to make things fit for my mistress. Soon she entered. I brought her a cup of water. A servant arrived with rice and fish and greens, fully cooked on someone else's fire. By the light of the lamp, I laid out dinner for my mistress.

She ate sparingly, said prayers, then went directly to her mat. Sleep was her way to escape the defeat and despair of this day, I think. I was left to myself to clean up.

This house had no hut out back, so when my work was done I unrolled a mat inside, as far apart from her as possible. I lay down, but sleep wouldn't come. Presently I sat up. My eyes travelled to the prone form of the Abbess. Already she was snoring! She seemed suddenly to be a complete failure as a mistress. I could not fathom why she hadn't recognized the danger at the nunnery immediately and ordered everyone to leave, and then followed, with me at her side. It was the duty of a mistress to safeguard those in her charge. I rebuked myself for not doing what the nuns had had the sense on their own to do that morning, run. I could have had my wish of the morning! I could have been down at the mountain's base now, in the old house, making amends to Father. Instead I was in the grip of these wicked people and their mysterious plots and machinations. The rightful King. Those were the words the commander had used for this Prince Darit. But we already had a rightful King. He had occupied the throne dais in the capital for many years.

I must say that what shocked me most, though, was how my mistress's resolve had crumbled at the instant that she herself was first threatened with violence. Lights had gone out in her eyes; she had turned weak and submissive. Even when Priest Sar announced that she would take part in rites upholding the false doctrine, she said nothing.

These thoughts tormented me like a swarm of bees, and I could not bear it. So I rose and went down the steps. Overhead shone the same late-night moon that had lit the mountainside the previous night. I noticed now that four guards were arrayed around the house. It was a risk not to go back inside, but I didn't care. I took a few steps away, testing my freedom. One of the guards followed, not getting too close, just keeping me in sight. I went a few steps further; so did he. I came to the wall of tall grass that lay just behind the house. Ahead was a narrow path through the grass, and so I entered. The guard did not follow, but called out something that I did not catch.

Afterwards, I realized that it was a warning. Just ten steps in, a shock – a great void. Had I gone any further, I would have tumbled off the western cliff. Instead, I stood trembling, spared, stooping to steady myself with hands to rock on either side. The moon had set the plain aglow in ghostly light. When I looked directly down, I could make out a small clearing with a tree to one side. It came to me that this was the place where the soldiers had broken up the hoisting of food. I noticed now that to my left a rope was secured around the girth of a boulder and that its strand ran down the cliff face.

I imagined climbing down this rope, leaving behind the Abbess and the struggle in which I had imagined I had some role. I could lower myself safely; the danger would soon be over. By escaping I would only be doing what so many other people had done.

My hands went to a rope to try its strength, but then I stopped. Another realisation had hit me. I was at the very spot where I had been tormented and threatened as a girl, the very spot where the Abbot's son and I had first come together. I can't say why, but this made me feel that I would be protected again, and that it was somehow Heaven's design that a dark act committed at this place should now be balanced by a coming one that was good. It was for me to stay until that good thing came to pass, by my hand or by someone else's. The someone else might be the son. I wondered whether he was right now sleeping in a house nearby. Indeed, I suddenly sensed his presence somewhere out in the darkness.

I returned to the house. From the doorway I glanced to the Abbess's sleeping form. She was quiet now. The moon shone on her through a window, allowing me to see that she was trembling in the grip of a dream. I stood watching, and suddenly I felt ashamed. I had judged so quickly, and with such selfishness. It seemed to me that, right as I watched, Heaven was instructing her on what she must do. And if Heaven was doing that, it must surely be demanding that I do my own duty and remain at her side. She needed me. Truly – had I not been with her today, she would have died on the point of a spear.

I knelt and said a prayer asking that the Abbess cast off the pall of defeat and regain her full mettle.

Part 4

Fortitude

From the day the man appears at the tower building site, the masons are trading theories about who he is and why he has come.

No one really believes the explanation that the foreman offers after a word with Priest Sar: Our visitor is a geomancer, here to confirm that the new tower is properly aligned with the cosmic axis. He is a guest of the Abbot and is to be given all due assistance. The men agree to do that, of course, but in subsequent days he rarely requests any such help. He ambles about the site on his own, keeping clear when stones are shifted from one place to another. He climbs the tower's scaffolding, he examines the palm leaf strips that bear the designs from which the men are working. Sometimes he scribbles notes on a piece of slate that he tucks away in a shoulder bag. He does not chat. Every effort to engage him in conversation dies out after hardly a word or two, and soon the men stop trying.

Most of them do hammer a bit harder than usual, dress a larger number of stones, to show what care they're taking with their tasks. But really, they wonder, why is it that the few words that we do get out of him have none of the flowery tone you'd expect from a man of such rank and expertise? Why does he not wear silk and gold? His garment is clean but plain and faintly worn at the hem, suggesting that his true occupation involves some kind of physical labour.

And he seems to betray a mason's sympathy with stone. Men who watch furtively as they work see him putting hands to fresh-cut blocks at the tower's base, fingers testing the firmness of the grain. One day he walks down to the quarry and spends an afternoon doing the same with sheets of stone that are still fast in the earth, yet to be birthed. A mason carelessly drops a hammer at the visitor's feet; his response is to scoop it up with a single deft motion and hand it back, handle first. He's had a hammer in his hands before, surely. He knows its weight and feel. So a theory flies about: He is a master mason and the Abbot is going to make him foreman.

Then one morning, the man does not appear. Work continues as before; the foreman says quiet prayers of thanks that perhaps his job is secure after all. The talk tapers off, but a week later, it resumes. In the house where the man had slept, a servant finds a tool in a corner, apparently left behind by accident. The servant is as curious about the visitor as everyone else, so he brings it to the building site. The men gather round to look. They note how small and delicate it is. It is a kind normally used for the scoring of sculpture.

25

In the Heart of the Adversary's Camp

What wonders the budding daylight revealed when I awoke. The house in which we'd been placed stood high enough on its stilts to allow a view over the tall grass. But beyond it I did not see the plain. Rather, I saw an undulating mat of clouds, their wispy fringes tinged pink by rays from our barely risen Lord the Sun. Only the peaks of far-off mountains jutted through; fields and forests below were cloaked, for whatever reason Heaven had chosen. I recalled mornings at our house at the stairway's base when the entire sky filled with clouds, and we went about our business, for however long, in a world grey and sombre. Yet I wondered now if on each of those days that dour colour and mood had been balanced, unknown to us, by this brightness and clarity on the upper side of the cloud mat.

I stepped across to the opposite window. From here the sight was the great lotus tower. Another surprise – I had thought it was fully completed, but in fact it was encased top to bottom in bamboo scaffolding. It looked too tall to be something that men had built, and yet I knew it was. I had seen the men coming and going, and certainly gods would not need scaffolding.

I could see too that the house in which we had slept was not entirely on its own. A short walk down the slope were five or six others of similar size, scattered about on terrain that was part stone sheet, part brush and tall grass. The scent of charcoal signalled that their occupants were up and beginning the day. Several more houses stood further up the slope from us and I realised that one, the largest and topmost, was the Abbot's. I looked away.

My mistress was stirring, so I hurried to get a fire of our own going for the morning meal.

She ate silently. I watched her surreptitiously, hopeful. But even with food in her stomach, her spirits did not return. Her eyes held to the floor as she chewed silently.

Later she rose and shuffled her way to the window that faced the tower.

'The Abbot's great project, almost finished,' she said, with bitterness that unnerved me.

'I had no idea, mistress, that it was so tall.'

'Too tall, too tall. A sign not of Heaven's glories, but the Abbot's vanity.'

Then she turned inside and, right there in front of me, broke down. 'Oh, Jorani! What are we going to do? We're prisoners! We'll never get out. I'm so sorry! I should have sent you running away with the nuns.'

I rose and stood before her, eyes to the floor. 'My place is with you, mistress.' I said that, but I was asking myself silently, where are the instructions that Heaven gave you in the moonlight last night?

'You are a gift, Jorani. You serve me so well, even at a time like this.'

I did not know how to respond. So I led her to her mat. 'Sit down, mistress. Let me get you more tea.' I turned my back and busied myself preparing it. From behind me came sobs. I knew that when I returned to her, I must have something constructive to say.

And then I did have something. Perhaps the spirit Naga had deemed that instructions, even for the Abbess, should flow through me, who for now had the more focused mind.

'Mistress, I thank Heaven that Ritisak is alive and retains his freedom.'

'But how can you know...?'

'Priest Sar said nothing about him last night. Ritisak is at the centre of Heaven's struggle, is he not? If he were dead or captured, the priest would have told us as a boast. No, Ritisak must have got away with everyone else.'

'Perhaps...' She was not willing to accept such a statement just yet, and I think she found it hard to accept it from a maid.

'And you are not a prisoner, mistress. Truly. You are a force in the heart of the enemy's camp. Surely you can do more from here than you could do from the nunnery. You were so isolated there.'

I wondered if she was listening, but I grew bold to sit down next to her. 'Please consider it, mistress! Before, you lived behind walls, wondering what was going on at the upper courts. Now you can see with your own eyes. You are at those courts.'

'Yes, but I will be forced to take part in their foul rites.'

I was worried she would begin weeping again. But then another idea came. 'Mistress, if you are present at those rites, perhaps you can do something to prevent them from having the effect that the Abbot intends.'

'What do you mean?' she asked scornfully. 'What could I do?'

That I could not answer. But I could see that she was now considering her own question. Then, a miracle. Her eyes lit up with the old gleam!

'Goodness, Jorani, you're right! Now, when will the things from the nunnery arrive?'

I did not know, of course, but at midday, four men climbed the steps of our house in turn and put loads of things down in places that I selected. My mistress sat with her back turned, saying not a word. We knew that Priest Sar would question the men, and it was now our intent to create in him the impression that she remained demoralised, and would do whatever task was put before her. She played this part well. It was all I could do, however, to behave as if I was terrified too. In fact I was not. My prayer of the previous night had been answered. I was no longer alone in confronting these people.

When they had gone, we examined the things carefully. Garments, writing board, teak boxes, kitchen implements, the portable shrine, and a certain gilded jar. The commander, at least, had kept his word. Nothing had been stolen.

26

The Supreme Linga

Two days later, Priest Sar returned to our house. In his specious way, he called up our steps that he had good news. 'Holy Mother, tomorrow morning the priests of our community will convene at the linga. We will stage a ceremony to bless with sacred water the texts of the true doctrine.'

We had known, of course, that he would come, and my mistress had decided it would be I who replied.

'Holiness, I beg your forgiveness for speaking, but I do so only to convey the will of the Abbess. She thanks you for coming. It will be her honour to attend.' I called out these words from inside, without appearing at the door, because a maid would be insulting a holy man by addressing him from above.

'Abbess, really, I am surprised! Again you let a servant speak for you? I feel I deserve your own words.'

Now it was my part to scurry down the steps and kneel in the dirt before the priest.

'Please, Holiness, forgive her!' I spoke in a loud whisper, as if afraid my words would carry up to her. 'Her spirits have not yet returned. I am told to convey to you that she remains deeply ashamed of her role in the events of recent months, of her failure to defend the just doctrine. Please, sir, she is mortified to the point that she finds it difficult even to speak, to eat, to do simple things. I beg that you understand.'

My head was down, so I could not see the priest's face, but I am sure he was smiling with cruel satisfaction.

'I do understand,' he replied. 'The events of two days ago were a severe trial for all of us, not the least a woman as holy as your mistress. I am sure that as she recovers she is thanking Heaven for its wisdom in removing the criminals from her midst and giving her the chance to pledge devotion to the true doctrine.'

'It is as you say, Holiness.'

To anyone else, I could never have told such lies in a convincing way, but with this priest I found full facility. I must say too that something invested this same ability in my mistress, because when we left the house the following day to attend the rite, I came close to thinking that her spirits had again flown off. How marred was that noble face by guilt and jumbled thinking (or so it seemed). How slowly she walked, barely half her normal gait, as if weighed down by a mountain of guilt. She muttered things to herself with such seeming veracity that I drew close to try to hear.

What I heard was this, in a hiss: 'Jorani, get away! You'll ruin it.'

The supreme linga of our temple of course normally resides in the First Court. But when the tower there was dismantled for replacement, priests removed the holy shaft to a chamber in the Second Court. It was to that place that we proceeded after performing ritual ablutions.

We approached the court's main hall of worship, a tall structure topped with red tiles. We mouthed brief prayers, then stepped through the door, crouching. We found ourselves between two rows of columns that led down to the end of the hall; beyond them was a door to a darkened chamber. Oil lamps flickered inside, and it was only then that I realised I was looking into the current home of the linga. It stood perhaps chest-high on a base of stone. I sank to a mat on the floor, having felt, if a maid can feel such a thing, the waves of the linga's energy on my cheeks. Palms together, I whispered a prayer asking forgiveness for daring look in its direction.

My mistress was unconcerned. 'It's all right, girl. Looking is permitted. Just do it with respect.'

Priests arrived. Later the Abbot shuffled in; it was of course a disappointment that his son was not with him. But after that, my mind went to the rite itself. From the priests, and from my mistress too, there came a chant in the language of mother India, which I later learned was a blessing to Our Lord Shiva: 'Hail, Lord of Three Eyes who nourishes and nurtures us and all beings. As the gardener frees the ripened cucumber from its creeper, may Our Lord liberate us from death and make us immortal. May Our Lord in his great mountaintop manifestation bestow blessings on us who dare approach.'

Again and again they repeated these words, and then, with no warning, they fell silent. Bells rang inside the linga chamber. The Abbot passed slowly through its door. With trembling hands, he raised a pitcher. I worried he would drop it, yet he managed to bring it to the top of the linga. He poured its water in a slow stream, chanting blessings as it made its way down the shaft's sides, changing light-hued stone to dark. Shiva's touch, I could feel, was sanctifying the water.

Priest Sar was on his knees at the linga, holding a silver pan. This he put to the lip of a conduit that from the shaft's base gave forth the holy water. It dripped slowly into the pan, which the priest held with the utmost respect and care. When the flow was complete, there were more blessings. The Abbot and Priest Sar emerged from the chamber and it was only now that I noticed the next focus of the rite. Outside the door was a low table on which were set four gilded jars, each with a whisk at its side, and two teak boxes of the type that store holy texts. Applying the same care, Priest Sar poured water from the silver pan into the jars, one after the other. There was yet more chanting, and then acolytes picked up the jars and placed one before each of three of priests in the hall – and one before my mistress.

After a suitable pause, one of the priests moved forward with his jar, dipped the whisk into its mouth, and with blessings cast what seemed a torrent of holy water onto the text boxes. The other two men did the same. Then it was my mistress's turn. She stepped to the boxes, cradling the jar like a child, and from it sent out a like soaking. The boxes were now quite wet; I wondered if holy water seeping inside would stain the texts.

The rite ended shortly afterwards and we repaired to the courtyard. My mistress signalled to me that we would keep going, back to the house, but Priest Sar was suddenly there at her side, saying that the master would speak with her.

The Abbot hobbled over. I stood behind the Abbess, fearful he would remember me, but he paid me no attention at all.

'Holy Sister,' he said, 'we welcome you back into the community. It is with deepest relief and affection that we see you have broken free of the grip of the heretics and are no longer their prisoner, either in body or spirit.'

The Abbess replied with proper meekness. 'It is with extreme gratitude that I acknowledge my Holy Brother's benevolence and wisdom. He could see that in my heart I was never one with the heretics, that it was only due to their soldiers, their wealth, and their threats that I was forced to pretend to side with them.'

The Abbot spent a moment longer looking at her. 'Yes, yes, that's how it was.'

I wondered if he had ever felt remorse for the long-ago trick he played on his sister. I wondered if she had ever accused him to his face of that offence. I would guess that the answer to both questions was no. For a moment, I tried to picture them as young brother and sister at the estate where they were born. I could not. I could only see them in their current stage, he an aged man facing death and trying first to see through a plan he had pursued all his adult life, she an aged woman whose only goal for now was to outwit him.

We were free to go. At the house, we climbed the steps as though everything were normal. But the moment we passed inside, the Abbess exclaimed: 'Give me the bag!'

From it she lifted a jar that was just like the four into which the sanctified water had been poured. It was in fact one of those four jars. In its place at the Second Court now was an identical jar in which had been delivered, those many days earlier, the last holy water that reached the nunnery.

The previous night, my mistress had given me that jar with instructions to go outside and fill it with the cleanest water I could find. Water from the sky, she said. So outside I went. The job did not take long. As I walked, rays from the moon glinted on something ahead. I hurried forward and found water that had collected in a depression in a sheet of stone. How clean, how pure it seemed – I dared dip a finger to test it. The glint was a summons, I was sure. So I scooped the water into the jar with a coconut cup.

In the house, the Abbess had prayed over this water at great length, seeking to imbue in it Heaven's support for the true doctrine. The next day the jar went with us to the rite, concealed in the bag that I carried. When the priests in the hall focused their attention on the texts in the boxes and the blessing they were receiving, I brought our jar silently out of the bag and placed the other inside.

Now the Abbess was praying over this one. When she finished, she sat back and let out a sigh. There was even a faint smile on her face. What relief I felt too.

'Mistress," I said, 'the danger is past!'

She looked at me, almost amused. 'Not past, Jorani. No, not past. But we have made progress. We have obstructed the infusion of magic into the Abbot's texts. His water carried that power when it was splashed, but ours followed and washed it away. His texts are still just texts, written out by his mortal hand and the mortal hands of his scribes. They have no standing in Heaven. The Abbot does not know this, but he will continue to try to advance his cause.'

'He does not know that, but, may I ask, mistress, does he know what lies in your heart?'

'I don't know. You saw how weak and infirm he is. He hopes to settle the change in doctrine before his death – he dares think the change will be accepted across the empire. Perhaps he is so convinced of its correctness that he can't conceive of anyone opposing it through honest motives. He is willing to accept any conversion to his views, no matter how unlikely a conversion might be. Or perhaps he grasps that I will never join with him, but that all that matters, in his view, is that I stated the opposite to the priestly community, in words and in my participation in the rite. With those acts, he feels, whatever authority I had has been vanquished.'

'But he was wrong, mistress!'

'Precisely!'

She smiled again and told me to bring tea. I did, but I could not help thinking that if Priest Sar suspected deception, he would not just leave us be.

27

The Masons' Labours

I stayed close to the house in ensuing days. But I learned things, because there came to be a frequent coming and going of people. It turned out that though the Naga masons had fled to the lowlands, the tower masons had not. They lived in a camp not far down the slope from us, near the edge of the western cliff at a place where the mountain's stone was particularly good for quarrying. They had suspended work during the fighting, but now were starting it up again and the trail to their workplace wound just past our front door. They came in groups every morning, hammers and chisels dangling from rope belts about their waists. When they reached the worksite, I would begin to hear the song of their tools against stone. Sometimes I saw these men high up on the tower's scaffolding, pointing this way and that, calling down, directing the hoisting of blocks with ropes that hung from the end of a stout wooden beam. It was remarkable – the men were as agile as monkeys up there, giving not a moment's thought to falling.

In the morning, with work and an impatient foreman waiting, the men were not in a mood to stop at the house. But it was different at day's end. Men who have finished a shift of heavy labour are first of all thirsty, so I began putting out cups beneath the house.

One day, an older mason stopped to avail himself. He slurped down the water in his cup with a single gulp. 'Please, sir,' I said, stepping forward, 'let me get you another. It's a small reward for your labours.' The second cup was drained almost as quickly.

After that he just stood, savouring the coolness of water in his insides. 'There was plenty of hard work today, young woman, you're right,' he said after a bit. 'But not for much longer. The work is almost done.'

'Really, sir? The scaffolding is still in place.'

He gave off a not unfriendly laugh. He would enjoy explaining. 'That can come down quickly. What matters is the stone that it covers and that is almost finished. The scaffolding, in fact, has just one more function to carry out.'

'What's that, sir?'

'Why, to bear the august feet of the Abbot! A final stone remains to go into its place in the tower's lotus crown. That act will complete the tower's fabric, and it will be performed by the hands of the Abbot himself in a ceremony.'

'The Abbot has the skills of a mason?'

'No, no, young woman.' He laughed again, at my question, but I think also at the notion of the Abbot with hammer and chisel. 'The chief mason will be there with him. The Abbot will merely push a wooden lever that will cause the stone to slide into place.'

'I see.'

'It is fitting that he should do it, because it is he who began this project.'

He asked for another cup of water. This one lasted longer, because a story that he proceeded to tell got in the way of drinking.

Five years earlier, the Abbot had called the senior masons together to tell them of the new central tower that he foresaw. Priest Sar, at the Abbot's side as always, unrolled a large palm leaf on which he had drawn up a plan at his master's direction. To the masons, it looked rather amateurish. 'Still,' said my visitor, 'we all felt that his vision reflected divine inspiration. But then we found the courage to point out that no tower in the empire had risen so high and that this was due not only to cost and labour but to limits in the strength and load-bearing abilities of stone. It has taken our forebears centuries, we told him, to learn precisely where Heaven has placed those limits.'

The Abbot listened to this, but he was not to be put off. He made some flattering statements about the genius and piety of these particular masons and how he was certain they could find ways that had eluded others. So they raised another objection: the stones required for construction on that scale would be too large to be brought into the courtyard in which the new tower would stand. The entryways weren't wide enough. So right then the Abbot proposed that a section of the courtyard's western gallery and wall be dismantled to open a path. The masons were of course unsettled by this idea. It is a very serious matter, they said, to dismantle part of a godly abode, even if the intention is to restore it as it was. But again the Abbot was not to be convinced.

So some weeks later, prayers were chanted, spells cast, and work on this preliminary job began. The western gallery and wall were taken apart, the stones numbered in chalk and stacked in a windy place just outside the courtyard. Through the resulting gap, newly cut stones were rolled on logs cut for the purpose, drawn with groans by labourers harnessed with ropes. Construction of the tower began. As it progressed, the master masons did prevail upon the Abbot to make some modifications to his design, but it remained essentially as first drawn.

'You might ask,' said the old mason, his cup still only half-finished, 'how could we commit ourselves to a plan in which we did not believe? Well, there were some of us who didn't commit. Some of us returned to the lowlands and looked for work down there. But others of us had families and debts and decided to stay. Just for the initial work—that's what most of us said. The Abbot helped in such decisions by offering wages that were higher than what we expected. Well, we worked and we became accustomed to those higher wages. With what we earned, houses were built in home villages, dowries were paid, debts to moneylenders were retired. And the construction did proceed smoothly. We could not deny that. Even as the tower grew taller, there were none of the accidents that some of the men had predicted. The project seemed blessed, in fact. Thus it was that many of us who had planned to stay just a year stayed two, then three, and before long this project had become our life work. Many of us began to think that the apprehensions of those years earlier had been misconceived. Now we have put the western gallery and wall back in place and are about to see the final fittings on the tower completed.'

He stopped and sipped again.

'Sir, it is a truly beautiful tower, if this girl can be allowed to say so.'

'She can indeed. And if I understand correctly, she had a role in making it so.'

'What do you mean?'

'I think you're a member of the Stairway Guide's family?'

'I am, sir!'

'And did you not, in years past, help the pilgrims put more than they intended into the donations box at the Entry Court?'

'Sir, whatever they put in, they put in because of goodness in their hearts and the encouragement of Heaven.'

He smiled. 'I'm sure that Heaven gave encouragement, but so did a girl who was standing there before them. Those higher wages that we got were due in part, I think, to your family's efforts on our behalf, and we are grateful for that.'

I smiled, taking comfort in knowing that these men considered me a friend.

'So,' said the mason, in a tone of wrapping up, 'I cast my lot here. I have no regrets. It would have been no easy task for a man of my age to find work in the lowlands. But thankfully, I won't have to look for a while.'

'There's going to be more work here?'

'Yes, though it will be of a different kind. The tower has thirty-six spots on ledges from which stone Nagas will look out. The images will be carved by sculptors, but there will be a need for people like me to quarry the stone and get it ready for carving. Hopefully, I will be one of the people selected to remain and do that work.'

Nagas often populate the towers of temples. I had seen them on the tower of the provincial temple that my mistress and I visited during our travels, the one where we made the rubbings. I welcomed the thought of Nagas inhabiting this tower as well. The spirit wife serpent, who might be listening to this very conversation, having heard her name mentioned, would be happy that so many other members of her clan would receive places of honour.

'Sir, when the time does come to make the selection, I believe that the sculptors will welcome your experience and diligence and beg you to stay on.'

'What flattery I'm hearing from you, young woman! Well, enough of it! It's time for me to get back down to the camp for the evening rice.'

When he'd gone, it occurred to me that he'd said nothing about the Lady's masons down on the plain, even though they were Naga specialists. If tensions continued to wane, if something resembling normal life resumed, would some of those men be called upon to help in this task? Perhaps if they came as individuals and not as a group, they'd be welcomed by the Abbot, or at least not bothered. I wondered if the old mason and others of his craft at the camp were somehow in touch with them.

28

The Abbot's Logic

Several days later, I was fetching water from the jar below the house when I caught sight of the commander walking in our direction. It was odd: He was taking a few steps, then going up on his toes, then walking a bit more, and it came to me what he was looking for. 'Good morning, sir,' I called. 'If it's a view of the plain that you want, try the path through the grass over there. But be careful. Just a few steps in, you'll come to the edge of the cliff.'

He gave a nod of acknowledgment, then entered the path. I waited for his return, pretending to tidy up things beneath the house.

When he emerged, he stepped over to the house. 'What a perch that is,' he declared. 'You can almost see the capital, I would think.'

'Yes, sir. It lies beyond the mountains that you see.'

'Really? But I saw no temple spires beyond the mountains. Nothing at all, really.'

'They're further than that, sir. But perhaps if you were to stand at the top of those mountains, you'd be able to see them.'

'You seem quite an expert on the subject,' he said in a friendly way. I got the feeling that beyond the ears of priests or my mistress, he could speak more freely.

'No, sir. But my mistress took me there last year.'

'Really?' I had risen again in his estimation. 'How long did it take? You were travelling by cart?'

'Yes, sir. It took about a week. You're going there, sir?'

'Yes, I will go, and so will many other soldiers. But not until our leader has come here and worshipped before the royal succession texts.'

I did not like hearing that, but I wanted to know more. 'Will that be soon?'

'He'll come in about ten days, I think.'

The commander made no sign to leave, so I brought him one of my cups of water. He seemed to welcome my company, never mind that I was a captive. I did my best to laugh and smile to sustain his attention. But after a while I was having difficulty keeping things up. What he told me took a sinister turn.

Most of the provinces to the north of us, he said, had joined what he called – and for this he assumed an officious tone, as if he were reciting words committed to memory – a grand movement of imperial salvation against the crimes of the false King. Armies were forming up. His own master, lord of an estate of sixteen thousand souls and two hundred elephants, had committed all his fighting men to the cause. All this the commander said, though each word was a capital insult to the dignity of our sovereign.

This movement had come to life at the empire's annual martial games, held six weeks earlier at an estate in the north. Sparking it was His Highness Prince Darit, whom the commander described as a valiant warrior and the King's son by his chief secondary wife. Prince Darit had declared his father's reign terminated because of repeated affronts to Heaven, corruption, and ruinous taxation of the estates. The justness of the cause was confirmed by the presence in the rebellion's ranks of an elephant in whose body resided the spirit of the King of one reign earlier, cruelly slain by the false monarch in order to take the throne. Prince Darit and his men had attacked the false monarch at the games, showing no fear, but their target escaped and fled back to Angkor. The rebellion was gaining support all over the empire, the commander said, and its forces would soon march on the capital. War would come quickly to an end; a new era of peace, justice, and harmony with Heaven would ensue.

'We are certain that Heaven intends this,' he said. 'What other outcome could there be when the movement has won the support of the august Lady Sray?'

The air went right out of me. He asked: 'Are you all right?'

I could not contain what I said next. 'Sir, we received the Lady at our nunnery and I can swear to you that the Lady's heart contains only peace and loyalty and serenity. She would never in any way support a movement such as you describe. Wherever this story has originated, it is untrue in every way.'

He looked hard at me, and I suddenly worried that I had misjudged him, and he was going to seize me and place me in a cage. I would be rolled in that cage on a cart to the capital, taunted by people in every village along the road.

But the moment passed, and he merely thanked me for the water and walked back down the hill.

I climbed the steps of the house to tell my mistress, but she had been eavesdropping all along.

'They call a concubine's son a prince!' she scoffed. 'Chief concubine or lesser concubine, it makes no difference. There is only one Crown Prince and it isn't this man Darit. And this – what do they call it, 'movement for imperial salvation' – what revolting words! It's just a bunch of traitors trying to get things that Heaven has refused to give them. If there's a gang of criminals around here, it's them! And to draw in the name of the Lady Sray!'

I was disappointed that she treated the Lady as an afterthought, but I said nothing.

She wasn't finished. 'They've struck an arrangement with the Abbot, it's clear. The claim of Darit will be fraudulently legitimised through the forging of texts to add to the royal depository here. They will show a bloodline through to him from the empire's founding sovereign.'

'I don't understand, mistress. If our King lacks a legitimate right to the throne' – it was frightening to say such words – 'how is it possible that his son can have such a right?'

'Precisely, young woman! Whatever justification they come up with, it will defy all logic and all teachings of the texts. But who knows, they could declare a finding that the soul of the deceased King has deeded over his regal rights to Darit, as evidenced by the presence of the holy elephant in the ranks of the rebellion. In exchange for legitimization, Darit will pledge to the Abbot that his heresy will be forgiven. No, not forgiven – it will be declared to be orthodoxy of the most blessed kind, drawn straight from the authority of the Vedas. It will be not concealed but celebrated and applied in every temple in the empire. All of this assumes, of course, that Heaven will allow His Majesty to be removed from the throne. It will not. This whole plot will be a failure, you will see. It can have no other end.'

'My mistress will need do nothing, then.' I said it, but I knew it was not true.

'Goodness, no, girl! Can't you see? We had some success against the texts of the false doctrine of abbot succession, but that's not enough. This time the challenge will be even bigger. We must find a way to take action against the false royal succession texts as well.'

I took up my broom, trembling, for lack of anything to say.

In following days, my mistress's spirits became more obdurate. She paced up and down inside, her mind churning through different ideas for how to accomplish this new goal. When she tired of that, she sat for hours at her writing board to replace texts that had been seized from her, me playing my role of assistant. 'The words are all present in my memory,' she told me. 'It's only a matter of summoning them and writing them down again.'

Her anger and energy made it difficult to be at her side all day. I yearned for a reason to get out. One day, one presented itself: I dropped one of our cooking bowls, breaking it. Within an hour, I was down our house's steps, asking permission from the guard to go and borrow another one. He shrugged; perhaps he felt that the Abbess was a sort of hostage for me as well as for Priest Sar – as long as the mistress was held, the servant would always return.

I went only as far as the next house down the slope. I called up the steps to make my presence known. There appeared at the door a young woman several years older than I, dressed in a simple village garment.

'Please,' I said, 'I have a request. I am from the house just there, and I have broken our cooking bowl. I beg your forgiveness, but I wonder if I might borrow one for a little while. Without a bowl, I cannot feed my mistress.'

'Let me ask.'

A somewhat older women came to the door and looked down towards me. She wore the white garment of a Brahmin, and a silver neck-piece. 'You are maid to Parvati, Abbess of the nunnery down the hill, are you not?'

'I am, ma'am.'

'Is your mistress all right?'

'She is, ma'am.' I did not know how much it was proper, or wise, to share, so I said nothing more.

'Well then, yes, you may borrow a bowl.' She turned to the young woman. 'Younger sister, could you please find one and give it to her?'

Younger sister! I said a silent prayer of astonished thanks. I will tell you what I was thinking: The young woman who first spoke to me is not a servant. She is a minor wife, a minor wife who is not a Brahmin.

When she descended the steps with the bowl, I looked extra closely at her garment and hair and way she carried herself. Everything I saw made me sure she was village-born, the same as me. Her manner of speaking, too, left me convinced of that.

When I returned to our house, my mistress took some interest in the interchange with the primary wife. I recounted it, but in such a slow and disjointed way that she tapped my wrist to focus my memory. But it would not focus. All I wanted to do was reflect that the priest had a minor wife who was not a Brahmin.

That evening I hurried my mistress along to finish her rice and settle down on her mat for the night. I blew out the lamp a half hour earlier than usual. Then, sitting in the dark with the mountaintop wind singing softly at the window sill, I reflected without distraction. I knew of course that Brahmin priests sometimes took multiple wives, like other kinds of men of rank, yet I had always assumed that all those wives must be Brahmins like the husband. But it was not so. It is easy to guess the fantasy that I was soon trying out that night. The time was some point in an idyllic future; the conflict at the temple had come to an end in some way favouring our side. I was established as a minor wife in the household of the son. Now of course he would have a primary wife of Brahmin blood, but she would be kind and supportive of me. She would assign me only the simpler household tasks, giving the rest to servants. She would accept that her husband would pass certain nights with me, and leave to him how often that would be. Now, I had no such night-time experience, and so these portions of my mental wanderings were less precise. But I did imagine his skin on mine, the tips of his fingers soft as they explored, his garment showing dull white as it lay aside in the darkness. I began to feel he was already here, his breath next to mine, and that I was experiencing his touch.

But then came the hint of a snore from across the room, and I shook off those thoughts. They were not fit for a holy woman's house. And in any case, what of my dream to resume as a stairway guide?

'Foolish! Foolish!' I whispered those words to myself.

The son was not with me on the mat, of course, and I began to wonder where in fact he was. There were not so many priestly houses at the top of the mountain, yet in our time here I had seen neither him nor anything that signalled his presence in one of them. I fell asleep that night in the grip of misgivings.

29

The Perfect Sweetness of Milk
from a Coconut

The bowl had been lent, not given, so it would have to go back. We needed a permanent replacement. I would not, of course, ask Priest Sar or his underlings to provide one. Though my mistress accepted eating the rice they provided, she would balk at making a request for anything extra. So one morning several days later, I left the house with an assignment to find a new one. With some silver in a bag, I walked to the houses below us and kept going, down the rocky slope, making as if there was no reason why I shouldn't. No one challenged me. I descended all the way to the market at the base of the northern stairway. There were a few soldiers there, but even they took no notice of me.

A cooking bowl is a substantial acquisition, so I spent some time going from vendor to vendor to see what was on offer. Many of these women I knew, and they greeted me warmly, whispering prayers for my safety. I told them what had happened to me and my mistress, and by the time I had settled on a bowl and placed it in my bag, I had learned quite a bit beyond the price and quality of earthenware. The nuns, the Naga masons, and the heir were indeed safe down on the plain. The women added that people such as themselves who had remained behind were in general safe too; the killings of that first day had stopped. The whole area was firmly in the control of Prince Darit's men, but the rebellion was not as widespread as the commander had suggested. There were stories that some nobles were publically declaring loyalty to His Majesty. But however true that was, it was having little effect here. The pretender's visit to the temple would in fact come in a few days' time. Some of the vendors were stocking up for sales to what they expected would be a large escort. Though their sympathies were with the King, they would not turn aside a chance to make some money. In fact, prices were already heading up in anticipation of it, though I paid normal rates because I was of the temple, never mind that I was a captive.

So as I prepared to climb back up to the house that morning, I felt I was the best-informed person on the mountaintop. Even as I'd talked with the vendor women, I was imagining myself presenting my mistress with these gleanings and drawing one of her smiles of approval. But then those thoughts ended abruptly. I saw Father.

He was perhaps thirty paces away, moving purposefully through the throng of market goers. I can't say how I'd failed to think I might run into him here. The mountaintop was back in the Abbot's hands and so it was only natural that Father would come up the stairway again, both to lead pilgrims and to retrieve his errant daughter.

My first instinct was to run. I no longer had the protection of darkness or the nunnery's threshold. Yet I didn't run, feeling sudden shame that I should treat Father as someone who was a danger. I stayed where I was, yet lacked the courage to call to him. But ten more paces, that was all it took – he caught sight of me.

I turned in his direction and put my head to the dust.

Above me, I heard: 'That won't be enough, Jorani. Now get up.' His voice boomed! Normally, it was a point of honour for him that members of our family never drew attention to ourselves in public.

I sprang up instantly. I stood before him, trembling, eyes to the ground.

'You're coming home now, do you understand?'

I nodded silently.

'Let's get going, then.'

He led me across the marketplace. No one dared acknowledge

they'd noticed this outburst; vendor women put their eyes to the ground, same as me. But I think I'm not exaggerating in saying that a hush fell over the entire market that morning.

Father headed to a shortcut trail that winds up through a wooded area to reach the eastern stairway. I followed, the bowl I'd bought feeling heavy in my bag.

'Please, Father, I...' I didn't know what I was going to say, only that I found the silence between us terrifying.

'Just keep walking.' This he said without turning to face me.

Again I did as told. Soon we were arriving at the place where the Nagas were to take their stone form.

I came to a stop. Father instantly sensed it and turned to face me. 'Go on, then. Down the steps. Right now.'

It was here that I finally found words, or rather, I was given them.

'Father, I must ask you something.'

'No! You can ask when we're down below.'

'Father, I must ask you, and ask you here.'

He stepped to me. I shut my eyes, expecting a blow, though I had never received one from him. Perhaps it was this sight, of his daughter cringing, preparing to accept a beating, that brought compassion into his heart despite all I had done to wrong him.

'Then ask me! What is it?'

The spirit wife Naga did not speak through my mouth that day. My voice did not change; I did not shudder and fall to the ground. But I do believe that she was with me and placed words in me to be given to Father as my own.

'I would like to know, Father, is it a person's first responsibility to obey a god or can it be to obey another person over the god's wishes?'

Whatever he was expecting, it wasn't this. 'It's the god who must be obeyed, of course! Provided that it's truly a god and not a demon masquerading as one.'

'What if the other person is the closest, most beloved person who can be imagined?'

'Still the responsibility is to the god.'

'There are no exceptions?'

'As I said, if it is a god, and not a demon. The actions that the god wishes will in some way bring about good for this other person. But that may take some time.'

I stood there quiet for a while.

I said: 'Father, I beg to tell you that your daughter is in this situation.'

'That can't be!'

'It can! You know that two gods inhabit the place where we're standing.'

'Of course.'

'I know it's vain, Father, but I believe that one of them has given me tasks that conflict with what I should do for you as your daughter.'

'You call it vain, but I...' Those words he practically spat out, but then something stilled him. I stood before him fearful again. But in stages there came over his face an expression of the deepest kind of relief. At first I thought that the Naga had voiced something to him as well, but later he told me that, no, it was entirely by what I had done, given him something he had craved for months, an explanation. Our estrangement was no longer the baffling handiwork of a daughter endangering herself and her family's honour and livelihood. Rather, it was part of a plan that straddled the world of humans and deities. The Naga's possession of Chantou had been its first manifestation. We owed so much to the protective beneficence of the serpent gods – movement up and down the mountainside free of accidents, the clean water in the stream by our house, the health and vigour in our bodies. It made perfect sense that our family would be called to serve them in unusual ways, and after Chantou my turn had come.

Father and I stepped away from the cliff's edge and sat down together on a rock. He listened as I recounted what I had done in the recent months. Some things I left out, because they would frighten him – I made no mention of the spear point at my belly in the nunnery that day. As I spoke, I sensed a further budding of sympathy in his heart. When I finished, he put arms around me. I hugged him back and for a while we wept together.

'You should have told me earlier, Jorani...'

'I had no way to, Father. I could not come out of the nunnery. I was so startled that night on the mountainside. And for so long I wasn't really sure of it myself.'

'I am ashamed,' he said. I was still in his embrace.

'Please, there is no need for shame, Father.'

'I should have known that my daughter would not do such things without a very serious reason.'

'Father, I'm the one who should be ashamed. Can you forgive me for staying quiet when you called for me on the mountainside? It was a daughter's duty to show herself and go with you.'

'It's a father's duty to understand, Jorani.'

'Well, it's past now, Father.'

'Yes, it is.' He stepped back to get a good look at me. I felt again like the little girl who rode on his shoulders.

'Well!' he said. 'Let's head down then.'

How is it that two people can be united one moment, and then apart the next? I did not know what to say now, so I delayed.

'Father, let's go drink some coconut juice. Like we always did after a climb.'

He agreed, though his face clouded over. We walked back down the shortcut trail to the marketplace, making random talk that masked this new barrier that we both sensed between us.

At the market, a vendor woman caught sight of us and whispered word to her neighbour. How strange this would seem to all of them. I would have to explain. But I put that thought aside as our favourite of the women cracked open a pair of coconuts and poured the milk into earthen cups.

We sat on her mat. Father took a sip from his cup, beaming as if he'd never tasted coconut milk before. 'Perfect sweetness, Jorani, isn't it?'

'Yes, Father. At this place it always tastes better than anywhere else.'

'And best of all today. Because my daughter is restored to me.'

I asked: 'How are the others down below, Father?'

'Everyone is fine. We have not been so busy, though. Most of the pilgrims have put off coming because of the troubles here, but some are starting to come again. Chantou misses you. Your brothers miss you. And of course Kamol misses you.'

'Yes.'

'He misses you perhaps more than any of us, Jorani, if we believe what he says. I don't let him help with the ascents just now, because he would be remembered here as one of the Naga masons' men, and there might be trouble.'

Kamol had not told Father about the confrontation with the commander, it seemed.

'But down there – there's no trouble, no trouble concerning anything. Kamol is a fine young man. He's waiting for you.'

'Father...'

'Jorani, I know that everything you have done was necessary in Heaven's eye. But I wonder now if the god might be willing to release you from further duty.'

'Really, it...'

'Let me continue. Our family has a long record of service to the Nagas. And now you have done what you have done. We could approach them and bow our heads and beg for a small gift, the selection of some other person to carry out the remaining necessary tasks on the mountaintop. We could pledge a special offering, half of our income for the creation of stone form for the holy serpents.'

How was I to respond? He was proposing the same supplication that I had myself thought up a few days earlier. Yet, hearing it from his mouth made me appreciate that it was against Heaven's will, at least for now. And also I was thinking that if he'd promised that I would be a guide again, climbing the stairway every day, how tempted I would have been. But I knew he would not make such an offer. Father's whole purpose would be to keep me in the safety of the base of the mountain. So I merely said: 'Father, half our income is too much.'

'Nonsense. A small price for a daughter returning home. I think the Naga couple would grant the request. They would acknowledge your service and also that a betrothed couple should not be kept apart. We could arrange a wedding in just a few days, Jorani. All it requires is a willing bride.'

'I'm sorry, Father. There isn't a willing bride. There cannot be one.'

That quieted him. He sat for a moment, then took my hand. His tears were going to come again. 'Oh, I know, Jorani, I know. This wedding can't happen now. What the god desires is for you to remain atop the mountain until this struggle is resolved. What you heard from my mouth just now is the ramblings of a father who worries for his daughter's safety, even if she is under the protection of a god.'

'We must believe, Father. The Nagas will continue to watch over our family's prosperity. They will keep me safe.'

He sat there, eyes down, pondering his cup. I looked to him, feeling the same outpouring of love that I had felt as a child when he embraced rather than punished me for the accident of the overturned lamp.

'Father, I must go.'

He said nothing.

'Please, please, understand. The spirit Naga wills it, but there are also the wishes of the Abbess. You gave me over to her that day, don't you remember? A contract exists, and she has not released me from it. She has given me many jobs that remain undone, and a good maid finishes whatever her mistress assigns. You want me to make you proud, don't you? Our family honours its obligations. When the work here is finished, I'll come back down. I promise. I want nothing more than to do that. And it won't be long.'

I rose and walked away, saddened that our reconciliation had come to this so quickly. But there was also contrition descending upon me. I had said nothing about the son. I had given Father to believe that my motives were all noble, nothing less than duty to god and mistress.

As my feet took me up the northern stairway's first steps, I felt Father's eyes on my back. I recalled the time those three years earlier when I had sensed them on me as I hurried up the first steps down by our house, sent on the errand for merit certificates.

30

The Twenty-Two Boxes

When I entered our house, the son was seated on a mat opposite my mistress. Our eyes connected for an instant. It was a shock, but instinct and training took hold and I went straight to the floor. I had thought about this moment many times, but nonetheless I was convinced now that whatever I did would be wrong. So I remained on the floor, face down. But as my wait lengthened, me picturing his face as I'd just seen it, I heard no departing footsteps. Then came the voice of the Abbess.

'You may raise your head, Jorani. We need some tea.'

Now it was no longer my decision what to do. I scurried off to the brazier and fanned its coals rather too hard, raising some ash into the air. Then I managed to calm myself, and got down to the business of making tea.

Behind me, I heard his voice. 'Please, let me say it again, Abbess. We are all so happy that you been brought back from the false doctrine. We look forward to your help in assuring that it is stamped out wherever it appears.'

I don't know why, but as I waited for the water to boil, I was feeling that if anything was false here, it was the way in which he was saying these words. It was the same stilted way in which the commander spoke when giving the formal name of the rebellion.

I filled the pot and brought it on a tray with two cups. After setting it down between them, I made to withdraw, but the Abbess stopped me.

'You will remain with us, Jorani. And Bouray, you may speak freely.'

His name. I had never heard it spoken.

Now he was speaking again, and in an earnest tone. 'That might be dangerous. There is no need to involve...'

She cut him off. 'What there is no need for is concealment. This maid has served me loyally, not only on domestic tasks but on many matters related to our campaign. She is brave, she is perceptive. She can keep secrets, and it is time that she knew what is happening here.'

I put my face to the floor in thanks for such praise, but the main emotion I felt was confusion. She told me to sit up and listen. 'Now,' she continued, addressing herself to the son again, 'continue what you were saying, please. You mentioned that the texts are stored in the Second Court, but in which library? There are two there. Is it the east or the west one?' She looked to me. 'I am referring to the texts of royal succession, Jorani.'

It took a moment for the son to reply. He seemed still reluctant. 'They are in the east library. The west one is used for primary texts related to the temple's own gods and liturgy. There are four other rooms in which texts are stored, but they are in the Third Court and they contain nothing concerning succession.'

The Abbess thought for a moment, then asked: 'Now in the east library, how are the texts arranged? I mean, how are they stored?'

'In boxes – like the ones you have here, but larger. There are twenty-two boxes in all.'

'Are the boxes labelled, perhaps by reign?'

'Yes.'

'And there are guards, I assume?'

'Yes. They are assigned by the priestly family that has responsibility for safeguarding the texts.'

These words I heard and comprehended, but much of what came after escaped me. My mind was occupied less by details of what was being said than by what the talk meant. The son was one of his father's opponents. He was meeting with my mistress under the guise of congratulating her for her conversion. I found myself studying the son without looking directly at him. I could again sense how relaxed and gentle he was, yet possessed of that same determination. He sat so near to me that I felt I should edge away. But I stayed put, looking up a bit now, counting his breaths, noticing how he tilted his head just slightly when answering a question. A golden necklace hung down to the centre of his chest. On other priests this type of jewellery seemed to me a sign of foreboding power and detachment; on the son it confirmed that he was beloved of Heaven. The downward cast of my eyes allowed me to take in other things in detail. For instance, his white Brahmin garment had a small grass stain on its hem; I wondered on what grass he had been sitting and when.

'...Jorani.'

My attention returned. 'Yes, mistress.'

'The time has come.'

'For what, mistress?'

'Why, to remove the relevant royal succession texts so they don't fall into the hands of this thug who wants to be King.'

She made the task sound simple, just a matter of deciding to do it.

'Bouray, you have stayed the proper amount of time. We will continue our discussion next time.'

'Yes, Abbess.'

With that, he rose and took his leave from her. He looked my way one more time, then was out the door.

Of course I immediately wondered when he would return. My mistress gave an answer. 'He'll be back tomorrow, Jorani. He's been given permission to come here to work with me on drafting texts that will be circulated to support the false doctrine. He will come back often, I think, and he is going to need your help.'

'For what, mistress?'

'Haven't you been listening? To bring out the royal texts. He will not be able to do it alone. There are too many, many more than we brought from the nunnery. You can help him, can you not?'

'Of course, mistress.'

I turned away. I could not let her see my face just now. But before long, I got control of myself and went about my work. I stole a glance her way; she was at a window, gazing out, giving no sign of suspicion that I was concealing something from her.

31

The Jewellery Case

T he son returned to the house the following afternoon, and the
next. He became a regular visitor, in fact. Sometimes my mistress
interrupted whatever she was doing and sat with him on the mat. They
spoke about broad theological questions or about details of the texts'
location inside the temple and the job of removing them. I wasn't
always sure – they switched back and forth between the common and
the holy language.

But other times when he arrived, the Abbess chose to remain
engrossed in whatever task she'd begun, and merely motioned that
he should sit down by himself. It was then for me to bring him tea.
Despite my many contrivances about a bond between us, I had no idea
how to converse with someone of his standing, so mostly I remained
silent. He smiled gratefully when I laid down the tea, as if I had
completed some enormous task that he did not deserve. Gradually
we progressed from 'thank you' and 'you are most welcome, sir' to
enquiries about each other's health. But it went no further. I had
been so sure of something before, but now, in his presence, I was not
sure what to make of his sympathetic tone. I knew that, unlike the
Abbess, some people of standing treat their servants kindly as a matter
of course, praising their work, offering thanks when attended. As a
child I had seen this more than once on the stairway between pilgrims
of noble blood and menials who accompanied them. But even then
I wondered how a servant was meant to respond, whether a reply in
kind would open the door to accusations of trying to take advantage.

So now I was determined not to disappoint the son in any such way. And yet still I could not give up the suspicion – perhaps I should say the hope – that his cordiality reflected more than a benevolent master's concern.

One day, I returned to the house to find Abbess and son again sitting together. She looked to me. 'Jorani, our guest has told me that there's a path through the grass and it leads to the cliff face behind the house. You know it, I believe?'

'I do, mistress. I went there on our first night in this house.'

'Really! You weren't afraid to stand at the cliff's edge?'

'No, mistress. There are rocks to hold on to.' The son nodded gravely, but said nothing. I was sure he was recalling what had happened there.

That was all. My mistress gave me no sign of why it mattered that I should know this place. She turned back to the son and the subject of the east library. I listened as best I could. Prayers, it seemed, were chanted twice a day before the texts and the gods who were honoured in these libraries. Once at midday, once by lamplight around two hours after sunset. These responsibilities were assigned by the caretaking family.

'You say that priests are assigned twelve-month terms at this duty?' the Abbess asked.

'Yes. The current terms will finish at the end of this month.'

'How advantageous for us.' I could tell she saw this as new confirmation that Heaven was assisting us. 'You would qualify for this duty?'

'It would be unusual for an Abbot's son to take it, but I think there's nothing in the texts that would bar it.'

'Yes, yes, you could do it. The gods would not object. Now, does the priest who has this duty bring anything into the library?'

'Palm leaves on which the day's prayers are written. It's his responsibility to select the proper ones and bring them in a bag to the library for chanting in front of the god.'

'I see.' A plan was forming.

Then she turned to me. 'Starting today, you will spend an hour a day at the son's house doing the chores of a maid.'

'What? But, yes, ma'am.'

'The maids who normally do his cleaning and washing fled the mountain during the hostilities. They have not returned. You will stand in for them.'

'Yes, ma'am.'

She eyed me for a moment, as if trying to read my mind. 'Well, don't you see what an opportunity their absence is for us?'

I did, but I knew she wanted to explain. 'If you are going to help in the task at hand, the real task, it will be useful for you to be known as someone who routinely passes in and out of his house. It may become necessary for you to carry things back and forth from his house to this one, or to other places.'

'Yes, ma'am. I understand. I'll do my best.'

An hour later, I was following him up the trail. He walked in front of me, remaining silent, as a master would.

His house, when we reached it, struck me as small but well kept. Just two rooms, with small trees on either side offering shade. Higher up the hill was his father's residence. From that I kept my eyes averted.

He entered; I followed. Inside, I saw a broom and went for it, but he put out a hand to stop me. 'Please, please, there is no need...' This was really the first time he had addressed me with anything other than pleasantries since the day the two boys tormented me. 'It is my avocation,' he said, 'to do the sweeping myself. And the other cleaning.'

I had never heard of such a thing, a man cleaning. 'Then what am I to do here, sir?'

'I'm not sure.'

I did not know what else to say, so I picked up the broom and began to sweep. After I had done one end of the room, I found my wits to say, 'Sir, I assume that people pass by this house sometime?'

'Yes, people do pass by.'

'I think it would seem strange if they looked in and saw a maid sitting on her hunkers, doing nothing. Maids are supposed to work. So I will work.'

He accepted that and sat down at his writing board. He studied a half-written text silently, sometimes pausing to write on a slate. The charcoal passed left and right. Somehow I felt he was play-acting, just as my pushing the broom left and right was play-acting, something to mask my disquiet. But that thought passed and soon I really did focus on the sweeping. I began to notice that, whatever my first impressions, the place had come to need a real cleaning since the other maids departed. In the eating area, the floors were stained. Dried-up grains of rice lay scattered about. Dust and cobwebs filled the corners and the sleeping mat looked as if it had never been shaken out. I wondered if perhaps he did in fact do the housework himself, such as it was done at all. I will confess that as I moved about I took an interest in details beyond questions of cleanliness. His silver drinking cup was slightly dented—had he dropped it, perhaps? His sleeping cloth was of a colour and weave that I had never seen. His wooden comb, lying near the sleeping area, had a few hairs caught in it. I resisted the urge to stick one in my waist.

Later I went beneath the house to his rain jar to draw water. This I used to clean the floor of the eating area and the sills of the windows. After an hour of applying myself this way, I was feeling more comfortable in his presence. I no longer stole looks in his direction. When I descended the house's steps to go back that day, I noticed that one of the guards who was normally seen outside the Abbess's house was now here. I walked past, pretending not to notice.

I returned the next day to find he was not at the house. I put aside my disappointment, though I could not help wondering if he had gone out so as to avoid being there with me. I looked around the house for jobs to do, because a good maid does not wait for instructions. Now, the son of course had jewellery, and this he kept in a teak box. I had seen it the first day, but did not open it. Now

I felt I should. I told myself that I would find in it something further needing cleaning or polishing, and that type of work was a maid's duty.

A jewellery case can contain not only wealth but secrets, yet I did not do what I should have done, wait for his return to ask permission. Rather, I knelt at the box and, murmuring a prayer, lifted the top. I would merely peek inside and see if there was something warranting a request for permission. Gold, silver, and jewels gleamed up at me. I instantly pressed the top back down, rather too hard. I looked about me, worried that unseen someones would accuse me of intending to steal. But in a few minutes my courage and curiosity returned. Inside were golden armbands, silver necklaces, ear pendants, rings. Some were jewel-studded. What elegance, what spiritual probity these shiny things possessed. Yet a closer look revealed that some of them had patches of tarnish. I smiled to myself – I had been right to check. I lifted the tray on which the precious things lay in the case, to see if polish was stored beneath. I had seen none elsewhere in the house. I did find a jar of polish, but I also found something else, a weighty object, or maybe several, wrapped in an old cloth. Carefully I lifted the folds of cloth away, expecting something of value.

What I found inside were fragments of pottery. How is it possible, but I knew immediately what they were. They were remnants of my water jar, the one the older Brahmin boy, the heir, had gleefully smashed on a rock. How many years had passed, yet I remembered the unusual green hue, the surface slightly rough to the touch. I sat turning the pieces in my fingers, edges sharp against my skin. The only explanation I could imagine for their presence in this box was that the son had gathered them up after I ran away.

Suddenly I felt I had no right to be looking at these things. I rewrapped the pieces as quickly as I could and closed the case.

The son returned a half hour later. He sat down at his writing board. I continued with my work, but my mind was of course on what was inside the box.

Normally I can hold my tongue. But before long words came spilling out.

'Sir, why do you have the fragments of my water jar?'

My broom had stopped its motions. I turned to face him. How brazen I was, but such was the strength of my shock and curiosity.

I saw that my question had brought great discomfort to his face.

'I apologise, sir. Truly! I had no right to look in the case. I thought there might be something inside to polish, that's all.' I quickly resumed my sweeping, pushing the broom so hard that it banged into a wall.

He was looking at me, I could tell. 'Please don't apologise, Jorani.'

'But I must.' I kept at my sweeping.

'No, please don't. You have done so much for me.'

'I merely clean your house, sir. Any girl can clean.'

'It's more than that.'

'Sir, I have no idea what you mean.'

'Jorani, perhaps you do? Some part of it, at least? But please, put down the broom. Sit with me here on this mat. I would like to explain.'

I did as I was told, but how conscious of myself I felt, sitting so close. I looked to the floor.

'Please, please,' he whispered, 'from now on, let it not be master and servant between us. I know that we must show that relationship to people who pass by, but there is no reason why it must be that way in private.'

'You frighten me, sir. I am in fact a servant.'

He ignored that. 'May I ask, Jorani, what is your earliest memory? The very first one.'

Why did he ask? 'I'm not sure, sir.' I wondered what would happen if I sprang up and ran away.

'Please, you can't remember at all?'

In fact I did know, and so I told him. 'Well, sir, I am sitting by the door of my house. It is midday and my father is behind me, tending to something. I'm not sure what. I can hear his footsteps here and there. But my attention is on some ants that are crossing the door's threshold in a line. They are the big black kind. One has become separated from the others. I put my finger to him, and he steps onto it. I put him down with his friends. In a moment he is continuing on his way with them, in the line.'

'A pleasant memory. Does it go on?'

'No, sir. It ends just there.'

'Now will you let me tell you mine? Will you listen?'

He was truly asking, and I nodded yes.

'Thank you. The story is rather different from yours. An old priest has taken me by the hand and is leading me off. I am so small that I am holding my hand up, like this, so that he can grasp it. I am turning around as I walk, looking back. I think it's because he has interrupted me eating something sweet, and I am looking back to this sweet thing, hoping it will still be there when I return. I have done something wrong in eating it. I don't know where he is taking me, but I don't want to go.'

'I am sorry, sir.'

'Well, that is kind of you, but there is no need to be sorry. I am just telling you what was my life from the earliest years. But, do you know, you helped me put that life behind me.'

'I don't know, sir. I don't know how that would be possible.'

'I will explain, if you will listen. Will you?'

Again, he was seeking my concurrence. How empathetic he was. I nodded that he should continue.

'Even before I was born, my father had decided that I would follow him as Abbot. And at a very young age I was given over to a group of hermit priests to begin my training. They lived off in the woods northwest of the temple on an isolated hillside so that there would be no distraction from their meditation and prayers. Probably you don't know the place. It's a half hour's walk beyond the nunnery. I remained there for many days at a time, sleeping on a special mat in the chief hermit's house, so that my training could proceed day and night. There was a woman who came to deliver food and do various cleaning tasks, perhaps once a week. I always tried to find a way to break away from whatever lesson I was being taught and go sit with her when she came. She was kind and attentive. When dusk fell and she went away, I tried to hide my tears from the priests. Perhaps once a month I was taken back to the house where I was born, to demonstrate to my father the things I had learned. I would sit before him and recite from memory a thousand-word passage from the Mahabharata. I would demonstrate writing skills with chalk or stylus, holding up the results for his inspection. I would say a new incantation, with certain words withheld, of course, because this was only a demonstration, not the actual practice of magic. After this, I would be given a brief time with my mother. She would sit stroking me, crying a bit, and then it was back to the hermitage in the woods.'

My heart was touched. 'Sir, I was in the company only of males for many years when I was young, but it wasn't like what you describe. They were my father and brothers. I did not learn the things that a girl learns from other females, but I was treated with love.'

'I'm sure you were. It shows in the character that you now possess.'

What a thing to say!

'Some of the hermits, Jorani, did the same with me, but they were first of all teachers tasked with imparting to me high levels of knowledge in short periods of time. Now, in my eighth year I was allowed to return to live in the house atop the mountain but my education continued. Each day I walked a short distance to a pavilion where one of the resident priests waited for me with a course of instruction. I was not allowed to associate with other boys, except when certain ones were brought in to take part in a joint lesson. They always deferred to me, letting me go first, praising my answers to the teachers' questions, though sometimes I could hear them whispering about me in mocking tones. As for girls, they were all kept at a distance. I was given to believe that I had no need to meet girls, that when I was older, a girl who would make a proper wife would be presented to me.

'This life was hard, but it seemed entirely natural to me. That is because I was told it was, so many times, by my father – it was the natural, required life for a future Abbot, he said. But as I grew older, I began to wonder if that was true. I think this was caused by the epics and commentaries that I was reading. I didn't tell anyone, but I found that what made the biggest impression on me was tales of the simple life. When Rama and Sita and his brother Lakshman are banished from the holy capital Ayodhaya, they feel no regret, no envy of those who remain behind. The Holy Three live in a hut that they construct of sticks and leaves in a clearing in the forest. They wash their own garments, they gather their own berries. They are rich in virtue, not in gold and silver. Heaven's touch is all around them and they find glory in it. To them the house in the clearing is the real Ayodhaya. At night I would lie awake thinking that this kind of life was what I aspired to, and that I would find it by remaining in the hermitage permanently. My father's house began to repel me. It was like the false Ayodhaya that Rama and his wife and brother had left – servants, gold, the finest fish and meat at every meal, constant flattery, distractions from spiritual quests. I could not see how living there in that way served the dictates of our faith.

'One morning, I was taken to my father's presence for another of those periodic demonstrations of learning. When I finished, my teachers withdrew and I was left alone with him. He praised my progress and began speaking of that time, still far in the future, when I would be invested with the sacred oaths and implements of his post. Some god guided me right at this moment and I interrupted my father with a confession: I viewed my future life as occurring in isolation at the hermitage on the hillside. I got no chance to explain because, oh how angry he became! His eyes bulged, his mouth opened wide. He pounded the floor, and he began a lecture in the sternest terms. I would continue my studies, I would look forward to the succession, I would make no further mention of this other path. Did I even understand the hardships of living at the hermitage? I said that I did; I had lived there. He laughed and said that because of who I was, I had always received better food there, a softer mat, even the domestic help of a woman from the village.

'After a while, he regained his calm. He told me that my desire showed pureness of spirit and was another sign that Heaven desired that I would lead the temple community, and not some other person. Put the hermitage out of your mind – use the meditation techniques that you have learned from the priests. Your place is here, this house! That was his message. When he finished, I rose and went outside. I felt confused and disheartened. I began to walk. I had no idea where I was going – I had never wandered like that before. After a while, I found myself in a deserted area west of the temple, near the cliff. Other boys had been here many times, I'm sure, but I had never been allowed such a simple outing. I walked through this area, and do you know what I came upon? I came upon a pair of Brahmin boys, supposedly blessed of Heaven, taking pleasure in tormenting a girl.'

He paused to make sure I grasped what he'd just said.

'You know what happened, Jorani. I got knocked down. But what a liberation it was! For the first time in my life, I was not flattered and fawned over. I was knocked down by that boy and I tasted dust in my mouth! For the first time in my life, I truly lived the teachings, in however small a way. I humbled myself and put the concerns of someone else before mine. Perhaps I am vain, but I did it at some physical risk, though that boy who struck me wasn't really so strong. I will tell you that I was disappointed when you ran off. I could not blame you – I could see that the experience had been nothing but frightening for you. Still, I regretted. Sitting and having a real conversations with you would have been another unknown experience for me. So what did I do after you left? I sat there for a little while, then I picked up those shards and brought them home with me. I wrapped them in cloth and placed them in my jewellery case. I wanted to preserve the memory of liberation from my station. And...I wanted to preserve my memory of you.'

What was I to say? 'I am happy that you did it, sir.'

'Must you call me sir?'

'I know of no other way to address you, sir. But I am sorry that I ran off. You're right – I was very frightened.'

'Yes, I had no right to expect you to stay a moment longer. But, please, let me finish the story. I did go back to my studies as my father had ordered. But I continued to harbour those unsettled feelings. I did not give up my hopes for a path to the reflective life. One thing stuck in my mind from my father's admonitions that day. He had said that Heaven did not want "some other person" to be Abbot. That seemed odd. There had never been any suggestion of some other person. It had always been me. I knew that succession normally passes through the maternal line, but I had always been led to believe that in this case there was no such person of that line, and that therefore the post could fall only to me. But who could my father mean? I began to wonder if this other person might in fact exist and whether his qualifications were really so deficient. The more I thought of this person, the more convinced I became that Heaven was opening a way for me to escape being Abbot.

'Now, there was one priest-instructor whom I felt close to, and at the end of a lesson one afternoon, I asked him about this. He frowned and didn't answer, but I pressed him that day and the next and finally he told me. There was a nephew who lived off the temple precincts, but no, he was not qualified. But why might people say he was? I pressed the priest for an answer. I had to know. Finally he told me that succession by the maternal line was old doctrine that had been exposed as false by religious authorities all over the empire. Heaven in fact intends that this inheritance should always pass to a son. He said all of this, this priest, yet I felt that he did not believe it. He would not speak further, and as we broke off the session that day, he whispered a request that I say nothing about this conversation to my father.

'It was around this time that Heaven intervened again. It caused this priest to bring the Abbess Parvati to my instruction pavilion for a lesson on the Yajur Veda. You may know that she is among the empire's foremost authorities on this scripture. At least, this was the reason the priest gave when my father found out she'd been there and banned her immediately from any further role in my education. She and I had only one session together. But there was no need for more. Right away I sensed a like mind in her. I declared to her that I believed Heaven did not intend me to be Abbot. She responded that I was correct, that there was an heir who met the requirements of bloodline. She would stand with me to see that the divine will was done here on the mountain.

'Though we did not meet again, we remained in communication. Notes were carried back and forth by acolytes whom she selected. I found the deepest satisfaction in this correspondence. I was able to express my hopes, my concerns, in perfect trust. I discovered that there were other people who shared my beliefs. It was not just her. There were many priests on the mountain, she said, who in their hearts opposed my father's plans but felt powerless to do anything. The priests feel deep affection for you, she said, and know that you have the correct character for the post, even if you lack the bloodline. But they use this affection as an excuse for inaction. How could they undermine the future of this boy they love so well? She told me not to reveal to any of them how I felt in my own heart. That would be dangerous.

'It was also through these notes that I learned more about the existence of Ritisak and his pure bloodline and that he was the boy who had knocked me down. The Abbess knew about the fight already, you see – Ritisak had boasted about it to her. And, let me say that through these communications I came to hear your name again. Ritisak had been quick to tell people that he had settled an insult made to him by Jorani, the Stairway Guide's daughter.

'I continued to ponder how I might direct my future. I knew that if one day I simply walked to the hermitage and declared my intention to live there, the priests inside would have nothing of it. They would send me back. No, I would have to go somewhere much further and keep it secret. But do you know? That thought frightened me deeply. I have never been off the mountain.'

'Never, sir?'

This I had trouble grasping. His mind, his intellect, his spirit had taken him to many places that I could never go, I was sure, but he had never had the simple satisfaction of putting one foot before the other for an hour or a day, had never known what it is to follow a trail trodden by many people before you, feeling the dust turning warmer as the sun rises higher in the sky, feeling the cool relief that comes from wading a stream, watching terrain and foliage change, and then reaching an entirely new place and new people.

'I could have shown you places to go, sir.'

He smiled. 'Yes, but I had not really made your acquaintance yet, had I? So after a while, I wrote to the Abbess about this. I asked if she would help me get to some place far away. But she replied that I had a greater duty. I must stay and work against the false doctrine and put it to an end. My father must be prevailed upon to renounce the doctrine of his own will, or else it would spread. He intended, she said, that it should be adopted at every temple in the empire! There were other Abbots, after all, who would nurse similar ambitions for their sons. Failing a renunciation by my father, she said, there must be some unmistakable signal from Heaven that it detests the so-called new superior way.

'I knew I could not change my father's mind, so I was left to consider what else I might do to put obstacles in his way or bring about this signal from Heaven. One afternoon, I was given to know something that I might do. I arrived at the big house to find Priest Sar there, showing my father some palm-leaf texts. The conversation stopped abruptly when I appeared; Priest Sar returned the texts to the box in which he had brought them. He withdrew. I was left with the feeling that these texts concerned me in some way. Now, I had seen that the box bore the seal of the western library; it also had a distinctive scratch on its lid. So the following day, I went to the western library. Unlike today, there were no guards standing over the texts, no one at all, in fact. I went inside and found the box easily. Among the texts in it was a new one of about forty strips' length. I read the opening passages. They sought Heaven's blessing for the new doctrine and forgiveness for the centuries of incorrect succession.

'Right then I felt that Heaven was delivering an instruction to me: Destroy these wicked things. I had arrived with a straw bag over my shoulder. I placed the offending texts in it, then closed the box and put it back against the wall just as I had found it. I was thinking like a criminal, you see, but it was for a holy purpose. I considered how to dispose of the texts. I could throw them over the cliff, but that would not destroy them right away, and they might be found. And the strips themselves would have received a blessing before the false words were placed on them, so I needed to destroy them in a dignified way. There came to mind the stone at the top of the eastern stairway, the place where old texts are burned. That would be it. I would need fire. So I went to a vacant cooking hut and took a jar of ash with a glowing coal; I would return the jar afterwards. Then I went to the stone, laid out the texts, said a prayer, and touched the coal to the first one. I blew until there was a flame. I fanned and in a few moments they were all burning. And then, Jorani, I looked up and saw you.'

'I remember.'

'For the second time, Heaven had brought us together at a very important time. And then we saw each other again an hour later. But even under my father's glare, you did not tell what I had done.'

'I did not. I felt an obligation to you, from the day when you freed me from those two boys. And I felt that a spirit was instructing me.'

'Perhaps this same spirit is instructing me.'

'I could not say, sir. But I hope you are correct. I have sometimes felt all alone in this god's service.'

I said those words looking directly at him. He nodded, as if he knew that feeling well. We sat in closeness for a moment more, then suddenly I shivered. I asked his permission to leave.

32

The Bird of Fair Feather

The next day, I found out there was much more to why the Abbot wanted the tower to be so tall.

I was alone in the son's house, finishing my work. I had run away the previous afternoon. But now I had got over my apprehensions and so when I heard him climbing the steps, I turned to the door believing that our talk would resume at the same intimate level. But his first word killed that thought.

'Garuda!' He said this with force that made me jump. 'It's all for Garuda, the Bird of Fair Feather!'

He did not explain immediately. Rather, he went to a window and stood looking out, trying to calm himself. I made tea and laid it at his place on the mat.

'Please, sir. You mustn't be upset.' My words sounded empty. How could I know what things would trouble him? 'Sit down and drink some of this.'

He did sit, apologizing for his abruptness, but then, before he could drink anything at all, the story came spilling out.

'Garuda! My father told us today. He sent an acolyte this afternoon to summon the priests to a meeting in the hall at the Second Court, do you know?'

'I don't know, sir.'

'Of course. Pardon me. But let me tell you. That was very unusual, so we all arrived wondering what it could be. We were surprised to see that the top men among the masons had been called too. After we had all sat down on our mats, my father entered the hall, helped along by a couple of servants. He began with a standard prayer, but it was clear from his demeanour that something out of the ordinary was coming. We found out very quickly. When the prayer was done, he gave a signal and Priest Sar unrolled a large palm leaf. It was a diagram of the new tower.'

He sipped at the tea. He did seem to be calming down, and I was glad for that. I said: 'It sounds very much like what happened a few years ago, sir, when the Abbot announced the plan for a new tower. One of the masons told me about it.'

'Yes, and it was like that today. When Priest Sar unrolled the palm leaf, we all leaned forward to try to see the details and there was general surprise – no, I would say shock – from those who were close enough to take it in. On each ledge where a stone Naga was supposed to be, this diagram showed a stone Garuda instead!

'My father knew of course that this would bring objections, I think even from the priests who've never strayed in loyalty, and so he began to speak immediately, giving instructions for the execution of this plan. His voice was so loud that it was as if he was trying to prevent anyone else from speaking. Masons would prepare thirty-six blocks of sandstone, he said. He would bless them, and then the masons would carve them into thirty-six images of the Bird of Fair Feather. These would be installed on the tower's ledges according to a schedule that he would devise. Priests would draft new liturgy by which Garuda would be honoured four times a day in the courtyard below. Another larger image of the Bird God would be erected in a chapel in the upper sanctuary. Water consecrated on the linga of the Lord of the Summit would be placed daily at its side.

I said: 'I have never heard that Garuda had a presence on the mountain.'

'He is here, Jorani, but in the correct, secondary rank and status as deemed by Heaven. There is an image of him in the Third Court. It is properly tended and honoured. But, do you see, now my father is promising the god that there will be much more for him here. I believe that my father intends to consecrate the new tower as the supreme sanctuary of Garuda for the world at large, reaching higher into the sky, closer to Heaven than any in the empire. From each level of the tower and from every side, the Bird of Fair Feather will gaze out in carved form. The tower will be his primary nest for eternity. And a god so honoured will think it a small thing to support the new doctrine of succession. That is my father's thinking, at least. He didn't say it, of course, but I'm sure of it.'

He thought a moment. 'My goodness, there's more! Garuda has powers of healing sickness!'

You will understand that all this made me very uneasy. We Khmers are born with the blood of Nagas in our veins. And Garuda is Naga's enemy — we all know that. Even in our own world, this conflict occurs every day. A hawk circles in the skies, watching, and then swoops down to catch a snake in its talons and devour it. Or a snake slithers up a tree and swallows the eggs that it finds in a nest. I had seen this strife many times growing up at the foot of the mountain. Had you asked me, I would have said that it seemed an even match. But up here was different. 'I feel, sir, that the Nagas will not allow what your father plans. They have been strong at our temple for so many years. They must be much stronger than Garuda.'

'I am sure they are doing their best to oppose it.'

I had not told him of my conviction that the female Naga was visiting me. Suddenly I wondered what else she might call on me to do.

'I know they are enemies, sir. But...but I don't know why.'

'It is because of a fight over the elixir of immortality, Jorani. Garuda and Naga are half-siblings. They used to get along, but now they fight.'

'It is not so different from people in our world.'

'Yes. And the fight began the way fights begin in the human world. There were once two wives of a sage. One of them desired children in great numbers, the other desired just a few. By Heaven's will, the first wife laid a thousand eggs that hatched into serpents, while the other laid only two, one of which hatched into the Bird of Fair Feather. Later on, Garuda's mother became enslaved to the serpents' mother as the result of a foolish bet in a game of dice. Garuda asked the serpents, what can I do to free her? They told him: Obtain the elixir of immortality and bring it to us. Garuda flew to Heaven. There he defied all manner of thunderbolts and sharp whirling knives and searing flames. He stole the holy potion from its guards. He took it down to the Nagas and placed it before them on a lawn of divinely blessed grass. Here it is, he said. I have done what you asked. Release my mother, then go perform your ablutions so that you can drink of the elixir. His mother went free. But when the serpents returned, washed and purified, they found that Garuda had whisked the elixir back to Heaven. They were so desperate for the taste of it that they licked the blades of the grass on which it had lain. They hoped they might absorb some lingering drops of its powers. In doing this, their tongues became divided like forks, as serpent tongues remain to this day. And ever since, they have viewed Garuda as their enemy and he has viewed them as his food.'

For a moment, I felt that I could taste that elixir and feel the sting of Garuda's betrayal.

'I think, sir, that I understand about the Naga masons.'

'What, exactly. If I may ask.'

'The reason they've been kept from their work. The Abbot agreed to the Lady Sray's offer to send the masons to carve the Naga couple at the eastern stairway. But I wonder if he intended all along to turn them instead to the work of glorifying Garuda. When the masons arrived, he refused to let them begin work on the Nagas and said that there were other important tasks that they must do first. He did not say what this other work was, but don't you think it was to carve Garuda?'

'Yes, yes! That must be it. My father is offering two gifts to the bird god. He is offering the tower nest and he's offering restraint of the power of the god's Naga rivals. But the Lady's masons resisted. We can be thankful for that.'

'And the tower masons, I think they will resist too. They are

Khmers like us and they know that Nagas' blood flows in their veins.'

He nodded. 'They did not directly refuse today, but they didn't agree either. When my father was finished, the master mason spoke for his men and said that carving Garuda requires skills and inspiration that they unfortunately lack. It was possible, he said, that he could send to the Capital for men who had these skills, but this would take time, and even in the capital, there aren't many of these artisans, because at most temples it is Nagas that are honoured on the towers. But my father interrupted him and said that he had already taken care of that question. A master sculptor specializing in Garuda images had come to visit and given his assurances that the job could be carried out. With that, the masons began trading glances. I asked afterward what that was about, and they said that a man had come some months earlier and spent several days at the worksite. They had been told he was an inspector from the royal household, but they now knew what his true purpose was.'

'The men will hold firm, sir. I am quite sure. They will oppose this.'

'I think you're right, Jorani. But please! You have listened to a very unfortunate story. I am sorry to have dampened your spirits.'

I wanted to say that he could never do that. But instead I sat as he sipped again at his tea. It had gone cold, so I replaced it with hot.

'You do too much for me, Jorani. You freshen my tea, you listen when I talk about things I've never talked about before.'

'It is my honour to listen, sir.'

'But that's very kind. But I hope that before too long I'll be the one who listens.'

That night, after I blew out the lamp at our house, the wife Naga again made known her presence. I came to understand there in the dark that she and her husband had not caused that pilgrim's fatal fall the day after Chantou's possession. These gods made their will known through omens and benevolent acts, not violence. It had been some other spirit that caused the fall – perhaps even Garuda, though I sensed no direct accusation. Whichever spirit it was had come down the slope to stir up trouble for the holy serpent couple who had seen to so many safe ascents for my family and pilgrims.

I rose from my mat just far enough to go into a prayerful position, my forehead to the floor. I recited words committing myself to the wife Naga's service and thanking her for the honour of choosing me.

With that done, I lay back down and how quickly my thoughts returned to the other subject that occupied me so often at mat time. This night I dwelt upon at what point Bouray might take his primary wife, and how long after that a minor wife might creep into the household. The two wives at the house below us seemed rather many years apart in age. Surely that did not mean that a like number of years would have to pass between the two weddings? Really, I had no idea, but it didn't matter. Before long I was at it again, spinning out fantasies of this life of domestic bliss as the husband's favoured one. On this night, I imagined some illness carrying off the elder sister shortly after my arrival. She would feel no pain, just close her eyes and be gone, headed for a life more elevated than this one. Shameful, I was. But then I put a stop to it. I had to. I now knew something of Bouray's life, and I could not avoid wondering if he had reached a level of spiritual achievement that would rule out marriage. He had said that he hoped he would listen to me, but nothing about on what. For a moment I heard myself describing to him methods of keeping charcoal dry or removing grass stains from a garment. He would listen closely. These were skills that would be useful in his future life of solitude in the forest.

It was time to make myself sleep. As I drifted away that night, I realized that for the first time, I had called him in my mind by his name, Bouray, and despite everything, that somehow made me feel closer to him.

33

Sharmistha's Passage in the Sky

The following week brought word from my mistress that Bouray had obtained the appointment to perform the cycle of prayers in each of the principle chambers of the temple's upper courts. The rites would proceed one day in one chamber, the next day in the next, over a total of twelve chambers. 'There will be no other priests present during these prayers,' the Abbess told me. 'The son will be alone with the absolute.'

She did not say it, but I'm sure she knew the precise day in which this sequence would bring him to pray over the texts of royal succession, and that this would occur before the arrival of Prince Darit.

'And there's something else, Jorani. I need you to have a word with the mason – that older one who's told you things about the building work. I'm sure he'll deny it, but I think his group must be in communication with the masons down on the plain. They're all of the same calling and craft, after all. Tell this man that I need to send a message down to the people below. Here it is – I've written it out.' She handed me a folded piece of palm leaf.

The next afternoon, I contrived to be working beneath the house when the man passed by on his way home from the temple courtyard. He stopped, and began chatting and drinking water in his usual way. But I wasn't really listening. I was shifting left and right to keep him between me and the gaze of the guard who stood outside our house. When the view was blocked, I put the note in his hand and whispered: 'Please, sir! This must go to your fellow masons below.' He pretended not to understand. But he did not give it back, instead tucking it into his waist.

How quickly things proceeded after that. Three days later, he put a note in my hand during another of these late-afternoon conversations. I gave it to the Abbess. She read it, a smile broadening on her face. 'Two days from now,' she said, 'when you go to the son's house, take a bag with you, a large one. Make sure it's clean.'

On the appointed day, I awoke at my normal time and began my work, yet the house did not grow light at its usual pace. I glanced out the window and understood. This was one of those days on which the clouds pass neither above nor below the temple, but straight through it, stealing even into its holy chambers. You walk about feeling the kiss of tiny droplets on your face and can see barely twenty paces ahead. I felt it was a good sign, a sign of support, because fewer people would see Bouray as he carried out his task.

Later, with bag in hand, I left for his house. There I went about my regular work, trying to remain tranquil, but each moment I was glancing out the door, wondering when he would arrive, or whether it might not be him at all but some fierce temple guard. Finally he did appear, stepping out of grey mist, carrying a rather bulky bag of his own. His climb up the house's steps was laboured, though he was trying to pretend the bag was light.

As he passed through the door, I hurried to put a writing board in place. His bag could not be set on the floor.

'There are more than I thought,' he said, putting it down. 'I'm worried there will be too many for you to carry.'

'I will manage it, sir.' I do believe I was stronger than he.

'I'll transfer them to your bag.'

That was proper. The hands of a servant girl could not touch such things.

He opened his bag carefully. The texts that were stacked inside looked different from any I had seen. They seemed weathered, almost like the stones of the temple itself, though I knew that they could not have been left in the open. It must be from age, or from the magical essence they contained. The thought of having these things in my possession, under my control, however briefly, was suddenly very troubling.

Yet I then felt something within me urging courage and promising protection. And so I placed my own bag alongside his. Stack by stack, he transferred the holy texts, pausing midway through the job to softly chant a prayer.

When he finished, I made to pick up the bag and leave. But he stopped me.

'It is a great thing that you do, Jorani. For Heaven and...for me.'

'For you, sir?'

'For me. You know it's my hope to leave the temple one day and live simply somewhere else. What you're doing today will bring that day closer, I am sure.'

'I hope so, sir.'

'You do it, but *why* do you do it, Jorani? I know that you feel a spirit has given you instructions, but when instructions like that come, many people find ways to pretend they don't hear. I've seen how you come and go around the temple grounds.' I wondered when he had been watching me. 'People like you. They don't stop you. You could get yourself down to the plain if you chose.'

'I have no choice but to stay here and help, sir. The spirit and my mistress both command it.'

I preferred this explanation to confessing that whatever I did was easier if I did it in his company. But how it wounded me to hear him talk about leaving. Right then, though he was sitting next to me, I imagined him walking a path through some distant forest, making his way to this new life of his, with me remaining back here, left to do nothing more than serve the Abbess. Then I wondered if a young Brahmin on such a quest might need a servant, and if that servant could be female and if that servant could be me, tailing along, cooking his food and drawing his water. The mendicant Brahmins who used to arrive at the stairway's base often had assistants, though most were children.

'I should go now, sir.'

I lifted the bag. It was indeed heavy. I took a step or two around the room to practice balancing its weight. Then I was descending the steps.

'Go safely, Jorani. I do not deserve you.'

Outside, the cloud-mist continued to darken the air; I welcomed its cover as I made my way toward our house, recalling his words.

'Jorani!'

I stopped abruptly. Standing not ten paces ahead was a man in outline in the mist. Priest Sar.

'Yes, Holiness!' I did my best to hide my alarm. But I was always nervous in the priest's presence, so perhaps he sensed nothing unusual in my behaviour.

'You're working hard, I see.' He stepped closer. 'That's quite a load you're carrying.'

'Yes, Holiness. The son's garments and some cooking things. We have a better supply of water at our house; I take them there to wash them. Separately from my mistress's, of course.'

'Of course. But what a burden! I suppose it can be difficult serving two masters, that is, a master and a mistress, at the same time.' He bared some teeth for a silent laugh.

'I do my best, Holiness. A servant can do no more.'

'And just to serve the one mistress must be quite a challenge.'

'I try, sir.'

'I've seen the ink stains on your fingers. You still help her as a scribe's assistant, do you?'

'I do, sir.'

He stepped closer still. I was sure he was going to seize my arm, but at the last instant he caught himself. 'Then tell me – and don't lie! She's still believes the false doctrine, doesn't she?'

'No, Holiness! My mistress never held it in her heart. She was forced to support it.'

'But she supported it for so long. Who was forcing her?'

'Why, Ritisak, Holiness! He threatened violence against her if she did not take his side. It was like that for years. She told me.'

It seemed a plausible explanation. I had no difficulty imagining him behaving that way. Priest Sar frowned, but seemed to accept it. 'You know a lot about your mistress. I will rely on you to disclose anything else that might interest me. Do you understand? You will tell me truthfully.'

'I am already truthful, Holiness.'

'So you say. But you want to return to the base of the mountain, don't you?'

'Of course, Holiness.'

'You want to return by walking down the stairway, not falling off the cliff, that cliff just behind your house?'

'*Yes, Holiness.*'

'Then keep in mind what I've just told you. You say you're just a servant, but you're quite an unusual servant. I have noticed.'

I stood before him, offering nothing more. A silence lengthened, and then he motioned that I could go. Off I went, heart pounding.

When I came through the door of our house, my mistress was on her feet, waiting. Just as I had done in the son's house, she had set out a writing board to receive the bag. I placed it there; she opened it with the same care that he had shown. She put both hands on the texts, closed her eyes in reverence, and I felt that their holy essence was filtering into her soul right as I watched. Then her eyes flew open, almost violently. She declared: 'We have in our possession, Jorani, the kernel of the imperial system. It is invested with power from which all authority of all kings, of all princes, of all priests flows.'

'Mistress, it is dangerous to keep such things here.'

'They will not stay here for long. Tonight you will see to their transfer and protection.'

I could only mutter agreement that I would do whatever she required.

I put out our lamp at the regular hour that night. But I did not lie down. Nor did the Abbess. We sat in the darkness, looking out the window that faced north. The wind was blowing hard now. It tousled the thatch over our heads and swept clouds and mist from the temple grounds.

'You see that constellation there, Jorani?' My mistress was gesturing out the window. 'I mean the one in which the stars zig and zag.'

'I do, mistress.'

'It is the celestial maiden Sharmistha, known for her service and sacrifice. May she be an inspiration for what we do tonight.'

'Yes, mistress.'

'Now be patient. We will wait until she has reached her highest point in the sky.'

This Sharmistha was quite low in the sky now. I lay back on my mat, sometimes watching, sometimes dozing. Each time I opened my eyes, she had edged barely a speck higher. With a prayer, I asked that she might move faster.

'Now, mistress?' Quite a few times I asked that as we waited in the dark.

'Not yet.'

Finally, the Abbess said: 'Now go.'

My instinct was to run, but I knew that, like Sharmistha, I should move slowly, with determination. In that way I crossed the room. Resting atop the writing board was the bag, which was tied shut by yarn, and by it lay a long rope. I took bag and rope in hand and descended our house's steps, slowly as before. On the ground, I walked in a direction that, if the guard across the trail was awake and saw me, would seem to be taking me to the privy behind the house. But once there, I kept going, those few extra steps to the wall of brush and the passageway through to the cliff face. I stepped into it and felt more secure in the embrace of foliage.

From the edge of a boulder, there came the wind's whistle. I prayed that the spirit that made it was friendly. At the passageway's end, I steadied myself by taking hold of rocks on either side, and leaned out over the abyss. Below, there was nothing! No light, no sign of any person. I wondered what I should do. My mistress had given no instruction for such a situation. I decided to wait.

From where I stood, I could not see Sharmistha, but I felt encouraged knowing that she was continuing her nightly transit across the sky. Perhaps she would offer special help.

Again and again, I looked down, hoping to see a lamp. And in its light, the form of Father. I had a hope that he would turn out to be the person taking custody of the sacred texts. I should not have done so, but right there, I shouted, 'Father, Father!' My voice could not compete with the wind to carry so far below, but I hoped that Sharmistha might send an assistant flying down to whisper in his ear that his daughter was looking at him at this very moment with the deepest devotion.

But he was not there, not then and not an hour later, when I began thinking that I should take the texts back to the house. I turned and crept along the path, but stopped short at the end. One of the guards, so often sleeping, was on his feet, loitering near the steps to our house. I would keep to where I was, and watch.

Yet he remained in his spot too, for an hour and another hour. Then, as the sun was just beginning to colour the sky beyond the temple, I was terrified to see the forms of four men advancing towards the house. When they drew closer I could see who they were – Priest Sar and assistants. They clambered up the steps without a word, followed by the guard who stood watch. It was like what had happened the day that the heir was seized at his mother's house. But for this instant, at least, I was free to move—no one was keeping guard outside the house. The bag bumping heavily against my hip, I raced to the left, into an area of bushes and sharp-edged rocks. I went as far as I could without coming upon another house. Then, murmuring a prayer for their protection, I placed the texts in a cavity between two rocks. They slid down into darkness and came to rest with a thump somewhere out of sight.

I stood for a moment and took stock. A shriek carried from our house. It was my mistress. 'Get your hands off!'

34

The Morality of Thieves

I raced up the steps and passed through the door. My mistress was standing like a cornered animal with her back to a wall, paralyzed by terror. Every patch of floor was covered with clothing, mats, and kitchenware thrown wildly from our household boxes. Two men were upending bedding and mats to see if anything lay underneath. Another had overturned my stove, apparently thinking that something was hidden in the ashes.

The man at the stove spoke. 'There's nothing here, sir.'

Those words were for Priest Sar, but he wasn't willing to accept them. Hitching up his garment, he bent down to pick through some cookware, then looked again into the box in which my mistress kept her texts. With each second, rage was building in him. But of course he found nothing. He stood up.

'Abbess, you know what we're looking for!'

'On Heaven's word, I don't.'

'You do! Where are they?'

'I can say nothing because I know nothing.'

'Perhaps I'm addressing these questions to the wrong person.' He turned to me – he had noticed me, then. 'The little servant girl! You were carrying a very large bag yesterday when I passed you.'

'Yes, sir. I was.'

'Garments and cookware to be washed, you said.'

'Yes, sir.'

'Where are they now?'

'I don't know exactly, sir.'

'*Why not?*'

'Because, sir, your men have turned everything upside down. Everything's mixed with everything else.'

Perhaps if I had responded in a more submissive way, he would not have said what next he said to his men.

'Take hold of the girl. Take her to the cliff and throw her off.'

I bolted for the door, but a man blocked my way.

The Abbess cried: 'You can't mean that!'

'I can and I do. Go on, men, take her away.'

'Priest Sar! This mountain is a holy place.'

'Yes, and its holiness is under threat. From thieves. And you may know that against thieves Heaven authorises us to employ the morality of thieves.'

'In what text does Heaven say such a thing? I demand to know!'

Now I made a run for the other side of the room – I think I intended to throw myself out the window. But one of the men caught me from behind and pinned my arms.

'Soften her up a bit first,' the priest said. 'Then she'll be more helpful.' He made a fist. 'Do it with one of these.'

The guard who held me was unsure how much force to apply. He had beaten many people before, I think, but probably never a young woman.

'Go on, hurry up,' urged the priest. 'Do it however you want.'

The guard brought the back of his hand hard against my face. For an instant, my sight went black.

'Stop this! Stop this!' The Abbess had got hold of my forearm and was pulling me to her.

'Again,' said the priest, calm even as he pushed my mistress aside. 'She'll talk. Do it harder. I want to see you do it harder.'

This time, it was his fist. My knees gave way. I remained standing only by the support of the guard behind me. My mouth warmed with the sweetish taste of blood.

'Hold her still!'

I had no preparation for what happened next. Priest Sar ripped away my garment. He knelt in front of me and with his right hand seized the inside of my thigh.

'Just a servant girl? No experience with men?' I kicked; he laughed and forced his hand higher. 'I've never believed it!'

'Priest Sar!'

I heard those two words, but not what came after them.

I awoke lying face up on the floor of the house. Something cool was dabbing at my lips.

'There! You'll feel better. It must hurt so much now, but it will stop.'

I opened my eyes. Bouray was kneeling next to me, a cloth stained in red in his hand. A sleep linen had been placed over my middle.

'I'm so happy you've woken up, Jorani.'

'Of course she has. This Jorani is as strong as a woman gets.' It was the Abbess, kneeling on the other side of me.

The memory came back. I tried to get up, thinking I should run. But all I did was spit out something. It was blood.

'It's all right,' Bouray said. 'Really. They're gone. They won't be back.' He smiled down on me, and I settled back on the mat.

'Sir, there's no need to stay. I'll be all right.' I said this because I was thinking quite clearly now. I knew that a request that he leave would mean he would stay.

'I'm sorry, but there is a need. You must rest, and have someone to see to you. Here, now take some water.' He put a cup to my lips.

How sweet and cool the water tasted. I lay back and now I did relax.

The Abbess crossed to the other side of the room to see to straightening up the debris.

Bouray looked to me: 'I should not have involved you in this, Jorani. I ask your forgiveness.'

'You did not involve me, sir. I was already involved. There is nothing to forgive.'

'But there is...'

'I cannot forgive a transgression that did not happen.'

He chose not to take it further and instead told me to close my eyes. I lay on the mat, feeling his closeness, yet his distance too as he maintained a respectable gap between us. He never touched me directly, only his cloth did, dabbing at my mouth and cheeks. I began to wish that the bleeding would not stop. But of course it did, quite soon, really.

Perhaps the Abbess had been watching for that. She returned and told him she would take over now. He declined, she repeated her request, and he gave in. But first he told me again how happy he was that I was all right.

As he descended the steps, I made to get up. There was no more need to fuss over me. But my mistress told me to stay where I was. She sat alongside me, dipping a cloth in a bowl of water that she had brought over, then cooing softly as she applied it to my face. I lay back again. There was no shortage of surprises on this day.

In a little bit I prevailed on her to tell me what had happened. The story I got was that in ransacking our house, the guards had made such a din that it carried up the hillside to Bouray's house. He came running to us. He burst through the door and never had she heard such words from his mouth. Villains! Cowards! Abusing a woman in a holy place! He told them get out before he brought down on them the worst curses you can imagine. Priest Sar went to his knees right there, stammering and perspiring. He tried to explain about a need to find missing texts, the most holy in the entire temple. Bouray did a very convincing job, my mistress said, of conveying shock and outrage over that, and then interrogating the priest as to how many texts were missing and since when exactly, and all the while continuing to berate him. You order your men to beat a young woman! Then you force yourself on her in that wicked way! All to cover up your own negligence in safeguarding the texts! The priest dared not talk back. He could not ignore the words of a man who would one day be his master, and in some ways already was. But Bouray also implied, the Abbess said, that if there was anything to be learned from her and from me, though he doubted there was, he would find it out through peaceful means and he would tell the proper authority, that is, his father. No, no! Priest Sar fairly blurted out those words. The Abbot doesn't know the texts are missing. Please! Then keep quiet about it, said Bouray. There's no need for him to know. I won't tell him, you won't tell him. We'll get the texts back, say the proper prayer of atonement, and no one will be the wiser.

With that, Bouray had secured my protection. The priest and his men withdrew like dogs that had lost a fight. But there was no saying how long they would stay away. As clever as Bouray had been, I could not help but think that Priest Sar would get to wondering why Bouray would suggest keeping the secret. I wondered too if I had hidden the texts well enough. Since he got no word of their location from us, Priest Sar would have his men looking day and night.

When I finally got to my feet, I glanced out the window and saw the very man who had struck me rooting around in some brush down the slope. He was terribly close to where I'd left the texts. I watched, unable to turn away, growing fearful every time he stepped closer to the hiding place, relieved when he moved the other way. Thankfully, the Abbess took me by the hand and moved me from the window. She did not ask where the texts were. She understood, I think, that it was better that she not know.

35

The Hidden Reason

One morning shortly after, the old mason gave me some important news during one of his afternoon stops. In two days' time, Prince Darit would arrive at the temple to undergo special accession rites to be conducted by the Abbot. As a supplementary honour, he would take part in the dedication of the new tower. The masons had received instructions to hurry their work so that the prince might climb the scaffolding with the Abbot and oversee the putting in place of the lotus crown's final stone.

When I told the Abbess, she made one of her mirthless smiles. 'I think we know now how Priest Sar discovered so quickly that the texts were missing. When word arrived that Darit was coming, he must have gone straight away to the library to begin preparing them for use in the rite. Just imagine how horrified he was to find they were missing!'

I got some pleasure doing so. 'What will he do when he can't find them?'

'I don't know – he can't even consider that outcome. The texts must be present during the rite. You see, the Abbot's scribes will have to create new texts that place Darit in the bloodline that began with our blessed King Jayavarman more than three centuries ago. Darit will take part in rites in which these will be invested with the full power of Heaven's will. The essence that the old texts contained will be transferred to the new texts, or at least that is how Darit and the Abbot will see it. Then the old will be taken to the obelisk on the cliff and burned.'

Briefly I pictured Bouray at that rock on that long-ago morning, burning his father's initial efforts to undermine Heaven's will.

Later that day, as I swept Bouray's house, I heard more. He had received his own instructions for the visit. He was to head a party that would greet Darit at the base of the northern stairway and lead him on the climb to the upper courts, with stops for prayers at shrines along the way. With the prayers completed, Darit would be taken to his lodgings, a guesthouse that was reserved for important visitors. He would have time to bathe and prepare for the evening meal, which would be taken at the Abbot's house. Senior figures from both sides would attend.

'And the Abbot requests the presence of the Abbess,' said Bouray. 'It must be as with the water rite at the linga. He thinks her presence will demonstrate that the entire temple community supports the new doctrine.'

'I hope she is able to pretend as well as the last time. You will be there?'

'Yes.'

'That will give us both courage.'

'You have plenty of that already.'

'But not like you. You proved it at the house with Priest Sar. I feel, sir, that I haven't thanked you adequately for that.'

'You have, you have. But in any case, it was easy. The words came naturally. It was for your sake, Jorani, so Heaven placed words in my mouth. It allowed me to provide protection that I owed you.'

'But you owed me nothing, sir. I owe you. It is you who have protected me, twice now, and both from the same threat, a fall over the face of the cliff. Today and that day in the past with the boys who broke the water jar.'

'It's hard to fathom. Both times it was that threat, wasn't it?'

'It was.'

'Well, I had no role in your exposure to the first threat, but in this new one, I did.'

'What do you mean, sir?'

'I mean that, were it not for me, you would not be facing this danger.'

'But I'm here because the Abbess summoned me to be her maid.'

'Yes, and there's a reason she summoned you and not someone else. You remember that I had only one tutoring session with the Abbess before my father ordered an end? But we continued to send notes back and forth. In one of them – no, more than one – I mentioned my encounters with a girl who seemed to me extraordinarily brave and yet gentle and endowed with a serene soul...'

'Please, sir...'

'No, no. Those are the terms in which I described you. I meant it. I suppose that in mentioning you, I hoped that we might somehow come together again. Jorani. I knew your name, and how it means radiant jewel.'

'There is nothing radiant...'

'But there is. But then the abbess told me that you had stopped coming to the mountaintop. It was a great disappointment to know that I had no chance of meeting you again.

'Two years went by, and then I got a note from the Abbess that ended with a mention that she was seeking a maid and could I recommend anyone now employed in the upper reaches. All the Brahmin houses had maids, as you know. I thought about it, thought some more, and then I said that I believed that the girl Jorani from down the stairway had all the attributes she was seeking. It was a selfish act on my part. I had no idea how you would feel about being brought to live atop the mountain, but I did it anyway.'

He looked to me for a reaction. I gave none because I was unsure how I felt.

He continued. 'Then came that day when I entered the meeting hall in the Third Court and saw you sitting next to the Abbess. It was my good fortune that my father was not looking in my direction just then. Otherwise he would have seen the shock on my face and begun asking questions.'

This caused me to smile. 'I remember you too, sir. I was waiting to see if you would attend the meeting.'

'Were you? By my memory, you showed no particular interest when you saw me. It made me sad for days afterwards.'

'I would have shown precisely the same surprise that you did if I hadn't known in advance that you would be there. That's the only reason. I had time to prepare, to preserve my demeanour.'

He seemed to like that answer. 'Well, it was a shock to me—as you saw.'

'I did, sir. You looked as though you had just discovered you were sitting on a scorpion.'

He laughed. 'Well, yes, the feeling was almost as strong as that. The Abbess hadn't told me you were in her service. So, after the meeting, I waited, thinking I might speak with you, but you had already gone outside and I felt you didn't want to see me. So I had a word with your mistress. I ended by saying I was very happy that you had come to the nunnery and how you had saved me from my father's anger that day at his house.'

I smiled again. The Abbess's first words of sympathy and warmth towards me had come in the days just after.

'The Abbess later sent me a note saying that she would go to the capital for a convocation of heads of nunneries. There was a hint about what she would do: she would seek out 'some things of interest' during the trip. Jorani, I will tell you that I paid little attention to that. I was only thinking that an Abbess takes her maid on a journey like that and there will be no chance that I'll see her for many weeks to come.'

'Sir, I had the same misgiving...'

'Did you?'

'I did. And you will recall that the next time I saw you was at the meeting from which I went running down the hill, carrying off the rubbings. I felt, sir, that you must hate me, for helping keep you from being Abbot.'

'No, it was not like that at all. I looked as you ran away, and I thought, there goes the girl who will open the way for the life that I've been hoping for.'

How I wished he hadn't said that. Again there came to me an image of him walking alone through a distant forest, headed to whatever that new life might be.

And so I turned and resumed my work, keeping my eyes away from him. In a few minutes I announced that I was done for the day. Then I was making my way back to the other house, almost running.

36

The Abbot's Banquet

Two days later, Prince Darit's arrival was marked by the striking of gongs in the lower courts. Throughout the day, we heard the sound again, at intervals marking his party's progress towards the summit along the processional avenue.

Dusk approached. Inside our house, I prepared my mistress for the welcoming banquet. As I did, I was thinking how much I would like not to go. However accustomed I had become to life in this place, I was still terrified of the Abbot.

An hour later, we arrived at the Abbot's house, me looking ahead nervously to see if the great man might be standing at that spot on the terrace from which he had interrogated me. But there was no sign of him. An acolyte showed us up the steps, then into a large room in which tables had been set with dining ware. Lamps burned, their flickers captured by gold-edged hangings at the windows. Our place was of course far from the larger tables at which the prince and Abbot would sit. Our only greeting came from Bouray, a furtive glance in our direction.

We put our faces down as the banquet's principals took their places. When I looked up, I saw that the man next to the Abbot was the prince. I knew that because of where he had been seated, but otherwise I could never have taken him for a man who aspired to be King. He was very young, wearing jewellery that even from where I sat looked garish and stolen. Already he was lounging back on an elbow as if he were at some drinking stall in the market. I was reminded, in fact, of the nephew and his air of petulance and wondered how it was that these men of such similar character were on opposite sides.

The Abbot looked wan and fatigued; his arms were even thinner than when last I'd seen him. He glanced toward Darit, and that put some life in him – he recoiled visibly at the young prince's breach of manners.

This was the first time the two men had been face-to-face. I wondered if the Abbot was having misgivings over placing his trust – his future, really – in the hands of this prince. But there was a banquet to put on, and after a while the Abbot called it to order. Speaking in the sacred language, he began introducing various of the priests of the temple to the visitor. Priest Sar was among them, of course, and gave a particularly long dip of the head to acknowledge the Abbot's words.

The prince's reaction was this: 'There's no reason to use the holy language, Abbot. We're all proud to be Khmers. We should speak Khmer.' I was left thinking the real reason was that he could not speak the holy language.

'Of course,' replied the Abbot, switching tongue. 'Now, you may know that we have a nunnery here. It is headed by the Abbess Parvati, who is deeply knowledgeable of the Yajur Veda and is consulted on this subject from nunneries, even some abbeys, all over the empire and in...'

My mistress dipped her head in acknowledgement, but Prince Darit cut in. 'You have many eminences here, Abbot. I can see that, I can sense the accomplishment in this room. But how long will it take them to complete the new texts that we need for the succession rite? I asked this afternoon and no one was able to say.'

That seemed to surprise the Abbot. He called on Priest Sar to answer.

'It's not possible to predict precisely...' He thought a moment, then continued. 'We must await Heaven's inspiration, and sometimes Heaven chooses to hold it back. Here atop the mountain, we know that the holy message cannot be hurried.'

The Abbot didn't like that answer. 'But in this case, you'll say the proper prayers to assure that the inspiration comes quickly, won't you, Priest Sar?' Clearly he wanted the visitors to finish their business here and leave.

'Yes, Holiness. We are doing our best.'

'Of course you are,' laughed Darit. 'But never mind. If Heaven's word doesn't come quickly to your men, we'll just write it up ourselves. We'll give your scribes spears and have them join the march on Angkor!'

For the wink of an eye, the Abbot was taken in. But then the prince gave a full-throated laugh, followed in kind by his retainers and then by the Abbot and the priests, though from them in a quieter, more dignified tone. Then, even before the noise calmed down, the prince learned back and began taking rice in his fingers, as if he were master of the temple.

The banquet proceeded in this fallacious spirit of good cheer. But before long I became aware of a tussle at the room's door. A man dressed in some kind of royal regalia was making to enter. A temple servant, with whispered words and hands to the man's forearms, was trying to hold him back. But the man broke away. He went to the floor, crawled straight to the Abbot, and with both hands presented a palm document. I understood now: He was a messenger.

The Abbot frowned, annoyed at the interruption, but he took the document and read. One by one, various changes came across him. His brow contracted. The frown became a look of bewilderment. Priest Sar, always attentive, moved quickly to his side. The Abbot lowered the document and looked up, as if at a loss.

All this happened without the prince taking notice. But then, as he lifted a cup of wine, his eye strayed to the Abbot.

'What is it?'

The Abbot took a breath. 'Well, it is this: The King, the false King, is dead!'

Wine sprayed straight out of the prince's mouth. *'What?'*

'Heaven has recalled him. It happened as he inspected construction at his mountain temple in the capital.'

'Impossible!' It was the Abbess, addressing me in a whisper.

'You're certain?' asked the prince. 'Where did the news come from?'

'From this man.' The Abbot gestured to the messenger, who remained on the floor beneath him. 'He has delivered an official palace bulletin.'

'That's all it says?'

'Yes.'

The prince sprang to his feet and kicked at the messenger. 'You! What else do you know?'

'Nothing, sir!'

'Go on, tell me – you were in the capital. What are people saying? They must be talking in the market! How did he die?'

'They say, sir, they say that there was a fall. His Majesty, I mean, the false King, was inspecting the upper tier of his mountain temple and he fell.'

'And how are the people responding?'

'Why, they are, they are...of course they're celebrating, sir.'

'What else, what else?'

'There is a separate message for the estates, sir. The requisition of men and materials for construction of the mountain temple is cancelled.'

The prince delivered another kick to the man, this one in celebration, then turned to the room with arms raised.

'Victory! Victory! Victory!'

In an instant all his soldiers were on their feet, joining in the chant, embracing one another, gulping at wine, splashing it on floors and hangings with joy that turned absolutely delirious. The priests in the room traded looks of bewilderment, unsure how men of their vocation should respond. With a nod to them, the Abbot struggled to his feet and joined in the victory chant.

I looked to my mistress, wondering if she would silence the room with a denunciation. But on her face was a look of abject hopelessness. She pulled at my wrist – we would leave. Women of holy orders could not of course take part in a martial celebration like this, so it was a convenient excuse to escape. But I was worried. She was beginning to show again that frightening paralysis of spirit.

As we walked, I stole a look over my shoulder for Bouray. He had stepped into a corridor where the others could not see him. He looked to me, conveying the deepest despair. I nodded. I hoped he would leave the house before someone took note of his sentiments.

'What tragedy, what tragedy!' The Abbess muttered these words as we went down the steps.

'Please, mistress, let's just go,' I whispered.

'How can Heaven have delivered this? We were getting so close!'

'The news must be wrong, mistress.' It was all I could think to say. Now she was weeping like a child. I seized her arm and propelled her into the darkness.

'It's over, it's over, Jorani. We have lost.'

As we hurried away, she continued to babble like this. I lent my arm to support her. Without it, I think she would have sunk to the ground along the trail.

We reached the house. And there we found the talkative mason waiting for us at the foot of the steps.

'Young woman, I am sorry to tell you, but your father is near death. We received word that he was wounded by a spear thrown by one of the Abbot's men. He begs that you come and see him before he departs this life.'

37

Descent

Of course I knew right away that I had to go to him. The succession struggle, Darit's hateful celebration, the Abbess's collapse – all of these suddenly seemed events unconnected to the life of the person I was, a maid. I even wondered if I had imagined the Naga's instructions. However it had happened, I had moved for so long in a world where I did not belong. I would return to Father. I had never imagined him as anything but physically vital, able to carry me up the stairway those countless times with hardly an extra breath. But now, as I tried to conjure up his image, the mangled bodies that I'd seen at the Entry Court forced their way into my mind's eye.

I'll go, I told the mason. I'll descend the stairway. But he said that would be dangerous – there were soldiers guarding it. If I came with him, I would be shown another way, tonight, in fact. I would be at Father's side by sunrise tomorrow.

My mistress barely listened to any of this. She climbed the steps to the house on her own. When I went to her a few minutes later, she was lying on her mat and did not respond to me. So I resolved to go without her permission. Surely Bouray would come here shortly and see to her.

In a few minutes, the mason and I were hurrying down the hillside trail in the dark, me trying to keep away thoughts of Father with a spear wound. Up ahead shone the lamps of the masons' settlement. There I was given over to the care of another mason and without a pause we moved down another trail at the settlement's far edge. Soon we emerged from the cover of trees. Straight ahead was the abyss.

'We're going to descend here,' the man told me. 'There's a narrow ledge that begins just over the edge. We are going to make our way along it. Do you see it?'

He went first. I followed, whispering a brief prayer to the spirits of this place. We descended at a tedious pace, facing the cliff's stone. My left foot advanced a hair along the ledge, my right took its place. After a while we came to a place where the cliff bulged out at waist level, the ledge passing underneath. How to proceed? This kind of obstacle was new to me. But I did not have time to puzzle it out. With skill of experience and use of unseen grips in the stone, my guide had already slipped past it. He reached back a hand and swung me expertly to the other side.

Further on, the ledge widened. We no longer had to move sideways. 'Just a bit more,' my guide told me, 'and we'll be on a real trail.'

I took that to mean a stretch of the trail along which I had led the soldiers that night. We would follow it all the way around the mountain slope to the stairway. But the trail that he meant, I soon found, was one that led steeply downwards. It was not always a trail, really. In places we had to jump from boulder to boulder.

It was well past midnight when we reached the base of the mountain and stepped out at the edge of some fallow paddy land.

'You did well,' the man said. 'With everyone else I've brought it's taken two or three times as long.'

I did not explain why, but just thanked him. He told me he would now head for a village to the south; I got the feeling there was a wife or girlfriend there. I would be on my own now. That was fine. Though I had never been to this side of the mountain, I had a sense of the direction that I would need to take.

We parted, wishing each other Heaven's protection. I made my way along a paddy dike. Pretty soon it came to a cart track. Heaven was helping me, it seemed. I strode quickly along the strip of soil between the wheel ruts. My thoughts again turned to Father, and whether Heaven would allow him to live until I arrived.

After an hour, I came to the village that lay near our house. Here and there a lamp burned, but otherwise there was no sign of life. The track led straight through, but I chose to circle the village, in case someone would see me and call out, even at this hour.

Finally, our house loomed in the darkness ahead. I began to run and I also began to cry.

At the steps, a male form stepped from the shadows. It was Kamol. 'Sweet Jorani!'

'This is not the time! How is he?'

Kamol hung his head. Panic took hold in me. 'No, no!' I cried. 'His spirit has left already! I'm too late!'

Kamol pulled me close. 'No, Jorani. Your father is fine. He's in the house, sleeping, as always.'

I pushed him away. 'But they said...' I was staring up at the house.

'They said it...they said it because I told them to.'

'I don't understand! I'm going to him.'

'Please, Jorani. There's no need. It was the only way to get you to come down. And now I've got you back. Finally!'

I pulled away to hurry up the steps. Peering inside, I caught sight of Father, lying on his mat. Chantou was next to him. All was as I'd seen a thousand times. Suddenly I felt like a little girl again, afraid my noisy feet on the steps would awaken my sleeping father.

I stole back down the steps and ran. Kamol was right behind me.

'Please, Jorani! Don't be angry.'

'Don't follow me!'

I entered the forest, but I had no idea where I was running to. After a few steps, I stopped and sat down on a rock, drawing my knees up to my chest. Kamol hung back.

I turned to him. 'How could you have made me think Father was dying! I nearly died of fright myself.'

Kamol said nothing.

'Does he know you did this?'

'No.'

'Does he know I was coming?'

'Yes. I told him that I'd sent you a message and you had agreed to come down.'

'And why does he think I'm coming down?'

As before, Kamol did not answer a very direct question and I felt anxious again.

Then out it came: 'Because...because of the wedding, Jorani! You and I will be married tomorrow!'

'No! I will not marry you.'

Finally, I had said it. But it did no good. 'Jorani, you must! Please, everything is arranged. Your father is expecting it, the village is expecting it. I will move to the house here. Later we will get our own. Just over there, I thought.' He pointed into the darkness; I did not do him the favour of looking.

He found the courage to come closer. 'Please, Jorani. I will make a good husband, I promise. You will see.'

He sat next to me, waiting for an answer. I opened my mouth to say something sharp, but found that I could not. Instead, I began to cry. 'Kamol, Kamol. I've been so cruel to you.'

'There is nothing cruel in your soul, Jorani. One who loves you can see that clearly.'

'And I love you as well, Kamol. But not in that way. I cannot marry you.'

'But I've asked you so many times, and you've never refused me.'

'Because I lacked the courage to tell you.'

'But I know you would come to love me. It might take time, that's all.'

'Kamol, no.'

'You say that, but I don't believe it!' He took my hand. 'I demand that you look me in the eye and declare that you don't love me!'

Instead I looked to the ground.

Normally a girl in this situation will explain calmly that her heart lies with someone else and to show how much she means it she will identify the man. Yet I knew I could not say that I would prefer to be joined with a Brahmin. It would be too cruel to Kamol, who would immediately think how he could not match the wealth, the comfort, the life free of the gutting of fish and the cleansing of braziers. But there was something else that kept me silent. Down here, off the mountaintop, from the vantage point of a rock in the forest with my family sleeping nearby, the whole idea seemed suddenly suspect, even ridiculous. I had seen that minor wife at the door of the priest's house up top, but I and everyone down here knew what can really be expected when a young village woman is drawn to the sleeping mat of a priest. She never stays long. Her prospects are ruined, so she gives up home and family and moves away to someplace where her background is unknown, though the people around her can guess. From that rock in the forest, I wondered if I could really expect to be the exception. It would not be only a matter of Bouray's feelings. I did feel confident they were real. But so many other barriers would stand in our way. Father would object. The Abbess would be scandalised.

So I said nothing about this to Kamol, knowing that the despair he would first feel would give way to earnest entreaties that I come to my senses about where things would end. I did not repeat my refusal of marriage, either, and that gave Kamol some hope. He moved closer and I did not stop him when he began to give me the story. He had told Father that he and I had been in communication through the masons, and that I had agreed to marry him and would come down the mountain. This news had of course caused elation in Father – Kamol repeated that particular fact to me three times. Preparations for a wedding had been made. It would be conducted the day after I returned. Kamol and his family members would process to our house bearing dowry gifts and the nuptial rites would follow.

By now the eastern sky was starting to show the first smudges of dawn. I rose, and we walked towards the house. Father was bathing at the jar, a torch burning nearby. How his face lit up when he saw me! He embraced me, tears flowing freely, then he called to Chantou and my brothers, who whooped and cheered when they caught sight of me. But how like a traitor I felt! And now totally without courage. I could say nothing to ruin their happiness. Instead, I broke down in tears, and they all took it as proof of how happy I was, how relieved to be back among them, safe at last from the conflict up top. And soon to be married too! Kamol stepped to my side and took my hand in front of all of them.

'Heaven has brought my bride down the mountain, just in time for the wedding.'

Off he went, to spread the word that I was back in the fold and to get ready for the ceremony.

Father stood looking at me. 'My daughter, returned to me unharmed. I've got to give thanks at the shrine.'

I tried to smile, but again I broke down.

'It's all right,' he said. 'Really! Cry all you want, it doesn't matter. It's a wonderful day for all of us. Our lives will be just as they were before.'

'I'll be able to guide the pilgrims again?'

'My girl Jorani – always with the same thought on her mind! But yes, that will resume. Just as soon as things are over and done with up top. I don't want you going up there with all those strange soldiers around.'

Chantou had nothing to say. All she did was embrace me.

The day progressed like that. Everyone at the house was so kind, so happy, so convinced of the rightness of this marriage that I began to feel that perhaps Heaven did intend it, that it was of a type ordained over the ages and I had no right to oppose it. Kamol was in fact a fine man; he would be the good husband that he pledged to be. We would have children. Heaven would smile on the family that was born from our union. And there would always be his strong pair of arms for pilgrims needing a ride upwards. How thankful I should be. A few hours earlier I had believed that Father was near death; now I was home with him and the rest of my family, everyone was elated, and I was about to become a wife.

This was very short notice for a wedding, of course, but the circumstances were unusual. That evening, one of Kamol's married sisters came from the village with a bridal garment and necklace. She took me inside and showed me how to put them on. Then she took me to the bathing jar and, murmuring prayers, helped make me clean and purified for the rites that would occur the following day.

That evening, with the lamp burning, Chantou rolled out my sleeping mat in my old spot and placed my linen on it. I lay down at peace with what was soon to happen. Almost at peace, I should say. I shed a few more tears through closed eyes, turning my head to the wall so that no one would see.

Perhaps you have guessed what happened during the night. The spirit of the wife Naga came to me again as I slept – I don't know how I had failed to foresee this – and set aside my affirmations of the previous hours. I never actually saw the Naga spirit in this dream. She chose to remain invisible that night, but she made known to me a thing more important than her image. I mean her determination. I awoke with a start before sunrise, perspiring, imbued with the conviction that whatever the family members sleeping around me believed, I could not marry Kamol. My responsibilities at this time were not to him or my family. They were to people and gods atop the mountain. I had to return.

And so I crept down the steps without awakening anyone.

I went first to the shrine behind the house, and knelt. 'Mother,' I whispered, 'I had planned to come to you this morning to tell you of my wedding and ask for your blessing. But instead I must ask that you be patient with me a while longer. Let me complete the task that the Naga wife has given me. Please help Kamol find solace in his heartbreak.'

With that I rose and moved silently away. First I walked, then I broke into a run. I was fully aware of the heart I was breaking, and the disgrace I was bringing upon my family. Yet still I ran. I won't say that I had put aside all doubts, but my belief outweighed whatever remaining apprehensions I had.

I followed the cart track by which I had come. It was still dark when I came to the spot where the mason and I had parted. I began the climb, guided by memory and sense of direction. It was early light when I came to the boulders that needed jumping between, and full light when I reached the narrow ledge.

I was confident of myself in every step along the ledge, except when I came to the place where the rock face jutted out. There was no hand of help this time. I looked over my shoulder, and saw below me the plain bathed in morning sunlight. I don't know why, but just then I wondered, what if I lost my balance and fell and I was only discovered some time later. What would Kamol feel? And Father? Would the hurt and disgrace that I had brought on them prevent them from grieving? I had no answer. So I took a breath and reached with my right hand, seeking a hole in the stone that would allow me a grip. A spirit guided my fingers. With hardly a thought, I swung my body around the jutting rock.

An hour later, I was kneeling before my mistress. But she had no interest in hearing what had happened.

'They have found the texts, Jorani! We have failed. The Abbot will conduct the transfer rite tomorrow and dedicate the tower.' She brought hands to her face and wept.

38

The Lotus Crown's Final Stone

How was it possible? My mistress's spirits had sunk even lower than when I had left her. She could barely speak. But piece by piece, she told me of the texts' discovery.

It was a simple story, really. The morning after I had left for the plain, one of Priest Sar's men began searching the rough area downhill from our house. He traipsed this way and that, back and forth, hopping from stone to stone. He kept at it hour after hour, afraid of returning to his master empty-handed. My mistress had just glanced out the window to check on him when he stepped on something sharp and jumped to the side in pain. I could picture the silent grin that brought to my mistress's face. But then the man went perfectly still. His eyes locked onto something in the rocks beneath him. It was the hole where I had hidden the texts. But for the sharp stone, he would not have found it. The Abbess could not fathom how Heaven had allowed this, but nonetheless it was fact. He pulled out the texts and rushed away to find his master, never mind his injured foot.

The texts' recovery meant that the tower dedication and the rite of the texts could be scheduled. Quickly, of course. Prince Darit was as eager as the Abbot for his force to leave the mountain and proceed to the Capital. And as with the banquet, the Abbot instructed all ranking members of the temple community to attend the dedication.

I tried to calm her. 'There will be another chance to take the texts back, mistress. Or perhaps Heaven will not accept the transfer of magic.

It will continue to recognise the old texts, even if they're destroyed.' I had no understanding of how such things work, but I made this and other arguments to try to restore her courage.

All of what I said she waved off. 'We have failed, Jorani. We have missed our chance.'

So it was that the following morning I passed with her through the small door in the western wall of the First Court. It was the first time I had set foot inside. I expected only silence and an abiding essence of Shiva. Yet what we stepped into was a noisy scene of fussing and preparation. Acolytes were hanging red and gold hangings across arcade windows that gave onto the courtyard. Priests were making ready a temporary teak altar. One of them, just at that moment, was upbraiding a junior one for forgetting some crucial element of the liturgical set-up – I couldn't hear what.

At the courtyard's centre, ignored for now, rose the tower. It drew my eye. Up close it was yet more glorious, even if still sheathed in scaffolding. Something new had been added: a bamboo platform up at the level of the unfinished lotus crown. Steps made of more bamboo wound round the tower, through the scaffolding, to give access to the platform. Their rise was quite gentle. Even a man as infirm as the Abbot would be able to ascend.

I put a supportive hand to my mistress. She walked as if half dead. That is the only way I can describe it. All energy had drained from her.

We were directed to a mat. As at those earlier ceremonies, our place was at a distance from the rite's focus of dignity. We sat with our backs to one of the windows of the courtyard's western side. An attendant came with cups of water. I sipped; my mistress left hers untouched. I looked up at the tower again, squinting. The late morning sun was brightening the sky beyond it. It was a day in which not one cloud ventured out.

When the rite's procession began, Priest Sar was first to pass through the courtyard's southern entryway. His face bore his familiar look of false piety. Behind him came two more priests, each bearing a polished teak box.

'The texts, old and new,' murmured the Abbess. 'One box for each kind.'

The Abbot, his gait laboured as always, followed leaning on his walking stick. Then came the prince and a collection of senior officers in the prince's fighting force. And Bouray. He looked as doleful as I know that we did. Somehow I had hoped he would find a way to put off the ceremony.

The procession passed in front of us to reach the courtyard's northern end. There the teak boxes were laid carefully down at the altar. Priest Sar placed offerings of fruit and lotus blossoms atop them, then stepped away. The texts would be fully blessed following the tower's dedication.

For that, the chief mason took the Abbot by the arm, and together, like an aged couple out for a walk, they trudged up the tower's bamboo steps. The second-ranking mason followed, then the prince. Even from where I sat, I could sense Darit's impatience with the ponderous pace of everything.

At the top, the two masons busied themselves with final preparations. Abbot and prince, however, stood motionless at their spots on the platform. We could all, I think, share in the awe they were experiencing. How different were these two men, but how similar their reactions to what their eyes were taking in, the entire world, all of creation laid out in every direction.

Bells rang. We put hands together in prayer as the Abbot began to chant verses of consecration. Most of it did not carry down to us, but near the end he raised his voice to deliver words that we all heard very clearly. 'When I push the lever and put in place this final stone, the greatest tower in the empire, abode to Our Lord Shiva, heavenly nest of the Bird of Fair Feather Garuda, will be completed. With this will forever be demonstrated the respect and adoration that reside in the hearts of everyone atop the holy mountain.'

He continued, but I was no longer listening. I was suddenly feeling a call in my heart to take action. For an instant I had a dreadful thought that I was meant to interrupt the rite. But then I realized it wasn't that. A servant girl would carry no authority. Her role was to bring about action by someone who would.

'Mistress!' I whispered. 'You cannot allow this to proceed. It defiles Heaven!'

Do you know, her eyes flew open. Her trance vanished. She turned and looked hard into my eyes. I shuddered. I do believe that in my eyes she saw the spirit wife Naga.

In an instant, she was on her feet!

'Sacrilege! Corruption! Abomination! By all authority invested in me, I curse this proceeding, I demand that it stop!'

So loud, so pugnacious was her voice that the Abbot did indeed stop. He peered down, disbelieving. The courtyard fell silent. How long that lasted, I can't recall, but then he recovered himself and his hand went to the wooden lever. He was a sick man, but he pushed it hard—he threw his whole weight into the task, really, as if to show how thoroughly he rejected what my mistress had shouted.

The crown's final stone shifted in response. But propelled by the Abbot's impulsive force, it slid past its intended hole, toward the crown's outer lip. 'Grab it, grab it!' That was the chief mason, shouting to his deputy. Both men thrust hands to the stone, but it was too heavy and continued past them. There came a loud, disturbing sound of two hostile surfaces grinding against one another. The stone passed over the crown's outer lip and fell with a deep and frightening thud to a ledge just below.

Birds took flight from niches in the tower's sides. My eyes followed them as they twisted and turned in the sunlight, wings fluttering. I wondered if they were birds, or the Bird of Fair Feather in multiple forms. Then I became aware of a strange low-pitched noise, a hidden rumble from within the tower. A moan, almost. A god was speaking.

As of its own accord, a stone broke away from the tower's side. It struck the courtyard pavement with terrifying force, splintering into fragments. One zipped straight to the heel of a priest, who sprung back in pain and surprise.

Prince Darit was hurrying down the bamboo steps. But the Abbot remained at the top, gripping a bamboo railing with both hands. He was intoning another prayer, I think, but the fight had gone out of his voice. Another stone split from the tower's side. 'Holiness! You'd better...' That was all I heard – the masons were imploring the Abbot to come down. One put a hand to him, but he shook it off angrily. The masons understood – he wasn't going. But they would. Down the steps they came in an undignified scramble.

All the time, the god inside was still speaking. The grunts and groans of the heavy labour of a massive shifting and rearranging of weight emerged from the tower.

'Mistress, we must...'

She was already getting to her feet, as were people all over the courtyard. Suddenly a section of scaffolding gave way, drawing cries of panic below. The platform on which the Abbot stood tilted abruptly; he struggled to remain on his feet. More stones fell. Prince Darit reached the steps' base and raced across the courtyard toward a group of his officers near the altar. As he ran, a falling stone struck his shoulder. He fell, yet got back up and reached his men. They all seemed paralyzed, their eyes on the top of the tower, where the Abbot still clung to a slender length of bamboo.

Then the tower itself came to life, as if it desired a new location and would move on its own. But its base was staying put, and only the top was moving, tipping, in fact, towards the south. Screams erupted all around. In my last memory of the Abbot, he is still on his feet, clutching that length of bamboo as if it would save him, and he is beginning to move earthward with the lotus crown that lacked but one piece.

'Mistress!' With all my strength, I pushed her through the courtyard window behind us. Something stung me in my side. We came tumbling down into the gallery's covered passageway. I tried to stand, but a succession of brutal shocks knocked me from my feet. Stones overhead shuddered; dark clouds of dust billowed in from the courtyard. The Abbess was face down on the floor, I dropped on top of her, eyes shut. I could hardly draw breath from the dust-fouled air. I was sure the stones of the passageway's vault would collapse onto us.

Yet this feeling passed in an instant. Silence set in. I looked up. Ahead of me, the passageway was filled with other prone people who had made it to safety. But there came maudlin cries from the courtyard. *'Help me over here!' 'Get it off me, get it off!'*

I glanced out the window. The sight I saw will stay with me forever. The tower was gone. In its place was a pile of huge stone blocks, lying randomly this way and that, many of them cracked or broken. Dust filled the air, but as the mountaintop's winds blew it away, horrors were exposed. Bodies lay twisted in various forms of mutilation and dismemberment. From beneath one block there protruded a bloodied, misshapen head.

I felt something warm on my side. A chip of stone was protruding from my skin, blood oozing around it. I turned to the Abbess and was surprised to see her sitting up. Her hair and body were grey with dust, but she seemed fully in control. Her first act was to pluck the chip from my side and toss it away.

'Did you see the teak boxes out there?'

'No, mistress.'

'Then go find them! I'm relying on you. Find both of them and bring them to me!'

'Yes, mistress.' That is what I said, and off I went, but first I would look for Bouray. Barely three steps from the window, I came across a body lying face down. Dread filled me as I stooped for a look, but then came cruel relief. It was Priest Sar. Nearby two acolytes were straining at a block to free someone trapped beneath. I stopped and lent my shoulder. The man rolled free, groaning, and I was relieved again – it was not Bouray. I went on, passing an acolyte in a daze, covered like everyone else in dust, his hand clutching a garment that was splattered red. How quickly I moved, checking every body that I could see. None were Bouray. But I knew that there were likely many other bodies that I could not see.

I stopped to catch my breath. Now I noticed that none of the falling stones had struck the altar. Yet the boxes were gone.

I ran to check the north side of the courtyard. My feet slid on the wetness of blood, but I did not fall. I noticed now that I was contributing to the blood underfoot. There were drips from the wound in my side, so I placed a hand over it. Still there was no sign of Bouray or the boxes. I moved through the courtyard's northern gate and stepped past the great linga – it was untended. In the hall behind it, sacred cups and hangings lay scattered on the floor. Roof tiles had fallen too. I passed between the two rows of columns, some of which leaned precariously now. I emerged into the Second Court's courtyard. Again, I saw no sign of what I was looking for. But, then, in the shadows of the passageway leading out, I saw Prince Darit, helped along by his men.

His energy, his bluster, were gone. No sooner had I spotted him than he fell heavily to the floor, panting. His shoulder was badly bloodied; I thought I saw the white of bone sticking out. Two men knelt at his side trying to get him to his feet. Two others stood nearby, each holding a teak box. I raced past them all, as if all I wanted was to get out. But I had a plan. I stopped in the outer doorway and looked back.

Darit had struggled to his feet and signalled that the group should move on.

I spoke. 'You cannot take the boxes.'

Darit looked at me, confused. Then he shrieked at his men to do something. One of them pulled a knife and moved towards me.

'You must leave the boxes!' I spoke so forcefully that the man stopped. I waved my hand, which was red with my own blood, and I think that disquieted him. 'Those texts are the sacred property of the

Lord of the Summit. Anyone who takes them beyond this door will die horribly and suffer punishment in the two worlds.'

'Do it,' Darit told his soldier. 'Use your knife, get her out of the way.'

Again, the man hesitated. Darit stumbled in my direction to deal with me himself. With one hand he seized my shoulder. He intended to shove me, but then my shoulder was all that was keeping him on his feet. He grasped wildly at me with his other hand, then collapsed, taking me to the floor.

I struggled free. 'You men have seen what happened to the Abbot,' I cried. 'A man much more powerful than any of you. It was a warning, a warning that your campaign does not meet Heaven's will.'

Darit was on his back, panting. 'I told you, let's go, let's go. Help me up.'

One of the officers put down his box. The second did the same with his. Then they picked up the prince and carried him out the door.

With that, I was alone. I crawled to the boxes and looked inside. Each was filled with holy texts. I said a prayer and threw myself over them. It was the only way I could think to protect them. I couldn't stand any more. More blood was flowing from my side. My vision was beginning to waver. Blackness closed in. It was in this place, in this state, that Bouray found me shortly afterward.

POSTSCRIPT

The Natural Way in a Family Succession

I now live again in the house at the base of the mountain. The tower's collapse two years ago is as clear in my memory as it was on the very day, though the only physical mark it left on me is a scar on my side, where that stone fragment drew blood after whizzing in through a passageway window.

On this particular morning, I am back in my role as guide for the women and children of a pilgrim party that is climbing the stairway. We have reached the final stretch of extreme steepness. At a lower section, I showed the party's two little girls how to clutch the ropes and pull themselves up, keeping toes pointed towards the steps. Their mother, a gentry woman from an estate south of the capital, keeps close behind them, nervous that her girls will fall, but I know they won't. I like these people; they seem to like me. Most of all, I like the work. It brings exactly the satisfaction that I recalled.

The soldiers have long since left the temple. The number of pilgrims coming has grown again to numbers almost equal to those of the old days. The tower's collapse and the unhappy history of conflict and heresy at this place have kept some pilgrims away, but others come specially to see the place where the great rebellion was turned back. Word has circulated that I was there when the tower fell, so on these climbs I am often asked to describe the day. I do as best I can. I say nothing about the Naga wife whom the Abbess saw in my eyes. But concerning something that was entirely of this world, the securing of the texts from Prince Darit, I do let them know. Some of the men smile indulgently and say they can't quite believe it. A young girl against five armed men! But I was there, and I know what happened, so this doesn't bother me.

'We're almost there! One, two, now!'

That's Father, leading the team that is lifting the conveyance of the only member of the party who requested a merit certificate, the gap-toothed grandfather. I do my best to conceal my amusement. The old gentleman's face is gripped by the silent fear that I saw so many times as a girl. But Father's team has safely negotiated all the previous steep sections, as always. If the passenger will be patient (and trusting) just a bit longer, he'll see that he'll be raised safely on this one as well.

The Abbess wept with joy that day when Bouray and I came to her, he carrying the two teak boxes. The tears flowed for us and for our safety (though I was still bleeding) but I must say, they flowed most of all for the recovery of the texts. Bring them straight to the house, she told us. There she kept them safe in the following days, guarding over them personally with a war club that Darit's men had left behind. The boxes, she said, would remain with her until proper authority was restored at the temple. In fact, she carried out that restoration herself, because no one came from the capital to take charge. She gathered up the temple's priests who had shown loyalty to the true doctrine. At her direction, they carried out rites that sent the former Abbot's soul on its journey to new life and in this life placed the nephew in his post. He remains there today. In the process, people on the mountain have learned a new word, 'regent.' When a King comes to the throne too young to rule, a regent stays at that King's side to make sure that decisions are properly taken and orders properly issued. It is that way here. The nephew is not too young in years, but it's clear that his judgement and character have not yet ripened to the point that he is ready to lead the mountaintop community on his own. The Abbess is back living in the nunnery, but we all know that every text, every proclamation, every initiative of any kind is put to her before action is taken. The priests around the nephew—rather, I should say, the Abbot – know that this is necessary and sometimes, I'm told, they must remind the Abbot himself rather forcefully. But so far, this arrangement is working. Everyone is optimistic that we have entered a new era in which peace and harmony will reign at the temple as Heaven intended. At least that is what we say to each other.

One of the new Abbot's first announcements, cleared by the Abbess, of course, was that there would be no immediate rebuilding of the tower. Heaven deems that the fallen stones should remain where they are, we were told, to give reminder of the peril of vainglory and the futility of rebellion against just doctrine and rule. Pilgrims whose rank was insufficient in the old days to ascend all the way to the First Court can now freely go that far, and see the fallen stones. Heaven spared the annex chamber that adjoined the tower at its north side. Inside is a shrine at which the supreme linga has been erected. There visitors pray to the Lord of the Summit to seek solace for the souls that were sent on their way on the day of the great collapse. No one has said it directly, but I think that pilgrims are happy that they're no longer solicited for silver for tower construction.

Some of the pilgrims ask me exactly where Prince Darit was standing when the tower came down. By a wooden altar that was specially built for that day, I tell them. You'll see it – like the stones, it has been left in place as a memorial. As for Darit, he had his men steal a cart but he made it only a day's travel north of the temple before he was seized and put in a cage. Do you know who did that? The commander, who changed sides once again.

The prince was kept in that cage for some time. People came to look at him through its bars, and despite his wounds, he tried with clever words to win them over to his side, but none were taken in. Everyone knew by now that his armies were breaking up, his soldiers trudging back to their home estates. We heard later that this had begun even before the tower's fall. You will recall that message from the capital to the estates announcing the King's death, but also a cancellation of quotas of labour and materials for construction of the King's mountain temple. The Abbess said it was the burden of these demands that had led many estates to support Darit in the first place. The Council of Brahmins in the palace in Angkor knew this as well and, with His Majesty no longer in this life, chose to try to end the rebellion by making this gesture of conciliation to the estates. It had begun to work, and the tower's fate was final confirmation that Heaven did not intend Darit to take the throne. Rather, it intended the nobleman whom the Council soon selected for the post. After a while, we stopped hearing news of Darit. He simply disappeared. There are many stories of what happened, but the most common is that he was put to death in the night and his body hidden in a place where it has never been found. Sometimes I am asked whether Darit's wandering spirit is ever sensed lurking in the tower's rubble. I reply that, no, it would not come to a place that had rejected the prince so firmly in life.

But news continues to arrive, to our family, at least, about Kamol. From the capital, because that is where he is now. When he learned that I had fled the house at the stairway's base that night and gone back up the mountain, he realised he could not remain. Giving no goodbyes, he left for Angkor. Good fortune greeted him there, as he deserved: on only his second day in the city he found work as a mason's assistant and he met a special girl. They married and there is already a child! Dear Kamol, sweet Kamol. I treated him so badly. I like to think that his move to the capital and his new life there were as easy as I have just described (and truly this is how they have been related to me) but I don't really know. Every time news of him reaches me, I feel a twinge of guilt. But how could I have disobeyed that order from the spirit Naga in my dream that night? Heaven did not intend that I marry him.

Father accepts that now. You will recall that when I arrived at the house early that morning, he did not know that Kamol had enticed me down with the lie about impending death. Father was furious when he learned that later on, and I think frightened too that some malevolent spirit might take such a lie as an opportunity to turn it into truth! I had never agreed to marry Kamol, which meant I wasn't breaking a promise. So, after the tower's fall, Father was more than pleased to take me back into the house.

Those two little pilgrim girls have now scrambled up the last few steps. Their mother is next. Then me. We are now at the top of the cliff, between the two Nagas, wife and husband. Not their spirits but their forms in stone, completed this year by the Lady Sray's masons. The holy serpents' necks are dressed with garlands, some fresh, some wilting; their hooded heads, fourteen in all, loom over us protectively. The girls and their mother kneel before the wife serpent to offer garlands of their own, which I had recommended that they obtain, for a small cost, from my family at the base of the mountain. This is a new service that my family provides. The Nagas are happy now. I can feel it. Garuda is satisfied too, though for this I must rely on the priests' word. That god is said to recognise that our temple was not intended as his great mountaintop nest. He will remain here, but in the same status as before, in the proper proportions of glory and influence concerning the holy serpents.

My peace of mind is back in its old proportion too, though it took considerable time. In the days following the collapse, I felt distraught over what I had done in the moments immediately before it. The chief mason survived, and he told people that had the Abbess not stood up and shouted her denunciation, the Abbot would not have grown angry, and would have pushed the lever only gently, as he had been shown, and the final stone of the lotus crown would have slid smoothly into its intended place. The great tower, fruit of ten years' labour, would still stand. Sixteen departed people would still breathe. When I heard these words, I kept quiet, because I knew that there was one earlier step in this sequence of cause and effect: Had a servant girl kept quiet, the Abbess would not have stood up and shouted her denunciation. People say that however many people died, it was clearly Heaven's intent. I know that's true, but I also could not stop feeling culpable when later I saw the wives and children of those who departed life that morning. I would turn away, experiencing a terrible agitation in my heart. I could not expunge the memories of bloodied bodies pinned under blocks. And then one night, as I lay trying to find sleep, I felt one more time the spirit Naga. But this time I felt her only as a kind of slithering out of me. I kept still, and I heard the soft sounds of her scales passing across the rocks and bushes outside the house. She was gone, but she had left in me one final awareness: she would not return. I let out a breath that night and wept. For with the Naga spirit went responsibility too. I had not been acting of my own will, I had been acting of hers, to carry Heaven's message. Had she not chosen me, she would have chosen someone else. I fell asleep quickly that night, and she did not appear in my dreams. I awoke the next morning feeling buoyed, even light-headed. My normal life could resume. To this day, when I say prayers before the stone wife Naga and leave garlands of my own, I feel that I am a worshipper like any other. I sense no special communication.

I never told anyone but Father that it was the wife Naga that was present in me, nor about my whispered pleading to the Abbess that day. And the Abbess never mentioned to me the words I had uttered nor the phantom she saw in my eyes. I can understand. As I told you, she is governing the temple now. She is known far and wide as the woman whom Heaven employed to end the rebellion and bring down the heretical tower. Her authority must be fully maintained, and it would suffer were people to know that the holy call for action originated in a maid, and not in herself. I don't say that as a boast or out of any kind of resentment – it is simply fact. But she did look on me differently after that day and she made no objection when I asked shortly afterwards to conclude my service to her and return below.

So everything is in harmony on the holy mountain, top and bottom. But I should not really say everything. Not yet.

'Up! Up! Push up!' That's Father again. He and his team are straining to lift the conveyance and its aged occupant to the top of the final section of steps. 'No, no—don't let it sag... Look out! *Higher, higher!*' Father throws an arm across to give extra support. I frown. I hope he's not about to repeat his joke about a certain member of the team needing a merit certificate himself.

In the hour after the tower's collapse, I was too stunned to think straight about much of anything. But as Bouray and I climbed the steps of the Abbess's house to deliver the two teak boxes for safekeeping, it came to me that the danger was finally past. But then came another realisation that caused my spirits to wilt. The end of danger meant there was no longer anything placing me and Bouray together.

My mistress soon dismissed us that day, and we descended the steps of the house. I turned to Bouray, preparing myself to say goodbye. Yet right there, by some miracle, I decided I would not. My hand went forward to his, just as his came to mine. Our fingers touched, then wrapped about each other, and for a moment we stood that way, silent, each with eyes on the other. Right there our future was sealed.

'We have never touched,' he said. We did not let go.

'In fact we have,' I replied, 'but only for practical things. You forget that you helped me to my feet just now in the temple.'

'You're right. I did.'

'And a long time ago you pulled me by my ankles at the cliff edge.'

'Well, I couldn't have let you fall off!'

We laughed. How strange and wonderful was a simple laugh.

But then I trembled.. With hardly a thought, I had just made a choice that would mean giving up my dream. There would be no life of service as a stairway guide. I would be Bouray's wife instead. I swallowed, and looked back to him, to assure myself that I truly wanted it this way.

How was it possible, but Bouray was reading my mind just then. With both hands he steadied me.

'Do you recall, Jorani, what you said to me that first time we met, when the two boys had left?'

'I said nothing at all. I ran away.'

'No, it wasn't like that. Here's what you said: "I am a guide and I will always be a guide."'

He had saved my jar's fragments, and also my words.

'We will be together, Jorani. We will have each other. And we will each have the life vocation that Heaven has been intending.'

So he proposed a preposterous idea.

So strong was the shock that I broke away from him and plopped myself down on the house's bottom step. Presently I looked up at him.

'Have you lost your mind? Have you ever seen the food we eat in our house? Do you have any idea how hard and worn our mats are?'

He met these questions with the dearest kind of laughter, and joined me on the step.

So, do you see, the member of the team whom Father is helping is Bouray!

We are married now. He is no longer a Brahmin. He underwent rites to shed his rank and his birth responsibilities. That was extremely unusual, so much so that the Abbess had to send to the capital for texts on how exactly to bring it about. But it was done. Now he wears the simple garment of a guide. He is the fourth pair of shoulders whenever there is a conveyance to carry up the stairway. His dream in the old days was to leave behind the luxury of the Brahmin life. He'd imagined it as a forest priest, not a stairway guide, but to him the challenge and satisfaction are the same.

Two years on, he has never expressed misgivings to me, and I don't believe he is concealing any. During the day he applies the arms and legs that Heaven gave him. At night he shares rice with me, and then a mat, though sometimes he falls asleep sooner than I would like. Still, we are content beyond all probability. What I will say is that if anyone is concealing something, it is me. At the odd moment, I wonder to myself what life would be had I prevailed upon him to remain a priest, and not take to the road but remain on the mountaintop, with me becoming the favoured second wife in his dwelling, savouring the soft mats and rich food, tasked with just the lightest duties of a household. That life will never happen and that's for the best. Bouray rebelled against it, and so would have I, though I can't say how long that might have taken.

The muscles on his arms have grown thicker, and his shoulders no longer bruise under the weight of the conveyance. Father, for all his hectoring, is recognising that Bouray has found his proper place and will become an accomplished guide. His approval did take time—nothing could seem farther from the natural than having a former priest as a son-in-law. But I knew that approval would come. My mother's spirit was much quicker to give her blessing. In fact, I sensed it the very first time that I knelt at the family shrine after returning to the base of the mountain. And of course Chantou is happy to have him. To her, Bouray is merely a kind-hearted young man who loves me and has joined the family. Lately she's been teaching him some of her country songs. I think she has no real appreciation of what he once was, nor the tragedy that occurred atop the mountain. I have never tried to explain these things to her.

My brother Bonarit gets on well with Bouray, though I know that there will always be a certain barrier between them. But one thing Bonarit doesn't worry about is rancour over who will become head of the family when the transition day eventually comes. Of all people, Bouray has proven that he has no intention of questioning the natural order of succession.

I am to have a child next year. I have not told him yet. It is only yesterday that I stole away to the village across the rice fields to be examined by the midwife there. I hope that our child will be a girl. I hope that I will be a good mother, and that my own mother will take an interest in her, and help her survive, and will plant in her the devotion to service on the stairway that I have always felt. And I hope that she will make her first ascent not when she is grown, but when she is still small enough to ride her father's shoulders. May people up top call her 'Little Champion Climber.'

HISTORICAL NOTE

I t's hard to imagine a setting more evocative of the absolute than the clifftop on which Preah Vihear temple stands. Winds whistle, clouds sail by, birds dart about on mysterious errands. The sky seems larger than you can recall, and more intensely blue. Five hundred metres below lies a plain of fields, forests, and hamlets, a beautiful yet ordinary world that seems somehow to accept a status subordinate to the holy mount.

The temples of Angkor are the most celebrated creations of Cambodia's fabled lost civilisation, the Khmer Empire. But scattered about other parts of mainland Southeast Asia are hundreds of lesser-known stone monuments built by people of this same ancient culture. Preah Vihear is the most spectacular of these and by far the most wondrously situated of all the empire's architectural creations. In 2008, the U.N. Educational, Scientific and Cultural Organisation (UNESCO) designated it a World Heritage Site.

The Khmers of the time were Hindus (or at least their aristocracy was) but what they created atop the cliff is an architectural depiction of something that exists in every belief system, the spiritual quest. The temple's defining feature is a gently rising processional avenue that takes the supplicant ever higher up the gradient of religious accomplishment. Five elaborate courts lie along the way, to be passed through and wondered at. Ritual bathing pools, terraces, soaring gables, stone Naga serpents, and sculpted scenes from Hindu epics further mark the ascent. The ultimate destination is the supreme sanctuary, abode of the god Shiva, known in this place as the Lord of the Summit. The cliff and thin air are just a few steps beyond.

Preah Vihear as depicted in a 1907 book by French archaeologist Étienne Lunet de Lajonquière.

I first visited Preah Vihear in 1974 and came away with the sense of rapture that it inspires in most every visitor. Years later, when I began writing history and fiction about the Khmer Empire, those feelings came back and I began to think about a novel set at the temple. My reading had turned up something that I missed on that first visit: an ancient Eastern Stairway leading up from the plain on the mountain's eastern side. This stuck in my mind, and I began to conceive a story built around a family with a hereditary vocation of escorting pilgrims during the ascent.

Given how steep the mountain is, I assumed that the stairway must run left, then right with switchbacks, like a modern mountain road. But when I saw the real thing for the first time, I realised how wrong that was. The ancient Khmers favoured straight lines in their architecture and so their stairway runs straight up the mountain with neither a zig nor a zag. As nature's slope becomes steeper, so does the stairway.

In the image above from a 1907 book by Étienne Lunet de Lajonquière, the structures that Jorani calls the Entry Court and the Northern Stairway show at the lower right. That's the First Court in the distance at the cliff's summit. The Eastern Stairway isn't depicted, but its final, mostly flat section would enter the image at the middle of the lower edge and lead to the Entry Court.

Some friends and I made the ascent on a dry-season morning in 2013, with frequent stops for rest and swigs from water bottles. We found the stairway well preserved in places, but in others it was crumbling or overgrown or had eroded away completely. As an archaeological relic, it's more a testament to the Khmers' brute strength than their artistic refinement. The steps are plain and utilitarian, with no carved embellishment. Some are made of stone hauled into place, while others were chiselled from living stone in the mountainside. Large stacked blocks, also unadorned, form a sort of gateway at the bottom. Similar blocks occur on either side of the stairway periodically during the ascent. Perhaps these served, like the courts of the temple

The base of the eastern stairway.

itself, to mark increasing stages of holiness as an ascent proceeds. That is, the stairway is another depiction of the spiritual quest, a lead-in for the elaborate one of the temple proper up top.

The Cambodian government has built a sturdy wooden staircase alongside the stairway, to which we modern climbers gratefully switched at impassable sections of the old way. Still, in a two-and-a-half-hour ascent, we worked up enough sweat to get an inkling of the faith, determination, and physical endurance that imbued the pilgrims who came here in the ancient era. At times I could almost sense them alongside us.

The temples of Angkor, which was the capital of the Khmer empire, stand about one hundred forty kilometres to the southwest. Though Preah Vihear is of their culture and era, it departs dramatically from them in design and orientation. This has caused no end of comment among scholars and tourists alike. Most of Angkor's temples are built on flatlands and through their own height and mass become Mount Meru, abode of the gods; Preah Vihear rests atop a natural Mount Meru. Angkor's temples are square or rectangular in plan and oriented east-west; Preah Vihear is linear (it extends about eight hundred metres end-to-end) and is oriented north-south. Angkor's temples were for the most part built by only one king; Preah Vihear seems to have enchanted king after king, resulting in a succession of expansions, upgrades, and enhancements on the mountaintop over the course of at least a century.

The temple stands apart too in having a special tragic story in recent times. History placed it right where two feuding modern-era countries, Cambodia and Thailand, rub up against each other. In 1962, a long and passionate fight in the United Nations' World Court in the Netherlands over ownership of the temple ended with a decision in Cambodia's favour and an order to Thailand to withdraw border police who were occupying the site. They moved, but just a few metres to the north. After the Cambodian civil war broke out in 1970, the temple became a front-line military position, battled over by faction after faction both for its status as a nationhood symbol and its extremely defensible high ground. When that war ended after a quarter century, the Thai-Cambodian feud resumed, resulting in hostilities in 2008 and 2011 that claimed dozens of lives. Thai shells exploded among the ruins, placing new scars on the temple's stones. You can read a full history of the temple, ancient and modern, in my 2015 book *Temple in the Clouds: Faith and Conflict at Preah Vihear*.

As of this writing, the temple has been at peace for five years, though heavily armed paramilitary police of the two sides still face each other at it across barbed wire. Let us hope that cool heads prevail and the quiet times continue. Guns and enmity have no place in this holy and historic place.

How old is Preah Vihear? Stone inscriptions, the prime source of knowledge of Khmer history, hint that some kind of religious community was present on the summit as of the ninth century. It can be conjectured that the empire's fourth king, Yashovarman I, built something at Preah Vihear, given that the site was within his realm and he was the rare Khmer king who liked to build atop real hills and mountains rather than creating his own (four hilltop temples in

An inscription at Preah Vihear.

the Angkor area date to his reign). I find that theory enticing, and so Jorani's family reveres this king as the temple's founder. The inscriptional record is much clearer and more detailed during later reigns. Texts recovered at the temple repeatedly

Shiva and Parvati atop the holy bull Nandi at Preah Vihear.

mention Suryavarman I, who held the throne from about 1010 to 1050 CE, indicating that he had a role in the construction and maintenance of the temple. Inscriptions dating from a century later suggest a similar interest by Suryavarman II, builder of Angkor Wat and the monarch of Jorani's time. One stone text from his era recounts that the aged Brahmin who crowned him visited Preah Vihear on royal business around the year 1120 to bring gifts such as hangings, golden bowls, and silk parasols, and to establish a new ashram.

The presence in the pavilions of lingas, the ritual phallic stones of Hinduism, show that the temple was dedicated to Shiva, as were most of the state temples of the empire. There is a linga outline chiselled into a boulder near the mountaintop. We get further confirmation from sculpture. Over one door, for instance, Shiva and his consort Parvati ride the holy bull Nandi. We can be sure that much of the ritual life of the temple involved the priestly tending of the lingas. Holy liquids, perhaps water, perhaps milk, were poured over these stones, then collected in sanctified form for use in further ritual at the temple and other places.

The temple seems also to have played a special role in the royal politics of the day: one inscription mentions that Preah Vihear included some kind of depository for texts that documented the lineages of kings back to the empire's founding. Khmer history had no shortage of rebellions and usurpers; one can imagine that preserving or destroying or forging these texts figured in some of these succession struggles. The texts' presence may also hint at why successive kings were interested in this place.

Like most of the temples of Angkor, Preah Vihear was abandoned to the elements at some unknown date as Khmer power waned (the empire's demise is commonly dated to 1431, when a Siamese army pillaged Angkor). When French colonial archaeologists began surveying the temple in the late nineteenth century, it was overgrown and largely deserted, visited only occasionally by people from nearby hamlets for special religious rites.

Beneath the foliage, however, the temple was found to be in an exceptional state of preservation. While many of Angkor's monuments had buckled and collapsed during the long untended centuries

The ruins of the primary tower.

because of weak foundations, Preah Vihear had the advantage of very solid underpinnings – the mountain is essentially one giant block of sandstone. But those early French visitors found a major exception to the general state of good repair: The primary tower, erected in the First Court, was just a jumble of huge fallen stones. There are a variety of theories explaining this, including earthquake, flawed engineering, and deliberate demolition whose purpose can only be guessed at. The explanation that Jorani offers is conjectural, but certainly consistent with what the visitor sees today.

The doctrine of matrilineal succession that figures so prominently in her story is documented in many inscriptions of the times. Notable among them is one that was found at Sdok Kok Thom, the temple that Jorani and the Abbess visit in search of textual support for their side of the struggle with the Abbot. It is another real place, located today in eastern Thailand near the border with Cambodia. Its inscription is the most important written record left behind by the ancient Khmers and was the subject of an earlier book of mine, *Stories in Stone: The Sdok Kok Thom Inscription & the Enigma of Khmer History.* Three hundred forty lines of Sanskrit and ancient Cambodian recount the history of a Brahmin family that served the kings of Angkor over the course of nine generations, starting with the empire's founder, Jayavarman II, around the year 800. In hearing the family's story, we hear the story of the empire itself, because successive patriarchs are recounted as present at key historical events. And over and over, the inscription states something that was clearly very important to the people of the time, that when the time came for succession in the priestly family, leadership passed not to a son of the patriarch, but to a sister's son. In the early eleventh century, for instance, the head was a priest called Shivacarya, son of his predecessor's sister. When he died, the matrilineal system was applied. *"A scion of this able, blessed female line was renowned under the name of Sadashiva, son of Shivacarya's sister, whose noble heart was ever Shiva's throne."* It was this Sadashiva who was in charge at the temple when the inscription was created around the year 1052.

There is no record of a family with a heredity vocation of escorting pilgrims up the Eastern Stairway. But it seems likely that ancient people got help with an ascent that was both physically demanding and potentially dangerous in terms of falls or encounters with unknown spirits. Certainly a vehicular road that was built in the early 2000s up the mountain's west side, rising very steeply and (as I had wrongly imagined of the stairway) winding left and right, is not travelled alone. Visitors go up with the drivers of motorbikes and pickups, who live off payments of Cambodian riel or U.S. dollars, the modern equivalent of the silver pebbles that are the livelihood of Jorani's family.

So Jorani and her family are fictional, but if you visit the clearing that is at the base of the Eastern Stairway today, you can easily imagine that a wooden house once stood there, flanked by a breezy pavilion in which pilgrims rested and sipped water from coconut cups to prepare physically and spiritually for a climb they had been anticipating for years.

The climb awaits you too, should you choose. The physical demands are considerable, but they will add a rich new dimension to your experience of one of the world's most remarkable beacons of the ancient past. The remains of the two stone Nagas, husband and wife, will greet you at the top of the final steep rise. Their heads are gone, but their long bodies extend in parallel away from the cliff line for many metres, defining an east-west walkway that channels you, as it channelled pilgrims of Jorani's time, towards the first sighting of the magnificent temple in the clouds.

John Burgess, October 2016